LOVE STORY (CONFIDENTIAL)

LOVE STORY (CONFIDENTIAL)

A HIDDEN SPRINGS NOVEL

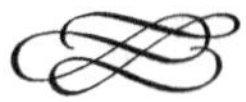

LISA MCLUCKIE

The Betty Press LLC
PO Box 241
Williams Bay, WI 53191
www.thebettypress.com
(262) 729-3231

ISBN-13: 978-1-941744-02-4
ISBN-10: 1-941744-02-8

For Andy, my hero.

PROLOGUE

"What are you doing?"

Startled, Tessa dropped her penny into the stream before the wish was done. She whispered the rest of the wish in a rush as the penny disappeared among the forget-me-nots, then spun to confront the interrupter.

"Who are you?" she demanded.

He was taller than she was, but then, everyone was taller than she was. He looked older, though, maybe two grades. He looked like a fourth grader. She did not trust fourth graders.

His grin caught her by surprise. It was the kind of smile that made you want to smile back, even when you were mad.

"I asked first," he said.

She crossed her arms, determined to resist. Her sister Mel had the same ability to charm herself out of trouble. All it took was a twinkly smile and you could get away with anything.

"Charm doesn't work on me," she said. "I'm immune."

The boy seemed startled by her pronouncement, but he

recovered quickly. He eased off on the smile and stuck out his hand for shaking.

"I'm RJ," he said.

Better, she thought. The handshake was very grown up.

"Tessa," she replied, and uncrossed her arms to shake his hand. "What do the letters stand for?" she asked.

"None of your business," he said.

Interesting. His real name must be really embarrassing.

"How old are you?" she asked.

"Ten," he answered. "How old are you?"

"Almost nine."

Really she was only eight and a quarter, but she liked to round up.

"So what were you doing?" he asked again. He seemed genuinely curious, so she decided to answer. Maybe she would forgive him for interrupting if he felt bad enough.

"I was wishing," she said matter-of-factly.

"For what?"

"None of your business." If he could say it, she could say it.

"Wishes are dumb."

"Boys are dumb," she said, and crossed her arms again. Maybe RJ stood for Real Jerk. "What are you doing here, anyway?"

She knew everybody in The Gardens, their neighborhood of exactly twenty houses surrounding the lakefront commons. If she didn't know him, he must be visiting—hopefully not for very long.

"I'm catching frogs," he said. "Obviously."

She wrinkled her nose. Frogs were disgusting.

"You can't catch frogs," she said. "They're too fast."

"Wanna bet?" he asked.

"Sure," she snapped back.

"My mom bought doughnuts at the diner. If I can't catch a frog, I'll let you have one."

There was only one diner in town, and they had the best doughnuts in the world.

"Sounds good to me," she said.

"What about you?" he asked. "If I catch a frog, what will you give me?"

She thought about that for a minute. She couldn't ask her mom to cook anything. Her mother was a terrible cook. She and her sisters, however, were pretty good.

"If you catch a frog, my sisters and I will make you chocolate-chip cookies."

He looked skeptical.

"How old are your sisters?" he asked.

"We're all nine. Almost," she added hastily.

"You can't all be the same age," he said.

Oh yeah, Mr. Know-it-all? He would feel really stupid when he met her sisters.

"Sure we can," said Tessa, pausing for dramatic effect. "We're triplets."

He laughed.

"Right. And I have superpowers."

"I'm serious," she insisted.

"Whatever." He shrugged. "If I catch a frog, I get cookies. Deal?"

"Deal," she said, and they shook on it.

She watched, fascinated, as he crept along the bank of the stream. He stopped and stayed very still for what seemed like forever. Then he grabbed something and hopped up, whooping so loudly she jumped back.

"Now that's how it's done," he crowed. "Wanna see?"

He moved toward her with his hand outstretched. She shook her head and backed up.

"We had a deal," he said. "I need to show you the proof so that you'll make me the cookies. No backing out because you never actually saw the frog."

"Ow!"

She had backed right into a tree. RJ stopped in front of her and opened his hand. Sure enough, there sat a tiny little frog, or maybe it was a toad. She didn't know. She didn't care. She needed to be away from the thing. Far, far away.

Just as she was about to make a run for it, the little creature jumped. She felt it land on her hair and started shrieking.

"Get it off! Get it off! Make it go away!"

The stupid boy was not helping. He was laughing so hard that he would probably pee his pants. When he fell to the ground because he was laughing so hard, she got mad. So mad, in fact, that she stopped being afraid. She looked down at RJ, narrowed her eyes, and pretended to sneeze. Her head snapped forward with just the right amount of force and the frog landed smack in the middle of RJ's forehead.

She smirked down at him.

Who was laughing now?

CHAPTER ONE

Memorial Day weekend, today

Tessa caught the package just before it hit her in the nose.

"Make a wish!" Mel said, laughing.

Tessa shot her sister a dirty look and turned the package over in the fading light, trying to figure out what it was. The nearby bonfire warmed her back, but it didn't make reading the label any easier. Tall shade trees blocked the last of the sun's rays, casting long shadows across the lakeside commons and painting the water in shades of fire. The Memorial Day barbecue marked the start of the summer season on the lake. Old friends gathered to catch up on everything that had happened during the year. Children roamed in packs, sorting out the pecking order for the summer. Teenagers hovered near the bonfire, too cool for ghost-in-the-graveyard, but not too old for s'mores.

When Tessa finally figured out what she held in her hands, she couldn't help smiling.

"Where did you find this?" she asked.

"Ah, the miracle of the Internet," said Mel. "You should try it sometime."

It was a sky lantern. Tessa hadn't seen one of these in (she quickly did the math in her head) eighteen years. Wow. They had all turned nine that year, and their friend Annabelle had ended her birthday party with what she had called wish lanterns, giving everyone an extra to take home.

Tessa's smile faded as Mel handed her a tiny pencil.

"For writing your wish," she said.

Tessa could hear the subtle challenge in her sister's voice. Mel should know better. Tessa didn't throw coins in fountains anymore, or look for four-leaf clovers, or search the sky for shooting stars. She had given up on wishing eighteen years ago, and she wasn't about to start again now.

"I'll just fly my lantern," said Tessa. "No need for wishing."

Mel refused to take the pencil back.

"Chicken?" she asked slyly.

"Of course not," Tessa retorted. "I just think wishing is a waste of time." She gave Mel a hard look. "You know that."

"So this should be no big deal, right?" Mel asked, gesturing to the paper lantern in Tessa's hand. "If you don't believe in wishes, who cares what you write? You could write anything."

"I don't need to prove anything," answered Tessa. She made a conscious effort not to clench her teeth.

"I see," said Mel, doing her best imitation of Tessa's therapist voice.

"What do you see?" snapped Tessa. She knew she was letting Mel get to her, but she couldn't help it. Her sister had been perfecting this technique for twenty-seven years and she was really, really good at it.

"Your words are saying that you don't believe in wishing," said Mel, still doing her 'therapist' impression, "but your behavior tells me that you do."

Tessa growled under her breath. She hated it when Mel was right. Mel raised an eyebrow, challenging her to deny it.

"Fine," said Tessa. "Let me demonstrate how much I don't care."

She ripped open the plastic sleeve and yanked out the folded lantern. She grabbed Mel by the shoulders, spun her around, and put the lantern on her back.

"Hold still," she ordered.

Using Mel as her writing desk, Tessa scribbled on the side of the lantern. She didn't think about it too much, writing the first thing that came into her head. Then she turned Mel back around, put the pencil in her hand, and snarled, "Happy now?"

"Yep," said Mel. She threw an arm around Tessa's tense shoulders and began walking her down to the tiny strip of beach. "Let's go fire these things up."

Tessa fought the urge to dig in her heels. All she really wanted to do was throw her lantern into the bonfire, but her inner voice echoed Mel's words: *What is your behavior telling Mel? What does it tell you?*

That decided it. She would prove to both Mel and herself that she truly didn't care about wishing anymore. She allowed Mel to lead her to the water's edge, where a small crowd had already gathered. Friends, neighbors, her parents, her other sister Callie—all of them stood around with their lanterns in various stages of assembly. Tessa put hers together without speaking, ignoring the lighthearted chatter that swirled around her. For most people, this was an amusing exercise, like buying a lottery ticket. For her, it was incredibly depressing, dredging up memories of The Year of Failed Wishes. It wasn't so much that she mourned the wishes. She mourned the girl who had done the wishing.

The nearly full moon had risen above the tree line on the far shore, providing the perfect backdrop for the lanterns as they rose into the air one by one. Someone passed her a lighter.

She used it to kindle her tiny flame and then handed it on to Mel. While she waited for the air inside her lantern to warm, she watched the early fliers rise higher and higher, wondering if any of them would tumble as hers had all those years ago, or go down in flames like Mel's. She hoped not.

At last her lantern was ready. Defiant, she lifted it to the moon and watched it rise. Mel followed suit and the two lanterns climbed side by side. A soft breeze caught them, carrying them farther and higher than the rest. It looked like their two lanterns might make it to the far end of the lake. When they were so far away that Tessa couldn't distinguish between their lanterns and the stars, she turned to face her sister, steeling herself for an I-told-you-so, but Mel surprised her, staying quiet for at least a minute before saying anything. When she spoke, she kept her eyes on the moon and her voice was suspiciously thick.

"So," she asked, "what did you wish for?"

Tessa wasn't sure how to answer.

"Don't want to jinx it?" Mel's voice sounded stronger and Tessa could see a half smile on her moonlit profile.

"It wasn't a wish," she admitted. "I'm done with those."

"So what was it?" asked Mel, finally turning to face her sister.

"A question," answered Tessa grimly. "Where the hell is my Prince Charming?"

RJ nursed his beer while he watched his friends and neighbors fuss over their sky lanterns. Thankfully, Mel had run out before she'd been able to saddle him with one. Craft projects weren't his thing, although he did enjoy watching everyone try to read and follow the directions in the dark. It looked like more fun than assembling IKEA furniture.

As he surveyed the crowd, he realized that all three of the

James triplets were up for the weekend. He had seen Mel, obviously, as she distributed the lanterns. She stood a few steps away from him now with Tessa. The third triplet, Callie, stood at the far end of the beach, but he couldn't identify the man she was with, or the boy. Holy crap, did she have a kid? Now he really felt old.

They hadn't changed much. They still looked very much alike: big green eyes, ghostly pale skin, and long honey-blond hair. Tessa twisted hers into a tight knot, Mel's flowed down her back like a river, and Callie's hung in a braid down her back. They were the same, but different, like the lake on different days. All three were still tiny and not particularly curvy, but RJ appreciated women of all shapes and sizes.

He watched as Mel and Tessa released their lanterns into the sky. All three James sisters in one place. Damn. He hadn't seen that trifecta in action since his final summer at the lake. Had it really been eight years? That had been his last summer of freedom, the one between sophomore and junior years of college. For the triplets and their posse of girlfriends, however, it had been the summer after high school graduation—their first taste of freedom, and all the wildness that went along with turning eighteen.

There had been a lot of skinny-dipping that summer.

He had managed to stay out of trouble by focusing his attention on the older girls, the ones who'd been closer to the end of college than the beginning. Oddly, though, his clearest memories were of Tessa. She had offered a running commentary on his early attempts at seduction, critiquing his flirting technique and offering practical suggestions for how to do better. To this day, whenever he approached an attractive woman, he tested his opening lines against his memory of Tessa.

WWTS: What would Tessa say?

As he approached her to say hello, he couldn't help overhearing the end of Tessa's exchange with Mel.

"Where the hell is my Prince Charming?"

How ironic that practical Tessa dreamed of fairy tales.

"Looking for me?" he drawled.

Tessa and Mel got one good look at him, long enough to realize who he was, and then the two of them dissolved into helpless laughter. He frowned, but it only made them laugh harder. Of all their possible reactions, he had not anticipated laughter. Charm was his specialty.

"RJ," gasped Tessa after several minutes of uncontrolled mirth, "what are you doing here?" She wiped tears from the corners of her eyes and struggled to get herself under control, only to lose it again when she met Mel's eyes.

"What, I'm not allowed to come home?" he asked. His knew he sounded grumpy, but he didn't bother to turn the charm back on. That had clearly backfired.

"No, it's not—" She stopped, took a breath, regrouped. "I thought you lived in California."

"I did," he answered simply, "and now I live here."

Tessa and Mel were avoiding each other's eyes and doing a crappy job of keeping straight faces.

"Really?" she asked, seeming genuinely surprised.

He could imagine all the questions that must be racing around in her head. *Why move back to the Midwest? What happened to change your mind?* He didn't really feel like explaining.

"So what's so funny?" he asked.

He had learned a few tricks in his years of lawyering. Take control of the conversation. Answer a question with a question. Tessa and Mel exchanged glances, then burst into giggles again, so he used another lawyer trick: patience. He crossed his arms and drummed his fingers on his bicep, waiting for an answer.

Mel gave his bicep an appreciative glance, but Tessa kept her eyes on his face.

"Sorry," she hiccupped. She shot a questioning glance at Mel, then took the lead in answering the question. "It's just that...well, you're sort of the opposite of Prince Charming."

"What are you talking about?" he objected, on the grounds that her answer was both insulting and flat-out wrong. "I've been told by *many* women that I'm both charming and easy on the eyes. What's not to like?"

"That's exactly the point," answered Tessa. "You've enjoyed the company of many—"

"Many!" echoed Mel.

"—women."

RJ couldn't follow her logic. He was well and truly baffled.

"And the problem is...?" He spread his arms wide in question.

Tessa sighed.

"Prince Charming is a one-woman kind of man, if you know what I mean," she explained.

"He makes one woman happy in many ways, rather than many women happy in one way," clarified Mel. Before he could protest, she added, "Yes, I'm suggesting you're a player."

He opened his mouth to speak, but no words came out. Tessa choked back a laugh.

"Mel means that in the nicest possible way," she said, giving Mel a reproving look. "You're not exactly known as the happily-ever-after type. Not that there's anything wrong with that," she added hastily, throwing up a hand to forestall any arguments.

He still had no words. Would the insults never end?

"I'm a happily-ever-after kind of girl, and Prince Charmings can be hard to find."

Finally he found his voice.

"So if I'm not Prince Charming, then who am I?" he

demanded, wanting to know exactly where he fit into this fairy-tale scheme.

Tessa and Mel looked at each other, considering their options.

"Jack and the Beanstalk?" proposed Tessa.

Mel immediately shook her head. "Grumpy the Dwarf!" she countered.

RJ frowned as they snickered together.

Then Tessa sucked in a breath. "Peter Pan," she whispered. Mel cocked her head, considering, then nodded her agreement. The two sisters turned to face him, their faces wearing identical expressions of smug triumph.

"Peter Pan," they announced.

"No way." He completely rejected their premise. He was not a boy playing at life. He was a man. A strong man. A hunter, even. "I think I merit at least the Huntsman from Snow White. Or what about the Wolf?" He liked that image, especially if Little Red Riding Hood was all grown up and naked under a red satin cloak. He grinned at them. "I'm the Big Bad Wolf."

Mel shook her head. "Nope," she said.

Tessa pursed her lips. "Sorry, but no."

He must have looked sad, or disappointed, or something, because all of a sudden they were trying to make him feel better.

"Don't worry," said Tessa, putting her hand on his forearm. He realized that his arms were still crossed, and his shoulders were actually a little tense. "Just because you're not Prince Charming doesn't mean you're not sexy. You are. Totally sexy, I mean."

"Superhot," agreed Mel, only she didn't look quite as earnest or, frankly, as honest as Tessa did.

"Superhot?" he queried, giving Mel his best cross-examination stare. She didn't even blink, just grinned at him.

"The hottest," she said, patting him on the shoulder. "I have to leave now or I might jump you, and that would be embarrassing. Wine?" she called to Tessa as she walked away.

"Yes, please," said Tessa.

Her hand was still on RJ's arm, and she was standing close enough that he could smell her shampoo—something with flowers or berries. For a moment he felt disoriented. This was Tessa, his baby sister's best friend. He should not be noticing how she smelled. Or the curve of her neck.

"You smell good," he said.

She was the one who had trained him all those years ago to give authentic compliments. From the way she smiled, she remembered.

"You're sweet," she answered, "but your superpowers won't work on me. I'm immune, remember?"

She looked up to meet his eyes, which must have thrown off her balance, because she swayed and held on tight to his arm.

"Too much to drink?" he asked.

She shook her head.

"I'm out of practice," she answered.

Or at least that's what it sounded like. He was about to ask her what she meant when his phone rang.

Tessa released the breath she had been holding when RJ turned away to take the call. Some things never changed. The sun rose in the morning, the wind blew across the water, and RJ made her shiver. He didn't do it on purpose. Flirting came as naturally to him as breathing. Unfortunately, she'd always had a weakness for his particular brand of charm.

Mel walked by and passed her a glass of wine, which gave her something to do while she waited. She would need to be careful or she would start acting like every other girl who looked too deeply into his eyes. Something about him made you want to kick your shoes off and let your hair down, maybe find a beach and a sunset. She could picture it all too easily. He would place a lei around her neck. Hand her a fruity drink with an umbrella in it. *Welcome to Fantasy Island.* She hid her smile when he glanced back at her. He offered a vacation from reality, and she was tempted to take it.

Growing up, she had managed to hide her shivers well. RJ had treated her like a younger sister. He had never turned the full force of his charm in her direction, so she had never actually tested her resistance. She had simply observed as he worked his magic.

Before she sank too deeply into daydreams, Tessa took a step back and breathed in the cool night air. The breeze coming across the water carried the memory of sailing and the promise of summer. She had always loved summer best, when she could spend her days out on the water and her nights staring up at the stars. Those were the years before 'real life' started, before the glow of streetlights crowded out the night sky.

RJ finished the call, and he looked upset. She shook off her odd mood and crooked an eyebrow at him.

He shook his head.

"It's nothing," he said.

She didn't need a psych degree to know that it was more than nothing, so she called him on it.

"Try again," she said.

He raked a hand through his shaggy hair, rubbed the back of his neck, and started talking.

"That was my racing crew, Walt, calling from the emergency room," he said.

"Is he okay?" she asked, swallowing her surprise. "Do you need to get over there?"

"No, he's fine. Nothing life-threatening," said RJ, looking almost comically glum. "His wife is with him."

"You were hoping for something more serious?" asked Tessa.

RJ barked out a laugh.

"Maybe," he said. "The idiot broke his foot playing soccer."

"How bad is it?" she asked, still mystified.

He shrugged.

"I think the meds were starting to kick in. He was fuzzy on the details. One thing was clear, however: He can't be my crew for a while. Maybe the whole season."

His face darkened, as if Walt had injured himself on purpose. She fought back a smile. RJ had always taken sailing a little too seriously.

"I'm sure you'll recover," she said. "What are you guys racing?"

"M-17s. Two-man crew." He sighed heavily. "This was supposed to be our year. We were going to sweep the whole series, but instead I have to break in somebody new, which is a giant pain in the ass."

"Oh come on," she protested. "There are tons of people who grew up sailing on the lake. Make some calls. You'll find someone."

He raised an eyebrow.

"Finding a sailor is not the problem," he said. "Finding someone good, who knows their stuff, and you can stand to spend every weekend with them? That's a whole lot harder."

"Sounds like dating," she said.

"If only it were that easy," he said, with a cocky grin. "I've tried mixing dating and sailing. When I start shouting orders, the ladies tend to jump ship."

She laughed. She couldn't help it. It was too easy to picture him yelling like a drill sergeant at a bikini-clad crewmate, and her making her escape in a graceful dive off the stern of the boat.

"You could do it," he said, suddenly serious.

She laughed harder, imagining herself in the bikini.

"Ah...no," she said when her laughter had subsided, but RJ

now had that gleam in his eye.

"Why not?" he asked. "You're the best sailor I know."

She shook her head. "I haven't sailed in years."

"Who cares?" he asked. "You used to sail circles around all of us, like you had your own private wind. It's not the kind of thing you forget."

The nostalgia came back, but with an edge this time. She *had* forgotten. No. Worse than that. She had deliberately put it out of her mind. Sailing was one of her favorite things in the world, and yet she hadn't given herself the time to do it since… She couldn't even remember the last time she had been out on the water.

The realization left a bitter taste in her mouth.

"No sailing for me," she said abruptly. "This is a make-or-break summer at work. I can't afford to take time away from that right now."

He nodded, thoughtful. She could almost see his mind working as he weighed her response and chose to back off. For the moment.

"Think about it," he said. "We could have a lot of fun together."

Tessa needed to get away from RJ and his powers of persuasion. Making a vague excuse about finding her sister, she headed for the end of the pier, hoping for a moment alone. The conversation with RJ and the strange wistfulness had left her off-balance. She needed to steady herself.

Maybe she had been cooped up in the city for too long. She had spent the endless winter shuttling back and forth between work and home with the occasional stop at the gym in between, breathing only the dry, recycled indoor air. Her entire life in Chicago was lived indoors. But tonight, for the first time in months, she could breathe deeply. Although the lake appeared calm, tiny ripples of water ran into the posts holding up the pier. She exhaled the city air, full of exhaust and the weight of too many people living too close together. The humidity stroked her skin, and the tension in her shoulders eased with every breath. She had a sudden urge to dip her toes in the chilly water and let down her ponytail.

Too late, she realized that someone else had already claimed her solitude. She found her mother at the end of the pier, contemplating the night sky from an Adirondack chair. Tessa settled in the empty chair beside her and resigned herself to conversation rather than quiet.

"Come to fetch me back to the party?" asked her mother.

"Actually, no," said Tessa. "I needed a break, and you found the best spot."

Dora smiled. Tessa had always thought her mother was beautiful, but in this light she looked almost surreal. Her long hair, a mix of blond and gray, turned silvery-white by moonlight as it fell past her shoulders. She wore a macramé poncho over tie-dyed leggings and moccasins, a fashion mash-up that only her mother could pull off. Tessa felt cold and vaguely frumpy in her well-worn jeans and plain white T-shirt.

"I was surprised to see you make a wish," said Dora.

Tessa grimaced.

"I shouldn't have let Mel get to me," she answered. "In any case, I didn't really make a wish. I asked a question."

When Dora looked over at her, one eyebrow raised, Tessa felt herself flush in the dark. Her mother still had frighteningly accurate mom-radar. Unable to explain her inner turmoil to herself, let alone to her mother, she answered with an evasion and a redirect.

"I asked for a status update on one of my old wishes, since none of them have come true yet," she said. "Did you do a lantern?"

"I did," answered Dora.

"And?" probed Tessa. "What did you wish for?"

Her mother paused before answering.

"Second chances."

Dora did not elaborate, and her brevity alone was enough to ping Tessa's own radar. Why would her mother need a second chance? She was living the dream: married to her first and only love, spending her summers running the sailing school and her winters doing her art. What could she possibly want to change? And why was her mother, the queen of over-sharing, suddenly reticent? Tessa opened her mouth to ask, but a sense of fair play stopped her. Her mother had let Tessa evade a direct question. The least she could do was return the favor.

"I'm a firm believer in second chances," said Tessa.

"Like Callie and Adam," murmured Dora. "It's nice that they got a second chance."

Tessa shot her mother a sharp glance.

"What do you mean?" she asked, keeping her voice carefully neutral. Callie had tried to keep her adolescent relationship with Adam a secret. Of course her sisters had figured it out, but had she confessed all to their mother? If not, Tessa didn't want to screw up her cover story.

Dora chuckled.

"You girls and your secrets. Mothers know a lot more than you think."

Tessa sincerely hoped that was not true.

"You're worried about her," said Dora.

"Aren't you?" she asked.

"Of course," said Dora. "I'm her mother. It's my job to worry."

"Adam brought her back to us," said Tessa. "I was beginning to think that would never happen."

Dora nodded slowly.

"She's still fragile, though," continued Tessa, "and if things with Adam go south..."

"They won't," said Dora.

"How can you be so sure?"

Her mother looked over at her, surprised.

"You're not?" she asked. "I can feel the difference in her. She and Adam anchor each other. They're stronger together than they were apart."

Tessa couldn't deny her mother's words, nor could she deny the jealous ache below her breastbone. She truly wanted her sister to be happy. And Callie seemed happy. Drunk in love. Insta-family. Professional success. Even a hound dog. She was a living, breathing country song—the happy kind, not the down-and-out kind.

Tessa wanted all those things for her sister. Problem was, she wanted them for herself, too. (Well, maybe not the hound dog. He seemed to drool a lot.) But each time she thought she was on the right track, her hopes of happily ever after turned out to be an illusion. They watched the stars together in silence while Tessa tried to unknot her tangled emotions.

"You're right," sighed Tessa. "I suppose I'm in the habit of worrying about her, and I need to stop."

"I saw you talking with RJ earlier," said Dora.

Tessa laughed under her breath. Clearly her mother was psychic, zeroing in on the key issues driving her restless mood. First Callie, now RJ.

"He's tempting me with an offer to crew for him this summer."

She didn't want to admit how much his offer appealed to her. Practical considerations couldn't compete with the fact that her body liked to shiver and her soul longed for the wind on the water. But she couldn't see how it would work.

"And the problem is...?" asked Dora.

Tessa sighed.

"Work, mostly," she said. "Not everybody can afford to take long weekends."

"You already know I think you work too much," her mother said with a snort. "Next?"

"It's not just the work," Tessa admitted. She hesitated briefly, then confessed. "I'm not sure I could resist RJ all summer."

"So why resist?" asked Dora.

"Mother!"

Dora laughed.

"You take relationships so seriously, sweetheart." Dora reached over to pat Tessa's hand. "Life is short. Enjoy it while you can. Not all relationships last forever—nor should they."

She said that last bit with a little more force than necessary, but before Tessa could quiz her about it, Dora stood up.

"Time to face the music," Dora muttered under her breath.

"What?"

"Nothing," said Dora. "I'm heading back. You take your break, sweetheart, and consider RJ's offer. You've worked hard to get where you are. It's time to have some fun."

Tessa studied the moonlight dancing on the water as she listened to her mother's retreating footsteps. There must be something odd in the lake air tonight. Only a few hours ago, she had been content with her life. Now, this sudden restlessness had illuminated the corners of her subconscious mind, revealing the shadows that she liked to ignore. Behind her pride and satisfaction in her work, she glimpsed deep resentment of the career that had kept her away from the lake. Hiding beneath her joy for Callie's happiness lurked a painful envy. She even begrudged her parents their happy marriage. They had won the happily-ever-after lottery, marrying young and still going strong after almost thirty years. Not everyone would be so lucky.

Maybe it had been a mistake to come up for the weekend. Sometimes it's easier to leave a door firmly closed, ignoring the 'what-ifs' and the 'might-have-beens.' Her little flight of fancy about RJ, for example, would not be easily forgotten. She would feel the sting of that memory on summer afternoons spent with clients rather than sailing. She smiled ruefully at the thought. It wasn't like this was the first time she had to decide between short-term pleasure and the long-term plan. Each time she was tempted to blow off the plan, she made the same choice. She sacrificed the present for the future, hoping one day it would all pay off.

As for her mother's advice, Tessa would love nothing more than to enjoy a summer at the lake, but she couldn't envision a way to do that without scuttling her career in the process.

Kat haunted the fringes of the bonfire. She should leave. It was time. The party had faded along with the sunset, but she couldn't seem to drag herself away. Nights like this demonstrated how solitary her life had become, and how much she craved the primitive comfort of company around a warm fire.

Both RJ and Callie had surprised her by extending an invitation to this neighborhood gathering. She had always been curious about the lake crowd, so she had accepted, if only to see what all the fuss was about. She had to admit, this small-scale gathering on the shore held much more appeal than the manic crush of big holiday weekends over at the municipal beach.

"Hey, landlady," said a familiar voice. She turned to find RJ standing beside her.

"Hey, favorite tenant," she responded lightly.

She could see the flash of his grin in the dark.

"Your one and only," he said.

Her decision to sublet spare office space to RJ had been a stroke of genius. She got a nice steady income stream and the company of a colleague in one nice, neat package. She hadn't realized quite how lonely she'd been at work until she suddenly had someone to talk to.

The evening had cooled, but he still wore only board shorts, a T-shirt, and flip-flops. She wondered when the California would wear off and he would finally admit that he lived in Wisconsin. He had been in denial since his return a few months ago, insisting on wearing shorts even in February, and trading hiking boots for flip-flops the moment the snow melted. She had only seen him in a suit and tie twice, and he hadn't looked happy about it. The fancy attire signaled that his mediation efforts had failed and he needed to appear in court. He cleaned up surprisingly well, though, taming his shaggy surfer cut with an excess of hair product and losing the scruff on his chin. If not for the gravelly voice and the megawatt grin, she might not have recognized him.

It was really too bad she didn't go for the scruffy surfer thing. He was prime dating material, despite the unfortunate obsession with sailing.

"Aren't you glad you came?" he asked. "This has to be more fun than weeding the garden. Wasn't that your big plan for the weekend?"

"I had a few other things on my list," she replied, skipping over his first question. He would be disappointed if she admitted the evening had made her melancholy.

"Such as…?"

"Oh, the usual. Napping, reading, doing laundry."

He groaned. "You have got to get out more."

"I like my life the way it is," she said. "Throw in the occasional date on Saturday night and I'll be perfectly happy."

"Done," he announced, but she shook her head.

"You're not eligible."

"Why not?" he asked.

"No offense, RJ, but even if you were my type, I have rules against dating my tenants and my colleagues. You're guilty on both counts."

"Wow," he said. "This is definitely not my night."

"Somehow, I think you'll recover," she reassured him. As far as she could tell, every other female in the county found him attractive. Their lack of chemistry was simply the exception that proved the rule.

"I never asked how the race went on Saturday. First of the season, right?" she asked.

"We won," he said, "but Walt broke his foot, so now I have no crew."

"In that case, congratulations and I'm sorry. Can't you find someone else to crew for you?"

"I'm working on it," he said thoughtfully, "but it will take some persuasion. Are you sure you don't want to learn how to sail?"

She smiled at that. Unlike all the lake rats, she had grown up on dry land, thank you very much. Her grandfather had been a landscaper, and her mom an amazing gardener. They had lived on the farm side of town, and she had never really understood everybody's obsession with the lake.

"There's a reason I'm called Kat, you know," she said. "I don't do water."

He couldn't have looked more horrified. She laughed.

"It's not a disease. Just a preference."

He shook his head in mock despair.

"It's a defect. Let me know when you're ready to remedy that."

"You'll be the first to know."

They watched the fire companionably for a minute or two before he spoke again.

"Have I thanked you lately for subletting the upstairs space to me?"

"It wasn't doing me much good as a storage space," she replied. "Besides, I like the help with the rent."

"It's more than the space, though," he said. "Starting over is never easy. You've given me a ton of moral support, and I appreciate that."

His openness made her uncomfortable, but he seemed to sense that and quickly turned the conversation back to business.

"You know, the short-term sublease is up soon, and I'd like to extend it, if that's cool with you," he said. "The space works well for me, and you can't beat the view."

She couldn't agree more. The view out her office window blew her mind every day. She could see all the way down Main Street to the park and the lake.

"You're welcome to stay. As subletters go, you're not nearly as much of a pain in the ass as I expected."

He grinned at her.

"Sweet," he said. "I'll draft the addendum and get it to you ASAP. Any chance you'll reconsider the espresso machine?"

Kat snorted.

"Not happening, RJ." She started walking away from the fire. It was definitely time to go home. "See you at work."

Memorial Day weekend, nineteen years ago

Tessa ignored the knock on the back door because she knew it had nothing to do with her. Any neighborhood kids would knock and then walk right in. The only people who knocked and waited were grown-ups and delivery people. She kept right on eating her lunch. Mel was curious, though, so she went to see who it was. Mel was always hoping that a package would be for her. It never was. It was always art supplies for their mother.

To Tessa's surprise, Mel came back through the mudroom door with two kids following her. The first was RJ, the boy from earlier this morning. A smaller girl trailed behind him. She looked scared. Probably her brother threw frogs on her head all the time, so of course she was scared. Tessa crossed her arms.

"What are you doing here?" she demanded.

Tessa hadn't told her sisters about either the boy or the frog, but that didn't matter. They crossed their arms, too. Callie shot her a questioning look. Tessa knew she was thinking about the girl standing behind RJ, but Tessa was still too mad at RJ to worry about the girl.

"I'm here for my cookies," he said, flashing all three of them that grin that made her want to uncross her arms. She gripped her elbows to make sure she didn't soften up. She could feel the messages her sisters were telegraphing. *Cookies? What is he talking about?*

"I don't make cookies for people who throw frogs on my head," she said.

"You made a bet," he insisted. "Would you want to disappoint my baby sister, Sunny?"

He tugged her in front of him, presenting her with a flourish as if she were a kitten or a puppy. She wriggled out of his grip and shot him a dirty look.

"I'm not a baby."

He said something in her ear and it must have been mean because she stepped away from him and crossed her arms, too. It was four against one, and he was the loser. RJ narrowed his eyes at Sunny before turning back to Tessa and her sisters.

"So you're backing out of the bet?" he asked.

Tessa smiled slowly.

"We'll be making cookies with Sunny this afternoon," she said, "and Sunny will decide whether or not she wants to share any with you."

He looked like he wanted to yell at all of them, but at that moment Tessa's mother walked into the kitchen.

"Hi kids," she said, then stopped short when she didn't recognize Sunny and RJ. "Girls, who are your new friends?"

"This is Sunny and her brother RJ," said Tessa. "Sunny is going to stay and bake cookies with us. RJ was just leaving."

He shot her an outraged look, but she just smiled sweetly back at him.

"What a wonderful plan," said her mother. "You can call me Mrs. James, or Miss Dora, or Dora, or really whatever you like. I don't mind. It's so nice to have new children up for the summer. Which family do you belong to? No, wait, let me guess. You must be Vi's grandchildren. She was saying the other day that you would be able to spend the whole summer up here, but she never mentioned how old you were. Why, Sunny, I think you're very close in age to the girls. Are you eight?"

Sunny and RJ blinked at the sudden silence. Sunny nodded, then ducked her head.

"Well that's perfect," continued Dora. "My girls can show you around, make sure you meet everyone. And RJ, you must be, what, twelve?"

He stood taller before admitting that he wasn't quite twelve yet. Tessa pressed her lips together to keep from saying something mean in front of her mother.

"Wonderful. There are a few boys your age. Evan Reese and his older brother Adam live on the other side of us, through the hedge. They arrived yesterday. I'm sure there must be a whole pack of boys roaming around. You'll need to keep an eye out for them."

Dora looked around the kitchen at the children staring silently back at her and smiled.

"Girls, let me know when you need help with the oven. Sunny and RJ, it was lovely to meet you."

With that, she disappeared back down the hall. Sunny and RJ stared after her, looking confused. Tessa just shook her head. Her mother had that effect on people. She did enough talking for two or three people, so you really didn't need to say anything. In fact, if you actually wanted to say something it could be tricky to find an opening. Tessa took advantage of their confusion to hustle RJ out the door.

"We'll bring Sunny home later," she said, and shut the screen door in his face.

When she got back into the kitchen, the four girls looked at each other, then they all started giggling.

"Did you see the look on his face?" asked Mel.

"I've never seen anybody boss RJ around," said Sunny. She looked really impressed.

"We'll boss him around for you anytime," said Tessa, slinging an arm around Sunny's shoulders. "Now let's make some cookies."

~

Memorial Day weekend, today

Tessa dodged tweens playing flashlight tag as she made her way back to the bonfire. The younger children and their parents had disappeared when the sun set, presumably to put the smallest ones to bed, leaving small clusters of teenagers and child-free adults around the bonfire. She stepped into the circle of firelight, grateful for the warmth.

What she really needed was food. A glass of wine on an empty stomach had left her feeling floaty. She had arrived late and missed the actual food at tonight's barbecue, so her best chance at dinner would be to head home and scrounge for left-overs, or to find Mel and convince her to go down to The Beach for a burger. Tessa was leaning toward the latter plan. There was no knowing how long leftovers had lingered in her parents' fridge.

As if summoned by her growling belly, RJ appeared beside her.

"S'more?" he asked, offering a plate with not one but two warm and melty s'mores on it.

"No wonder women fall at your feet," she said with a smile. "How can I resist?"

He grinned as she reached over to take one.

"Resistance is futile."

He claimed the second s'more and they sat down side by side on a split-log bench, munching their treats and staring at the fire. The man was definitely charming, and she had to admit he knew his way around a marshmallow. Hers was perfectly toasted: brown and bubbly on the outside, liquid on the inside, and not a hint of char. It took patience to achieve the perfect marshmallow—not something she would have expected from RJ.

His shoulder warmed her side as much as the fire warmed her face, melting her insides like marshmallow even as she licked the real thing off her fingers. She looked up to catch him watching her, and she self-consciously sucked the last smudges of chocolate off her thumb. His face was difficult to read in the firelight, but she could swear that he smiled as he licked his own fingers. Predictably, she shivered, and in response he wrapped his free arm around her.

"Cold?" he asked.

She nodded, even though it was a convenient lie. Her shivers had nothing to do with the temperature.

"I'll grab a jacket from the house," he said.

"No, don't," she said, before he could move. "I'll be fine."

If he had been anyone else, she would have gently shrugged off the half embrace. She would have nipped the flirtation in the bud and returned to the house to get her own jacket. But for some reason, with RJ, she stayed right where she was. She didn't want to stop the flirtation. She didn't want to be practical, or levelheaded, or think about the long term. She wanted to enjoy this moment without judgment or questions.

What the hell, she thought, and leaned her head on his shoulder. This was RJ. He didn't have a sleazy bone in his body. That's why women loved him. And it had been so damn long since a guy had offered simple comfort without strings or complications or expectations that she couldn't resist. He rubbed his hand absently up and down her arm, offering warmth through friction. Each stroke melted her brain a bit more. This was why she needed to be careful. This man was her kryptonite. Beautiful, warm, dangerous kryptonite.

"So how's your family?" asked Tessa.

"Pretty much the same," he answered.

"That bad, huh?"

RJ sighed. "We lost Pops right before Christmas."

"I heard," she said. "I'm sorry. How's Nana Vi doing?"

"She's okay. At least she and Dad are speaking now. She and I talk on Sundays, and I go down every month or so and take her out to brunch."

"Does she ever come up here?"

"Not yet," said RJ, "but I'm working on it."

"Is that why you came back?" asked Tessa.

"Let's just say that it was time for a change, and when I found out that Pops left me the lake house, I knew this was where I needed to be."

There was more to that story, but this didn't seem like the moment to interrogate him. Maybe Sunny would fill her in.

"How's Sunny doing?" she asked. "She's been so busy with the kids that we don't talk as often as we used to."

"The kids are doing great. They've come down to see me once or twice since I made the move back here. I don't know how she does it. Will works nonstop, so she's basically on her own with the little guys. They're very...energetic."

Tessa laughed. "I remember. The last time I saw them I needed a nap afterward."

She gazed at the familiar faces in the dwindling crowd. She

had known so many of these people her whole life, and now her childhood friends were getting married and starting their own families. She wanted to be a part of the daisy chain of generations. She wanted to watch her children and grandchildren play flashlight tag after the bonfire. Maybe that was why all her relationships ended before they could get off the ground. She was trying to plug the guys into her preplanned life, and of course none of them fit, which left her with a dilemma. Did she give up the dream, or give up the search? A question with no good answer.

"You know," she said, "I think you've dated every single girl here except me and my sisters. Girls our age, I mean." She paused, turning the idea over in her head. "Why is that?"

"You want the charming answer or the real answer?" he asked.

She looked up at him, intrigued. She had expected a charming answer because, well, he was RJ. She hadn't expected him to admit that there might be more.

"Both, of course," she said. "Charm first, please."

He had to pull together his serious face before replying.

"How could I possibly choose among the three loveliest ladies in the neighborhood?"

She snickered. "That was good," she said. "Maybe a little cliché, but still quite effective."

"It's a cliché for a reason," he said.

"Why not just admit that you couldn't tell us apart?" she asked.

"Don't be ridiculous. I've always been able tell you apart," he said. "Some guys couldn't. I never understood why they fell for it when you would pretend to be one of your sisters."

She looked up at him in surprise. They had only pulled the switch a handful of times, and—as far as they knew—nobody had ever picked up on it.

"We called it 'the boyfriend test,'" she said.

"Seriously?"

She nodded. "We decided that we would only date people who could tell us apart, and if we had any doubts, we would switch places and test them." She wrinkled her nose. "That's how I ended up with Roger Hall as my first kiss. To this day I think Mel knew the kiss was coming and used the boyfriend test as a way to get out of it." She lowered her voice, still slightly grossed out by the memory. "He was *not* a good kisser."

"Teenage boys rarely are," he said wryly.

"So what's the real reason?" she asked. She studied his face, on the alert for a joke, but he seemed completely relaxed and open.

"I'm sure this will come as no surprise. I don't do the 'happily ever after' thing. You do."

She nodded slowly. "That's true," she said. "White picket fence, two-point-five children, matching track suits—I want the whole package."

"And you know that vision gives me hives, right?"

She grinned. "Want to hear about the two dogs and the rescue kittens?"

He covered his face in mock horror. "No, please, make it stop!"

"I get it," she said, laughing. "Other girls are fine, but I give you hives."

"The hives are only the symptom," he said. "The problem is that you don't do light and easy, and I don't go deep. You would get hurt, and I would hate that."

She had forgotten about his insight. In many ways, he saw people more clearly than she did, even though she did it for a living.

"I only date women if I believe they can keep it light. I've only been wrong a few times, and it wasn't pretty."

Weren't they a pair? He folded before he could lose, and while she was holding out for a sure thing. They lived on opposite ends of the spectrum, neither of them willing to risk their heart. It was sad, really. Possibly even pathetic.

"Sail with me," he said abruptly.

"Why?" she asked.

"Because I think we would make an amazing team," he answered.

The words wound themselves around her heart and squeezed. It wasn't just what he said, but how he said it. The fire and the wine and the strong arm around her shoulder conspired to change her mind. She understood all too well why women fell for him. She wanted to say yes—to anything.

"I wish I could," she whispered, "but this is a big summer for me at work. Make-or-break, you know what I mean?"

He sighed.

"If you change your mind, will you call me?" he asked. "I would love to sail with you."

"Well hello, Tessa. I didn't expect to see you here."

Tessa tensed, all of her work-stress returning in a single jolt.

"You okay?" murmured RJ. He gave her shoulder an extra squeeze.

"Fine," she whispered, but it came out more like a defeated sigh. She looked up slowly.

"Hey, Brock." She kept her voice neutral and light. "Long time no see."

Long time meaning not since Thursday afternoon, when he had left work early to make the long weekend longer.

"You remember Helen, don't you?" he asked. "Sweetheart, come say hello."

Tessa groaned softly as she stood up, the side that had been pressed against RJ suddenly chilled. She used to babysit for Helen. As the girl—she must be twenty-three or twenty-four by now—circled the bonfire to join Brock, Tessa couldn't help feeling sorry for her. Once she got a good look behind Brock's smooth facade, she would find little to hold her interest. For the moment, however, they were a matched set, both overdressed, ready for the country club rather than a casual barbecue.

"Hello," cooed Helen. "Tessa, it's been ages."

"It has," she agreed blandly, submitting to a light hug and some air kisses.

"Oh, and RJ, is that really you?"

He got the same greeting, only the hug was full-snuggle and the kisses were real. Tessa raised an eyebrow but didn't comment. RJ could (and did) date whomever he pleased. The real mystery, for Tessa anyway, was what voodoo he used to make former girlfriends walk away happy. Brock must have been wondering the same thing. She could see his jaw clench in the firelight.

Once Helen released him, RJ moved back to Tessa's side and put his arm around her again. She relaxed, grateful for both the warmth and the moral support. People would probably assume that she and RJ were dating now, but she couldn't bring herself to care.

"Brock, Helen," said RJ. "Nice race yesterday."

Tessa bit the inside of her cheek. She could tell by the look on Brock's face that RJ had beaten them. Helen shot RJ an annoyed glance and sprang to Brock's defense.

"I suppose Brock's mind wasn't fully on the race," she said. "Have you heard the news?"

"What news?" Tessa asked cautiously. She didn't like Brock's smug expression.

"Brock has been promoted at work," she gushed. "He'll have sole responsibility for launching the Hammond Center's new couples counseling program. Can you imagine? Such a huge responsibility. I only hope it doesn't interfere with the rest of the sailing season."

Tessa stared blankly at Helen, her stunned brain trying to

process the words.

That was *her* job. *Her* program. She had put together the initial proposal, done all the research, laid the groundwork. She had met with Brock's father only last week to convince him that she should lead the new initiative. He had said he would consider it. Apparently he had considered it for all of thirty seconds.

Her career plan shimmered in her mind before it faded away. She had been chasing a mirage.

"Congratulations, Brock," she managed to say in a halfway-normal voice. "Your father must be very proud."

Polite words, but she knew—and Brock knew—that it was a dig. He would never openly acknowledge her contribution to the project, and he would never admit that he got this big promotion based on nepotism rather than merit.

"Tessa works for Brock," Helen explained to RJ, "at the family's counseling center in Lake Forest."

Helen's helpful words may have been directed at RJ, but Tessa acknowledged the return fire. She didn't remember Helen being cruel as a child and wondered what exactly Brock had told her. If this news turned out to be true—if Brock was really going to be her boss—then she would need to start job-hunting immediately.

"We'll launch the center in the fall," said Brock, "which means—between sailing and work—it's going to be a crazy summer."

"I'm sure," she murmured. She didn't trust herself to say more.

"In fact," he said, as if the idea had just occurred to him, "I wonder if you might be interested in taking on some of my clients? I'll need to cut back on counseling hours now that I have ongoing management responsibilities."

If Tessa clenched her teeth any harder, they would crumble into dust in her mouth. She forced her jaw to unlock.

"Wow, Brock, I don't know what to say," she hedged.

"Say yes, so that I have enough practice time to beat this guy in the next race." He gestured to RJ with a laugh that sounded forced. More than anything, Brock hated to lose.

RJ must be able to tell how upset she was. She could hide it from Brock and Helen, but she couldn't hide it from him. Her entire body had gone tense, and she felt like his arm was the only thing holding her together.

Maybe Brock had screwed her over, career-wise. Maybe all her careful planning was for naught. Maybe—she fought the urge to vomit—Brock was indeed now her boss. However, that didn't mean that she needed to play along. She had many tools in her arsenal, and passive-aggressive resistance was just the one she needed right now. She leaned her head on RJ's shoulder, looked up at Brock, and smiled.

"I'm afraid I'll have to say no, Brock," she said breezily. "I've just agreed to crew for RJ for the rest of the season. It will be all I can do to manage my current clients and still make it up here for the races."

She could feel RJ's chuckle as he squeezed her arm and then, to her delight, kissed the top of her head. She reveled in the warmth that flowed down her body even as she kept her eyes on Brock.

"Pity," he bit out.

"I'm sure one of the other counselors will be happy to help you out."

She should be miserable, mourning the destruction of her carefully laid plans. Instead she felt light. Any lighter and she would float away on the breeze like one of the wish lanterns.

"In that case, we'll see you on the lake," he snapped.

He turned on his heel and strode away, tugging Helen along in his wake.

Tessa had just hammered the first nail in her professional coffin. Oddly, she found that she looked forward to doing it again. Brock had hijacked her career plan. She owed him no loyalty. She would use up all her vacation days, find a new job, and partner with RJ to kick Brock's sorry ass on the water.

"Leave it to Brock to keep preppy alive," murmured RJ as Brock and Helen disappeared into the darkness.

She snickered, then turned in his arms and gave him a huge hug. He wrapped both arms around her. He was big and warm and the muscled planes of his chest felt incredibly good against her forehead. It was all she could do to keep from purring.

She pulled back before she could embarrass herself. The cool night air helped to clear her head, as did RJ's next words.

"Do you seriously work for him?" he asked, releasing her and shoving his hands into his pockets. "That must suck."

It felt so good to laugh about it. She felt free. Cold, but free. She crossed her arms and rubbed them to make up for the loss of RJ's body heat.

"Until today, I technically worked *with* him. We were colleagues, but I guess this promotion will make him my boss." She made a face. "It does suck."

"I'm surprised that Helen's dating him," said RJ. He shook his head. "She's a sweetheart. What do women see in him?"

"I have no idea," she muttered, unable to keep the sarcasm out of her voice.

He glanced at her, then did a double take.

"Did you...?"

"What, are you a freaking mind reader?" she snapped, hugging herself tighter. "It was a brief lapse in judgment, never to be repeated. Trust me."

He laughed. She gave him the evil eye and he managed to control the laughter, but he couldn't quite pull a straight face. The fact that she had dated Brock—however briefly—was humiliating enough without RJ's finding it so hilarious.

"We will never speak of it again," he promised, his voice solemn but his lips still twitching.

"No, we won't," she agreed.

"I have to admit," he said. "I'm really glad Brock pissed you off. You needed a special incentive to be my crew for the summer."

"You're lucky I have a temper."

"We are going to have the best time," he said.

And she believed him.

"You're freezing," said RJ. "I'm going to find you a jacket."

He took off before Tessa could object again and jogged toward his house in the darkness. The words echoed in his mind, still a surprise after six months. *His house.* The permanence of home ownership was something he'd always avoided, until his grandfather had made the decision for him. Sometimes RJ wondered if Pops had known that he was throwing RJ a lifeline when he most needed one. If he couldn't have his grandfather back, he would honor the old man's faith in him by taking care of the house and not turning into a douchebag like his dad. He would also look out for Nana Vi. She was putting up a strong front after losing Pops, but it wasn't good for her to spend so much time alone in her apartment downtown. He needed to convince her to come up to the lake.

He found a windbreaker hanging inside the kitchen door and grabbed it for himself. For Tessa, he scored a thick, heavy fleece out of the hall closet. As he jogged back toward the bonfire, he realized that he was grinning in the dark like an idiot. Talk about luck. Not only had he solved his crew problem, but he had solved it with one of his favorite people, and a freakishly talented sailor to boot.

He had to admit that he was a little uneasy about the unexpected chemistry between them. After however many years away, he was finding it difficult to classify her as an extra little sister. He knew her, and yet he didn't. She was a mystery wrapped up in the familiar. If she had been any other woman, he would already be pouring on the charm, but this was Tessa. She had always been immune. Besides, she still wanted that white picket fence, and to him, it still looked like window dressing on a prison.

It all added up to a hands-off protocol, no matter how tempting the sizzle.

RJ found Tessa toasting her hands at the fading bonfire. He walked up behind her and wrapped the fleece around her shoulders, positioning it so that she could easily slip her arms into the sleeves. She snuggled into it, and he couldn't resist closing his arms around her, warming her back while the fire warmed the front of her. He rested his chin on the top of her head and ignored the mocking voice of his conscience. *Hands off?*

"Better?" he asked.

She nodded and leaned back against him. He acknowledged his body's response, then did his best to shut it down.

"We should talk calendar at some point," he murmured. "Make sure all the race dates work for you. And we need to find some time to practice. You'll be rusty."

"I hope you don't regret asking me," she said. "I've developed a burning need to kick Brock's ass."

He chuckled. "No regrets here. When we win that trophy, and Brock has to smile and clap and pretend to congratulate us, you'll know you made the right decision."

She couldn't help but laugh with him.

"I don't remember Brock being this much of a prick," said RJ. "What went wrong?"

She shrugged within the circle of his arms. "I don't know. Somewhere along the line he went from cocky to jerk, and it took me too long to figure it out."

"How long did you guys date?" he asked curiously. He could barely stand to be around the guy for five minutes.

"Not long," she said grimly. "Long enough. I don't want to talk about Brock. I want to talk strategy and ground rules."

Tessa moved out of his arms, turning to face him. He was about to ask what she meant by 'ground rules' when someone ducked under his arm and cozied up against his side. He blinked down at the newcomer in surprise. It was little Heidi Steffan. He felt suddenly ancient. Heidi was frozen in his memory at about seven, chubby with curly pigtails and half her teeth missing. He wasn't prepared to deal with the twenty-year-old Heidi, fully grown and full of purpose.

"Hey RJ," she purred, completely ignoring Tessa. "I hear you need a new crew. Want to teach me how to sail?"

Tessa's eyes widened. He could only imagine what she was thinking. RJ eased himself gently away from Heidi, giving her an avuncular pat on the back.

"Sorry to disappoint, but I'm all set," he said, monitoring Tessa's reaction more closely than Heidi's.

"What? How?" she pouted prettily. "I really want to learn how to sail."

"I'm sure you'll find someone to teach you," he soothed. "It just won't be me."

After a little more coddling, Heidi drifted away, disappointed but not, thankfully, angry. Angry women made RJ very uncomfortable.

"Want to walk down by the water?" he asked Tessa. She nodded. Together, they wandered down to the little strip of rocky beach, stopping occasionally to say good night to the neighbors heading in the other direction. By the time they reached their destination, they had the beach to themselves. They stood side by side, looking out over the lake while the night breeze stirred up the unmistakable scent of the shoreline. Some might smell only dead fish and wet leaves, but to him it spoke of water, wind, and freedom.

"If we're going to do this," she said softly, "let's lay out some ground rules."

"What did you have in mind?" He had no idea what she was talking about, but it sounded very mysterious.

She took a deep breath before she spoke.

"The last time we spent any real time together was, what, eight years ago?"

He nodded. His last summer at the lake. The summer he and Tessa had tried to keep Sunny from self-destructing.

"A lot has happened since then," she continued. "People change. They grow up." She wrapped the fleece more tightly around herself and looked up at him in the moonlight. "Things between us feel different now."

He studied her face as he debated what to say. He would be lying if he said nothing had changed, but talking about it might make it harder to ignore.

"Does that bother you?" he asked.

"No, but it worries me," she answered. "I'm not sure what to do about it."

He grinned at that. "If you were anyone else, I would have several excellent suggestions." Maybe they could breeze through this. Laugh it off.

"I figured as much," she said with half a smile.

"You don't want to hear them?" he asked, hoping she would follow his lead and keep things light.

"Well, that's the problem," she said. "I find that I do want to hear them."

His body reacted to her answer before his brain caught up. The surge of lust took him by surprise, filling his head with images of Tessa in his bed. He could see it too clearly, her blond hair spilling across the pillows, her eyelids heavy. She would lose that tight control and maddening calm and slowly melt in his arms. He caught himself reaching for her and stopped. This was not the time for touching. Hands off. That was the protocol.

"You have no idea how tempting that is," he said, "but it's

still a bad idea."

"Because I can't do light and easy."

He nodded. She moved closer, which made it hard for him to think clearly.

"What if I really want to give it a try?" she asked.

He shook his head slowly. There was a reason they shouldn't do this. Something really important. Unfortunately, his brain had fogged up to the point that he couldn't seem to grab hold of a coherent thought.

"You don't think I can do it?"

That was it. That was the reason. He nodded.

"What if I promise?" she said. Her voice was calm and even, but there was a hint of a smile to it.

"Promise what?" he asked. He reached for her hips, but he wasn't sure if he intended to pull her closer or keep her away. She slid her hands up his chest until they rested on his heart.

"I promise that I'll end it cleanly," she said, "before things get ugly."

He started to object, but she kept talking.

"Years from now, when I'm married to the perfect man with my two-point-five kids and my white picket fence, and you're dating some sexy sailor, we'll laugh about that crazy summer when we had an affair. We'll still be friends, and we won't have any regrets."

She stared up at him. He could feel her willing him to say yes.

"You can be very persuasive," he said. He told his conscience to shut the hell up and let him handle this.

She grinned at that. "Some people might even call me 'charming.'"

He pulled her hips against his, which caught her by surprise.

"Those are some pretty big promises," he said. God, she felt good. "Are you sure you can keep them?"

She nodded slowly.

"I'm a professional counselor, remember? I know how these things work."

He was pretty sure that was bullshit, but he really wanted to believe her.

"You said something about ground rules," he said, trying to keep his head on straight.

"Only one," she said. "Don't try to talk me into anything before I'm ready. I've never had a summer fling before, and I don't want to rush it."

He stared at her for a long minute before he answered. This was going to end in disaster. He should let go of her right now and walk away. But she gave him that long, slow smile and he was done.

"As you wish."

All she could think was, *Oh my God he's quoting 'The Princess Bride.'* She had no idea how long she stood there blinking at him in the moonlight, her hands clutching his jacket. Then she realized that he was waiting for her to make a move. He was waiting for *her* to kiss *him*.

"Oh, there you are, Tessa dear."

It took a few seconds for Tessa to realize that the voice belonged to her mother. She thunked her forehead down on RJ's chest. If she didn't answer, maybe her mother would go away.

"Hi, Mrs. James," said RJ. He didn't tense up or push her away. He just stood there, perfectly comfortable, while she hid in the circle of his arms and pretended her mother hadn't just busted them.

"RJ, dear, I thought that might be you."

Her mother thought she might be almost hooking up with somebody else? Tessa groaned and pushed herself away from RJ's warm chest. He kept one arm firmly around her waist as she turned to face her mother.

"How is your law practice going? I hear good things about your work."

"Thanks. I'm glad to hear that," said RJ diplomatically. "Things are going better than I ever expected."

Her mother probably had the inside scoop on all the local divorces.

"So few young people come back here after college," said Dora. "It's too bad, really, but all the good jobs are in the cities, and of course the social life. It's not so easy to find a date up here. Speaking of dates—"

"Mom." Tessa interrupted before her mother could go down that rabbit hole. "Did you need me for something?"

"Oh, right," said Dora. "I wanted to let you know that I'm heading up to the house. Mel walked into town for a drink with some of the young people. She asked me to tell you. Callie left with Adam and Danny a while ago, and your Dad and Zeke went back to the house."

"Don't wait up," said Tessa. "I'll catch up with Mel after RJ and I figure out the sailing schedule."

Tessa couldn't see her mother's face in the darkness, but she could imagine her smug expression all too easily.

"Take your time, dear," fluttered Dora. "Don't worry about us."

Her mother disappeared in the direction of the house and Tessa eased herself away from RJ. There was a part of her—a really big part, to be honest—that wanted to make the first move and let RJ kiss her into stupidity. But the moment was gone, and along with it her courage. She was new to this whole 'summer fling' business, and no matter how tempting he might be, she needed to go slow. No rush, no regrets.

"So when is the next race?" she asked, using practical considerations to put some distance between them. She couldn't read his face at all now with the moon at his back, and maybe that was for the best. She couldn't think clearly when she looked into his eyes.

"Next Saturday," he answered. "Most of the races are on Saturdays. A couple of them got pushed to Sunday for one reason or another. There's also a big regatta the week of the Fourth, if you can take some extra days off."

"I have a lot of vacation days," she said. "I'm sure I can make it work. I should be able to rearrange my schedule to take this Friday off, for practice."

"Sounds good."

"I'm going to catch up with Mel," she said. She needed to leave before she changed her mind and decided to rush into things. She started to unzip the fleece so that she could give it back to him, but he put his hand over hers.

"Keep it," he said. "You can give it back the next time I see you."

The moment his hand engulfed hers, her brain shut down. She stood motionless, more aware of the rise and fall of his chest than of her own shallow breaths. She had no idea how long they stood there. Two breaths? Ten? She hung suspended between fear and want, unable to choose.

When he finally let go, she decided that the ground-rule thing had been a really stupid idea. She shoved her hands in the pockets of the fleece and started to back away again.

"Thanks," she said. "I look forward to sailing with you, Skipper."

"I prefer 'Captain,'" he said with mock severity, "and I believe the correct word is sailing 'under' me."

"We'll see about that," she said with a laugh.

She threw the words over her shoulder as she walked away, unable to hide the skip in her step. Sure, she had butterflies in her belly, but she could tell already that this was going to be fun.

CHAPTER TWO

June, nineteen years ago

TESSA, CALLIE, AND MEL MARCHED INTO THE KITCHEN. TESSA held a wriggling bundle of fur in her arms, and her sisters flanked her, presenting a united front. Their mother was at the counter, stirring something in a Crock-Pot that might eventually be dinner. She was going through a slow-cooker phase. She glanced over her shoulder and did a double take when she caught sight of the puppy.

"Oh, what a sweet puppy!" she exclaimed, leaving the spoon in the crock-pot and coming over to scratch its head. "Whose is he?" she asked.

Mel stepped forward, gave her mother her most charming smile, and prepared to persuade.

"He's ours," she announced.

Tessa crossed her fingers under the puppy's butt. For a moment her mother blinked at the three of them, then she burst out laughing.

"Oh, that's a good one," she chuckled. "I was not expecting that. Seriously, who does he belong to?"

"Seriously, he belongs to us," insisted Mel.

Her mother cocked her head to one side, studying Mel's face, then the matching faces of her sisters. At some point she realized her daughters were not kidding and she sighed.

"Oh, girls, we've talked about this. No pets until you turn ten. Don't think you can get me to change my mind so easily, no matter how cute the puppy."

Tessa could feel tears filling her eyes and she blinked, hoping they would start falling right away. Her chest swelled up with the injustice of it all. This little puppy needed a home, and they had a home, so why was her mother being so unreasonable?

"But mom—" pleaded Mel.

Her mother was already shaking her head at the three of them.

"Where did the puppy come from?" she asked. "I'll call and explain and we'll give him back so that another family can have a chance."

"No," said Tessa. "No." She said it louder the second time, then turned on her heel and marched right back out of the kitchen with the puppy. Mel and Callie stayed behind to continue pleading the case. When her sneakers hit the dirt in the back yard, Tessa took off running down the shore path and hid with the puppy under the troll bridge. Sunny found her there a minute later.

"I saw you running," she said, out of breath herself. "What's going on? Oh! A puppy."

Sunny immediately began petting him and cooing over him. Tessa sniffled, torn between anger and despair.

"My mother says we can't keep him," said Tessa, "but he needs a home. He doesn't have anybody else in the world."

"That's not fair," said Sunny. "Look how he loves you. You have to keep him."

The puppy at that point was climbing out of Tessa's arms and into Sunny's lap, which delighted her.

Tessa shook her head sadly.

"I don't think my mom is going to change her mind," she said.

"Well if you can't keep him, then I'll keep him," Sunny declared.

"Do you really think your mom would let you?" asked Tessa.

"Yes," said Sunny. She sounded confident, but Tessa could tell that she was faking.

"Let's go ask," said Tessa, before Sunny could lose her nerve.

Together they hurried over to Sunny's house, where Sunny found her mother and grandmother in the kitchen. Nana Vi had been up since dawn, but Sunny's mom had just wandered downstairs. She liked to sleep late in the summertime. She lounged at the kitchen table in a silky kimono that gaped open. Tessa tried not to look, because she was pretty sure Sunny's mom wasn't wearing anything underneath.

"Mom, Mom, Mom." Sunny bounced with excitement, unable to hold on to the puppy, who then leaped to the floor and began sniffing around the kitchen. Nana Vi laughed, but Sunny's mom groaned and covered her eyes.

"Sunny, please tell me that there is not a muddy puppy roaming around the kitchen."

"There is! There is!" exclaimed Sunny, still bouncing and now clapping as well.

"Please return it to its rightful owner immediately," ordered her mother. Sunny's bouncing slowed down.

"I am the rightful owner," said Sunny. Tessa nearly burst with pride. Her friend wasn't usually brave enough to say things like that out loud.

"No you are not," said her mother. Sunny deflated a little

more and the bouncing stopped.

"But mom, he needs a home," she said.

"And he will have one," said her mother, "but it won't be ours."

Nana Vi had been watching this whole exchange and when Sunny's mom said 'ours' she stiffened.

"Actually, Nancy," said Vi, "this is my home, and I must say I've been meaning to get a dog for ages. Just never found the right one."

She crossed the room to scoop up the puppy, who promptly licked her face. She smiled conspiratorially at Sunny.

"What do you think, Sunny? Is this the puppy I've been looking for?"

Sunny grinned and nodded. Tessa had to admit that Sunny had the coolest grandmother in the world. Not that Tessa had any grandparents for comparison, but Nana Vi was still the coolest.

Nancy gave Nana Vi a scary look, then rose from the table.

"Whatever," she said. "Let's be very clear that the dog will not be coming home with us at the end of the summer."

She swept out of the kitchen, leaving the puppy-lovers behind to crow over their victory.

"Can we really keep him, Nana?" asked Sunny. "You really mean it?"

Nana Vi ruffled Sunny's curls.

"I mean everything I say, missy, and I am keeping this dog. Will you help me feed him?" Sunny nodded. "How about teaching him how to do tricks?" Sunny nodded again. "Good," said Nana Vi. "When I'm done cleaning the kitchen we'll go to the store and get some puppy supplies. Now you girls take him outside to play until I'm ready to go."

The girls tumbled outside, puppy following behind, and they sat in the shade of a tall maple throwing sticks for him, still unable to believe their good fortune.

"What should we call him?" asked Sunny. "Did you name him already?"

Tessa shook her head. They sat in silence while they thought about it for a minute.

"Spot?" proposed Sunny.

Tessa cocked her head to one side, studying the puppy as he tried to chew through the stick.

"He doesn't really have any spots," she observed.

"Oh, right," said Sunny.

"What about Lucky?" asked Tessa. "It's pretty lucky that you get to keep him."

Sunny smiled.

"I like it," she said.

Tessa nodded her agreement.

"Lucky it is."

Tuesday after Memorial Day, today

Tessa typed the last of her notes about the previous session and closed the file, only to stare at the mystery of her calendar all over again. The receptionists at the Hammond Center rarely used the special features of their high-end appointment-booking system, but someone had taken the time to mark her next appointment with an ominous red flag. Whoever had booked the appointment for this unnamed new client had over-ridden the standard time blocks and allotted two full hours for the visit, including a fifteen-minute pre-meeting with Dr. Hammond himself. Only VIPs got this treatment, but she was too low on the ladder to work with anybody exciting. She checked her watch one last time, then pushed back her chair. There was only one way to find out what was going on.

Gliding through the hall—there was no way to walk on the

thick, padded carpet without gliding—Tessa approached the inner sanctum. Dr. Hammond's assistant saw her coming and pressed a button on the sleek black desk phone.

"Miss James is here," she murmured.

Dr. James. Tessa had to bite down hard to stop herself from making the correction. She had worked her ass off for that PhD, and here of all places she expected people to call her Dr. James. However, she was not foolish enough to piss off Dr. Hammond's assistant.

"Send her in," replied the voice from the speaker.

Tessa obeyed Dr. Hammond's command automatically, heading toward the door to his office even as his assistant gestured in that direction. The door opened as she approached. She stepped into the posh office and stopped short. The person who had opened the office door was the general counsel for the Hammond Center.

This could not be good.

"Sit," said Dr. Hammond.

She paused before complying. What would his next command be? Roll over? Play dead? She sat in one of the two cushioned leather chairs facing his desk, and the attorney claimed the other.

"Miss James," began Dr. Hammond, "we find ourselves in an awkward situation. An old friend contacted me to ask for help in assessing his mother's state of mind. She refused point blank to see any of our therapists until she learned that you were on staff. Do you know a woman named Viola Foster?"

Tessa didn't bother to hide her surprise.

"Does she have a grandson named RJ?"

"She does," answered Dr. Hammond. He nodded at the attorney. "Excellent. I'm glad we can confirm the connection. I've known her son Robert—RJ's father—for many years. Despite his move to California we've kept in touch. You may have heard that her husband died about six months ago."

Tessa nodded, wondering what was going on with Nana Vi. RJ had said that she was doing okay, but his father, it seemed, did not agree. That was worrisome enough on its own. Even more concerning was how she was supposed to help.

"Since losing her husband, Mrs. Foster has displayed some unusual behavior. According to reports, she talks to her dead husband as if he were there with her, and she refuses to speak about him in the past tense. Robert is understandably concerned about her, but it's difficult for him to monitor or assess the situation from California. She lives alone in the apartment she and her husband shared for decades. She still drives. In fact, she drove herself here today. She's waiting in your office now."

"Sir, with all due respect—"

"Let me guess," he interrupted. "You're about to express ethical qualms about how you shouldn't take on a patient with whom you have a personal relationship."

She nodded.

"And if a personal relationship is the only scenario in which she will accept help?"

"I'm sure I can persuade her to—"

"You're welcome to try," interrupted Dr. Hammond. For a therapist, he was surprisingly cynical. "If, however, she refuses to work with anyone else, I expect you to make the assessment."

Her eyes widened. She wasn't sure she could bring herself to declare Nana Vi incompetent, even if she had gone completely off the deep end. Another thought occurred to her.

"Is the family aware that I'm the one who will be meeting with her?" she asked.

"Robert has asked that this assessment remain confidential."

"So the rest of the family doesn't know," she pressed.

"They do not," replied Dr. Hammond.

"And Mr. Foster? Does he know that I'm the practitioner?"

Given the role she had played in his domestic disintegration, she doubted he would approve of her going anywhere near his mother.

"He does."

She gave Dr. Hammond a hard stare. He didn't seem to be lying. She looked over at the attorney, who had remained silent all this time. He nodded in confirmation. She was mystified. RJ's dad must be very, very worried about Nana Vi if he was willing to let Tessa meet with her. Her heart sank. The last thing she wanted was to be the catalyst for yet another Foster family crisis. However, it didn't seem like she had much choice in the matter.

"I'll talk to her," said Tessa. "If I can persuade her to see someone else, someone more impartial, I will."

"Very well," said Dr. Hammond. "In that case, hand her off to Brock."

Tessa held herself very still. There was no chance in hell that she would place a fragile Nana Vi in Brock's care, but she couldn't exactly say that to Brock's own father. If she had any doubts about the need for an escape plan, Dr. Hammond was graciously removing them. She would help Nana Vi—as her friend, not her therapist—and then she would move on.

Tessa hurried back to her office. The gentle lighting and layered neutral textures of the Hammond Center had been designed to soothe, but they did nothing to calm her swirling thoughts. Memories of Nana Vi, and Sunny, and RJ, and fractured families, and fragile friends, and all her regrets, all her wishes jumbled together. She needed to get a grip.

The door to her office stood ajar, and Tessa could see the back of one petite shoulder through the opening. As promised, Nana Vi was already waiting. Tessa stopped a few feet away and took a calming breath. She mentally swept her swirling thoughts into a pile and then imagined scooping them into a box and closing it up. She would deal with it—all of it—later.

Squaring her shoulders, she stepped calmly into her office.

It was a good thing she had taken a moment to prepare herself, because the change in Nana Vi was radical enough to take her breath away. She hadn't seen Vi since last summer, when her husband was still alive and they were both up at the lake. Now she looked like an echo of herself, so fragile that a strong gust of wind would knock her over. The moment she recognized Tessa, though, a light came into her eyes.

"Well, look at you," she said, standing up with surprising agility and clasping Tessa by the shoulders. She examined Tessa closely, gave a sharp nod, and then kissed her on both cheeks. Tessa embraced her gently. The elderly woman might look fragile, but her grip remained strong and she smelled good. Although Tessa didn't have any grandparents of her own, Nana Vi was her honorary fairy godmother, and she was suddenly overwhelmed with relief that Vi had insisted upon seeing her for this evaluation.

Tessa closed the office door for privacy.

"Come sit on the couch with me and tell me what's going on," she said, ushering Vi to the couch where they sat they sat side by side.

"I'm here because my son thinks I'm crazy," said Vi.

"And why would he think that?" asked Tessa. She kept her expression innocent, but Nana Vi cackled anyway. People had been calling her crazy for years. She had never been particularly good at following the rules.

"Because I talk to dead people," she answered.

"I see," said Tessa. She waited for the rest of the explanation.

"Do you practice that in the mirror?" asked Vi.

"What?"

"The therapist stuff. 'I see,'" she mocked. "Tell me you practice the poker face."

Tessa nodded, no longer trying to hide her smile.

"It's part of the training," she teased. "I took a class."

"Ha," said Vi. "I knew it."

"I can see that you haven't changed," said Tessa. "You've always been crazy, so what's the big deal now? Which dead people are you talking to, and more importantly, are they talking back?"

Vi looked down at her hands and began spinning her engagement ring around her finger. She had lost enough weight that it rattled loose against the wedding band, only the swell of her knuckle keeping both rings from falling off.

"Nana, you need to tell me what's going on. I can't help if you don't tell me."

Vi gave her a sharp look, then looked back down at her hands. Tessa waited. In truth, she had never practiced her poker face in the mirror, but she had certainly practiced waiting for her clients to open up. She didn't have to wait long for Vi, though. Patience had never been one of her virtues.

"I talk to Robert," she muttered. "Senior."

"You miss him," said Tessa.

"Of course I miss him," snapped Vi. "We were married for sixty years. I talked with him every single day for sixty years. I'm not going to stop now just because he's dead. I'll be joining him soon enough."

Tessa swallowed but the lump in her throat wouldn't go away. If she ever found a love strong enough to last sixty years, she wouldn't stop talking to her husband either, not even if he was dead.

"Did you tell that to Robert Junior?" she asked softly. "It doesn't sound crazy to me."

"Not exactly," admitted Vi.

"What exactly did you tell him?"

"I told him to mind his own fucking business," said Vi.

Tessa snorted. She had forgotten Vi's foul mouth.

"How did he find out about it in the first place?" asked Tessa. "Isn't he in California?"

When Vi looked away, clearly uncomfortable, Tessa knew she was on to something interesting.

"I didn't know he had a spy," she said. "The cleaning girl, Kaja. She comes every morning to help. She ratted me out."

Tessa waited until Vi looked back at her.

"She heard you talking to your husband?"

Vi nodded.

"What kinds of things do you talk about?" asked Tessa.

"Normal things," answered Vi, clearly on the defensive. "We read the morning paper, and we'll point out interesting articles or funny little things that catch our attention. He has such a sly sense of humor…"

Tessa blinked back the tears that threatened to fall.

"Does he still make you laugh?"

Vi nodded.

"It's easy to imagine what he would say. Sometimes I like to think that he's whispering in my ear."

They sat in silence for a few minutes. Tessa's heart hurt for Nana Vi. She wanted to learn more, and she wanted to talk to this Kaja who saw her every day, but first impressions were important, and her first impression was strong.

"I don't think you're crazy," said Tessa. "Just sad. There's nothing wrong with being sad."

Vi looked her right in the eye and the depth of the grief she saw took Tessa's breath away.

"You're damn right I'm sad," she said. "How long am I supposed to wait around before I can be with him again? I'd like to get this over with."

"Get what over with?" asked Tessa. Her whole body prickled with warning.

"Life."

CHAPTER THREE

July, nineteen years ago

"I'M BORED," SAID TESSA.

She and Sunny had been wading in the cool shade under the troll bridge while Lucky lounged on the ledge, but Tessa had had enough. She sat down on the ledge beside Lucky and pulled her feet out of the water, wrapping her arms around her knees and wiggling her toes. Sunny sat beside her and matched her pose. Tessa looked back and forth between her own naked toes and Sunny's brightly painted ones. She frowned.

"I want to paint my toenails," she said.

"I thought your mom wouldn't let you," said Sunny.

Tessa frowned even more.

"It's not fair that you can paint your toes and I can't."

"I know," said Sunny.

"Where does your mom keep her nail polish?" asked Tessa.

"In her bathroom," said Sunny, "but I don't think—"

"Please," begged Tessa. "We'll be really careful, and we won't spill any, and it's not like it's permanent. If my mom is really mad, we can take it back off again."

Sunny still looked doubtful, but Tessa could tell she was thinking about it.

"Please," repeated Tessa, using her best puppy eyes this time.

"I don't want your mom to be mad at me," she said.

"She won't. I promise," said Tessa. "She'll be mad at me for breaking the rule, but not you."

"Are you sure?"

"Positive."

Tessa held her breath while Sunny made her decision.

"Fine," said Sunny. "But you had better be right about your mom."

"Thank you," said Tessa, putting her arm around Sunny's shoulders and squeezing. "Let's go do it right now."

Tessa was out from under the bridge and heading toward Sunny's house before her friend could even catch her breath. Sunny ran to catch up and Lucky trotted along behind them. Most everybody else was down at the pier swimming, so they didn't run into any grown-ups along the way. Tessa knew that Sunny wasn't completely on board with this plan. All it would take was one question from a grown-up and she would change her mind.

This summer was turning out to be really interesting. She had never had a friend outside of her sisters before. Now, for the first time in her life, she had her own friend, and her own secrets. It made her world feel bigger.

"Nana Vi and Pops went out for the afternoon, and my mom is taking a nap," said Sunny, "but I know where she keeps everything. We can tiptoe past her and into the bathroom. The bottles of nail polish are in the little closet behind the bath-room door."

They snuck into the house through the porch door and tiptoed down the hall to Sunny's mom's bedroom. She slept in the only bedroom on the main level. Everyone else slept upstairs. Tessa let Sunny take the lead and followed Sunny's cues to keep quiet. Her mom was supposed to be sleeping, but as they got close they could hear noises coming from the bedroom. From the expression on Sunny's face, Tessa could tell that she was also confused by the noise. Maybe her mom was watching TV.

Sunny gently pushed the door open and the two of them stood frozen in the doorway. Sunny's mom was totally naked, straddling their friend Annabelle's dad as if she were riding a horse. He had his eyes closed and didn't even notice the girls. Sunny's mom had her back to the door. Her hands gripped his shoulders as she rode him, pounding on his lap in a way that made no sense. His hands clutched her breasts. Tessa wondered why they were panting, and if it hurt to have your boobs squeezed like that. They both looked like they were in pain. They started to make some louder noises, then yelled together, then Sunny's mom collapsed in a heap on top of Annabelle's dad, and the only noise was the sound of them breathing.

"Mom?"

Sunny's voice was really quiet, but she might as well have yelled. Her mother levitated off the bed. Annabelle's dad put his hands over his face like maybe he was going to cry and rolled onto his side. Tessa was glad that he turned away because she did not want to see his private parts again.

"Get out!" screamed Sunny's mom. She pushed them backwards into the hallway and they stumbled against the far wall. She leaned in until her nose almost touched Sunny's. "Don't you ever say a word about this to anybody, do you understand?"

Sunny nodded. Then her mother spun around, took two steps back into the bedroom, and slammed the door in their faces.

They heard the lock click, and then a thump as something bumped against the door and slid down it. It sounded like maybe Sunny's mom was crying. Tessa reached over and took Sunny by the hand. They were both shaking. Tessa pulled Sunny down the hall and led her back to the troll bridge, Lucky at their heels. They sat under the bridge for what seemed like hours. RJ found them there. Sunny wouldn't speak. Tessa tried to explain what had happened, even though it still didn't make a lot of sense. To their relief, RJ went away to investigate. They stayed right where they were until the shadows stretched out on the grass and Nana Vi came to find them.

Today

RJ walked home from work, savoring every second of his five-minute commute. It was his favorite part of the day. After weeks of rain and overcast skies, the entire neighborhood had exploded with color. The earliest bulbs had faded, giving way to the second wave, mostly irises and tulips. People had spent Memorial Day weekend cleaning up their gardens and filling up their planters and flower boxes with annuals. The trees were in full leaf, the grass freshly mowed, and he could smell the lake even though it was still a few blocks away. It couldn't be more different from the desert browns and forced greens of California, and there was nowhere he would rather be.

People thought he was crazy for giving up the flash of L.A., but there was something soul-crushing about spending two and a half hours every day in your car, sucking exhaust, and bored out of your skull. It doesn't matter how close you live to the ocean if you only see it for five minutes in the morning. Long hours at the office do not a good surfer make. Besides, as much as he had loved surfing and sailing on the ocean, he loved the lake more. Here in Hidden Springs he got to sail all summer long on his own terms. No business suits. No partner track. No golden handcuffs.

God, he loved it here.

When he saw his sister's car parked in his driveway, he paused, then picked up the pace. He took the back steps two at a time and burst into the kitchen, only to find it empty. He dropped his messenger bag on the couch on his way through, stepped out onto the front porch, and almost immediately spotted her frizzy halo down at the lakefront. He crossed the commons at a jog, slowing as he approached.

He didn't need to worry. He could tell from her body language that she was okay. His nephews crawled in the sand at her feet, building sandcastles in the glorified sandbox they called a beach.

She turned as he drew close and her face lit up.

"Hey there, big brother," she said. He caught her in a hug as his nephews popped up from their work and started peppering him with questions.

"Uncle RJ, want to see what we made? It's a castle! And a river! Will you help me with the bucket? Here, you hold it—"

It was a good thing that RJ wore flip-flops to work, because seconds later he was ankle-deep in the water, scooping up a bucketful and then hustling back up to the castle to pour it slowly into the moat so that it could flow down the river and back into the lake. It was tiring work, river-making, and he needed to be quick on his feet to keep the flow going. Oscar and Huck helped, using tiny buckets, and between the three of them they kept the thing going for at least five minutes.

Sunny watched the three boys (yes, she was including RJ in that head count) from the edge of the beach, but she didn't join in their fun. It takes a light heart to build a sandcastle. Hers didn't qualify. She had hoped that coming down to the lake would allow her to leave her heartache behind, but so far it wasn't working. Instead, her sore heart wrapped itself in layer upon layer of memory, which only made it heavier than before.

The hardest part of parenting was the fact that it didn't let up, even when the foundation of your life shook beneath your feet. No matter how much everything might suck, the kids still needed you to show up. No excuses. No days off. The only way to find your balance was to find yourself some backup. So here she was, back in the place where her own childhood had gone off the rails, hoping she could keep things on track for her little guys. Hoping RJ would be able to help her find her feet again.

She didn't need to solve all her problems today. That would be impossible, in any case. She needed to steady herself, and think, and take things one moment at a time. Luckily, this moment couldn't be better. The end of May was always dicey, weather-wise, but today they had the gift of sunshine and soft air and ridiculously clear water. Even the mayflies weren't bad this year, especially with the breeze coming off the lake. Their home up in Madison might not be as urban as New York, but it was still a city, and it felt good to get away from the buzz of the crowd.

The sight of RJ with the boys made her want to laugh and cry all at the same time. If she could only borrow a little bit of RJ's inner child and sprinkle it like fairy dust on her husband, maybe things could be different.

RJ threw in the towel first.

"Oh, no!" he yelled, with as much drama as possible. He pretended to trip in slow motion and dumped his full bucket of water right onto the heads of his nephews. The water was still really cold, and there was much shrieking before they all fell into a heap on the beach. Sunny stood above them, hands on her hips, shaking her head.

"You couldn't have waited until they had their suits on?" she asked.

"Where's the fun in that?"

"No fun," said Oscar, looking just like his mom as he put his hands on his hips and shook his head right back at her, even though he was lying on his back on the sand.

"Again! Again!" shouted Huck.

RJ tickled him silly and then stood up, brushing off the sand and grinning unrepentantly at his sister.

"Who's hungry?" he asked.

Two little boys popped up from the sand, suddenly starving.

"My fridge is pretty much empty," he said, "but this is a special occasion. What do you say we go out for some pizza?"

Whoops of joy ensued. The little boys ran across the commons back to the house, while RJ trailed behind with Sunny. She watched them go, a wistful half smile on her face, but she didn't say anything to explain their unexpected visit.

"Good to see you, sis," he said.

"Likewise," she answered.

He stifled a sigh. No explanation meant that things were complicated. He would give her a free pass for now, but they would talk later, after the boys were asleep. No matter how bad things were, he needed to know.

"Tessa, sweetheart, I'm so glad you picked up."

"Hi, Mom," she sighed. "What's up?"

Tessa had answered the phone without checking the caller ID. Big mistake. Her last client of the day was due in less than ten minutes, and she still hadn't been able to write a single word about her meeting with Nana Vi. She should have let the call go to voicemail. Tessa closed her eyes and her notebook.

Maybe she would have better luck distilling her thoughts tonight.

"Well, honey, I wanted to ask you a tiny favor."

Tessa stifled a groan. Her mother had never in her life asked for a tiny favor. They always mushroomed into something far larger and more time-consuming than advertised.

"What is it?" she asked cautiously.

Her mother laughed.

"Nothing crazy, silly. Didn't you say that you were coming back up on Thursday night?"

"Ye-e-e-s," answered Tessa.

"I was hoping that you could pick me up at the airport on your way up. I land at about five in the afternoon. By the time I get my bag and walk outside, it will probably be six o'clock. I hate to ask your father to drive all the way down to get me when you'll be heading up anyway. You know how your father is about driving in traffic."

Actually, Tessa knew how her *mother* was when her father drove in traffic. Her running commentary, gasps of terror, attempts to use the invisible passenger-side brake pedal, and death grip on the armrest were more than any driver should have to endure. She would pick up her mother, if only to spare her father the trauma.

"Sure, Mom. I can pick you up. Can you ask Dad to email me the flight details so I have them handy?"

"Of course. Thank you, darling girl. Now I know you have to work so I won't keep you—"

"Wait a sec, Mom, you never said where you were going."

Tessa hadn't even thought to be suspicious until her mother tried to end the phone call. Her mother was *never* the one to end a phone call. The woman could chat for days.

"Oh," said her mother, clearly unprepared. "I'm going to visit an old friend in New York City. She's in the hospital and she asked me to come visit. How could I say no?"

"You have a friend in New York?" asked Tessa. She had never, not even once, heard her mother talk about a friend in New York City. Instead of answering the question, her mother tried to redirect.

"Darling, I just had the best idea. You know that the sailing school is getting ready for classes to start next week? The director is wonderful, and of course she'll call me with any questions, but may I give them your number, just in case there's some kind of crisis?"

Tessa hadn't even realized that it was prep week. Not only did her mother have a secret friend in New York, but this friend was important enough for Dora to blow off prep week. What the hell?

"Of course I'll help, Mom, but you do realize I'm almost two hours away, right? If it's really an emergency, I'm not going to be very useful."

"Of course, of course," fluttered Dora. "I'm not talking about fire or blood. They would call 911 for that. It's all the other things that come up, the everyday crises, really, that need a calm presence to sort out. Your father will be busy wrapping things up at the grade school, and he really doesn't know anything about sailing. I thought you would be a much better choice."

"Mom, how many phone calls are we talking about? They're not going to call me five or six times a day, are they? I won't be able to answer half the time."

"I know, I know," said Dora, "but humor me in this. I hate being away during prep week, and I'll feel better knowing that they have someone else they can call if they can't reach me."

"Why wouldn't they be able to reach you? You have a cell phone."

"Yes, but I don't know how things will be at the hospital, darling. You know how they have rules about cell phones." Her mother rushed to forestall further questions. "I know you have clients, so I won't keep you on the phone, but don't forget about your father's retirement party. You'll be here, won't you, on Saturday night?"

"Yes, Mom," said Tessa. "It's been on my calendar for months."

She clamped down on her raging curiosity. Maybe she could get some details out of her mother on the ride up from the airport, or after a glass of wine at the party. For now, she would let her mother think she had gotten away with...whatever it was she was getting away with.

"Thank you again, darling," said her mother. "And let me say that I'm so pleased you'll be back out on the water. RJ is such a talented young sailor. You two are well matched."

The way Dora said it made Tessa squirm.

"Yes, well, it's only for the summer," she said, "so don't start dreaming about trophies and publicity for the school."

Or wedding bells and grandchildren.

Dora laughed, for real this time. "I do like trophies and publicity."

"I know," said Tessa, suddenly wistful for all those summers where the only thing she worried about was the next race and the cutest boy. "Trust me, I know."

"Gotta run, sweetheart, but I'll see you this weekend."

After her mother had hung up, Tessa stared thoughtfully at the phone. She had three minutes left before her next session. On impulse, she dialed Callie's cell. Callie had just spent the month with Mom and Dad. Maybe she would know something about this New York trip. But Callie's phone went straight to voicemail, and Tessa hung up without leaving a message. Something was up with her parents, and she needed to find out more. Maybe spending weekends at the lake this summer was not such a crazy idea, after all.

CHAPTER FOUR

July, nineteen years ago

RJ STOOD IN THE DOORWAY OF HIS MOTHER'S ROOM, WATCHING her as she emptied drawers and threw armfuls of clothing into a suitcase. He couldn't breathe. All he could do was watch as she stormed around the room, leaving a trail of tears and destruction in her path.

He wasn't sure what to think about Tessa's story. It was hard enough to imagine his mom naked. Imagining her with Annabelle's dad was flat-out impossible. And yet, how could he not believe it? The two girls might not understand what they had seen, but he was old enough to get it. Something major had happened. He couldn't deny it, and neither could his mother.

She caught sight of him in the doorway and froze. Nothing moved in the room except for the rise and fall of her chest as she tried to stop crying, and the single sock that dropped from the pile of clothes in her arms.

"Leave me alone," she said. Her voice was harsh. It was the one she used when she was fighting with his dad. She had never used it on RJ before.

"Mom...," he began, then stopped. He didn't know what to ask. Everything felt wrong. "Are we leaving? Should I pack, too?"

"No," she said. "I'm leaving. You're staying."

She resumed her packing.

"Where are you going?" he asked.

"Away," she said. This time she did not stop moving around the room. "Your father needs to learn that he can *not*"—she emphasized the word by jamming clothing into the corners of the suitcase—"control me. I am not a doll that he can take out and play with whenever he likes, and then throw in the back of the closet when he discovers a pretty new one. He can *not*"—this time she slammed the closet door—"ship me off to live under the supervision of his mother while he enjoys his freedom in the city. There is no way in hell that I'm going to turn into a compliant little Stepford wife. Ever."

RJ stared at her. He had no idea what she was talking about. He watched as she tried to close the suitcase, muttering under her breath. It didn't look like it was going to work, but she tucked in all the loose ends, used her body weight to press the top down, and managed to pull the zipper all the way around the edges. She stood up, flushed but triumphant.

She was really leaving.

"Don't go," he whispered.

"What did you say?" she asked.

He could see the answer in her eyes, but he couldn't stop himself from asking again. He needed her. Sunny needed her. She couldn't just go away.

"Don't go." He said it louder this time, but it didn't make a difference.

"I'm going," she said. There was no room for negotiation when she used that voice.

He felt light, like maybe panic was helium and in a few minutes he would be so full of it that he could float away. He held onto the doorframe to anchor himself, but had to let go when she left the bedroom, dragging her suitcase behind her. He leaned against the hallway wall and watched her disappear into the kitchen.He heard the squeak of the back door and the thump of the suitcase as she pulled it down the back steps. With each thump, he slid a little lower down the wall until he finally hit the floor. He steadied himself on the smooth wood. His stomach grew heavy, weighing him down. So strange, to feel light and heavy at the same time.

He didn't move, just listened to the sounds of his mother leaving. He heard the trunk. The car door. The sound of the engine turning over. He heard his mother put the car in reverse, back out of the parking space, and drive away. After the sound of the engine had faded into the distance, he could hear lots of other things. Kids outside. Birds. Every now and then a shriek and a splash from the direction of the water. He couldn't seem to move, so he sat and listened.

It was a warm afternoon, and muggy, so eventually RJ laid his head down on the cool wood floor and closed his eyes. He didn't want to think about what had just happened, or what would happen next. He wanted everything to go back the way it was before. After a while, he fell asleep, and that was where Nana Vi found him.

Today

RJ flopped onto the couch after the little boys had gone to bed. For all their protests about not being tired, they had nearly fallen asleep in the bathtub, and had conked out completely the minute their still-damp heads had hit their pillows. Sunny landed beside him on the couch.

"Peace at last," she said.

"Amen, sister," he answered.

They stared out the front windows at the lake, neither of them feeling the need to say anything. RJ was hoping that she would offer an explanation for her visit, but as the minutes ticked by it became clear that she was not going to make any confessions. He would either have to be very sneaky or very direct if he wanted to find out what was going on.

His phone rang, breaking the silence. He dug it out of his back pocket and checked the caller ID.

"It's Mom," he said. "Does she know you're here?"

Sunny gave him a panicked look and shook her head. He sighed and answered.

"Hey, Mom."

"Your father has crossed the line this time."

"I'm fine, Mom. How are you?" he replied, rolling his eyes in Sunny's direction.

"I'm serious, RJ. I need you to speak with your father. The situation is completely unacceptable."

"What is it this time?" he asked.

"Apparently, your father has decided—with no warning at all—to stop paying the bill for the Neiman Marcus card." RJ could hear the familiar tremor in her voice, the one that meant she was so angry that she might cry. "Do you have any idea how humiliating it is to have your card declined? Do you? I'll never be able to show my face there again."

He made the appropriate soothing noises and waited for her to wind down. The insult was fresh, so this would take a while. Sunny was no fool. She recognized the tone of her mother's voice even if she couldn't hear the exact words. She gave RJ a tiny wave and fled the room. Traitor. He wished that he could escape, too, but he had long ago accepted his role as family mediator. Hell, he was good at it. He just hoped that one of these days they would let him mediate their divorce. Nineteen years of torture was long enough.

When his mother finally let him go, after extracting his promise to fix things, he found Sunny in the kitchen pulling together something that looked like dinner. She handed him a beer from the fridge and they clinked bottles.

"To family," she said.

He couldn't quite bring himself to echo her words, so he leaned back against the counter and took a long pull of the cold beer. She laughed.

"That bad, huh?"

"You don't want to know," he answered, and he didn't want to tell her. The implosion of their parents' marriage had nearly destroyed Sunny. He would do whatever he needed to do to shield her from the never-ending torture of their separation. She did much better when she kept her distance, and they both knew it.

She gave him a crooked smile. "You always were the smart one."

"You going to tell me why you're here?" he asked.

She looked down at her feet, then back up at him. "I'd rather not," she said.

He didn't like that answer, but he wasn't sure how much to push.

"Where's Will?"

"At home," she said carefully.

"And will he be joining you here?"

She shook her head. He wanted to push, but the shimmer of tears in her eyes stopped him. He really hoped that Will hadn't done something stupid. RJ liked Will and didn't want to have to kill him.

"You know, at some point you have to tell me what's going on," he said.

"I know," she whispered. "Just not yet, okay?"

"Okay," he said, and wrapped her up in a big hug.

He couldn't make it better if he didn't know what was going

on, but had learned the hard way not to push when his sister was feeling fragile. If he wanted to help, he would need to be patient.

Sunny sagged against RJ in relief. He wasn't going to make her explain. She knew she had to tell him at some point, but she also knew exactly what he would say. He wasn't a big believer in marriage to begin with, so at the first hint of trouble, he would advise an amicable parting, before things got ugly. Trouble was, there were two kids in the middle of her troubles with Will, and she would do anything to make sure they didn't get hurt. She didn't want them to grow up shuttling between two parents. Her own experience had left too many scars. She wanted to work things out with Will, and she didn't want to have to fight through her brother's objections along the way.

She needed to fix this all by herself.

Tessa mulled over the chaos of her life as she fought traffic on her way to O'Hare on Thursday night. She should never have agreed to pick up her mom at the airport. They would both have made it to the lake faster if her Mom had taken a cab to the train and Tessa had taken the back roads. Instead she got to enjoy three hours of heavy traffic and self-analysis after a painfully long day at work.

Lovely.

Her worst fears had been confirmed at the staff meeting on Wednesday, when Dr. Hammond, Brock's father, had announced that Brock would be heading up the new couples counseling program. Tessa had celebrated Wednesday night by updating her resume, then drinking half a bottle of Chardonnay and psychoanalyzing the contestants on *The Bach-*

elor. It should be easy enough to find another counseling job at another center, but instead of looking forward to a fresh start, she dreaded it.

Only last week, her life had been simple, her plan clear. Today she was doubting her career choice, her judgment, and her approach to relationships. Everything had changed at the barbecue.

She had been trained to pay attention to behavior, so she couldn't help but observe her own. People can delude themselves just as easily as they can fool others, but if you pay attention to what people do, rather than what they say, you'll know their true desires. Apparently Tessa desired an affair with RJ. She had made him a bold promise even though she knew full well she couldn't keep it. She wanted this affair so much that she was planning to hide a world of heartbreak from RJ at the end. Maybe she could pull it off. Maybe not.

There was only one way to find out.

By the time she broke free of the gridlock to make the exit at O'Hare, she was half an hour late. Her mother had already collected her suitcase and was waiting outside. Tessa found her on the first go-round, and within moments had her mother safely installed in the passenger seat and her suitcase in the trunk. Oddly, instead of the usual flow of chatter from her mother, Tessa got exactly one sentence.

"Thanks for picking me up, sweetheart."

At first, Tessa was grateful for the silence because it helped her focus on not crashing, but after twenty minutes, when they had cleared the toll and were moving smoothly, if slowly, with the traffic heading north, she began to worry.

"So," she said casually, "how was the trip?"

"It was great."

Tessa waited, but Dora did not elaborate.

"It was pretty quiet here," offered Tessa. "No panicked phone calls from the sailing school."

Dora nodded absently, her eyes on the scenery out her window.

"Remind me again who you went to visit?" prompted Tessa.

Her mother had not, of course, told her the name of her friend, but Tessa figured her chances of learning something were much better if she pretended otherwise.

"She's an old friend," hedged Dora. "You've never met her."

"What's her name?" asked Tessa.

Her mother hesitated before answering. "Lauren," she said.

"Why is she in the hospital?"

"Congestive heart failure," said Dora.

This was like pulling teeth. Luckily, Tessa had learned a few tricks in her day job.

"Where do you know her from?" she asked. She planned to keep asking questions until her mother admitted that she didn't want to answer.

"We met in my hometown," Dora responded carefully. "We used to sail together."

More and more interesting. Tessa could count on one hand the number of times that her mother had volunteered information about her years growing up on Long Island. It was as if her life had begun when she had moved to Chicago for art school and met their father. She never, ever spoke about her life before Luke.

Tessa and her sisters had learned to avoid asking questions about the past because it seemed to upset both Dora and Luke, but for the first time it occurred to Tessa that maybe the time had come to ask. Something had happened to separate both of her parents from their families. That kind of emotional baggage can get heavy after too many years carrying it around, and her parents must be tired. Whatever had happened, no matter how awful, she and her sisters could handle it.

"You know," said Tessa, "you don't talk very much about

your life before you moved to Chicago. Maybe this summer you could share some stories with us."

Dora was quiet for a few moments, continuing to stare out the window as the miles rolled by.

"Maybe I could," she murmured, so softly that Tessa wondered if she had really said the words or if it was wishful thinking on her part. But then her mother continued. "Maybe it's time. I've been thinking that you girls should know more about...everything."

"I'd like to hear it," she said, keeping her voice neutral, "whenever you're ready."

Dora looked over at her, a tiny furrow between her eyebrows.

"Don't try your Jedi mind tricks on me, young lady," she said severely. "I'll spill my secrets in my own time."

Tessa tried to keep a straight face, totally failed, and then they were both laughing.

"You know I don't actually use mind tricks, right Mom?" she asked. Her mother had always been suspicious of her chosen profession.

"Right, honey," said Dora. "And I don't use guilt to get what I want."

CHAPTER FIVE

July, nineteen years ago

Lucky's ears perked up. Tessa listened hard and after a few seconds she too heard footsteps approaching on the gravel path. She put a hand on Lucky's back to shush him, but he slipped away, darted out from under the bridge, and greeted the newcomer with enthusiastic barking. Seconds later, Nana Vi appeared in the archway, bent over so that she could look underneath. When she spied the girls, she got down on her hands and knees and crawled over to join them on the concrete ledge. She sat, wrapped her arms around her knees, and studied them intently.

"You girls okay?" she asked.

They nodded. Even though she wasn't feeling particularly okay, Tessa knew that 'yes' was the right answer.

"Is my mom okay?" whispered Sunny.

Vi's face softened and she reached out to tuck Sunny's flyaway curls behind one ear.

"She's fine," said Vi, "or at least, she will be."

"I didn't mean to—"

"Hush, now. You didn't do anything wrong."

"But she said—"

Sunny broke off when Nana's expression turned stern.

"No matter what she said, this isn't your fault, honey. Your mama loves you very much, but she makes mistakes like everyone else. This is a big one, no doubt, and you and RJ will stay right here at the lake with me and Pops until your parents can sort everything out."

"Is she still mad at me?" asked Sunny.

This time the look on Nana Vi's face made Tessa want to run and hide.

"The only person your mama should be mad at is herself," said Vi sharply. "She's a grown woman and should know better. In any case, she's gone away for a little while, so you don't need to worry about whether or not she's mad. You need to worry about whether or not you're hungry."

Tessa couldn't imagine eating right now. Her stomach was in knots.

"You girls come back to the house soon. I'm going to get started on dinner."

With that, Vi unfolded herself and crawled back out from under the bridge. Lucky followed in order to give her a proper send-off, then returned to snuggle up against Sunny.

Tessa watched Sunny's face crumple and her eyes fill with tears. This was all Tessa's fault. If she hadn't been so determined to break the rules, none of this would have happened.

"I'll fix it," said Tessa.

Sunny sniffled and looked over at her.

"How?" she asked. "My mom is already gone."

"I'll find a way," said Tessa. "There must be a way to make the grown-ups forget all about it."

"Maybe we could find a wishing well," said Sunny. She squeezed Lucky and hiccuped, which made them both smile.

"Or a four-leaf clover," said Tessa.

"Or a shooting star," said Sunny.

Tessa could feel the hope bubbling up inside her.

"Or a rainbow," she said.

"My birthday is coming up," said Sunny. "I could use my birthday wish."

Tessa put an arm around Sunny's shoulders and squeezed. She had felt small and scared all afternoon, but now she felt like there was something she could do to make things right.

"We'll both use all our wishes," said Tessa, "until everything is back to normal."

~

Today

Sunny paused outside The Law Offices of Katherine Rodriguez. A part of her really wanted to go in and get some answers, but the other half of her was so terrified of those answers that she couldn't convince her hand to open the door. She hadn't ever met Kat in person. When you spend summers at the lake, you only meet kids who live near the water, not the ones who live in town or out on the surrounding farms. Tessa had talked about Kat during high school, mostly about how gorgeous she was. There had been some drama involving Kat toward the end of high school, but Sunny had been in the midst of her own drama at that point, and if Tessa had told her the details she had no memory of it.

Whatever had happened in high school, RJ said nice things about Kat now. She worked with kids and she helped families. That's what Sunny needed, if she could only work up the courage to ask. The problem was solved for her when the door opened. The woman standing before her must be Kat. She was probably six feet tall in her high heels and stunningly gorgeous.

Sunny considered running, but she couldn't make herself do that either.

"Come on in," said the woman, taking Sunny by the hand and leading her over to the couch in the waiting area. Sunny followed automatically, taking the seat she was offered. The woman took the seat on the far side of the coffee table.

"I'm Kat," she confirmed. "And you are?"

"Sunny."

"RJ's sister?" she asked.

Sunny nodded.

"If you're looking for RJ, he took the afternoon off to tinker with his sailboat."

"I know," said Sunny.

Kat studied her for a moment, then said, "You're not looking for RJ, are you?"

Sunny shook her head slowly, unsure of how to begin. She wasn't even sure Kat would be able to help her. If she worked with RJ, would she be obligated to tell him about their conversation? Or could it stay secret if Sunny officially became her client? Sunny swallowed hard at the thought of making anything official. She forced herself to breathe slowly so that she wouldn't throw up.

"Why don't you tell me what's going on? Maybe I can help."

She seemed so nice. Why was it so hard to say it out loud? Sunny cleared her throat.

"If I ask you something, can we keep it just between us? I mean, does RJ need to find out that we talked?"

"If you'd rather keep our conversation confidential, then it's confidential. I have to warn you, though, that there's always a chance someone at the diner saw you come in, and they might mention it to RJ."

"That's okay," said Sunny. "I can tell him I came looking for him, forgetting that he would be out."

Sunny stopped talking. She wasn't really sure where to start, so she sat there for a minute, trying to pull her thoughts together. She appreciated the fact that Kat didn't bug her. She must have a lot of practice at this.

"Things are complicated right now with my husband, Will," she began. *Complicated.* Funny how so much heartache could be wrapped up inside one little word. "I'm really worried that—"

Her voice broke, but she cleared her throat and pushed through the overwhelming urge to cry. She needed to keep her act together, if not for her own sake then for the kids.

"I'm worried that if we can't work things out, we'll end up fighting over custody of the kids. I don't want to drag them through it, but I also don't want to give them up. I don't know anything about how this all works, and I was hoping you could tell me."

"That's a big question," said Kat. "It doesn't have a simple answer."

"I know." Sunny looked down at her hands and spun her engagement ring around her finger. She loved the way the wedding ring held the engagement ring in place. She really didn't want to take them off.

"Maybe it would be helpful if I talked about best case, worst case, and the way things usually go," Kat offered.

"Yes, please," said Sunny. She curled up on the couch and wrapped her arms around her knees, bracing herself for a harsh dose of reality.

"You live in Madison, right?" asked Kat. Sunny nodded, and she continued. "So we don't have to worry about the laws in other states. We only need to worry about Wisconsin. If things go south, you and your husband would both have custody of the kids, meaning you would work together to make important decisions about their future. The thing you're worried about is called placement, and the only rule about placement is to do what's in the best interests of the children. So, best case, you and your husband get along pretty well and you live near each other, which makes it easy to work out a sharing schedule. The kids see a lot of both parents, the judge doesn't have to get involved, and everybody is happy."

"And the worst case?" asked Sunny.

"Worst case, you and your husband are so angry with each other that you're not speaking. Each of you demands full-time placement, accusing the other of being an unfit parent. A guardian ad litem represents the kids, and the judge comes up with a placement arrangement that you hate. Depending on how persuasive the unfit parent argument is, the judge may require that all visits be supervised."

Sunny could feel the stirrings of panic rise up inside her chest. It wouldn't get that bad. It couldn't get that bad. No matter what, Will knew that she loved the boys. He would never try to keep her from seeing them.

"Most of the time," continued Kat, "we end up somewhere in the middle. Nobody is completely happy with the final arrangement, but nobody hates it either. Sometimes couples get creative. I know of one couple who took turns living in the family home. They accepted disruption in their own lives rather than asking the kids to deal with it. But that's less common."

Sunny could feel Kat watching her, but she didn't know what else to ask. Her head was already spinning.

"Let me ask you something," said Kat. "How do things work in your family right now? Who watches the kids?"

"I do," said Sunny. "They're only four and two, so they aren't in school yet. They both attend a preschool program three mornings a week, but otherwise they're with me."

"And your husband works full-time?"

Sunny nodded.

"In that case," said Kat, "unless you've done something horrible, it's unlikely a judge would disrupt the day-to-day lives of the kids. The most likely placement arrangement would have the boys with you during the week and caring for them during the day. They would spend time with your husband when he is available."

Sunny could feel a weight lift from her chest. She took a deep breath and swiped a stray tear from the corner of her eye.

"Do you really think so?"

Kat shrugged. "I don't know the details of your situation," she said, "so this is all just speculation. That said, I see a lot of these cases, so I've got a pretty good feel for how things work out. Unless there is something unusual about your circumstances, these things are usually worked out in a reasonable way."

"Thank you," said Sunny. "I was working myself into a panic thinking that the person with the best lawyer could 'win' the kids, and that terrified me."

"Divorce is hard enough," said Kat with a gentle smile. "No need to make it worse."

Sunny uncurled from the couch. She hadn't realized she was gripping her own elbows so hard until she saw the red marks fading on her arms.

"You can call me anytime, you know," said Kat as they both stood. She picked up a business card from the credenza on the side wall and handed it to Sunny. "RJ does not need to know."

"Thanks," repeated Sunny.

She slipped out the door and into the sunshine, feeling a hundred times lighter than when she had walked in. She still didn't want to admit that things with Will could come to an end, but at least now when she thought about it, she didn't go immediately into panic mode. She and Will needed to figure things out, and they would. She just needed to convince him to listen.

.   .   .

Kat stared at the door that had closed behind Sunny. That had been...unexpected. She knew only the basics about RJ's sister. She was younger than he was, and she had married young, but he talked about it like it was a good thing. He seemed reassured that someone was looking out for his baby sister even when he wasn't around. He kept photos of his nephews upstairs on his desk, and whenever he talked about them—the nephews or his sister—he smiled.

Kat often wondered what it would be like to have a sibling. She had friends and colleagues, but no family left. She was all alone in the world. Despite her pride in making her own way, she couldn't deny that it was lonely. One day, maybe, she would find the right person and start a family of her own, but only if she was absolutely sure. She knew well how badly things could go wrong, both from her own experience and from the clients she saw every day.

The fact that Sunny had chosen to seek out Kat for advice rather than her own brother, now that was interesting. RJ was so approachable it seemed impossible that his own sister wouldn't confide in him. Then again, Sunny sounded like she wanted to work things out, and Kat would bet good money that RJ's advice would be to cut and run. Maybe Sunny's behavior made sense after all.

Kat stood abruptly. If Sunny needed someone in her corner, Kat would be there. That was her specialty.

RJ checked the weather radar on his phone as they sat down at an unclaimed table in Lucy's Diner on Friday. At best, they had a window of about two hours to sail before the storm, and that was pushing it. Damn it. He should have checked the weather this morning and rearranged his day. He should have waited until later this afternoon to call his father. He hadn't wanted to think about work or family while he was out on the water. He wanted a clear head this afternoon. Tessa was going to be enough of a distraction all on her own, but now they might not even get a chance to sail.

"Hot date?" asked Tessa, looking pointedly at his phone.

"Yep," he replied, giving her a broad wink, "but you'd be hotter if you were wearing a bikini."

The smart remark earned him a laugh.

"I was checking the radar," he said. "It looks like we only have about two hours before some bad weather blows in."

"Well, what are we waiting for?" she asked, standing abruptly. "Let's get out there."

With perfect timing, her stomach grumbled again in protest. This time he laughed.

"We need to eat," he said, but he also rose. "Why don't we order some sandwiches to go?"

They grabbed sandwiches at the counter and were out the door in record time. They ate on the way, riding together in RJ's car. As he drove one-handed through town, he tried to wrap his head around the idea of a summer affair with Tessa. He had been thinking about it all week, and frankly his body was fully in favor of giving it a try. However, he liked her too much to mess with her. He liked the open, friendly way that she looked at him, and the straightforward enjoyment in her face when they were together. No games. They were friends, and as much as he would love to sleep with her, he really didn't want to screw up a good thing.

Besides, if he broke Tessa's heart, Sunny would kill him. If they were going to give this a try, Tessa would have to convince him that she really could keep it light.

Over at the yacht club, things were quiet. A couple of people were bringing their boats in for the day, but nobody was crazy enough to go back out. He checked the radar again.

"I still think we have about two hours," he said. "Are you

okay with doing this? I don't want to push too hard on your first time out."

"I'm not a rookie, RJ. Strong wind doesn't scare me."

He grinned.

"Well, then, let's get out there."

She was good. Really good. He had known she would be competent. She had grown up at the sailing school, after all, so rigging a boat was second nature for her. Even on an unfamiliar model, she seemed perfectly at ease. All it took was a quick glance at him to confirm that she was getting the setup right, and she had it done. Between the two of them, they had the boat in the water in under fifteen minutes. As they pushed away from the pier, he gave her a nod of respect.

"How long has it been?" he asked, pitching his voice so that she could hear him over the whip of the sails and the slap of the water against the hull.

"Too long," she answered. "Once I started grad school, it's been all work and no sailing. I've only been up for the occasional weekend, and there never seemed to be a good time to get out on the water."

RJ adjusted the trim of the mainsail, then tacked so that they would head across the lake toward the bay.

"Sounds like you weren't trying very hard," he said as they ducked under the boom and repositioned themselves on the other side of the boat. She was quiet for so long he wondered if she had even heard the question.

"I guess I wasn't," she said at last. "Maybe I was afraid that the occasional sail wouldn't be enough. I didn't want any distractions. For me, sailing is definitely a distraction."

"And now?" he asked. "Can you handle the distraction?"

He was dying to know what she was thinking. Did she still want an affair? Could she really keep things light? She grinned at him, as if she could read his mind.

"Oh, I can handle it," she answered. "Can you?"

Her eyes narrowed as she issued the challenge, and damn if she wasn't the sexiest thing he had ever seen.

"Count on it," he said. "Distraction is my middle name."

Tessa couldn't help the little bubble of joy that rose up inside her.She was back on the water, grinning like an idiot at RJ, who was fun and charming and sexy and no wonder women fell into bed with him. The wind played with her ponytail, tossing it from side to side and whipping her in the face. She anchored the jib sheet between her knees and secured her ponytail inside her baseball cap. She relaxed into the familiar routine and they sailed in silence for a while, periodically adjusting the trim as the wind carried them across the lake.

It truly was the perfect day to be out on the water. The sun warmed their backs without frying them. Fluffy white clouds raced across the sky. The wind held strong and steady, kicking up a few whitecaps. She could see the rough weather coming from the northeast and monitored the bank of dark clouds in the distance. Storms didn't usually come in from that direction, so she didn't have a good sense of its speed. She was guessing maybe half an hour before they should turn back. She loved a challenging sail, but she wasn't stupid. Lightning and water don't mix well.

She laughed out loud. How had she managed to stay away for so long?

They worked their way across the lake, tacking back and forth, moving upwind toward the point where the shore curved into the bay. After reaching their goal, they turned east, sailing across the mouth of the bay. They worked well together, as if they had sailed together for years. She didn't question it. She didn't need to understand this to enjoy it. They were having fun.

When they reached the far side of the bay, they changed

course to head downwind in the final stretch back toward the yacht club. She hoisted the spinnaker, loving the moment that it caught the wind and stretched tight, the bright rainbow of color a glorious contrast to the pure white of the mainsail and the jib. After securing it, she looked over her shoulder to check on the dark clouds, and was dismayed to realize they had picked up speed. She met RJ's eyes.

"We're cutting it close," he said, his voice tight.

All they could do was make a run for it. The wind grew stronger, transforming the lake into a sea of whitecaps. Neither of them smiled as they raced the storm across the lake.

RJ lined them up perfectly for the final approach to the pier. Tessa hauled in the spinnaker. RJ dropped the mainsail and the jib and let momentum carry them the last few yards. Tessa leapt off the bow, bowline in hand, and steadied the boat while RJ jumped off and raced up the pier to get the trailer in position. They wrestled the boat onto the trailer and hauled it safely out just as the first giant raindrops began to splatter on the ground. Together they pulled the trailer back to their parking spot beside the big storage building. They quickly rolled up the sails and stowed them. She jumped when lightning shot across the sky accompanied by a palpable crack of thunder. RJ grabbed her hand and together they ducked into the storage building through the open garage door as the skies opened up.

Tessa stood at the open door of the storage building and watched the rain pour down. She had always loved thunderstorms—the more intense the better. As a kid, she would sit on the sun porch during a storm so that she could be a part of the action without, as her mother put it, getting herself killed for the thrill of it. But that was years ago, before college, and work, and life happened.

She reached out and let the raindrops pelt her open palms. She felt fully awake for the first time in years, her entire body alive with energy. RJ came up behind her and threw an arm around her shoulder. They both stared at the wall of falling water broken only by her hands. The heat of his body contrasted nicely with the cool air flowing in through the over-sized garage door.

"Have you ever danced in the rain?" he murmured in her ear.

His question reverberated all the way down to her toes. She swallowed hard and shook her head, slowly lowering her hands to her sides.

"I usually just watch," she admitted.

"You should try it sometime," he said, leaning in so that she felt his breath on her ear. Her brain stuttered to a halt and her body dissolved into one giant shiver.

What the hell was her problem? She had been waiting her whole life for this spark. She should be grabbing him with both hands and refusing to let go until they were both naked. Instead, she stood there like an idiot, frozen with indecision. What exactly was she afraid of? Was it fear of the unknown? Fear of being just another conquest? Maybe it was simply fear of future pain. As the thunder rumbled around them, she reached one very simple conclusion: whatever her problem was, she needed to get over it.

After a few minutes of torrential downpour, the rain mellowed into a gentler shower and they made a run for the clubhouse. Once inside, she gasped at the chill from the air-conditioning and shook off the soaking as best she could.

The bar was crowded with disappointed sailors, some of whom called out greetings or gave RJ flack about staying out too long. Most had watched their hasty return from the windows overlooking the lakefront. RJ elbowed his way into a spot at the center, closer to the bartender, in order to secure some drinks. Tessa hung back and sighed inwardly, knowing how quickly gossip would fly through town. It wasn't that she minded being linked with RJ. She just liked her privacy. There was a reason she had left Hidden Springs for the anonymity of the city. Gossip and innuendo could suck the joy out of life. Realistically, though, if she wanted to enjoy the summer, she would need to remember how to live with the talk.

No matter what you do in a small town, there's talk.

"That was quite a show you put on," said Brock.

Tessa turned to find him leaning against the end of the bar. Her mouth tightened. She hadn't seen him since the staff meeting earlier in the week where his big promotion had been announced and he had officially become her boss. Just thinking about it made her eye twitch. Tessa kept her expression neutral and resigned herself to making polite conversation until RJ got back.

"We managed to squeeze in some great sailing before the storm hit," said Tessa.

"Have you seen the weather reports for this weekend?" he asked.

She shook her head.

"Looks like Sunday's race may be rained out."

"Relieved?" asked RJ as he walked up with their drinks. "Chardonnay, right?" he whispered in her ear.

RJ's question made Tessa smile in spite of herself. He had remembered her favorite type of wine, a thoughtful little trick that she herself had taught him. Damn, he was good. The student had become the master. He placed the glass of wine in her hand and remained standing behind her. The warmth of his body helped to offset the chill of the air-conditioning. She resisted the urge to lean against him, though. She would face Brock on her own two feet.

"No. You?" returned Brock. "Personally, I was looking forward to a rematch."

"Right," said RJ, making his skepticism clear.

Brock had never taken teasing well, but instead of giving as good as he got, he shifted focus to take his frustration out on Tessa. Maybe he saw her as an easier target. She recognized Brock's pattern and she was getting tired of it.

"I'm surprised that you can afford the time away from work," said Brock.

"I've accumulated some vacation days," said Tessa smoothly. "It helps that many of my clients are on vacation as well."

Really, the practice went into hibernation in the summer. If it weren't for all the partners taking extra time off, everybody's schedule would be light.

"I guess I'm surprised that my father would approve the time off," said Brock, his voice tight. "After all, with the new center opening, there's a lot of work to be done. It's all hands on deck."

The way he said it, you would think that he was going to be working eighty-hour weeks all summer in order to make it happen. That, however, was ridiculous. He would be taking off every Friday and most Thursday afternoons, leaving it to the rest of the staff (to her) to pick up the slack.

"He didn't seem concerned," said Tessa. "He must have a lot of faith in your abilities." Tessa kept her voice even as she said it, wishing she had the guts to tell Brock to jump off a cliff.

"I'll have to talk with him about that," said Brock, before turning on his heel and walking away, leaving his half-full glass of scotch behind on the bar.

Tessa looked at RJ, who raised an eyebrow in question. She giggled, and suddenly they were both laughing. She knew that she should be worried about her backup plan, but right now she couldn't seem to care.

"I guess I'm in trouble," she said.

"Maybe," said RJ. "Have you ever wondered what it would take to get fired?"

She laughed again, remembering the look on Brock's face. If she was going down, she might as well go down in flames.

"All the time," she answered.

CHAPTER SIX

March, eighteen years ago

THE GRANDFATHER CLOCK IN THE HALL TICKED TOWARD
midnight. Tessa concentrated on the sound, wishing time could
go faster. Her ninth birthday could not come soon enough.
Everything had gone wrong this year. Tonight was her big
chance to make it all right again.

She forced herself to wait until the hall clock struck
midnight. Her sisters did not understand how important
tonight was, and if she woke them too soon they would make
noise, which would wake up Mom and Dad, and then the
whole plan would be ruined. Her sisters were excited about
sneaking out of the house in the middle of the night, but they
didn't really believe in wishing like Tessa did. Or at least, the
way Tessa used to believe. After almost a year of failed wishes,
she had started to have doubts.

Still, if ever wishes were going to work, it would be tonight.
Three sisters. Three birthday wishes. Three times three for
their nine years. Their magic would never be stronger.

When the clock finally struck twelve, Tessa crept over to

Mel's bed and gently shook her shoulder. Mel popped up, fully awake and ready to go. Callie, however, was not so easy. She snored right through Tessa's gentle shake. It took a firm poke in the back from Mel to get her moving.

The girls crept down the stairs and through the kitchen to the mudroom, avoiding all the creaky floorboards along the way. They pulled on their winter gear right over their pajamas and Tessa led the way out the back door. They wouldn't even need the flashlight tucked into Callie's pocket. The full moon lit their way. Although spring had technically arrived, frost coated the stepping-stones that led down to the lake, making them extra-slippery. Callie held on to Mel's arm, and Mel held on to Tessa's. If one went down, they would all go down together.

When they reached the rocky little beach at the front edge of the commons, Tessa knelt on the sand and tugged off her mittens. She pulled her wish lantern out of her pocket and started putting it together. Callie and Mel followed her lead.

Assembling the lanterns in the dark, with freezing fingers, took longer than Tessa had expected. She wanted to get this right, so she didn't let anything distract her, not the cold breeze tickling her ears, not Callie's fidgets, and definitely not Mel's grumbled complaints. This was important. Her stomach knotted up, not so much with excitement as nerves. She felt like she might throw up, so she swallowed hard and kept her mouth shut tight.

Finally, when all three wish lanterns sat before them on the sand, Tessa pulled a crumpled paper from her pocket and smoothed it out.

"Do you really think it will work?" asked Callie doubtfully. "I've never heard of a Moon Goddess from China."

"Of course it will," snapped Tessa. "I got the spell from Annabelle, and Annabelle's mom got her from China, and the magic is from China, so it *has* to work."

Callie and Mel might have their doubts, but Tessa was

sure. Nobody else could make magical wishes like the three of them, because nobody else had three birthdays on the same day. Three times three. This would work. She could feel it.

"Let's do this," said Mel. "I can't feel my fingers."

Tessa glared at Mel, then cleared her throat.

O Goddess of the darkest night,
O Goddess of the brightest moon,
Hear us on our night of birth,
We will send our wishes soon.
Catch the fire that floats on air.
Learn our deepest secret wishes.
If they please you, keep them close.
If not, let them swim with fishes.

Mel broke the spooky silence first.

"Are we supposed to say Amen or something like that?" she asked.

Callie giggled.

Tessa glared at them both this time. She wondered if hitting Mel would screw up the magic. It was very tempting, but she couldn't risk it.

"Just light the lanterns," she ordered.

Mel fumbled with the lighter, clicking it until the flame finally sparked and stayed on. She lit Tessa's lantern first, then Callie's, then finally her own. The girls stood and held their wishes in front of them, waiting for the tiny candles to warm the air inside.

Before everything went wrong, Tessa used to wish for silly stuff, like Prince Charming, or superpowers, or more wishes. Those never worked, because they weren't real wishes. This one came from her heart.

Tessa thought about the words she had written so carefully

on her lantern in her best cursive writing: *Please make every-thing go back to the way it was before.*

Since that horrible day last summer, she had only wished for this one thing. So far none of the wishes had worked—not yet, anyway. She had tried everything: Clovers. Shooting stars. Fountains. Rainbows. Eyelashes. This time would be different, though. Tessa could feel the magic in her bones.

She had ruined her friend's life, and tonight she would fix it.

Tessa's lantern rose first, floating into the sky and charting a crooked path toward the full moon. Mel's followed, then Callie's. They watched, silent, as the three wishes drifted apart, carried by competing breezes. She could feel her heart rising higher and higher along with her wish, moving away from her sisters' lanterns, finding its own way to the Moon Goddess.

Then her lantern lurched. Tessa choked back a cry. She watched as her lantern tumbled end-over-end into the frigid lake water. The Moon Goddess could not have sent a stronger message: *Wish Denied.* Callie put an arm around Tessa's shoulders, trying to make her feel better without saying anything out loud, but it didn't help.

Tessa squeezed her eyes shut, pushing the tears back into their spouts. She wouldn't cry over a stupid wish to a stupid Moon Goddess. Tessa would find a way to fix things all by herself.

She opened her eyes just in time to see Mel's lantern go down in flames. It had tilted so far to one side that the candle flame licked the paper and the entire lantern caught fire. It burned quickly. Only the bamboo frame landed in the water, followed by a few charred scraps of paper fluttering behind. Tessa reached over and put an arm around Mel.

"Shit," said Mel, showing off her newest swear word.

"I'm sorry," Tessa whispered. Maybe the Moon Goddess didn't like them.

"Who cares," said Mel. "I don't think Chinese magic can work for us, anyway. We're not from China."

The girls fell silent as they watched Callie's lantern continue to rise, the flame flickering but staying strong. The lantern rose so high and so far that Tessa could barely see it against the backdrop of stars. Then it floated across the face of the full moon and disappeared.

The girls gasped in shock.

"Did you see that?" squeaked Tessa. "It worked. The Goddess took your wish."

She was dying to know what Callie had wished for, but she didn't ask. If there was even a small chance that magic could work for one of them, she didn't want to jinx it.

"It just disappeared," whispered Callie. "It was there, and then it wasn't."

"I don't know if that was magic," said Mel, "but it was pretty cool."

They watched the moon together in silence until a cloud covered it, then tromped back up to the house. Tessa trailed behind, dragging a heavy heart behind her. She wanted to be happy for Callie—really she did—but disappointment overwhelmed her. She had been so sure that the birthday magic would work for all of them.

But that didn't mean she was giving up. She straightened her shoulders. Big girls don't need magic. She would make things right all by herself.

Today

Tessa and her mother sat on the screened-in porch the following afternoon and watched the rain. They had brought their coffee out here to sit and chat but had fallen silent. She and RJ had hoped to squeeze in another practice round today, but the rain was so peaceful that Tessa couldn't regret missing out. Rainy days made her thoughtful, and Tessa had a lot to think about after her exchange with Brock yesterday.

The job had never been perfect. She had always known that it couldn't last forever. It was a family business, after all, and she wasn't family. She had no intention of being a second-class citizen for her entire career. Brock had distracted her for a few months with the dream of building a couples counseling center, but she could see now that he had been using her energy and enthusiasm for his own ends. If she refused to be his minion, he would find an excuse to get rid of her. The hard work was done, and now he could afford to cut her loose.

She smiled grimly to herself. If Brock thought the easy part was over then he was delusional. Opening a new business, in counseling or any other field, took hard work and savvy marketing. People wouldn't trust you with their troubles just because you built a fancy office and offered fancy coffee. Couples counseling required a delicate balance between the needs of the individual and the needs of the couple. Her smile widened. Maybe she could keep her job long enough to watch Brock crash and burn.

"What's got you smiling, honey?" asked her mother.

"Just thinking about what I want to be when I grow up," she answered lightly. No need to reveal her vindictive streak.

"I suppose I should think about that, too," said Dora with a little laugh.

Tessa looked over at her mother and raised her eyebrows. Her mother gave her a lopsided shrug.

"Who wants to be a grown-up? It sounds so final, like you have nothing left to learn. I try to keep an open mind and follow my heart where it leads me."

Tilting her head to one side, Tessa considered her mother's answer.

"Did you follow your heart to New York City?"

"I suppose I did," said Dora. Tessa bit her tongue and waited, and sure enough her mother continued. "Lauren and I...we go back a long time. The doctors tell her she could live for several more years, but she's convinced that she won't last the summer." Dora sighed. "When she asked me to visit, I couldn't say no."

"Why would you want to?" Tessa asked.

"I closed the door on that part of my life a long time ago," said Dora, "and I thought it was forever. I never would have guessed that she would be the one to open it again, and now that she has, I don't know what I should do."

"What do you *want* to do?" asked Tessa. "What does your heart say?"

Her mother's smile was bittersweet.

"If only I knew," she mused. "Maybe it's just your father's retirement that has me so muddled. It's such a big turning point."

Her mother was changing the subject, and Tessa followed her lead. No need to push.

"I like his friend Zeke," said Tessa, "although it's odd that we've never heard of him before."

She gave her mother her best innocent look, but her mother was no dummy. She knew exactly what Tessa was wondering. Why had her parents been so silent about their past? It was as if their lives had begun the day they met.

"Ah, Zeke," said her mother. "Now that's an interesting development."

"Dad never talked about him. Never even mentioned him."

Her mother glanced over, her expression thoughtful, then looked back out at the rain. Tessa waited, hoping her mother would fill in some of the blanks. Her father was different around his friend. More alive, somehow. Oddly, her father's newfound energy made her feel guilty. It was beginning to look like her father had set aside his dream in order to raise a family. Maybe her mother had done the same.

"Your father and I agreed that we needed a fresh start when we had you girls. Maybe that was the wrong decision, but it felt right at the time."

"And now that the past has come knocking?" asked Tessa.

"We'll have to wait and see," said her mother, abruptly standing up. "Now I need to run some errands. Do you need anything from the store?"

Startled, Tessa couldn't think of a thing to say. Before she knew it her mother had slipped into the kitchen and made her escape.

Tessa thought back over their conversation as she listened to the car rumble away up the drive. Her parents didn't need to bury the past anymore. She and her sisters were all grown up. They didn't need protecting. What they really needed was to understand, and that couldn't happen unless they got their parents talking.

Brunch. Tomorrow morning. Lucy's Diner.

Her sisters would arrive later this afternoon for the party. She would fill them in on what she had uncovered, see if Callie had learned anything during her month at home, and together they would hatch a plan for Sunday morning.

It was like high school all over again, only they were out of practice. Tessa, Callie, and Mel had grown up sharing the bathroom at the top of the stairs. Their mother had always insisted that the ancient tile and plumbing were charming, but the girls were not so sure they liked charming. The mirror was minuscule, the old-fashioned sink provided no counter space, and you couldn't flush the toilet while anybody was in the shower. With Mel up for the weekend and Callie at home instead of at

Adam's, bathroom access was limited. So here they were, trying to remember the dance but mostly getting in each other's way.

As soon as Mel moved away from the mirror, Tessa dove in to throw on some makeup. Callie had given up completely and was using the mirror on the back of her closet door. Tessa liked having the sink handy in case she botched the job.

"I'm worried about Mom and Dad," said Tessa. She was about to put some mascara on when Mel grabbed her by the shoulder.

"Why?" asked Mel. "What happened?"

Tessa sighed and carefully moved the mascara brush away from her face. Mel was already overreacting. She turned around to calm her sister.

"Nothing serious, I promise. I just have this feeling…"

"Shit," said Mel.

"What?"

"I hate it when you have 'a feeling,'" said Mel. "Remember when you had 'a feeling' about Kat? That did not turn out well."

"But I…but she…this is totally different." Tessa didn't know what else to say.

"Really?" asked Mel. "What do you know so far?"

Callie poked her head into the bathroom.

"What's going on?" she asked. Tessa pulled her into the bathroom and shut the door. Now they really were back in high school.

"Everybody calm down," said Tessa. "I don't want to turn this into a huge thing."

Mel raised an eyebrow and looked pointedly at the closed door to the bathroom.

"Whatever," sighed Tessa.

"What's the thing?" asked Callie, biting back a smile.

"We don't have all day," said Mel. "Party starts in an hour, and we're supposed to get there early."

Tessa ran a hand through her hair, feeling very mature as she resisted the urge to throttle her sister.

"It's just a feeling I have," she began, giving Mel the evil eye. "Did you know about Mom's trip to New York?"

Callie and Mel shook their heads.

"Well," Tessa continued, "Mom just made a quick trip to visit an old friend, someone I've never even heard of."

"Lauren," said Callie softly.

"You know about her," demanded Tessa. "Who is she?"

"She's an old friend of Mom's," answered Callie. "She's very sick."

"Have you heard of her?" Tessa directed the question at Mel, who shook her head.

"I expect Mom and Dad have met a lot of people over the course of their lives, and we don't know half of them," said Mel. "Maybe more than half."

"She took time off during prep week, and she didn't seem like herself when I picked her up from the airport," said Tessa. "She seemed…"

"Quiet?" supplied Callie.

Tessa nodded. "Exactly."

Callie nodded her head slowly.

"How do you know about Lauren?" asked Tessa. "Did Mom tell you about her? Did she say anything about her past?"

Callie studied her fingernails and a blush started to creep up her neck.

"I found some old letters," she began. "I read them." She looked up at her sisters and the guilt on her face was clear. "I know I shouldn't have done it, and I still feel sick about it, but Mom was acting so weird and I wanted to know what was going on. I never imagined…"

"What?" demanded Mel. "You never imagined what?"

Mel had never been very patient.

"Secrets," said Callie. "It never occurred to me that Mom

and Dad might have secrets. I'm still not sure how I feel about it."

"So what was in the letters?" demanded Mel. "What's the big secret?"

"It's not so much the letters," said Callie. "They're just updates on Lauren's life and her kids. Pictures. Funny stories. Nothing secret-worthy."

"So why didn't she ever talk about it?" asked Tessa.

When Callie didn't answer right away, Tessa could feel the knot in her stomach twist tighter.

Callie flushed. "I'm not sure how much of this I'm supposed to be telling you," she said.

"All of it," said Mel. "Obviously."

"When Mom found out I read the letters, she was pissed."

Mel chuckled at that, because usually when their mom was angry, it blew over in about thirty seconds.

"No," said Callie, "not like that. She didn't freak out at all. She got quiet, which was much worse. I've never seen her like that."

"Did she explain?" asked Tessa.

"Eventually," said Callie. "I always thought that Dad was her first love, but it turns out she had an affair with a married man before she left New York."

"What?" Mel yelped.

"Quiet," hissed Callie. "She didn't say much about it, only that it was Lauren's husband, and Lauren knew about it, and it was messy and complicated and she needed to leave. So she left. She moved to Chicago and met Dad and lived happily ever after."

Callie looked like she might throw up.

"Holy crap," said Mel. "How long were you planning on keeping that to yourself?"

Callie looked down at her hands.

"I don't know," she said. "Mom said she would never have

brought it up if I hadn't found the letters. She never said whether or not I could tell you, and it felt weird to tell you."

Tessa thought about how strange it must be for her mother to revisit her former life after all this time. Of course she was acting odd. She had a lot on her mind.

"I guess this explains the mystery, then," said Mel.

"Some of it, anyway," said Tessa.

"What do you mean?" asked Callie.

"I feel like there's more going on with Mom and Dad than we really understand. Neither of them have ever talked about their lives before they met, and now all of a sudden they both have old friends from the past popping up? It's weird. I feel like we need to start asking questions. We're old enough to handle the answers."

"I think you're right," said Callie. "The more time I spend with Dad and his friend Zeke, the more questions I have. Mom's not the only one with secrets."

"Now hold on," said Mel. "Maybe there are some things they don't want to share?"

Tessa and Callie gave her identical looks of scorn.

"This is supposed to be a family, Mel," said Tessa. "Secrets have no place here."

They both burst out laughing at Mel's horrified expression.

"Oh, keep your secrets," said Tessa. "We'll get them out of you eventually."

"Not going to happen," said Mel.

Tessa shook her head. "Everyone has secrets. Sometimes big. Sometimes small. But here's the thing. Secrets—especially the big ones—can really screw you up if you keep them for too long. Not that I think Mom is screwed up. I just... Things feel off and I'm worried. I need you to pay attention, keep your eyes and ears open, and let me know what you think tomorrow after brunch."

"Brunch?" asked Mel.

"Lucy's. Ten o'clock."

Callie smiled. "I bet Adam and Danny would join us. Danny will do almost anything for those doughnuts."

"Do you mind if we keep it just family?" asked Tessa carefully. Callie's relationship with Adam was still so new that Callie wanted to spend every possible moment with him and his nephew, but that would defeat the purpose of having brunch in the first place. "Adam and Danny are great, but Mom and Dad will be on best behavior with company, and I want to see them act like themselves."

Callie nodded. "It's okay," she said. "I'll be here for a few more days, and I'll spend most of the rest of that time with the two of them, anyway."

"Are we done with the secret bathroom conference yet?" asked Mel. "I have some serious work to do before I'm ready for prime time."

"We're done," said Tessa. "Remember: Eyes and ears open."

"Got it," said Mel.

Callie grinned and saluted.

"Yes, sir."

RJ kicked his feet up on the couch and scowled at the dark sky. The rain had faded to a misty gloom after ruining his day. There wasn't even a hint of wind to make it interesting. He hated days like this.

Sunny had gone upstairs to wake the boys from their rest time, which was unfortunate because he appreciated the calm after the chaos of this morning. He loved his nephews. He found, however, that they were best enjoyed in small doses, with lots of rest time in between.

If only Sunny would tell him what was really going on with Will. All he'd been able to get from her so far was that they needed time apart and she didn't know how long she and the boys would be staying. He understood how things could go wrong in a marriage. It was his business, after all. What he didn't understand was how Sunny could let this drag on while the kids were stuck in the middle. She and Will needed to end this now, before it got any uglier. Before the kids got hurt.

As he mulled over his options for dealing with Sunny, he realized that he didn't need to figure it out alone. If anybody could help him with Sunny, it would be Tessa. There was a chance, though, that Sunny had already confided in her and sworn her to secrecy. If only there were some way to get Tessa's input without asking her to spill any secrets.

A slow smile spread across his face when he realized he knew exactly what to do. While Sunny was still out of earshot, he pulled his phone from his pocket and dialed Tessa's number.

"Tess, it's RJ. You got a sec?"

"Sure," she answered.

He could tell that she was outside somewhere because he could hear wind and water right through the phone. He could also hear movement from upstairs, so he knew he didn't have much time.

"Listen, I need to ask your advice about something."

"Really?" she asked. "Sounds intriguing. Is this sailing-related?"

"It's relationship-related. I need to pick your counselor brain."

She was silent for a moment, then said, "I thought you weren't in a relationship."

"Not for me," he said with a laugh. "God, no. I would never...never mind. It's for...a client."

He was pretty sure he heard a sigh over the sound of the wind.

"This could get complicated, RJ," she hedged. "What exactly do you need?"

"Help."

"How much help?"

"Well," he said slowly, "I guess I could get by with some advice to start, but there's a chance that some sort of sing-Kumbayah intervention will be required."

"I can see the slippery slope stretching out in front of me," she said.

He heard waves again.

"Where are you?" he asked.

"On the shore path, walking over to my dad's retirement party. Want to come?"

"Sure," he said. "Where exactly?"

"We'll be upstairs at The Beach. Why don't you stop by and you can fill me in on the details."

"Done," he said. "See you in a few."

He hung up just as small feet began thumping down the stairs.

"Hey, sis," he called. "I need to go out for a little while."

Tessa and her sisters huddled at the far end of the bar. They were ducking, for the moment anyway, all their old grade-school teachers, who seemed to enjoy fussing over the triplets almost as much as they liked to tell embarrassing stories about their father. He had been the music teacher for the past thirty years, which provided plenty of material for his roast. For the moment, the teacher group had gathered by the front windows overlooking the lake and ordered another pitcher of beer. The girls kept their distance and enjoyed the reprieve.

"Did you ever think that Mrs. Rogers would still be teaching?" asked Mel. "She was ancient when we were there."

"She couldn't have been that old," replied Tessa tartly.

"We've been out of grade school for fifteen years, and she's still going strong. I bet she just went gray early."

"Did you know she used to dye her hair red and go on a road trip on her Harley every summer?" asked Callie, laughing at the disbelief on her sisters' faces. "It's true," she continued. "She lives about half an hour away, so it wasn't like we were going to run into her at the grocery store. Apparently she has a wild streak, but as a teacher she can only let loose in the summertime. I saw the pictures once in her desk drawer and asked Dad about them."

"A Harley?" asked Tessa, eyeing Mrs. Rogers speculatively. "I wonder what else we don't know."

They were quiet for a moment, their imaginations running wild. Finally Mel shook her head and turned back to her sisters.

"What's Dad going to do now that he's retired?" asked Mel. She and Tessa turned to Callie, figuring she was most likely to know. Callie and their father had the music bond gluing them together.

Callie shrugged. "Not sure, but I think he might start spending time in Nashville."

Tessa almost dropped her beer. She caught it right before it slipped through her fingers.

"Seriously?" she asked. "Would Mom go with him? Who would run the sailing school?"

Tessa blinked, realizing that there was an easy answer to that question. She needed to be on her guard or her mother would maneuver her into taking over. Not that the idea wasn't appealing, but she had a career and student loans to think about. The sailing school wasn't part of the plan.

Callie shrugged again. "No clue. And don't go bugging them about it. I'm just guessing."

"Based on what?" Tessa asked.

"Based on Dad's friend Zeke putting on the hard sell and

trying to talk him into it." She paused to take a drink. "Dad didn't say no, and Mom didn't say anything at all."

The three of them turned to stare at Luke, who seemed happy but flustered by the ribbing from his colleagues, and at Dora, who sat beside him, smiling gently and looking peaceful. What the hell was going on?

"What about you?" asked Tessa. "Are you going to be spending time in Nashville, too? Or will you stay here most of the time?"

Callie got a dreamy look on her face. Tessa and Mel looked at each other and rolled their eyes.

"What?" asked Callie. "What did I do?"

"You got the look," said Tessa with a smile.

"The Happily Ever After look," agreed Mel. "It's revolting."

Callie laughed, delighted.

"I don't know exactly how it's going to work," she said. "We're going to play it by ear."

"Hot guy, three o'clock," said Mel.

Tessa and Callie turned reflexively toward the entrance and Tessa smiled. She couldn't help it. Mel was right. RJ *was* hot, with his too-long California hair, his scruffy face, and his hard, lean body wrapped in board shorts and a weathered polo shirt. She zoned out for a minute, wondering if his chest was still smooth and tan like it had been in high school, or if he had a dusting of hair across his chest, in the same golden brown as the hair on his head, only the hair on his chest would be curly and springy and lead inevitably downward until...

"Holy shit, you have the hots for RJ!" accused Mel.

Tessa blushed. "Shut up."

The object of her lustful thoughts had spotted them and was approaching. The last thing RJ needed to hear was how hot he was. He knew that already.

Callie's mouth had frozen in a tiny O of surprise, and Tessa reached over to poke her. She needed to wipe the startled look off her face before RJ got close enough to ask questions. Of course her sisters were surprised. The three of them had snickered at RJ's harem all through their high school summers, and when RJ had broken hearts by accident, they had helped to pick up the pieces. The idea that one of them would fall for his legendary charm was ridiculous.

RJ met her eyes and grinned and she felt that old familiar shiver.

Ridiculous.

RJ liked the way that Tessa blushed as he approached. She swallowed hard, like she was thinking about sex and trying not to show it. He let her stew in her sexy thoughts while he made nice with her sisters.

"Mel, it's been too long," he said smoothly, giving her a light embrace and just enough eye contact on release to let her know that she looked good tonight. He didn't need to say it out loud. Mel knew she looked good. "You still painting?" he asked casually. Guys had always screwed up with Mel, focusing on her hotness rather than her talent.

Sure enough, she gave him her real smile, not the fake one.

"RJ, honey, I'll paint you anytime."

He grinned. Mel was as good at this game as he was.

Then he turned his attention to Callie, giving her a quick hug as well. He kept it brotherly, because she had the vibe going on that women get when they're off the market. He thought he had seen her with someone at the barbecue.

"Callie, you look happy. Who's the lucky man?" he asked.

She smiled.

"Adam," she answered. "You remember Adam Reese?"

He paused, startled, then smoothed over the hitch.

"I do," he said. "Great guy."

Sometimes he forgot that they were all adults now, and the

old high school rules no longer applied. So what if Callie was a few years younger than RJ and Adam a few years older? They were all grown-ups now.

"I agree," she said. Callie didn't smile easily, but when she did, she glowed. An image flashed through his mind of Tessa smiling like that at him, and his throat tightened. He tried to shake it off, but still felt unsettled.

Seeing all three James sisters together, he couldn't help but notice how they had changed. Sure, they still looked alike. They always would. But over the last eight years, they had each come into their own. Mel was still hell on heels. Callie was still the quiet one. And then there was Tessa. Something about her had always snagged his attention. Maybe it was the straight, no-nonsense posture, as if she had no idea how small she was. Maybe it was the way she organized everyone around her. The thing that fascinated him most, though, was the way she looked at him, as if she could see straight through to his secrets. Not that he had secrets. Hell, he was an open book.

"Hey, Tess," he said. "Are you sure you want to talk about work stuff now? I don't want to take you away from the party."

She smiled—her everyday smile—as a burst of laughter came from across the room.

"Dad's getting roasted by his soon-to-be-former colleagues. It's an inside game at this point. Why don't we go out on the deck and see if we get rained on?"

She poured a beer for RJ and then led the way out to the deck. He loved the way she moved. She was smooth, like wind moving across the water. He also found himself distracted by the sway of her hips and tried to remember the ground rules. He was allowed to look, right? He just needed to wait for her go-ahead before there was any touching. He could do that.

Out on the deck, she pulled out a chair and sat, putting her feet up on the railing. He followed suit. The lake stretched out before them, mirroring the dark gray sky. He watched the wind dance across the surface and felt a stray raindrop hit his forehead.

"So what's on your mind?" she asked. "The doctor is in."

"I have some difficult clients."

"Do I get to ask who?" she asked.

"Nope."

She nodded and waited for him to continue. He appreciated her respect for confidentiality, especially in a small town. He felt a twinge of guilt for using the term 'clients' to refer to his sister and brother-in-law, but he was wandering in a gray area here. If he hinted that this might involve Sunny, Tessa would be pissed.

"Usually, when I work with a couple," he began, "they're still speaking to each other. If they weren't, they wouldn't want a mediator. In this particular case, though, things are complicated. They're not speaking, but they also can't afford two separate attorneys. They have two little kids, so they really need to be able to talk to each other. I'd like to be able to help them, but I don't know where to start."

"What are you hoping I can do?" she asked. "I've never consulted on a divorce case before. Most of my clients want to make things work again. At least they're trying. I'm not sure I know where to start, either."

He shrugged. "I was hoping that you could give me some tips. Maybe I can borrow your therapist voodoo to get them talking. There must be some way to get them to put their bullshit aside and focus on what's best for the kids."

She nodded slowly, and he could tell that he had caught her interest.

"It's worth a shot," she said. Then she looked at him out of the corner of her eye and smiled. "Standard terms, by the way. If this works, you owe me doughnuts."

"Deal."

Just like old times.

"How urgent is this?" she asked. "I'd like to bounce some ideas off people in the office with more post-divorce experience. Can you wait until next weekend for ideas?"

"I think so," he said. "They seem to be in a holding pattern right now, so we have some time."

Mel leaned out the deck door.

"Tess, it's time for karaoke."

"Coming." Tessa turned to RJ. "Want to join the fun?"

"Definitely not," he said. "I'll escape while I can, but I'll see you tomorrow afternoon for the race."

"Until tomorrow, then."

CHAPTER SEVEN

Labor Day weekend, nineteen years ago

"It will work," said Tessa.

Sunny shrugged and flopped back on the grass. The sun had gone down, but Tessa didn't need to see Sunny's face to know that she was feeling defeated. She had been moping around all night. She didn't want to play flashlight tag, and she had zero interest in catching fireflies.

"Whatever," said Sunny.

Tessa wanted to shake her. This was their last chance to wish together. Tomorrow, Sunny would go back to the city, and her whole life would change. Her dad had moved into a new apartment. Sunny and RJ would live with their mom during the week and with their dad on the weekends. Nana Vi had told the kids about the plan because Sunny's mom and dad were staying far away from Hidden Springs. Neither one of them was willing to drive up to pick up the kids. Instead, Nana Vi was going to put Sunny and RJ on the train tomorrow morning, all by themselves, and their mom would meet them at the train station downtown. Nana Vi wasn't happy about any of it. Tessa and

Sunny had eavesdropped while Vi was talking to Sunny's dad, and she had used a lot of swear words.

Tessa had spent most of July at the public library reading about wishes and spells. She and Sunny had tried all the usual stuff, but so far it wasn't working. The time had come to get creative. Tessa had always liked the idea of a message in a bottle, but if you wanted that message to get to a higher power, you probably had to burn it. So Tessa wrote their wish on a piece of paper, then folded it into the shape of a boat and prepared to launch it in the stream.

They would have to get the timing right. If she lit the boat on fire too soon, it would burn up and sink before it reached the lake, which was the closest thing they had to an ocean. If she tried to light it when it was already in the water, it might float away or get too wet for lighting.

Sunny wasn't going to be much help on this one. She lay on the grass staring up at the stars and humming softly to herself. Tessa was going to have to handle this wish on her own.

Tessa clicked the lighter a few times and had just gotten the flame to hold when she heard Nana Vi's voice behind her.

"What do you think you're doing, young lady?"

Startled, Tessa dropped the lighter. It bounced off her knee and landed in the grass. She turned around to find Nana Vi looking down at the two of them, her hands on her hips.

"Well?" she asked.

"We were wishing," said Tessa.

"For what?" demanded Vi.

Tessa clamped her lips together and refused to answer. The one sure way to spoil a wish was to say it out loud. Tessa couldn't see the expression on Vi's face, but she could hear the chuckle.

"Not going to tell me, are you?" she said.

Tessa shook her head.

"That's fine," said Vi. "You do what you need to do. I wanted to let you know that the bonfire has died down enough to make s'mores. You ladies come along when you're ready."

She turned to walk away, but turned back almost immediately.

"One more thing," she said. "I know you girls like to make wishes, but fairies and gods and magic don't make dreams come true. People do." Vi said it with conviction, like she was speaking from experience.

She turned on her heel and walked away, leaving Tessa gaping at her retreating back. What kind of grandmother doesn't believe in wishes? Or fairies? Wasn't that a requirement?

"She's right," said Sunny.

Tessa had almost forgotten her friend lying next to her in the grass.

"How can you say that?" asked Tessa.

"We've been wishing for a month and it hasn't worked," said Sunny. "I'm tired of wishing."

"Well, I'm not," said Tessa.

Defiant, she retrieved the lighter and clicked it until it flamed, then set fire to her little wish-boat. She set it gently in the stream and watched as it floated under the bridge and toward the open water. The flame flared highest just as the boat spilled out into the lake, and then the flame slowly died as the boat bobbed and swirled at the mouth of the stream.

"I don't give up," said Tessa, "and neither should you."

Today

Tessa woke to more gray skies and drizzle on Sunday morning. She checked the weather on her phone, and there was a chance that it would clear up before the race that afternoon, but she wasn't going to hold her breath. Even if the race happened, it would be cold and wet out there on the water. Not that she minded a little exposure to the elements, but she had been hoping for a sunnier start to the season.

Even the late sleepers (really, just Mel) were up by ten, so they made it over to Lucy's Diner before the after-church rush. They were able to snag a table in the back, which suited Tessa just fine. If they sat too close to the main entrance, they would be interrupted every two minutes by old friends. This was much better.

She waited until everyone had placed their orders and had coffee or tea in front of them before she snuck in the first question. A softball, really, designed to get everybody talking.

"So Dad, now that you're officially retired, what's your plan? Are you going to take up golf and start looking for a condo in Florida?"

He laughed. "Somehow I don't think golf is my game, honey."

Tessa waited for her mother to jump in. This was exactly the type of question that she loved, and one where she should certainly have an opinion. But Dora stayed quiet, simply looking at Luke with a half smile on her face.

"Then what is your game?" probed Tessa.

Luke dodged her question by taking a slow sip of his coffee. She knew that trick. She waited.

"I've been thinking about spending part of the year in Nashville," he said at last. Tessa met Callie's eyes and nodded. If Callie hadn't given them a heads up, she and Mel would be falling off their chairs in shock right now. Even so, the fact that Luke would mention the plan so casually came as a surprise. Dora showed no visible reaction, which was even more mystifying.

Mel may not have fallen off her chair, but she was still shaken.

"Nashville?" she asked. "I know country music is your thing, but you're seriously thinking about moving there? What the hell would Mom do in Nashville?"

Luke tipped his head to one side and deflected that question to Dora.

"I don't know," answered Dora. "I'm not sure there's much for me in Nashville, but that doesn't mean your father can't go. He would get a real kick out of immersing himself in his songwriting and reconnecting with all his music friends."

All three girls stared blankly at her. Had she really just suggested that she and Dad spend time apart? It didn't compute. Tessa let the stunned silence stretch out, hoping her mother would compulsively fill it. She did not disappoint.

"Darlings, don't look so scared. If your father wants to devote time to his music career now that he's done with teaching, it would be awful of me to hold him back, don't you think? Honestly, your father and I have been together for thirty years. I think we can handle some time away from each other without self-destructing."

Tessa nodded slowly and Dora narrowed her eyes at her.

"Don't nod at me, missy. I can see the wheels turning inside that head of yours, and they need to stop right now."

Mel snickered, and Callie bit her lip to hide a smile. Even Luke leaned back in his chair, crossed his arms, and grinned at Dora.

"What?" her mother demanded. "Tessa was using her mind tricks on me and I won't have it."

"Dora, honey, it's not a trick if everybody knows she's doing it. If you don't want to talk, you don't have to talk."

"Well," said Dora in a huff. "I'd like to see you say nothing when she does the nod and the 'hmmm' in your direction."

Luke laughed. Dora frowned at him, crossed her arms, and clamped her mouth shut.

When the three girls burst into laughter, Dora had a hard

time staying grumpy, but Tessa could tell that she was still unsettled. There were things her mother didn't want to share. Tessa didn't need to know all her mother's secrets, of course, but it would be nice if she didn't suddenly have so many of them. Her parents had been together forever, and Tessa worried about what would happen if they started spending time apart.

A buzz from her pocket distracted her.

The race is on. See you at the yacht club at 2pm. - RJ

She frowned. Change was coming, and though her parents might be ready for it, she was not.

Instead of leaving brunch all together, they ended up filtering out in groups. Her parents left first, taking care of the check on their way out. Now that the drizzle had stopped and the skies were clearing, they planned to walk home the long way. Callie bailed next, mostly because she wanted to get back to Adam. That left Tessa and Mel to fight over the last doughnut.

Mel looked at the doughnut, then raised an eyebrow.

"Rock-paper-scissors?" she asked.

"Let's split it," said Tessa.

Lucy hustled up with a refresher on the coffee.

"You girls take your time," she said. "We still have half an hour before church lets out."

She was off and away before they could reply, so they stayed where they were, sipping coffee and each eating their half of the doughnut.

"What do you think about Callie and Adam?" asked Mel.

Tessa gave a one-shoulder shrug. "I love seeing her happy," she said.

"But?"

"I worry."

"Me, too," said Mel.

They didn't have to say more. Callie may have forgiven and forgotten whatever had ended the first round of her relationship with Adam, but Tessa and Mel had lived through the aftermath. They had watched their sister shut down, drifting farther and farther away until neither of them could reach her. It wasn't that Tessa didn't like Adam. In a way, he had brought Callie back to them. But her happiness depended on him, and Tessa didn't even want to think about what would happen if things went south again. Given a choice, she would choose the calm stability of her parents' marriage. It might not be exciting, but it had stood the test of time.

"Do you think Mom and Dad were like that when they first got together?" Tessa asked. "They've always been so steady. It's hard to imagine them crazy in love."

Mel wrinkled her forehead, then shook her head.

"No way to know for sure," she said, "but I can't see it. This weirdness about Nashville is the closest thing I've seen to them fighting, and it's not even fighting. I'm not sure what it is. I'm still trying to wrap my head around Dad's ties to the music business. All these years we thought he was kidding about his country music connections. Makes you wonder what else we don't know."

"Maybe Mom is a spy," said Tessa.

Mel snorted. "Mom is the worst secret-keeper of all time. Can you imagine?"

"Um, no," laughed Tessa.

"And on that note..."

Mel pushed back her chair and together they headed toward the door.

Tessa stopped abruptly outside. Mel crashed into her and they both had to grab the railing to stay upright.

"What the hell?" snapped Mel.

"Sorry," mumbled Tessa, but it was too late.

They found themselves face to face with Kat Rodriguez. Callie had already made her peace with Kat, and Mel had run into her at the barbecue, but Tessa hadn't seen her since high school. She was still tall and gorgeous, of course. Her sisters had mentioned that part. Even in casual weekend-wear, she looked like she had stepped from the pages of a catalog. Her long dark hair was twisted into a knot and held in place by two sticks. Tessa almost laughed out loud when she saw the hairstyle, only because she could not get her hair to do that no matter how hard she tried. Kat's gorgeousness was nothing new. She had been making Tessa feel small and frumpy since freshman year of high school. Why stop now?

Something had changed, though. There was something fundamentally different about her, and it took Tessa a second to identify it. Confidence. She seemed completely unfazed by the chance encounter, which only highlighted Tessa's own unease.

Kat gave them a level stare, then nodded politely.

"Hi, ladies," she said. Her voice was neutral, but there was no welcome on her face.

Tessa straightened up, knowing she would never be as tall as Kat, but wishing that she had worn something with a heel. Every inch helps, particularly when you have guilt weighing you down.

"Hi, Kitty. I mean Kat," said Tessa. Callie had told her about Kat's switch to a more mature nickname. "It's been a long time."

"It has," Kat agreed.

She wasn't making this any less awkward. If anything, she seemed to be enjoying Tessa's obvious discomfort. Mel was no use. She was using Tessa as a human shield. What they really needed was a graceful exit. A chance to regroup and then have a do-over, so they could talk things through and make their peace like mature adults.

"Well," Tessa fumbled, "it's good to see you. We should catch up. Get together for a drink or something."

Tessa couldn't believe the words that had just fallen out of her mouth. She should be able to keep her cool in a tense situation. This verbal vomit was completely unacceptable. Mel gave her a sharp jab to the back, but Tessa ignored her. If she thought going out for drinks was such a bad idea, then she could step up and do some talking.

Kat smiled like she knew exactly what was going on inside Tessa's head. Instead of letting them off the hook, she said, "I'd like that. How about next weekend? Will you be around?"

Tessa nodded like the idiot she was.

"Great," said Kat. "Friday night. I'll look forward to it."

And with that, she swept past them and into Lucy's Diner, leaving Tessa and Mel bobbing in her wake.

"What the hell was that?" hissed Mel. She grabbed Tessa by the elbow and started dragging her toward the park.

"I don't know," said Tessa. Her voice came out as a squeak.

"We could have gotten through that with a simple 'hello, nice to see you, good-bye,' but no." Her voice got louder the farther away they got from the diner. "You had to go and turn it into a thing. With drinks. What were you thinking?"

Tessa didn't know what to say. If her sisters had asked her yesterday what she planned to do when she finally ran into Kat, she would have said exactly what Mel suggested: *Hello. Nice to see you. Good-bye.* Sure, they had a lot of baggage that they could probably sort through, but was it really necessary? Did they really see each other that often? Sometimes it was okay to let the past stay in the past, and that wasn't just a cop-out. That was a real therapeutic choice. If the past wasn't causing anybody any trouble, then just leave it alone.

Apparently her subconscious disagreed with that plan, because they were now going to have drinks with Kat next weekend, and almost certainly sort through some baggage.

It was going to be a disaster.

Tessa liked watching RJ work. He moved through the well-practiced steps as they rigged the boat, smooth and efficient, unhurried, his hands capable and experienced. The muscles in his forearms flexed with each movement, leading her thoughts away from sailing and toward temptation. She wrestled with the question that had plagued her for the last few nights: Was she ready for this? He represented both risk and reward tangled together in one irresistible package. She was at war with herself, fear and temptation battling it out. She knew, deep down, that temptation would win, but fear wasn't giving up without a fight.

The funny thing was, she wasn't nervous about sailing at all. What with the battle raging inside her, she couldn't spare any stress at all for her first race in years. She attached the spinnaker sheets and waited for RJ to do his final check. The time had come to relax and have fun, and damn it, she was going to have fun.

So when RJ pulled a classic 'smooth move' and came up behind her, wrapping his arms around her waist as they surveyed their work, she let him. She relaxed against the warm wall of muscle and enjoyed the support of his arms. She told her inner critic to shut up as her skin prickled with goose bumps and the hair on the back of her arms stood up. She liked this, and she didn't want to analyze it to death.

RJ seemed to sense her mood, because he also relaxed, some of the pre-race tension easing out of his muscles. He leaned forward to whisper softly in her ear, "We are going to kick some serious ass today."

She smiled to herself. Okay, so maybe his mind wasn't completely on her. Maybe he was embracing her out of habit while the race consumed his thoughts. She didn't really care. If she was serious about this affair with RJ, she would need to go into it with her eyes open. She wanted to learn from his experience. That was the whole point. If she couldn't stomach the idea that other women had come before her and more would come after, then she should get the hell out. Resentment had no place here.

So she let her fears drift away on the breeze. She closed her eyes, breathed him in, and promised herself that she would let the afternoon unfold. She would focus on this moment, and then the next moment, and then the one after that. She would enjoy the day. Tomorrow could wait.

CHAPTER EIGHT

RJ DIDN'T KNOW WHAT HAD COME OVER TESSA TODAY, BUT HE liked it. She was usually wound up tight, but today she was completely relaxed. Maybe it was the prospect of sailing, or spending a few days away from the city, or his charm and wit (yeah, right). Maybe it was all of those things. He didn't really care. All he knew was that she was relaxed, her head was in the game, and she didn't startle every time he touched her.

As they worked together to rig the boat, he found ways to brush against her indoor-pale skin. Every time it looked like she might need extra muscle, he was there to help out. He even got away with tucking a stray strand of hair behind her ear. All she did was smile at him and continue to prep the boat. All too soon, the work was done and they walked the trailer down to the water for launching. He wasn't sure if he would be able to touch her at all on the boat, but damned if he wasn't going to try.

The clouds had cleared, revealing a deep blue sky that turned the lake an impossibly deep blue as well. The earlier rain meant fewer speedboats out on the water, leaving the field of battle wide open. The oversized orange buoys that marked the course had already been placed, but the motorboat carrying the race officials still sat tied up at the pier. The brisk, unpredictable wind kicked up chop and added a hint of excitement to the day. With wind like this, there was a healthy chance that someone would capsize. He didn't usually worry about that, counting on his skill and the weight of his crew to keep them upright, but Tessa wasn't exactly good ballast. She might weigh 115 with her life jacket on. No matter how far they hiked out today, if the boat wanted to go over, it was going to go over.

It was going to be a hell of a race.

There were only seven boats in the race today, a little thin for his taste, but at least Brock and Helen were among the competition. They would be racing an L4 pattern and finishing downwind. Helen gave them a wave as they neared the starting line, but Brock ignored them completely. RJ smiled. If Brock was ignoring him, it meant that RJ had succeeded in getting under his skin. Brock was likely to lose focus and do stupid shit, and there was nothing RJ liked better than a stupid opponent.

What RJ didn't count on was the distraction he had brought on board his own vessel. Even though Tessa had next to zero experience on this particular class of boat, she had sailed all her life. He didn't need to draw her attention to the trim of the jib. Before he could say a word she was adjusting it, easing out the sheet until she hit the sweet spot. Watching her handle herself so competently made him hard as a rock. He adjusted himself and almost lost his grip on the main sheet.

He was going to have to stop thinking about Tessa and start thinking about sailing if he wanted to win this race.

He forced himself to look away from Tessa's neckline and survey the field. The beginning of any race could be a free-for-all, but today they were all synced up as they headed toward the line. He heard the gun signaling the start of the race as they crossed the imaginary line between the two orange markers.

Game on.

This first leg would be the easy part. They had timed the start perfectly and held the lead all the way up the first leg, but they ran into trouble as they rounded the mark. RJ misjudged the wind speed, or maybe it changed on him, and they missed the lay line. By the time they had their act together again, they had fallen back to second. He clenched his jaw to keep from swearing out loud. They had plenty of time to recapture the lead.

RJ managed to keep his focus on the race, and by the time they approached the upwind mark for a second time they were running in first. He almost laughed out loud at his luck in convincing Tessa to crew for him. She was an amazing sailor, and she looked good doing it. The spray had caught her more than once, so her board shorts were soaked and clinging to her thighs. He couldn't help but admire the cut of the muscles in those thighs as she braced herself and hiked out even further, doing what little she could to keep them on the best angle of heel. Even more intriguing were the rivulets of water cruising down her neck and disappearing behind the collar of her windbreaker. When the race was over, he would be happy to unzip the windbreaker and help her dry off. It was the least he could do, really.

"RJ! Incoming. Nine o'clock."

The urgency in Tessa's voice snapped him back to reality. While he had been taking a mental vacation, another boat, crewed by two teenagers, had caught up with them. They were making great time, and he cursed when he realized that they were on starboard and had the right-of-way. He was going to have to gybe early.

"Fuck, fuck, fuck," he muttered under his breath.

"Sorry," said Tessa over her shoulder. "I was looking ahead at the mark. I should have seen them coming."

He appreciated her attempt to make him feel better, but it was his responsibility to monitor the field.

"Let's do this," he said. "Ready?"

"Yep," she called back.

He pulled the tiller toward him and ducked under the boom as it swung across the boat. Tessa did a beautiful job of releasing the spinnaker, and then several things went wrong at once. The wind caught the spinnaker and yanked the boat forward. He lost his footing, slipped, and fell hard against the tiller. The boat turned sharply, and before he could shout a warning they were both in the water.

He should have been furious—at himself for blowing the gybe, at the teenagers for forcing the move, at himself again for missing their play—but all it took to defuse his anger was one look at Tessa's outraged face as she sputtered beside him in the water.

"Stop laughing, you idiot, and help me get this boat back up," she ordered, teeth chattering. She splashed him, which only made him laugh harder.

He sobered as he realized her lips were already showing a blue-purple undertone. He needed to get her out of the frigid water. He swam to the tip of the mast, supporting it so that the boat wouldn't turtle. Tessa climbed into the hull, uncleating the lines so that the wind couldn't catch the sails immediately after they righted the boat. When she was ready, he lifted the tip of the mast out of the water, relying on the added buoyancy of his life vest to make it happen. She straddled the side of the hull and transferred her weight toward the sideboard that pierced the bottom of the boat and now stuck out sideways. She handled her end beautifully, keeping her weight balanced so that as the boat flipped in slow motion back to vertical, she ended up in the boat rather than back in the water. He scrambled gracelessly back in and they stared at each other, two drowned rats with the limp sail fluttering between them.

She was the one who started laughing this time. Anybody else would have been pissed as hell, ready to rip him a new one, but not Tessa. Sopping wet and blue with cold, she was the most beautiful thing he had ever seen.

"We're going to need to work on that gybe," she said, still giggling. "There is no way in hell I'm touching that water again until after the Fourth of July."

"Agreed," he said. "Certain parts of my anatomy may take that long to recover."

That set her off again, and he smiled and shook his head as they sorted through the lines, untangling them as needed. When things were put back to rights, he set a course for the yacht club. Technically, they would also cross the finish line, but they were so far behind at this point that it was more a formality than anything else. Still, he'd prefer last place to no place.

As they trailed behind the pack, they could see that Brock was about to win the race. The spinnakers made it easy to distinguish the competitors, even from a distance. RJ grimaced, but he said nothing. Tessa also stayed silent except for a barely audible snort of annoyance. She was too cold at this point to talk much. Even if she tried, he wasn't sure he would be able to hear her over the chattering of her teeth.

When they reached the shore, a group of stragglers and spectators—including his friend Walt, clumsy in his walking cast—helped them to haul the boat out of the water. He was grateful for the assistance. The cold had started to affect him as well, and he wasn't sure he could get his stiff hands to do the work. Tessa was shaking so hard she could barely stand. Someone threw a blanket around her and she gave a nice little moan of relief.

"I've got this, man," said Walt. "You go dry off."

"You sure?" asked RJ. "You're not exactly a hundred percent yourself."

"At least I'm not blue," Walt retorted. "The sails need time to dry anyway. Get out of here. I've got it."

"Thanks," said RJ. "I owe you one."

"I'll put it on your tab," said Walt.

RJ threw his arm around Tessa and together they walked up toward the parking lot. They paused beside the patio outside the bar. Most of the sailors, drink in hand, had spilled out into the sunshine to enjoy his ignominious finish. He took their good-natured ribbing with a grin. Brock and Helen sat at the center of the group, basking in the victory and both looking a bit smug for RJ's taste. He gave them a mock salute, knowing that it would tweak Brock.

"Congratulations on the victory," he said, keeping any hint of sarcasm out of his voice. Nothing irritates a bad winner more than a good sport. "Can't wait for the next go-round."

"I'm surprised you're so eager for another spanking," said Brock.

Tessa sighed. They had been so close to making their escape, but now the manly posturing would begin. Brock was on his second drink already. His voice had thickened and his words were beginning to slur. She resigned herself to the delay and looked up at RJ, who raised an eyebrow at Brock's remark, then smiled slowly. Her insides warmed a few degrees and she decided that she could survive for a couple more minutes.

"Now, Brock," he drawled, "there's no need to go all 'Fifty Shades' on me. I'm looking for friendly rivalry here. Nothing kinky."

The crowd laughed and Brock's neck flushed. His grip around Helen's shoulders tightened so much that she flinched. Tessa, wrapped in both the blanket and RJ's arm, could do little more than watch the train wreck happen.

"I'm not surprised you made a mistake today," said Brock,

giving Tessa a look that was half sneer, half leer. "With a distraction like that on board, I'm surprised you finished at all."

Ick. She could brush off Brock's remark because she didn't care, but she was pissed off on behalf of Helen. As Brock's crew, she had helped him win the race, and she didn't deserve to be publicly insulted, whether it was direct or implied. Unfortunately, Tessa couldn't think of a snappy comeback that would make the situation any better. Damn if RJ wasn't right on top of it, though.

"While I agree," said RJ loud enough for the crowd to hear, "that my crew possesses great beauty in addition to great skill, I would never blame her for my mistakes. After all," said RJ, making a courtly gesture in Helen's direction, "you also have a great distraction on board, and she seems to have enhanced your performance rather than diminished it."

Helen blushed. Brock flushed a darker shade of red. Tessa even felt a warm glow wash over her, despite the fact that she knew RJ's remark was calculated. The man was brilliant. He had managed to compliment Helen, give her the credit for Brock's victory, compliment Tessa, shoulder all the blame himself, and make Brock look like an asshole all in one fell swoop. The crowd actually applauded his gallantry. Tessa caught him giving Brock a smug smile. No doubt payback from Brock would be a bitch, but Tessa found herself looking forward to it.

"Until next time," said RJ, saluting Brock again and then moving on toward the truck.

Tessa muttered "Bravo!" under her breath. She would have said more, but they ran smack into the teenagers from the race. The two were a matched set, most likely brothers. One looked to be about eighteen, the other around fifteen or sixteen. In a blink, she recognized them.

"Steve and Mike, right?" she asked. She had taught at the sailing school during her college summers. These boys had both been her students. Of course, they had been significantly shorter then. Now they both towered over her, tall enough to meet RJ eye to eye. Steve, the older brother, had grown into his arms and legs, but Mike was still gangly. "Nice racing out there." She offered her hand and they each shook it in turn. "We'll have to watch out for you two this season."

At her smile, they both turned a sweet shade of pink around the ears.

"Thanks," said the older one, extending his hand to RJ as well.

RJ nodded as he shook the boy's hand. "Well played, gentlemen," he replied. "See you next weekend?"

The boys nodded.

"Until then," said RJ, and hustled her to the truck before anybody else could stop them.

Once they reached the truck, he tucked her into the passenger seat, buckling her seatbelt right around the blanket so that she didn't have to unwrap her arms. He pressed a button on the door. She was too chilled to care what it did.

"The seat heater will kick on in a sec," he said. "You all right?" He smoothed a few damp tendrils of hair behind her ears.

She nodded, even as the familiar shivers danced down her neck.

"Liar," he said, chuckling, then closed her door and walked around to the driver's side.

She wasn't shivering because of the cold anymore, but out of habit she kept that information to herself. She simply sat back and relaxed into the rapidly warming seat, vowing that her next car would have seat heaters because, really, how had she survived so long without them? She allowed her eyes to drift shut and surrendered to the dreamy haze. It wasn't until he pulled up behind his house that she began to rouse herself.

"No front-door service?" she asked, then yawned. She didn't mind the short walk home, but he was usually more chivalrous.

He didn't answer. Instead, he shut off the truck and got out, walking around to open her door before she could wriggle out of the blanket. He released her from the seatbelt and then picked her right up out of the seat, carrying her in his arms like a bride, or a load of laundry. She couldn't get her arms out from under the blanket. He used his hip to shut the truck door and carried her toward the back door of his house. As he walked, he shifted her weight in his arms, which nudged her face into his neck. She breathed him in, struggling to remember the question that had been on the tip of her tongue, but the second she thought about her tongue, she found that her lips had parted so that she could taste him.

Beneath her lips, the skin of his neck was cool, still chilled from their unexpected swim. He tasted like fresh air and lake water. He shifted her again in his arms as they went up the back steps. She let her mouth move down the taut muscle on the side of his neck until it reached the curve of his shoulder. She tested it with her teeth, not biting really, just...exploring. He growled low in his throat, and she smiled against his skin, turning her head so that it rested on his shoulder and she could breathe the warm air rising from the neckline of his shirt. The man must have one hell of an onboard heater.

Clarity returned when he pushed open the back door and shouting exploded around them.

"Uncle RJ! Uncle RJ! What did you bring?"

"Is it a present?"

"Whatever it is, it's big."

"RJ, do you need a hand?" asked a grown-up voice.

"Sunny!" Tessa yelped, recognizing the voice. She tried to

twist out of RJ's arms and almost knocked the two of them to the kitchen floor.

"It's alive!" screeched one of the kids.

"Tessa?" said Sunny. "Are you okay? Why is RJ carrying you? Why are you all wet?"

Sunny steadied both of them while Tessa untangled herself from the blanket. RJ stepped back and leaned against the kitchen wall.

"Sailing mishap," he explained.

"Sounds like hazing to me," said Sunny.

Tessa gave her a wet hug. "When did you get here?" she asked.

"Thursday," answered Sunny.

She shot RJ an annoyed look, wondering why he had neglected to tell her that her best friend was in town. Then again, her best friend hadn't called her, either, so she couldn't put all the blame on him. She gave Sunny another wet hug and decided to put all the blame on RJ anyway.

"It's so good to see you. Wait, these can't be the boys," said Tessa, stepping back to get a good look. "What have you been feeding them? They're so big!"

They stood taller at her remark, even as they hovered close to Sunny's legs. The last time she had seen them, Oscar had been the size of Huck, and Huck had been a tiny baby. Her mind still boggled at the idea of Sunny as a mom. Technically, Tessa was older than Sunny by a few months, yet now she felt younger, as if Sunny had grown up all the way and Tessa was stuck partway there.

"How old are you guys now?" she asked.

"Four," announced Oscar, holding up four fingers to match.

Little Huck held up four fingers as well.

"Really?" Tessa asked Huck. "You're four, too?"

He nodded solemnly. Oscar shook his head in disagreement. Sunny bit back a smile and wiggled two fingers behind Huck's head.

"Sorry we couldn't come out to watch the race," said Sunny. "Can't miss nap time."

"You didn't miss much," said RJ, "except me dunking Tessa. Speaking of which—" He grabbed one of Tessa's hands and pulled it toward him for a closer look. "Your fingernails are still blue. We need to get you warmed up."

"Hot tub?" suggested Sunny, but RJ shook his head.

"I wish," he said. "It's out of commission for now. I'm thinking she needs the big bathtub upstairs."

"Bath time!" yelled Huck.

Sunny shook her head.

"Not for you, buddy. We're going to the park, remember?"

"Park," he repeated. He looked torn, not sure if he should be mad about missing tub time or excited about the trip to the park. Excitement won. Sunny grabbed an enormous mom-bag from the kitchen counter and started herding the boys toward the door.

"Let's go, team, before it decides to rain again." She grinned at Tessa. "You around tonight? I bought wine at the grocery store."

"I have to head back to the city tonight," said Tessa, "but I'll try to catch you before I go."

Tessa watched Sunny herd the boys down the stairs and load up the car. After they drove away, the silence that filled the kitchen felt as loud as the chaos had been a few minutes before. Slowly, she turned to face RJ.

"Bath time?" she asked.

"Come with me," said RJ, tugging on Tessa's blue-fingered hand until she followed him out of the kitchen and up the stairs. When he pulled her into the bathroom with the big tub, she realized that he was completely serious. He turned on the taps and let the water run over his hand, testing the temperature. All thoughts of Sunny and the boys fled her mind. Even the chill that had settled into her bones faded into unimportance. There was plenty of room in that tub for two adults. Her belly started to burn, and her brain exploded in panic.

She wasn't ready. It was too soon. She still wasn't sure she could handle an affair, much less dive into one with no lead-up at all. Well, okay, there had been some lead-up, and she had been kissing his neck—okay, devouring his neck—on the way into the house, but she was not herself. Her brain was not functioning properly. She couldn't be held responsible for her actions. Could she? And if he simply undressed her and put her in the tub, would she stop him? Already the fire in her belly was spreading lower and her brain was starting to melt.

She started babbling.

"RJ, please, let's not rush this. I mean, I know I was… sending another message entirely while you carried me inside, but really, now that I've had a second to think about it, I know for sure that I'm not ready for this. At all. Maybe that makes me a big chicken, but I just can't do it. You could probably talk me into it. Hell, I *know* you could talk me into it, but I think it would be a mistake. I think I would regret it tomorrow. Can you understand that? Am I making any sense at all?"

She forced herself to shut up and wait for his answer, all the while trying to clamp down on the babble that continued unabated in her head. He sat facing her on the edge of the tub, one hand still monitoring the water temperature as he studied her face. He seemed to take forever to answer, but that might have had something to do with her state of panic.

"Not really," he said.

She blinked at him.

"But you promised," she accused.

He shook the water off his hand as he stood up.

"Tess, you need to relax. I'm not going to talk you into anything. We are not going to do anything that you're not ready for. Out on the water today, I dunked you, and that's on me. It's my responsibility to make sure you get warm again."

"But—" she sputtered. "You don't need to... That doesn't mean I'm going to climb into a bathtub with you."

He sighed.

"Your lack of trust is disheartening," he said, then gave her a quick wink. "But I forgive you."

Before she could come up with an appropriate response, he pulled open a drawer full of spare bathing suits.

"Take your pick," he said. He turned to leave the room again, pausing in the doorway. "I'll be back in two minutes. If you don't have a suit on, I'll be happy to help."

He left her gaping at the closed door.

RJ knocked before reentering the bathroom. He figured if he just walked in, Tessa might scream or something. Sure enough, she squeaked when he came in, even though he had knocked. Maybe she had missed the knock over the sound of the water still filling the tub. She sat on the edge of one end of the tub, dipping her feet in the water. The red one-piece suit she had chosen was a little loose and gaped nicely at the neckline. She looked relieved to see him wearing a bathing suit as well. What, she thought he would strut around in all his glory when she was in panic mode? He shut the door behind him to keep the warm air inside and walked over to the side of the tub.

"You okay?" he asked.

She nodded, wary, and he shook his head with a laugh.

"I'm not going to eat you, you know."

He really wanted to add 'not today' to that remark, but figured there was a good chance she would run for the hills if he starting joking about stuff like that.

"Okay," she answered, so softly that he could barely hear her above the water.

She had managed to immerse her legs all the way up to mid-calf. He took a seat at the opposite end of the tub and dipped his legs in as well. The lukewarm water burned his still-chilled skin, but he dealt with the sting and within moments had adjusted to the temperature. Leaning forward, he checked the temperature of the water at the faucet, which was positioned at the midpoint of the tub, halfway between them. His toes still tingled, so he didn't bump up the temperature yet.

He watched Tessa with his peripheral vision. She seemed to be relaxing, although he couldn't be sure. He lowered himself slowly into the tub, suppressing a hiss as his valuables hit the water. Tessa was watching him now instead of her knees, so he raised an eyebrow in challenge. She gave him a frown and started to lower herself into the tub as well. She took a lot more time, but eventually they were both in the tub, facing each other, their legs resting side by side in the swirling water.

Now that they had both adjusted to the temperature, he added some more hot to the mix and grabbed a bottle of bubble bath sitting behind the faucet. Maybe she would be less self-conscious with some camouflage. He could feel Tessa's eyes on him as he poured a healthy dose of the bubble stuff into the stream of water coming from the faucet. The bubbles foamed up and within seconds their bodies were hidden from view, leaving only heads and shoulders visible.

When the water reached the safety drain, he turned off the taps. The lights were too bright. He wished he had thought to dim them, or turn half of them off. The silence surrounded them. Would have been nice to pipe in some low music, too, but that might have pushed Tessa over the edge into panic. No need to set the scene for seduction. RJ had something much more nefarious in mind.

Temptation.

. . .

Tessa tried to relax. The hot water helped, but she worried about the bubbles. The red bathing suit provided little defense against the liquid seduction. It hung loose on her body, exposing way too much skin and allowing eddies of heat to slide beneath the fabric. She studied the foam as if it might hold the answer to all her worries, but it told her nothing, just tried to soothe her with its softness and the fizzy sound of bubbles bursting.

It had been eight years since she had last seen RJ shirtless, and the years had been good to him. His leanness had turned into layers of solid muscle. The dusting of hair across his chest was new, narrowing to a trail before disappearing beneath the waistband of his board shorts. The tattoos were a surprise. One circled his bicep. The other, on his back, she had only glimpsed briefly in the mirror. Now the bubbles hid his body from view, but she promised herself that she would get a closer look later.

She nearly jumped out of her skin when RJ's hand, hidden beneath the surface, clasped her ankle. His mouth quirked at her reaction, but his eyes held challenge.

"We're not going to have sex today." He said it casually, as if he were saying, *We're not going to play cards today.* The words should have hit her like a bucket of cold water, but instead her body surged with heat.

"I made a promise," he said, "and I'm going to keep it. You're not ready, and I won't try to talk you into it."

She sucked in a breath, the air so heavy and humid that breathing took effort.

"What if I try to change your mind?" she asked. The words were out of her mouth before she realized what she was think-ing, much less saying. She would have blushed, but her skin was already so flushed from the warm water that it wasn't possible.

He smiled at that, one of those long, slow smiles that made her melty and nervous all at once.

"No sex," he repeated. "Even if you beg."

At his words, a shiver ran down the length of her body.

Oh dear God, she was going to beg.

He began to caress her ankle, his fingers moving in slow circles, then strolling down to massage the arch of her foot. She heard a sound and realized that she had made a happy little sigh. She slid a bit lower into the water.

The man was brilliant. He had drawn a line in the sand, evil genius that he was, and now instead of being completely terrified, she felt safe and powerful, and she longed to stretch her toe across that line, just to see what would happen.

When he reached over with his other hand to rearrange her legs, she didn't object. She helped, in fact, letting him float one leg over his so that, beneath the veil of foam, she opened up to him. His legs were long, and he rearranged them as well so that his feet rested one on either side of her hips. Her legs rested on top of his, draped so that her feet nestled against the outside of his thighs. He held one foot in each hand now. Her awareness condensed until she felt only the motion of his thumbs on the arches of her feet, each rhythmic circle sending waves of sensation upward along her legs. The waves collided at the top, leaving her speechless.

His hands eventually abandoned her feet to stroke her calves, all the way up to the vulnerable hollow behind her knees. She sank lower into the warm water, wanting to give him more, but the bubbles tickling her nose stopped her. She closed her eyes and let the sensations roll through her. He eased her legs open wider so that her knees rested on the sides of the tub and stroked her from knees to toes and back again. She moaned softly and tried to scoot close to him, but found that her hips were wedged firmly between his feet. She made an impatient sound in the back of her throat.

"Look at me, Tessa," he murmured.

She opened her eyes just enough to glare at him. The lights were too bright.

"We're not going to have sex today."

He looked like he thought this whole situation was pretty damned funny.

"You don't need to keep saying that," she snapped. "I got it."

She wriggled free and made a move to stand up—if he was going to be a jerk, she wasn't going to stay in the tub—but he put out a hand to stop her.

"You might be more comfortable over here," he suggested. He tugged her gently toward him.

Her heart stuttered inside her chest, then began thumping so loudly she wondered if he could hear it too.

"Come here," he said, and she did.

Her earlier movement had started the water sloshing around the tub. This time she moved more slowly, using the extra time to breathe. He settled her gently in front of him. She leaned back against his chest, her head on his shoulder, her arms sinking down to rest on his thighs, her legs lined up inside his. He wrapped one arm around her and pulled her back against him. She stilled, both shocked and thrilled by the massive erection pressing against her back.

She wasn't the only one who wanted more.

After that, she couldn't think clearly anymore. She had to close her eyes to shut out the glare of the lights. His mouth did something to her ear, distracting her with the heat of his breath and the nip of his teeth. His hands moved up to slip the straps of the one-piece off her shoulders. He moved too slowly. Why didn't he move faster? She wanted more. Now. Instead, he slowed down. He held the shoulder straps taut so that she could feel the top edge of the suit moving down her breasts, millimeter by millimeter, until they caught on her nipples. She forgot to breathe, waiting for him to release the tension.

When he let go, her breasts floated free beneath the thinning layer of bubbles. She could feel each tiny bubble as it popped against her skin. Then, as she sucked in a breath, he took one breast in each hand and began to caress them. She clutched his thighs and whimpered. She needed to move, but when she pressed back against him he froze, his grip on her breasts tightening. She did it again. This time he slid one arm around her waist and with the other hand grabbed her thigh, pinning her against him so that she couldn't move.

"Stop," he growled in her ear.

"I can't," she whispered, trying again to move her hips.

He laughed, a low rumble that she felt with her body. She leaned her head to the side so that he could more easily do whatever he pleased with her neck. When she began to massage his thighs, his growl of satisfaction inspired her to keep going, determined to drive him just as insane as she was. He released her waist and his hand moved up to reclaim one breast. His other hand, the one imprisoning her thigh, also loosened its grip and began to stroke the inside of her thighs, echoing the motion of her hands on his body. With each stroke, he came closer and closer to her center, but no matter how wide she opened her legs, he refused to move beyond the edge of the bathing suit.

He was doing it on purpose. Torturing her. She stopped stroking his legs and instead pressed herself back against him, moving her hips in exactly the right way to torture him back. He made a frustrated noise that pleased her, then startled her by switching hands, tormenting the other breast. His other hand now took up the underwater torment, approaching and retreating until her breathing grew ragged. When he traced the edge of the suit with his fingers, barely disturbing the edge of the fabric, she reached her limit. She grabbed his hand and put it exactly where she wanted it.

"Please," she whispered.

Suddenly both his hands were there, between her legs, beneath the suit. His feet somehow pinned her own against the side of the tub, holding her legs wide apart. The fingers of one hand plunged inside her while the other hand circled hard, holding her against him as she fell apart in his arms.

When it was over, when his fingers gentled to move in lazy circles and she twitched from delicious aftershocks, she blinked and opened her eyes, only to be blinded again by the bathroom lights. Most of the bubbles were gone, and she wondered at the sight of their entwined legs, hers still splayed wide apart. The shoulder straps of the suit had sunk down to her elbows while her breasts broke the surface of the water, a few stray bubbles clinging to her nipples. RJ's arms circled her, his hands disappearing from between her thighs. She couldn't believe she was looking at her own body, and that she wasn't having some kind of panic attack. She couldn't even be bothered to feel embarrassed, or self-conscious. All she felt was complete and total satisfaction.

She sighed contentedly and RJ kissed her neck in response.

"Feeling more comfortable now?" he asked.

She nodded, then realized that he was still hard as a rock. She ran her hands gently along the muscles of his thighs.

"What about you?" she asked. "You don't seem very comfortable …yet."

He nipped her ear.

"We're not having sex today," he murmured.

"I know," she replied, "but that's—"

"No buts," he interrupted. "I'm fine. You're not going to have any regrets about this. You're not going to wonder if I talked you into anything, or if you got caught up in the moment, or if you felt obligated to return a favor. I can wait."

She frowned, following his logic but not liking it one bit. It didn't feel right to leave him hanging. She opened her mouth to argue some more, but he beat her to it.

"You're going to think about this afternoon every second…of every minute…of every day." His hands moved to match his words, providing lovely emphasis, and her insides clenched, already wanting another turn. "You're going to be distracted at work, and very, very lonely at home in your bed." She nodded, and he kept moving his hands in that slow rhythm. She tried to squeeze her thighs together to ease the sweet ache, but he wouldn't let her. "You're going to wonder just how good the real thing will be. All. Week. Long." She nodded, her grip tightening on his thighs. He began pressing the fingers of one hand inside her, slowly, gently, matching the rhythm of those endless circles. "And next weekend," he continued, whispering the words directly into her ear so that she shivered and her back arched, her nipples rock hard and aching to be touched, but she didn't want him to touch them because then he would have to stop what he was doing between her legs, and she never, ever wanted him to stop. "Next weekend, when you come back, you'll know exactly—" The motion of his hands grew more fierce and insistent. "—what you want."

She came again, shuddering and bucking against him as he drove her over the edge. She yelled his name. She clutched the edge of the tub while her body freaked out and water splashed everywhere. She had never—It didn't matter. With RJ, she might as well throw the rulebook out the window.

This time, when she had recovered, he gently removed his hands from beneath the bathing suit and caressed her body in long strokes intended to calm rather than arouse. The water had cooled, so they climbed out. He grabbed a towel and quickly dried off, then left the room to give her privacy that she no longer wanted or needed. She stripped off the too-large suit and dried off, then wrapped the towel around herself. Her clothes were still wet, but as she was wondering what she should do about that, he knocked, then cracked open the door and stuck a hand through the opening, offering a pair of sweat pants and a sweatshirt. She smiled. Talented *and* thoughtful.

The perfect man.

He was right. She was going to think about this interlude all week long, not that she needed much time for reflection or debate. There was no longer a shred of doubt in her mind.

She knew exactly what she wanted.

CHAPTER NINE

TESSA HAD ALWAYS LOVED THE TROLL BRIDGE THAT MARKED THE far edge of The Gardens. It had a stone and concrete foundation, so it felt sturdy and safe. The wrought-iron railing had been replaced last year, and the new line of spikes across the top made it look a little dangerous. There were three steps up and three steps down. You could stand in the middle of the bridge, drop flowers into the stream below, and watch them float downstream into the lake. The shore path went up and over the bridge, continuing down the lakeshore until it disappeared into the willow trees at the point.

Tessa and Sunny had claimed the bridge as their own private hideaway. The high schoolers were too big to fit comfortably in the shady arch beneath it, and too cool to hang out under bridges anyway. Mel didn't like sitting on the damp concrete ledge that formed the bank of the stream or leaning against the rough stonework of the archway. Callie had cut her head once on one of the pieces of iron that poked out of the underside of the bridge and now she flat-out refused to go underneath. The smaller kids were too afraid to go anywhere near it. This might have something to do with the stories Tessa and Sunny had told them about the trolls who lived in a secret cave beneath the bridge and ate little children for dinner. (They were very good storytellers.) As a result, they pretty much had the bridge to themselves, and it became their special place.

On this particular afternoon, Nana Vi sent Tessa to search for Sunny, and Tessa knew exactly where to start looking. As Tessa approached the bridge, Lucky came bounding out from underneath to greet her with joyful barks and licking. She followed him back to the base of the bridge and ducked underneath. As she had expected, Sunny sat in the cool shade. Her feet dangled in the stream and she was wiggling a bunch of forget-me-nots back and forth with her toes. Her face was red and streaked with tears, and she really needed a tissue.

"I'm not going back," said Sunny.

"Fine with me," said Tessa. She knew better than to argue with Sunny when she was in this mood.

"That lady is not my mom and I do not have to be nice to her."

"Don't worry. Nana Vi kicked her out."

"Nana did what?"

"I didn't mean to listen, but I was looking for you, and I came in the porch like usual, only Nana and your dad and that girl were in the kitchen yelling at each other."

Tessa knew that she should have turned right around and left, but Sunny was like her extra sister, and Nana was the closest thing she had to a grandmother. She had heard the yelling and panicked and hid on the porch to make sure it all turned out okay.

"What did they say?" asked Sunny.

"I didn't hear the beginning," said Tessa, "but when I got there Nana was yelling at your dad about how this was all hard enough without him making it worse and bringing a lady-friend here. Your dad said something about being a man with needs and your Nana told him to suck it up. She said she wouldn't allow his lady-friend to stay in the house. Then the lady-friend started crying and saying she wanted to go home, so your dad said he would take her home. And then your Nana told him not to come back until he was serious about being a dad."

"And then what?" whispered Sunny, her eyes round.

"And then he left," said Tessa. "The girl went, too, so I guess he took her home."

"She lives in Chicago," said Sunny.

"That's pretty far."

"Do you think he'll come back?" asked Sunny.

Sunny's dad was supposed to spend the whole week with her and RJ. They spent their summers at the lake, which gave them a break from the back-and-forth life back in the city. During the school year, their parents took turns being in charge, which was weird, but Tessa figured taking turns was better than fighting. Of course, getting along was also better than fighting, but Sunny's parents didn't seem to know how to do that.

"I don't know," said Tessa. "I waited until it was all quiet, and then I pretended that I just got there. Nana didn't say anything about your dad. She just told me to go find you and bring you home."

Sunny sniffled.

"He was going to take me sailing," she said.

"I can take you sailing," offered Tessa.

Sunny shook her head sadly and resumed playing with the forget-me-nots. "It wouldn't be the same."

She was right, of course. Sailing with her dad was a special outing. Sailing with Tessa was an everyday thing. Tessa wanted to fix things for Sunny, but it seemed like no matter how hard she tried, they only got worse.

Tessa wrapped her arms around her knees and they sat together in silence for a long time. Lucky flopped beside them on the cool concrete, happy to be out of the sun for a while. When Sunny's sniffles had faded, they both splashed their faces with cold water from the stream and headed back to Nana's house. If they were very lucky, there would be brownies. Nana liked to bake when she was angry.

Today

Tessa pulled into the parking lot behind Nana Vi's condo building and found an open spot. The upscale property sat right on the shores of Lake Michigan, the manicured grounds creating an unexpected break in the endless chain of lakefront mansions that anchored the north shore suburbs. She wasn't sure if a home visit was the right move, but after last week's session with Nana Vi she was worried. She wouldn't call Nana Vi suicidal, exactly, or she would have alerted the family. It was more like Vi was on her own deathwatch, impatient for the event even if she was unwilling to make it happen. People in that frame of mind could be unpredictable and perhaps a little careless of their own safety. She had also walked away from that first meeting with a sense of unease. Nana Vi hadn't told her everything.

She had eventually reached the cleaning girl, Kaja, on her cell phone, but the conversation had left Tessa with more questions than answers. Kaja's English wasn't great, and she was clearly worried that Tessa worked for immigration rather than for Mr. Foster in California. All Tessa had managed to take away from the conversation was the fact that Kaja thought it was "not right" for Mrs. Foster to talk to the dead Mr. Foster.

The doorman called Vi to make sure that Tessa was

expected, then directed Tessa to the elevators. Like the Hammond Center, Vi's building was very posh. The decor aimed for antique and classic but didn't quite hit the mark, the excessive use of gilt and mirrors hinting instead at the early '80s, and when you looked closely, you could see that everything was worn around the edges.

Tessa knocked on Vi's door and Vi opened it immediately.

"What are you waiting for? Come in, come in."

Vi hustled her inside and took her by the elbow, steering her through the hall to the living room. Tessa stopped short when the view hit her, and Vi chuckled by her side.

"Some view, isn't it?" she said smugly.

Tessa nodded.

'Some view' didn't quite capture it. The condo had floor-to-ceiling windows looking out onto Lake Michigan. The building itself was perhaps a hundred yards from the water's edge, with only grass and gardens on the strip of land in between. Here on the tenth floor, not even the handful of ancient oaks could block the view. Tessa sank down onto the couch and soaked it in.

"I'm never leaving," she murmured, and Vi laughed in delight.

"Me either," she said. "Do you want some coffee?"

Tessa nodded, and Vi disappeared into the kitchen to fetch it. She returned a moment later with a tray containing two steaming mugs of coffee, cream, sugar, and a small plate of cookies. Tessa smiled when she saw them. Some things never changed. Vi always had cookies in the house. Her favorites were the long, thin pirouettes. Tessa munched one before sipping her coffee.

"I understand you got quite a dunking on Sunday," said Vi.

Tessa raised her eyebrows over the rim of her coffee mug.

"RJ calls me every Sunday night," she explained. "He's a good boy."

Nodding her agreement, Tessa ignored the flush that raced through her body at the memory of the way RJ had helped her to warm up after the dunking. This was neither the time nor the place. Vi was sharp, though, and she must have caught the hint of a blush because her eyes narrowed speculatively.

"We had fun," said Tessa blandly, but Nana Vi was no dummy.

"Now, don't you let him get fresh with you, missy," said Vi firmly. "That boy is too charming for his own good. A new girl every week and here he is almost thirty and no great-grandbabies in sight. If he thinks he can treat you that way, then he and I need to have a little talk."

Tessa almost snorted her coffee. If anything, Vi was getting more outspoken as she got older.

"Don't worry, Vi," she said. "We laid out some ground rules. He's not allowed to use his charm on me."

Vi still looked skeptical, so Tessa decided to give her a taste of her own medicine.

"Maybe you should be warning RJ about me," she said. "I'm not looking for anything serious, but I hear he's great in the sack."

That earned her a loud cackle from Vi.

"That's my girl," she said. "You give him hell."

Tessa shook her head in exasperation.

"I can only imagine what you were like as a girl," she said. "No wonder Robert was crazy about you."

"He was," said Vi. "He is."

They sat in silence for a moment before Tessa spoke again.

"So what are your plans for today?" she asked.

"Nothing much," shrugged Vi. "Robert and I were just reading the paper, and then later I'll take a walk by the water. We don't really get out much anymore."

Tessa noted Vi's use of 'we' but didn't comment on it. The habits of a lifetime were hard to break.

"Anything good in the paper this morning?" she asked.

Vi pursed her lips, then put down her coffee cup.

"We didn't get very far into it," she said, "but I'll fetch it and we can take a look."

Curious to see the rest of the place, Tessa trailed behind Vi and stopped in the doorway of the kitchen. Vi was still chattering away, but Tessa couldn't make sense of her words anymore. Her eyes were fixed on the man seated at the kitchen table. Was he...? But how...?

Vi was folding the paper up to carry it back to the living room when she saw Tessa's face.

"Tessa, honey, what is it? You're white as a sheet. Oh—" Vi looked from Tessa to the figure at the table and then back to Tessa. She laid the paper back on the table and started to fuss with it, making sure it was perfectly folded and tucked back together.

"Vi, who's this?" Tessa asked. She couldn't quite make her voice work, so it came out low and husky.

Vi straightened, pride and defiance in every inch of her body.

"Why, this is Robert, of course."

Tessa walked slowly around the kitchen table and tried to understand what she was seeing. Now that the initial shock had worn off, she understood that this wasn't an actual person, but some kind of dummy dressed up as Vi's late husband. Her heart was pounding as she finally understood why Kaja had been so concerned. Vi wasn't just talking to her dead husband. She was pretending he was still alive.

Now standing beside Vi, Tessa wrapped an arm around her petite shoulders and gave her a gentle squeeze.

"You know that this isn't really Robert, right? Please tell me you understand that."

Vi stiffened within the circle of her arm, then reached down, snatched up the newspaper, and stalked out of the kitchen. Tessa followed more slowly behind. Vi slapped the tightly folded paper onto the coffee table and walked instead to the wall of windows, where she stood staring out at the water. Tessa chose to return to her seat, where she waited for Vi to recover. Direct confrontation was a risky choice, but one that suited Vi's personality. She would have little patience with a more subtle approach.

"Vi?" asked Tessa. She kept her voice gentle but firm. She wasn't going to let Vi off the hook.

The older woman turned to face Tessa and crossed her arms.

"What do you want me to say?" she demanded. "I know it's only a dummy. I know my Robert is gone." Her voice cracked and she cleared her throat. "What I want to know is why everybody cares so much about what I do in the privacy of my own home. So I prefer to talk to a shadow rather than thin air. Who cares? I'm not hurting anyone."

"Did you explain that to Robert Junior?" asked Tessa.

"Of course not," she snapped back. "He destroyed his own marriage. How could he possibly understand how I feel?"

"You make an excellent point," said Tessa.

Vi snorted, then walked slowly over to her chair, easing herself slowly into the seat, as if all her strength had left her.

"That boy should tend to his own garden before he starts criticizing mine."

"He may not understand marriage, but he's still your son. He lost his father. Do you think he might be afraid of losing his mother, too?"

"I'm right here," muttered Vi.

"How often do you go out?" asked Tessa.

Vi shrugged.

"I see," said Tessa.

That earned her a sharp look.

"If you have something to say, missy, just say it. Let's not have any of that 'I see' business."

"Fine," said Tessa. "Robert is dead. You are not. What do you suppose he would say if he knew you were hiding away in your home waiting to die?"

Tessa felt a twinge of guilt. She had hurt Vi's feelings, but these things needed to be said, and Vi had always been one for plain speaking. She simply preferred to be on the giving rather than the receiving end.

Vi twisted her wedding ring around a few times before she answered.

"He would be furious."

"He would," agreed Tessa, which only made Vi's mouth tighten around the corners.

"But I'm furious, too," she said firmly. "He's the one who left me, so he can be as angry as he wants. If he's that pissed off, he can come back and get me."

"It's hard to fight with someone who won't fight back," said Tessa.

Vi nodded curtly.

"How long are you planning to continue your protest?" asked Tessa.

"As long as it takes," said Vi. Her anger had taken on a bit of a pout.

"To what?" asked Tessa. "To die?"

All she got in response was a stubbornly lifted chin. She couldn't help it; she laughed.

"What's so funny?" snapped Vi.

"I've seen that expression before, you know," said Tessa. "That's exactly what Huck does when you tell him it's time to go to bed."

Vi huffed at the comparison.

"I am not a sulky toddler."

Tessa raised an eyebrow. Vi needed to get angry at somebody who was alive.

"Could have fooled me."

"It's time for you to leave," said Vi. She marched toward the front door without looking back to see if Tessa would follow. Tessa did, but she took her own sweet time. She wanted Vi good and riled before she left.

"Thank you for the coffee," said Tessa.

Vi had opened the door and was standing there waiting to hustle her out. She didn't respond, just stood there, her posture ramrod straight, waiting for Tessa to make her exit. Tessa leaned down and gave her a kiss on the cheek.

"See you soon," she said, and slipped out the door.

Vi didn't exactly slam the door shut behind her, but it was close. Tessa chuckled on her way to the elevator. She would be back, and next time she would bring reinforcements.

Would the week never end?

Tessa kept it together—for the most part—during the day. Her clients needed her full attention, and only occasionally did she shift in her seat, recross her legs, or lose her train of thought. The nights, however, were another story. Nothing about her normal routine felt normal anymore. 'Normally' she stopped at the gym on the way home, but now her workout only made her more aware of every inch of her body. 'Normally' she found the repetition of each exercise in the equipment circuit soothing. Calming, even. Now, however, every exercise was a form of sensual torture. All that thrusting and panting, the long slow burn in her muscles, the quivers that told her she was nearing her limit, and the delicious relief of exhaustion. The gym seemed practically pornographic. The shower afterward didn't help. Too many bubbles sliding down her body. She barely made it through her Monday workout and didn't dare go back on Tuesday.

She also found that dinner took forever to prepare. She kept losing track of what she was doing, realizing with a start that she had been staring into space for who knows how long rather than chopping the carrot in front of her. And why would she want to chop a carrot? She had done a fine job of scraping it. The long strokes felt right, and she liked the firm weight of it in her hand. It was only when she couldn't bear to cut it that she realized she was losing her mind.

The man truly was an evil genius. She was counting the minutes until she could get him alone.

Never before had she allowed a man to take possession of her senses like this, but then, never before had a man unlocked the secrets of her body. Until recently, she had thought she had the only key. She found that she couldn't quite remember the ho-hum sexual encounters of her past. They had faded to the point that they felt like something she had once read in a book. This obsession with RJ was so vivid, so intense, that it overshadowed everything else. Even her own attempts to take the edge off left her wanting more.

By Friday morning she was nearing the end of her rope. She had no idea how she would get RJ to herself with Sunny and the boys still visiting, but she would find a way. Her last client appointment was scheduled for two o'clock, and after that she intended to fly out the door and break the speed limit all the way up to the lake. Her bag was packed, her plants watered, her apartment locked up tight. The only thing standing between her and freedom were four client appointments. She could do that.

Just as she was about to go fetch her first client from the waiting room, Brock appeared in the doorway of her office.

"Good morning," he said.

Something in his tone of voice alerted her that he was up to no good.

"Brock," she responded. "Can I help you with something? I have a client waiting."

"This won't take long," he said, stepping into her office without waiting for an invitation.

She tensed and leaned forward in her seat, pretending to check something on her computer screen rather than tip her head back to look up at him. When it became clear that he was waiting for that tiny act of submission, she scooted her chair back and stood to face him.

"What do you need, Brock?"

She kept her voice neutral, but her body language made it clear that she didn't have time for his games.

"We're going to have a meeting this afternoon to discuss the plan and timeline for opening the new center. You need to be there."

So this was how things were going to be now that Brock was in charge.

"I'm leaving at three today," she said. No apologies. No waffling. Brock was letting her know how he planned to run things, and she responded in kind.

"You'll need to change your plans," he replied.

She gave him a tight smile.

"I'm unwilling to do that."

The expression on his face would have made her laugh if she weren't so tightly wound up. He looked like he was trying to play the role of weary principal to her version of uncooperative student. This from the guy who had been begging for her help only a few months before. She didn't have the patience for it.

"That's...disappointing."

Her smile widened.

"I'm sure you'll muddle through without me," she said. "And now, I need to meet my client."

She skipped the good-byes, walked around Brock, and exited her office. She didn't even have an adrenaline rush from the confrontation. All she felt was relief.

RJ tried to keep busy, and the distraction of his nephews certainly helped, but eventually he conceded that his plan had backfired. Instead of driving Tessa crazy, he had driven himself over the edge. He just couldn't get over the revelation of this whole new side of Tessa. She had always been the practical one, offering great advice but completely immune to his charm. Despite the fact that they hadn't seen each other in years, she probably knew him better than most of his friends, certainly better than any other woman. There had never been any bull-shit between them. You might argue that they had been too honest with one another, but at least there had never been any games. Even now, as they explored this new territory, she didn't let his charm come between them. She was worried. He could see that. But she was also incredibly courageous.

As RJ walked home from the office on Friday afternoon, he started to wonder if he should call a halt to this whole thing before it went any further. He had the uneasy feeling that Tessa wouldn't be able to keep her promise, and it didn't seem fair to continue knowing that she would get hurt in the end. He didn't want to destroy both their friendship and her illusions at the same time. One way or another he needed to make a decision because she would be here tonight. Once they crossed the line, sexually speaking, there would be no going back.

He took the back steps two at a time. In the kitchen, he found Sunny and the boys eating an early dinner, which dissolved into chaos for a few moments in celebration of his return.

"RJ, I'm so glad you're home," said Sunny when things had

settled back down. She gave him her 'sunny' smile, the one that had earned her the nickname, and he sighed.

"Yes," he said.

"What?" she asked. "I didn't ask you a question."

He shook his head.

"Whatever it is you need, yes," he said. "You would have talked me into it anyway. I'm just saving you the trouble."

Her smile widened even more, if that was possible. She gave him a giant kiss on the cheek as he sat down.

"You're the best."

"So what is it that I'm doing?"

She laughed. "I was going to ask you to watch the boys tonight so that I can go out with some friends. You are absolutely the best. Don't worry. They're really easy. They'll both be asleep by eight, I promise."

This did not bode well for his plans with Tessa.

"Sunny, I'm not really qualified—"

"You'll be great. No qualifications required."

She didn't even let him object properly.

"Where are you going?" he asked, not that it mattered. She was going to leave him alone with the little terrors. Alone and defenseless.

"We're meeting at The Beach," she said, "so we don't have to worry about driving."

"Are you sure—?"

"Positive," said Sunny. "And don't worry. You'll have backup. I texted Tessa and she's agreed to share kid duty with you."

RJ saw the smug look on her face but let it slide. His sister was no dummy. She had picked up on the vibes between him and Tessa and used it to her advantage. There was no way he would try to weasel out now. He was about to give her a hard time when his phone rang.

One glance at the caller ID told him that he should let it go straight to voicemail. Sunny saw the expression on his face and gave him a lopsided smile full of sympathy.

"Mom or Dad?" she asked.

Resigned to the inevitable, he accepted the call as he stood up from the kitchen table.

"Dad," he said tersely into the phone. Sunny mouthed 'good luck' and then grabbed Huck's hand to stop him from throwing a handful of peas at Oscar. RJ walked through the living room and onto the front porch.

"Son," said his dad on the other end of the line.

"What do you need?" he asked. Like his mother, his father always needed something. Whereas with Sunny, RJ's default answer was yes, his default response to his father happened to be no. Forever and always, no.

"Can't a guy call to check in on his son?"

"It would be a first," said RJ. "Why don't you cut to the chase?"

"Fine," said his father. "I need you to invite your mother to the lake for the Fourth of July."

RJ let his silence speak for itself. His father used silence right back at him. RJ broke first.

"You can't be serious," said RJ. "She hasn't been here since… She hasn't been here in nineteen years. What makes you think I can persuade her to come now?"

"She'll come to visit her grandchildren," said his father, "and you'll make sure she stays in one place long enough for me to talk with her."

"Are you finally going to end it?" asked RJ, unable to keep the bitterness out of his voice.

"On the contrary," he replied. "It's time that Nancy and I put all this nonsense behind us."

RJ shook his head. His father wasn't making any sense.

"And then what?" he asked. "Live happily ever after?"

"You never know," said his father.

"This is bullshit," said RJ. "I don't know what the hell you're up to, but I can tell you one thing: This is the last time you use me as the go-between. I'll get her here, you two will talk, and from that moment forward you leave me out of it. Whatever 'it' is. Understood?"

"Understood."

RJ didn't have time to get over his shock and anger before his father ended the call. He stood staring out at the water for a few minutes, trying to calm down and understand what was going on, but he couldn't wrap his head around it.

"That was quick," said Sunny when RJ returned to the kitchen. "What did he want?"

RJ explained and he saw his own confusion reflected in her face.

"Are you actually going to do it?" asked Sunny. "The last thing we need is a repeat of all the drama..."

Her voice trailed off and RJ fought to keep his expression neutral. All that drama had sent Sunny into a destructive spiral of self-blame and self-medication. He and Tessa had finally gotten through to her, but it had been touch and go for a while. If his parents—or at least his father—wanted to hash things out after nineteen years, that was their business, and he would make sure they were alone when it all went down. He would not put Sunny at risk again.

"Hell, yes, I'm going to do it," he said. "You and I have been in the middle for too long."

Tessa stopped to get gas halfway up to the lake and saw a missed text from Sunny.

Couple of my girlfriends from Madison are in town tonight. Any chance you could help RJ babysit so I can sneak out for dinner and a drink?

How could she say no? Sunny needed to get out and have some fun, and she wouldn't be able to do that unless she knew the boys were in good hands. RJ was great with the boys, as long as he was in 'fun uncle' mode. He didn't have a lot of experience being the one in charge. Tessa, on the other hand, had mastered the art of babysitting by age eleven. With a sigh, she replied.

I'm on it. Should be there just after five. Soon enough?

So much for getting RJ alone. Now they would need to wait until Sunny got home before they could find some real privacy. Sunny replied:

Perfect. I'm meeting them at five, so I'll miss you, but RJ will only have to survive a few minutes on his own. Thank you!!! You are a goddess.

Tessa smiled and shook her head.

Anytime.

While she was in the middle of this exchange, she got a text from Mel.

Drinks with Kat. 9pm at The Beach. Don't make me go alone.

Tessa groaned. She had completely forgotten their impromptu invitation to Kat last weekend. Mel must have worked out the details, and now they were stuck. She didn't even consider using babysitting as an excuse to get out of it. Mel would kill her.

I'll be there. Helping RJ babysit tonight. Meet you at home at 8:30 and we can head out from there.

Tessa got back on the road and tried to resign herself to the new plan for the evening. If anything, the delay reconfirmed how very much she wanted to take things to the next level with RJ. She just needed the chance to show him.

Tessa arrived about twenty minutes after Sunny left, and RJ had never been so glad to see anyone in his entire life. His nephews were so excited about 'guys night' that they had lost their minds. Whatever magic Sunny used to control their behavior had left the building along with her. At this point, it was all about damage control. Paper airplanes had seemed like a brilliant distraction as Sunny was walking out the door, but he had never realized that featherlight paper airplanes, when thrown with sufficient force and chased with sufficient enthusiasm, could cause this much damage. So far they had destroyed a vase filled with dried flowers, a frog paperweight, and possibly the hearing in his left ear.

"Hi guys," she said as she breezed through the back door. "I don't think you heard me knocking."

The boys immediately launched their paper airplanes at her, one heading directly for her face. She made an impressive midair catch, saving her eyesight in the process, and grabbed the second airplane from its landing spot on the kitchen counter. Taking quick stock of the situation, she said, "What do you say we take this party outside and see how far these airplanes can fly?"

She led the boys out the front porch toward the commons, holding the paper airplanes high above her head until everyone was safely outside. As she passed RJ, who lay defeated on the floor next to the couch, she chuckled.

"On your feet, soldier," she called over her shoulder. "The sooner we tire them out, the sooner we can have some time to ourselves."

He groaned as he rolled to his side and hauled himself to his feet. Two small boys would not defeat him.

CHAPTER TEN

AN HOUR LATER, RJ AND TESSA CREPT DOWN THE STAIRS, AFRAID that the slightest noise would wake the tiny terrors who now slept in the bunk bed upstairs. Tessa, his angel of mercy, had tired them out on the commons, and then she and RJ had supervised a lengthy bath in the smaller bathtub. The little boys had lobbied hard for the big bathtub, but Tessa and RJ had taken one look at each other, then marched the boys to the smaller one down the hall. After two rounds of toothbrushing and several thousand storybooks, the boys' eyelids had started to droop. If they could only keep the house perfectly quiet until the boys fell all the way to sleep, they would be golden.

RJ grabbed a bottle of Chardonnay from the fridge and handed it to Tessa along with an opener and a couple of wine glasses.

"Relax," he whispered. "Pour the wine. I'll be out in a second."

She disappeared into the living room while he put together a weak attempt at appetizers. He found cheese and crackers and he sliced an apple to go alongside. It wasn't fancy, and it wasn't dinner, but it would tide them over until they figured out what they wanted to eat. He found her leaning back on the couch with her feet up on the coffee table, wine in hand, eyes closed. She heard him coming and opened one eye, smiling when she saw the snacks.

"My hero," she said, keeping her voice low. "How did you know I was starving?"

"Psychic," he answered. He took the seat beside her, picked up the glass of wine that she had poured for him, and sat back with a sigh of relief. After the explosive sound and energy of his nephews, the silence was blissful.

He spent a few minutes lamenting the failure of his grand plan for tonight. Being in the same room with Tessa was enough to put him on alert, but given their babysitting responsibilities, this would have to be a rated-G evening. Maybe, once they were sure the boys were asleep, they could progress to PG, but that was as far as he was comfortable going. Huck might be too young to care what he saw if he came downstairs looking for his mama, but Oscar would have questions. Lots of questions.

So instead of imagining Tessa naked, or trying to get her naked, he distracted himself with his other problem.

"Have you had a chance to think about my difficult clients?" he asked. "Any suggestions?"

She turned sideways on the couch to face him and folded one leg to make herself comfortable.

"In fact, I have," she said, "and the first step is to open the lines of communication."

"Easier said than done," he said.

"I know, I know," she said. "But what if you start out with something more like homework? Don't ask them to talk to each other yet. Ask them to write down the story of how they first met, or what attracted them to each other in the first place, or what they appreciate most about the other person as a parent.

No pressure. No decisions about the future. Just focus on the positive and use that as your foundation."

"What good will that do?" he asked. "Won't it just make them realize how awful things are now?"

"Maybe," she said, "but I think it will also soften them up, especially when you have them read each other's stories."

"Wait. What?" said RJ. "There's no way they would agree to that."

"I wouldn't ask them ahead of time," said Tessa. "They wouldn't be able to write anything down. They'd be too self-conscious, worried about what the other will think when they read it. Once their story is written, though, once it's separate from them, they'll be more willing to share it, particularly if they're dying of curiosity to know what the other person has written."

His skepticism must have shown on his face, because she gave a weary sigh.

"Let's try an experiment," she said. "Do you have paper and a couple of pens?"

"Sure," he said, and got up to go find some in the kitchen. He would be happy to do whatever she asked, particularly if it kept his mind off all the things they *weren't* doing, but he couldn't promise to believe it would work.

Once they were settled again on the couch, she gave him instructions.

"Write down ten things you love about me," she said. "Don't overthink it. Just write down the first ten things that come to mind."

He stared at her blankly for a minute. She rolled her eyes.

"If the word 'love' makes you uncomfortable, let's reclassify it to 'like.' Write down ten things you *like* about me."

"Ten?" he asked. Was she crazy? Not that he didn't like her, but he had to think of ten specific things?

She was starting to look annoyed.

"Is it really that hard?" she asked. "Ten things. And no cheating by listing my ten toes, or something dumb like that. Ten real things."

He suppressed a smile. She was definitely a mindreader. As soon as she had confirmed the ten, he was already thinking fingers. Or toes. Or other body parts. As if continuing to read his thoughts, she narrowed her eyes at him.

"No more than three things on the list can be body parts," she said sternly.

"Yes, ma'am," he murmured. Was she going to be this bossy in bed? He seriously hoped so.

It took him a minute to get started. He was distracted by the way she chewed on her thumb while she was thinking. That got him thinking about kissing, and how they hadn't really done any kissing, despite the adventure in the tub last week. As much as he wanted to help his sister, he considered putting aside his pen and paper and distracting Tessa by demonstrating exactly what he was thinking about. But then she glanced up, caught him staring, and raised her eyebrow.

He gave her a mock salute and turned his attention to writing. They wrote in silence. With each item he added to his list, his curiosity grew. There was something irresistible in the knowledge that she was writing down ten things about him, and that no more than three of them could be body parts. She had been completely and totally right, damn it. He was dying to see her list.

When they had both finished, she smiled smugly.

"Want to trade?" she asked.

He didn't pretend to deny her victory. He simply tossed his paper into her lap and held out a hand, demanding hers. She handed it over, then chuckled.

"You know that this was only a demo exercise, right?" she asked, her expression oh-so-innocent. "You could make up anything. It doesn't have to be true."

"What?"

She laughed out loud at his reaction.

"Gotcha," she said.

He shook his head and smoothed out her paper so that he could read her answers. She damn well better have answered the questions seriously, or he was going to be pissed.

The first thing he noticed was the rhythm of her neat, compact handwriting. Funny how well it suited her personality. His own handwriting was legible, but it would never be described as neat. He watched her face as she started to read his list, but she had her therapist mask on and he couldn't tell what she was thinking. Frustrated, he turned his attention to her list.

Ten Things I Love About You

1. Your shoulders

2. Your confidence

3. Your smarts

4. The way you look out for your sister

5. The way you play with your nephews

6. Your kindness

7. The way you sail

8. The way you walk

9. Your integrity

10. Your restraint

He read the list several times, trying to wrap his head around the fact that these words described him. She must be writing about someone else—someone much kinder and gentler than RJ. He had expected something about his looks, or his charm, or maybe his skills in the bathtub, but she had skipped those entirely. He shifted position, suddenly uncomfortable. Her list had knocked him off balance and he didn't know what to do next.

. . .

Tessa began to wonder if this little demonstration had been such a bright idea after all. In order to participate, she had to make herself vulnerable, which turned out to be both more interesting and more uncomfortable than she had anticipated. It served her right, though, for thinking that it would be easy. She would have more empathy now for her clients when she asked them to step outside their comfort zones.

She handed her list to RJ, hoping that he would tread lightly. RJ would never hurt her feelings on purpose, but vulnerability might make him clumsy. She picked up his list from her lap and braced herself. Maybe he took the exercise seriously, but chances were that he had tried to charm his way through. If he did, that would tell her a lot about what she could expect from their summer fling. She took a deep breath and began reading.

Ten Things I ~~Like~~ Love About You
1. Your eyes
2. Your neck
3. Your toes (all ten of them)

She laughed. Couldn't help it.

4. Your laugh
5. Your honesty
6. The sounds you made in the bathtub last week
7. The way you love your family
8. Your competitive streak
9. Your courage
10. The way you see me

Tessa bit her lip but refused to let herself look at RJ. She wasn't ready to see his reaction to her list, and she didn't want to weird him out by letting him see the confusion on her face. This exercise was supposed to prove a point, but she hadn't really thought it through. She hadn't realized how it might change things between them. Up until now, it had been easy to keep things light. Neither of them wanted to screw up their friendship. Neither of them wanted to get hurt.

Now, however, she had opened a door. Okay, maybe a window. Either way, she had altered their course, and she had no idea how to proceed from here. She could only hope for the best and steel herself for the worst.

She couldn't get over the fact that he had taken her by surprise. For a guy who coasted through relationships, he had really opened up on paper. Sure, there was charm here, but he had also shared something very real. Her brain must be fogged by lust. She wasn't thinking clearly these days. Most of her brain cells were busy floating in memories of last weekend, or plotting how she would take RJ to bed and have her way with him.

God, she hoped he still wanted to do that. She hoped she hadn't panicked him with her list, because the more she learned about the man RJ had become, the one hidden beneath the charm, the more she liked him.

He had finished reading her list. She could tell from his body language in her peripheral vision. Now he was waiting for her to finish. He was waiting to see what she would do.

She schooled her face into a neutral expression, then set his list on the coffee table and met his eyes. He looked shell-shocked. She probably did, too. She tugged her letter from his hands and set it on the coffee table as well. He cleared his throat.

"Tessa," he said.

"Yes?" she asked as she began to unbutton her blouse.

He seemed unable to put words together, so she stopped

halfway down, far enough so that he could clearly see the lacy bra she had chosen this morning with him in mind. He swallowed hard.

"Tessa, I…"

She slowly moved toward him and his words trailed off.

"Yes?" she asked again as she positioned herself astride him and rolled her hips, adjusting her position until it felt just right. He didn't answer, but he did stretch his legs out on the couch and grip both sides of her waist, as if he were afraid she might try to leave or something crazy like that. She continued unbuttoning her shirt, taking her time, waiting for his answer. When he still didn't speak, she cocked an eyebrow at him.

"What, no charm?" she asked.

She let the shirt slide down her shoulders and his fingers bit into her hips, grinding her against him in a very satisfying way. She braced her hands in the couch pillows on either side of his shoulders and leaned forward, making sure he got a very close look at the lacy bra before putting her lips against his ear and whispering.

"I liked your list very much."

Then she nipped at his earlobe, and he came unleashed.

He growled as he turned his face in to her neck, kissing and biting and licking his way down past her collarbone until he reached the edge of the lace. His hands slid up her sides but instead of removing the lacy barrier, he simply yanked the cups down under her breasts so that he could have immediate access. She gasped as he took one nipple into his mouth and found the other with his fingers. It was all she could do to clutch the pillows and hold on.His hands found their way back to her hips and he rocked her against him, the rhythm of his hips and his mouth sending her in a now-familiar direction.

And someone knocked at the door.

Startled, she froze, blinking. Must—reconnect—brain.

She heard another tap-tap-tap at the kitchen door, and then

the squeak of the door as it opened. She ducked down, landing hard on RJ's chest. He made an 'oof' sound as she knocked the wind out of him, but when he caught his breath he started shaking with silent laughter. Apparently he found this all very amusing, but then, he was probably used to getting caught with half-naked women. She frantically scooped her boobs back into her bra. To him this must be no big deal. She, however, had zero experience with this type of situation and had no desire to be caught half naked.

"Yoo-hoo, anybody home?"

Especially not by her mother.

Tessa groaned softly and thumped her head several times on RJ's chest. He laughed more, and even mid-freak-out she had to appreciate the feeling of rock-solid man laughing beneath her. Before her mother could catch them all tangled up in one another, Tessa scooted backwards until she was sitting at the far end of the couch by RJ's feet, shrugging her blouse back on as she went. He smiled and pulled himself lazily into a sitting position at the opposite end of the couch. Her fingers flew up the front of the blouse, and she could only hope that she had buttoned herself evenly. God knew what her hair must look like. At least she had been on top. She flushed all over again. She had been on top of RJ, ready to rip his clothes off and have her way with him. Was it possible to feel both triumphant and mortified at the same time? For Pete's sake, there were children sleeping upstairs.

"In here, Mom," she called, loud enough for Dora to hear but—she hoped—not loud enough to wake the boys. Dora appeared at the kitchen door.

"Tessa, honey, is that you?" she asked. She took one look at the two of them on the couch and smiled.

"Hi, Mrs. James," said RJ. He didn't look the least bit embarrassed.

"Well hi there, RJ," she said. "What are you two kids up to?"

"We're working," said Tessa. *Giant lie.* "I'm helping RJ with a case."

This tidbit succeeded in distracting her mother. Fresh gossip trumped old news every time.

"Really?" she asked, taking a step closer to the couch. "Which case?"

"You're going to have to figure this one out on your own, Mom," answered Tessa, grateful that the distraction had worked. "Lawyer-client privilege and all that. It's confidential."

"Right, right," she muttered, but then perked up. "So between sailing and the case, it looks like you two will be spending a lot of time together."

Tessa nodded cautiously. RJ did the same.

"Wonderful!" crowed her mother. "It's so nice to have you up here on the weekends, and RJ, sweetie, it's so nice to have you around, too. You know, after that business with your parents, I worried that you kids would never want to come back here, which is a shame, really, to lose all those happy memories because of some bad behavior on the part of the grown-ups. I hope things work out so you can stay."

"Thanks, Mrs. J," said RJ.

Most people would think that RJ was completely unaffected by the mention of his parents, but Tessa knew better. She had seen too much of their drama firsthand, and she caught the set of his jaw and the tension that spread over his shoulders. She did not want to think about RJ's childhood right now. She wanted to focus on his adulthood. She wanted to feel the stubble on his jaw, peel off his T-shirt, and massage the tension right out of his shoulders.

Dora gave RJ a sweet smile, then turned back to Tessa.

"Well, I'll just leave you two...colleagues...alone then. Get to work, you two," she said as she turned to leave. She stopped in the doorway and turned back with a question. "Don't rush home, Tessa dear. Your father and I have already had dinner. Leftovers are in the fridge if you want some."

Tessa could feel the blush climbing her neck. Could her mother be any more obvious?

"Sounds great," she said. "I'll be home soon."

Her mother looked disappointed.

"All right, then," she said. "See you later, dear. Nice to see you, RJ."

When the kitchen door squeaked shut, RJ burst out laughing. Tessa groaned and nailed him in the face with a pillow, but he kept right on laughing. She flopped sideways with a dramatic sigh, wishing that the couch would swallow her up. She had thought that the days of her mother embarrassing her were over, but apparently she was wrong.

"I love your mother," said RJ, still chuckling.

"I used to," said Tessa. She and her mother would definitely be having a talk this evening. "What was she doing here, anyway?" she said grumpily.

RJ paused at that, cocking his head to one side. "I have no idea," he said at last. "She never said."

"I'll ask her," said Tessa. "Later."

"And right now?" asked RJ, giving her a wicked grin. "What were we talking about when your mother popped in? Oh, right," he said, lying back down and putting his hands behind his head. "I was being very careful not to rush you, or talk you into anything that you don't want to do."

His tone was joking, but the heat in his eyes was absolutely serious, and Tessa's breath caught. She still couldn't quite believe that she and RJ... She gave herself a mental shake. This was really happening, and she needed to get a grip. She was going to enjoy a summer fling, damn it, and he was going to make it amazing. And then, at the end of the summer, he was going to show her how to break things off gracefully, so that nobody got hurt. What could be simpler?

Tessa eased forward until she lay on top of him again, the length of her body pressed against his, one of his legs tucked in between hers. She held herself up on her forearms so that she could watch his face while she bossed him around.

"I want those hands below deck, sailor," she commanded. He obliged by running his hands down the length of her back and then securing her hips.

"Aye, aye, Captain," he said.

Before he could make any further smartass comments, she lowered her mouth to his and claimed it for her own.

RJ had one last coherent thought: Tessa should always be in charge. He kept his head together this time, barely, and made sure she kept her clothes on. *Rated G*, he reminded himself. She gave herself over to the heat growing between them, holding nothing back, which left him to be the responsible one, damn it. She kept trying to take off his shirt, or unbutton her own, and he eventually had to roll her over and pin her hands above her head.

"We are babysitting," he said. "Clothes stay on."

She raised her eyebrows at his mock-serious scolding.

"Or what?" she asked. "Spanking?"

"Tempting," he growled. He let one hand wander down and take possession of her breast, earning a breathy moan when he ran his thumb across her nipple. "However, that sounds like more of an incentive than a deterrent."

"Mm-hmmm," she sighed, and arched her back to give him better access.

"Let's put it this way," he said, giving her his best sexy smile. "If you can't behave, you'll have to go home. Alone."

"When you put it that way," she murmured, "it's hard to argue with you."

"Good," he said, and brought his mouth down on hers.

He released her hands and adjusted his position so he could cup her face with his hands, focusing all his attention on the exploration of her mouth. He stroked his fingers along the line of her cheekbones, then buried his hands in her hair. She wriggled beneath him so that she could wrap her legs around his waist, hooking her feet and pulling him closer. And then his phone rang.

The custom ringtone sliced right through the heat. His mother had the world's worst timing.

If he didn't answer, he knew perfectly well that she would keep calling and calling. His cell phone was in the other room, but by the time he could get his hands on it and throw it out the window, this moment with Tessa would be ruined.

His hands, currently cupping Tessa's glorious ass, paused in their exploration. She whimpered a protest against his mouth. She had no idea how much he wanted to stay in this moment. He kneaded her backside, grinding her against his hard-on, and was rewarded with a shuddery moan. He didn't want rated-G. He wanted rated-X. Now.

Let it ring, he thought as he held Tessa against him, each roll of his hips earning another shudder, another moan of pleasure. They were worse than a pair of teenagers, dry-humping on the couch while they were supposed to be babysitting. It seemed to be working, though. She was completely out of her mind, and he refused to let his mother kill the moment for both of them. The phone went silent. RJ let Tessa take the lead, following her rhythm, until all at once she fell apart in his arms.

He almost went with her. Frankly, it would have been a relief, but at that moment his phone started ringing again, and the cold slap in the face was enough to yank his own satisfaction firmly out of reach. He ground his teeth together, anchoring Tessa in his arms until she calmed. After a moment, he rolled to one side and looked down at her. She blinked up at him.

"Wow," she whispered. "Just…wow."

He grinned. Couldn't help it. Never in his life had he imagined that he would put that sleepy, sultry look on Tessa's face. Gently, he ran a hand through her hair. She continued to stare at him, bemused.

"Hey there, beautiful," he murmured.

She blushed.

"You got me again," she said, and he could hear the surprise in her voice.

"Of course I did," he answered, feeling insulted. If there was one thing in this world that he excelled at—besides sailing—it was giving pleasure to women. It was kind of his thing.

"Nobody has ever…I mean, I haven't…" She didn't finish her sentence, but he could pretty easily fill in the blanks.

"Never?" he asked, raising an eyebrow. She blushed harder, but didn't look away. Instead, she smiled wryly.

"Not with anybody else in the room," she said, and then grinned sheepishly.

He tried to keep the shock off his face. Not that she would resort to self-service, but at the ineptitude of the men in her past. Women's bodies weren't all that hard to figure out. Hell, there must be handbooks. He had to assume it was lack of effort, and that pissed him off.

His phone rang again, and she got a furrow between her eyebrows.

"Who keeps calling?" she asked.

"My mother," he sighed.

"Your mother's ringtone is the theme music for the Wicked Witch of the West?" She gave him a look that clearly stated she did not find his choice of ringtone as funny as he did.

He tried his get-out-of-trouble grin, but as usual it didn't work on Tessa.

"Don't you think you should answer it?" she asked. "She's called three times now. It might be an emergency."

RJ shook his head.

"Trust me," he said. "It's not an emergency."

"Oh," said Tessa, and thankfully left it alone. He did not feel like explaining his mother or his fucked-up family to Tessa right now. He had a hard enough time figuring it out for himself.

She eased slowly off the couch. He could tell that she was going to leave. He knew the vibe because usually he was the one leaving. When she had straightened her clothing and pulled herself back together, she picked up his list, folded it, and put it in her pocket.

"I want to read it again," she said. He liked the sexy smile that went along with her words. He wanted to read her list again, too. Then he wanted to get her naked for a long, long time.

"What are you doing after the race tomorrow?" he asked.

"I'm open," she said. "Do you have something in mind?"

He nodded slowly and was rewarded with that sexy smile again.

"What about Sunny?" she asked. "Won't she be here? I mean, I'd love to see her, but we wouldn't exactly be alone."

"She said something about taking the boys down to Chicago to see my mom."

"Oh?" she said, sounding intrigued.

"Overnight," he said.

"Oh...," she repeated, but this time it came out more like a sigh. "I'll look forward to it," she said, then ducked her head. "And thanks," she added.

This last bit came with a hint of shyness. Usually he was the one doing the thanking, but given his aching balls, he'd take whatever he could get.

"Anytime," he answered. The salacious look that accompanied his answer made her laugh.

"I've gotta go," she said. "I almost forgot, but Mel and I have plans."

"You're going to leave me alone with the boys? I thought you were my backup."

"I think you can handle it from here," said Tessa. "Don't make any loud noises. And call your mom."

At that moment the phone rang again and he winced. He wondered if there was a setting on his phone that would make all his mother's phone calls go straight to voicemail. He would need to look into that. Tessa raised an eyebrow and nodded toward the sound of his phone in the other room.

RJ would have loved to pull her back down on top of him, but instead, he stood and walked with her into the kitchen so he could grab his phone off the charger. He really did need to deal with his mother.

"Until tomorrow," she said.

"Aye, aye, Captain." He gave her a cheeky salute.

When she had closed the door, he grinned. Tessa James was going to twist him up into a pretzel, and he was going to enjoy every single second.

Kat entered through the side door at The Beach. Once upon a time she would have enjoyed making an entrance, but these days she preferred to survey the crowd first and for the most part stay on the sidelines. A quick scan of the bar told her that the summer season had begun in earnest. She recognized only a handful people. The rest, upwards of fifty of them, were clearly tourists. She expanded her scan to include the pool table and the bar-height tables around the edges of the room, but didn't see Tessa and Mel anywhere. As she eased down the side of the bar, Kat caught sight of Sunny playing darts with a group of friends, but still didn't see Tessa or Mel at any of the tables on the lower level by the main door. It was only when she turned around that she spotted them. The matching pair had chosen a high table tucked into a corner, exactly the one she would have chosen herself, where they could watch all the action and still retain a sense of privacy. They caught sight of her just as she saw them, and together they waved her over.

No turning back now.

Kat signaled that she was going to grab a drink at the bar first, then found a spot where she could break in between two groups of women, effectively blocking any get-to-know-you attempts by the guys at the bar. It was a madhouse, but she didn't mind waiting until Nick, the bartender, could get to her. She needed to gather her thoughts and decide what she wanted out of this conversation with Tessa and Mel. Who knows what had possessed her the other day? She had caught the two of them off guard, and they had handled it so badly that Kat hadn't been able to resist tightening the screws. Was it wrong to take satisfaction in their discomfort?

She didn't blame them for pressing the self-destruct button on her life. Most days, it felt like it had all happened a hundred years ago to someone else. But every now and then something would bring it all back. It might be a story on the news, or a conversation with one of her client families. She never knew what the trigger would be, only that on those days the past weighed her down, and she wondered if she would ever truly be free of it.

Nick handed her a Corona with a slice of lime shoved into the neck of the bottle. She left him some cash on the bar and headed over to their table, taking the seat by the window.

"Want some pizza?" asked Tessa.

The two of them had barely made a dent in the small pizza. Only one row of tiny squares was missing. Looked like they were one beer ahead of her, though, which should make for interesting conversation.

"No, thanks," said Kat. "Just ate."

Tessa and Mel looked at each other. Kat imagined that they were playing some kind of psychic rock-paper-scissors to decide who had to talk first. Tessa lost.

"So how long have you been back in town?" asked Tessa.

"Three years," said Kat. "I'm surprised we didn't run into each other sooner."

"I haven't been up much in the past few years," said Tessa. "Things have been crazy with work."

Mel coughed to cover up a verdict of 'lame' and Tessa shot her a dirty look.

"What did you end up doing after you left here?" asked Tessa. "Nobody ever told us if you were okay."

Kat swirled her beer while she thought about how to answer—if she even wanted to answer. She generally avoided talking about the aftermath of her mother's death because it had been a very dark couple of years. Once she had reached the other side, she didn't like to look back.

Before she could formulate a reply, Sunny appeared at her side. She was clearly a few beers ahead of all of them. She doled out hugs all around, plopped onto the last empty barstool, and thunked her elbows onto the table. When she looked at Kat curiously, Kat knew she was in trouble.

"I interrupted right before you were going to answer," she said. "Tell us your story."

Kat seriously considered leaving without any explanation at all, but she had gotten herself into this situation, and she would accept her karmic justice with good grace. That didn't mean she had to offer up much detail, however.

"Things were tough for a few years after my mom died," she

said. Understatement of the century. "I finished high school up near Milwaukee, and then continued on right into college. I didn't have a lot going on in my life then, so I managed to finish college in three years." The truth was a lot closer to 'didn't want to have time to think about anything,' but these girls didn't need to know that. "Then came law school, and internships, and the realization that I wanted to build my own practice and focus on helping families in trouble."

"That's amazing," said Sunny.

Kat shifted uncomfortably on her stool. Nothing about those years had been amazing.

"Why here?" asked Tessa.

That was the real question, wasn't it? Why circle back to the source of so much pain? This was definitely a question that she didn't want Tessa exploring too deeply.

Kat shrugged. "It seemed like the right move."

They were silent for a moment, then Tessa said, "I'm so sorry about everything that happened."

"Everything was going to go to shit at some point," said Kat. "Not much you could have done to stop the train wreck."

The beer was not sitting well in Kat's stomach. This was the last thing she wanted to be talking about tonight, but the curiosity on Sunny's face made it clear that more questions were coming. Time to change the subject.

"Where are the kids tonight?" asked Kat.

Sunny and Tessa shared a smile. Conversation successfully redirected.

"RJ is babysitting," said Sunny. Tessa nodded a confirmation.

"Are you sure that's safe?" asked Kat. "RJ's a sweetheart, but I'm not sure he has any childcare skills."

"That's the lame excuse he tried to give me," said Sunny scornfully, "but I sent him some reinforcements so he couldn't weasel out of helping."

"It was a tough assignment, but we survived. The kids were sleeping when I left."

"Was RJ sleeping, too?" asked Sunny.

Tessa shook her head. "Nope. He had to call your mom about something."

The laughter faded from Sunny's face.

"He needs to stop being her middleman," said Sunny. "He tries too hard to protect me, and it's driving him crazy."

"That's what big brothers do," said Tessa with a shrug.

Sunny scowled. "He needs to chill out on the overprotection. I'm all grown up now, and I can stand up for myself."

"He worries about you," said Tessa gently. "I worry about you."

At that, Sunny's expression went from open to closed. Kat knew in that moment that Sunny hadn't confided in Tessa. Not yet. And she wasn't ready to bare her soul right now, either. Instead she glanced around the room, looking for the group of friends from the dart game. When she spotted them, she began to ease off her stool.

"I should go," said Sunny. "Don't want to blow off my ladies."

"You sure you don't want to have a beer with us?" asked Tessa. "I feel like we haven't had much time to catch up."

Tessa's question had the opposite effect from the one she intended. Instead of staying, Sunny sped up her departure.

"Thanks again for helping with the kids tonight," said Sunny. "He really couldn't have done it without you." She slipped behind Kat and started to walk away.

"See you soon," called Tessa. She did not look happy to see Sunny go.

"What's up with her?" asked Mel.

Tessa shook her head slowly as she watched Sunny rejoin her friends.

"Don't know yet. She doesn't want to tell me."

"Maybe you need to leave this one alone," said Kat.

In her head, the words had sounded neutral, but when she spoke them out loud, she sounded like an overprotective mama cat.

"Or not," said Tessa.

Great. Now Kat was on Tessa's radar. The last thing she wanted to do was let on that Sunny had confided in a near-stranger.

"Not every problem can be fixed," said Kat.

Damn it, she still sounded snarly.

"I've known Sunny almost all my life," said Tessa carefully. "I have a pretty good sense of when to help and when to step back."

"You're right, of course," said Kat.

She took one last sip of her beer and reached a decision. This meet-up had been a terrible idea. She didn't want to dig around in her own baggage, and she definitely didn't want to make life any harder for Sunny. It was time to go. She stood up, pushing her barstool away from the table.

"Look, this has been fun," said Kat, "but it's been a hell of a week. I'm heading home."

Her abrupt decision took Tessa and Mel by surprise. They didn't even manage to say good-bye as she turned to leave. She had made it a few steps away when one last thought occurred to her and she turned back.

"First do no harm, okay? That's all I ask."

Tessa looked stricken, but she nodded, and Mel nodded, too. That would have to be good enough. The last thing any of them needed was another intervention gone wrong.

CHAPTER ELEVEN

August, fourteen years ago

TESSA SAT CRISS-CROSS ON THE LEDGE UNDERNEATH THE TROLL
bridge, pencil in hand, diary open, but she had already lost her
train of thought. The muggy afternoon made her sleepy.
Instead of fighting it, she leaned back against the rough stone
arch and let her mind wander. She had almost dozed off when
she heard the murmur of voices coming down the path. Instead
of passing over the bridge and continuing down the path, the
voices detoured and stopped along the bank of the stream, just
out of her line of sight. Curious, she set aside her diary and
pencil and leaned forward to get a better view. They were
standing so close to the bridge that she couldn't see their heads,
but one of set of legs was clearly RJ's. She recognized the swim
shorts and his flip-flops. The other legs looked like they might
belong to Holly Banks, at least from this angle. Holly always
wore pretty sandals, and just yesterday she had painted her
toenails bright pink. The girl shifted and Tessa got a good look
at her toes.

Yep. Definitely Holly.

Tessa could hear every word of their conversation. She briefly considered letting them know she was there, but decided against it. If they were dumb enough to talk near the troll bridge without checking underneath, they deserved to be overheard. Besides, it wasn't like they were talking about anything interesting.

That is, until all of sudden they were. Just as Tessa was losing interest, RJ asked Holly to watch the fireworks with him. Tessa rose up onto her knees so that she could hear better, her head brushing the underside of the bridge's arch.

"Like a date?" asked Holly.

"Yeah," said RJ.

Tessa felt a flutter deep in her belly and held her breath. If he were asking Tessa—not that he would ever ask his little sister's friend on a date—she would definitely say yes. Thinking about it made her flush from her forehead to her toes. But Holly was one of the popular girls, two years older than Tessa and impossibly perfect. She didn't need braces or glasses and she never blushed. She had completely skipped her awkward phase, and now that she had finished her freshman year of high school, she oozed confidence. Sometimes Tessa fantasized that the only place Holly was perfect was here at the lake, and that when she left to go back to her school-year home, she lost all her confidence and turned awkward and shy like a normal girl. It probably wasn't true, but it made Tessa feel better to imagine it.

"Sure," said Holly, after pausing long enough to make RJ— and Tessa—nervous.

"Cool," he said. He leaned against the arch of the bridge, his legs only inches from Tessa's face. She held her breath and began to ease backward. She imagined that he was staring deeply into Holly's eyes, and her stomach tightened all over again. She couldn't be sure from her vantage point, but that's what she would want to happen if she were Holly.

"See you later, then," said Holly. She sounded unsure of herself, so Tessa decided that RJ had definitely been staring into her eyes. Tessa's knees always went watery when he looked at her for too long. Then Holly walked away, leaving RJ alone beside the bridge.

"Score," he crowed softly.

She giggled, then froze when he dropped into a crouch and pinned her down with his eyes.

"Tessa" he said. It sounded like an accusation.

She suddenly felt guilty and, given the angry look on his face, a little bit scared. She tried to scoot backward as he crawled under the bridge, but she was still on her knees, her head too close to the stonework, and her hair had snagged on one of the pieces of iron that stuck out. She blinked back the sting of tears and tried to untangle herself. She couldn't see, so she had to do it by feel. She tried to look casual.

"Um, actually, no, it's..." Which one should she throw under the bus? "Mel."

She tried to put some sass into her voice. If she was going to sacrifice Mel, she might as well do a good impression.

"Nice try," he said, "but I'm not stupid."

Everybody else got them confused. Why not him? She scowled at him. If only her hair would come unstuck she could get away from him.

"How much did you hear?"

"Pretty much everything," she admitted, then stuck out her chin as much as she could, given her predicament. "It wasn't really that interesting."

He glared at her.

"It's rude to eavesdrop on a private conversation, you know," he said.

"You interrupted my privacy," she pointed out. "I come here to get away from everybody."

"You should have told us you were here," he said.

"And miss the show?" she asked. She still hadn't managed to free her hair, and she was finding it very difficult to keep pretending like nothing was wrong.

"What are you doing?" he asked.

She could feel the blush creeping up her neck, which only made everything worse.

"My hair is stuck," she admitted.

"Let me give you a hand," he said, but the smirk that went with the offer took all of the niceness away.

"It's fine," she snapped. "I've got it."

He started helping anyway. She felt confused when he got too close, so she tried to move away.

"You're making it worse," he said. "Hold still."

He cradled her cheek with one hand to hold her head still, and with the other he ran his fingers through her hair, starting at her forehead and gently combing backwards until he reached the snag. She held her breath while he worked through the tangle. Then suddenly she was free. She dropped down onto her bottom and scooted backward. It took a minute for her breathing to even out. He had never touched her before, not really. If she had been standing up she would have melted into a puddle at his feet. As it was, she could only hope that none of her inner freak-out showed on her face. He seemed completely unaffected as he sat down on the ledge and looped his arms around his knees.

"So you thought it was pretty funny, huh?"

It took her a second to realize that he was talking about her eavesdropping again. He was going to pretend like he didn't care, but she knew that he did.

"Only at the end," she said.

"If you tell Sunny about this..."

"I won't," she promised.

"Good. She's annoying enough as it is."

Tessa understood annoying sisters, but she really didn't

understand the whole dating thing. The boys in her class only cared about sports and fart jokes. She honestly didn't know why some of her friends were so obsessed with 'going out' with them. It wasn't like they were going to 'go' anywhere.

"I was pretty smooth, there, wasn't I?" he asked.

He looked awfully pleased with himself, and apparently he expected her to congratulate him or something.

"You did okay, I guess." She used the same know-it-all voice that Sunny used when she wanted to make her brother mad.

"I was amazing," he said. "And she said yes, so it worked, so shut up."

Tessa gave him a half shrug.

"Fine. If you want to think you were awesome, you go right ahead."

She gave him ten seconds to explode. He made it to three.

"What is that supposed to mean?"

"Oh, nothing," said Tessa. "I've seen guys do better, that's all."

"How?" he demanded.

She made him wait.

"You really want to know?"

"Just tell me, damn it."

She knew she had hooked him because he was starting to swear. Now she needed to think of something to say.

"First of all," she began, "you need more confidence. I could tell that you were nervous, and that will make the girl nervous, too. It's better to be confident."

"I am confident," he said. "And anyway, how the hell am I supposed to be confident if I don't know what she's going to say?"

"I don't know," she snapped back. "Fake it, I guess."

He didn't say anything for a while, and she worried that she'd gone too far. As annoying as RJ could be, she liked hanging out with his little sister and she didn't want things to be weird when she was over at their house.

"What else?" he asked.

She sat up straighter, surprised that he was taking her seriously. She scrambled to think of a second piece of advice.

"You need to notice details, like what flavor of ice cream she likes. Then instead of asking her out for ice cream, you can offer to get her favorite kind."

"Isn't that creepy?" he asked.

She shook her head impatiently.

"Of course not," she said. "It's considerate. It shows that you pay attention and you're not just interested in her boobs."

He gave her a quick grin.

"And what if I *am* only interested in her boobs?"

Tessa gave him her best disgusted look.

"Then you're an idiot and I shouldn't be giving you any tips."

"Why does liking boobs make me an idiot?"

"Boobs are just things stuck onto your chest. They have nothing to do with who you are. You may be an idiot, but Holly's not. She wants to hang out with a guy who sees her insides."

"Okay, so how do I show her I'm that guy?"

Tessa mulled that one over for a minute before answering.

"Don't ever mention how she looks," she said at last.

"Never?"

"Every other guy will tell her how pretty she is. You tell her something real. Show her that you notice who she *is*, not how she *looks*."

He looked skeptical.

"It will work," she insisted.

He still looked skeptical.

"Fine." She crossed her arms and tried to look superior.

"Don't believe me. Keep doing what you're doing. I'm sure you have everything completely figured out."

"It doesn't make sense," he said. "My mom loves it when I notice how she looks."

"She's a grown-up," said Tessa, shrugging philosophically, "and she really likes to dress up. Holly's not like that, which you would know if you were paying attention."

"Fine," he said. "I'll consider trying it your way." He turned to crawl out from under the bridge, then looked back at her. "If it doesn't work, you owe me cookies."

"And if it works?" She cocked one eyebrow, like she had been practicing in the mirror.

"Doughnuts."

"Deal."

~

Today

The next day dawned bright and clear. It could not have been more perfect for sailing—sunny, breezy, and finally starting to feel like summer. RJ and Tessa drove over to the yacht club together, hitched up the boat, and headed out. There was no race for the series this weekend, so RJ had entered an interlake regatta on a different lake about half an hour away. There should be a greater number of competitors, but they would also see the usual suspects from their own series. Conditions would be different on the larger, shallower body of water, but no less challenging. He promised himself that he would not dunk Tessa again. He didn't want to derail their plans for afterward.

Tessa seemed relaxed today, which was, frankly, a relief. Sex can complicate things fast, and while they had not yet done the deed, they were clearly moving in that direction. If Tessa were freaking out about it, he would slow things down, maybe even pull the plug, but instead she seemed calm and maybe even happy. They shared an easy silence on the way over, letting the radio provide a soundtrack. Every now and then she looked over at him with a secret smile, and he wondered if she was thinking about their last encounter or imagining their next one. He got hard just thinking about it. He would need to figure out a way to keep his head on straight until the race was over. Then she could do whatever she wanted with him and he would take it like a man.

They were among the first to arrive and scored a great parking spot close to the water.

"So what's our strategy?" asked Tessa as they began their prep.

The half-raised mainsail hid her from view, so he leaned over to look at her around the side of the mast.

"We win?" he suggested.

"But how?" she responded. "What's the plan?"

He thought about that for a minute. He loved to sail, and he was good at it, but it didn't usually involve a plan.

"Is this a trick question?" he asked.

She laughed.

"I guess that answers my question," she said.

He scowled to himself, wondering what the hell there was to plan. You sail faster than the others. You take advantage of wind shifts as they arise. That's the plan.

When she finished on her side of the boat, she walked around the stern and joined him.

"Would you like to suggest a strategy, smarty-pants?" he asked.

She raised an eyebrow, then shrugged.

"I have a couple of ideas."

He crossed his arms.

"Let's hear them," he said.

She looked around, as if she were going to reveal something

top secret, but they were early and there was nobody nearby. When she came closer, and stood only inches away from him so that she could speak softly and not be overheard, he decided he didn't mind a little cloak-and-dagger action. In fact…

She grabbed his hands as he reached for her hips.

"Don't distract me."

He grinned. He liked distracting her. She was smart, though, and didn't let go of his hands.

"Brock doesn't make good decisions when he's angry," she said.

"I've noticed," said RJ. At least ten different tweaks sprang to mind, each of which would easily piss off Brock. This was going to be fun. "What else?" He could tell by the look on her face that there was more.

"The teenagers," she said. "They're good, but I'm betting I can throw them off their game. I was thinking of a wardrobe malfunction."

He choked.

"What?" he asked. He must have heard her wrong.

She very slowly unbuttoned her linen blouse to reveal the tiniest red bikini top he had ever seen. As he watched, her nipples hardened. He tried to touch them, but realized that Tessa still held his hands. He dragged his eyes up to meet hers and realized that she was just as turned on as he was. Unfortunately, she could still think clearly.

"This is the worst bikini," she said breathlessly. "I swear I can hardly keep it on."

He swallowed.

"You realize that distracting those teenagers is an extremely risky strategy," he growled.

"Why is that?"

"Let's imagine for a moment that you're half naked on the boat. The teenagers won't be the only ones distracted," he said. "Chances are very high that we will crash and drown."

"Oh," she breathed. "Maybe I should keep my shirt on, then. For safety."

"For safety," he agreed.

"Okay, then," she said, stepping closer, so that their joined hands were pinned in between her chest and his.

He could feel her nipples press into the backs of his hands. With a quick twist, he freed his hands, using one to pull her closer and the other to slide inside her open shirtfront to cup her breast. He dragged the tiny triangle of fabric to the side, revealing one very aroused nipple. She watched him do it, then looked up at him with those wide eyes. He couldn't help himself. He dragged his thumb across her nipple again, this time watching her face and earning a sexy whimper from the back of her throat. He kept up the torture until the whimper turned into a moan. He was in the process of sliding her shirt off her shoulder when he heard the crunch of tires on gravel. It took him a few seconds to remember that they were standing outside next to the half-rigged boat in a parking lot.

They jumped apart, and she steadied herself on the side of the boat before adjusting her top and frantically re-buttoning her shirt.

"Don't distract me on the boat," he said gruffly, and she nodded, her eyes wide.

"No distractions," she agreed.

They finished rigging the boat without speaking or making eye contact. For safety.

The tires rolling across the gravel parking lot belonged to Brock and Helen. Tessa blinked away the last of the sensual haze and put Operation Angry Brock into action.

"Hi, Helen," called Tessa as she approached their now-parked truck and trailer. She didn't offer a greeting to Brock. Rather than deliberately snubbing him, she pretended that she didn't notice him standing on the far side of their boat. She could see him scowling in her peripheral vision. After chatting with Helen for a minute or two, she pretended to notice Brock for the first time.

"Oh, Brock, hi," she said. "I'm sorry. I didn't see you there."

She could almost hear him grinding his teeth.

RJ chose that moment to join the group, greeting Brock with a nod, but Helen got a kiss on the cheek before RJ stepped back to slide an arm around Tessa. He had subtly staked a claim on both women, and Brock's instinctive, primal reaction was a joy to behold. Tessa could practically see the steam coming out his ears. She smiled in satisfaction before turning to RJ.

"I guess we had better get the boat in the water," she said.

"See you out there," RJ called to Brock. "May the best man win."

Tessa rolled her eyes at RJ's parting shot. As if he and Brock would be sailing out there all by their manly selves. Helen caught her reaction and suppressed a giggle, but RJ and Brock were oblivious. They were engaged in some kind of macho stare-down. She tugged on RJ's shirt as she turned to leave.

"RJ," she muttered. "Cut it out."

He came reluctantly, as if he would rather stay and beat the crap out of Brock. Tessa couldn't figure out why his reaction to Brock had gone from playful to intense all of a sudden.

"You dated him? Really?" asked RJ.

She sighed.

"Yes."

"For how long?" he persisted.

"A couple of months."

If he wanted to interrogate her while they got the boat into the water, she wasn't going to make it easy for him.

"Why?" RJ sounded truly mystified.

"He can be charming, too, you know." She needed to

remind him that charm was not necessarily a good thing. She needed some reminding herself. "It's not like he came with a warning label. We were working together on a project. He's smart and good-looking and charming and confident. It took me a while to figure out that he was also a jerk."

"And you never...?"

She stopped in her tracks and let out a huff of disgust. He stopped as well and turned to face her.

"Is that what this is about?" she demanded. "You want to know if we slept together? You need me to stroke your ego and tell you that you're already better in the sack than he is, before we've even gone there?"

He crossed his arms and looked genuinely angry.

"This is not about me," he said, his voice pitched low for privacy but still intense. "I'm trying to understand why an amazing woman like you would put up with a prick like that for a day, let alone a month. What the hell, Tessa?"

She opened and closed her mouth a few times like a fish before she could put a coherent sentence together. She was as good at deluding herself as anybody else, but that didn't make her feel any less foolish.

"He needed me," she said at last, "and I..." She swallowed. "I mistook that for more. I let myself imagine that we had so much in common, when really he just wanted me to do all the work."

A hot ball of anger blocked her throat. She tried to swallow it, but it wouldn't go away, and worse, she could feel the sting of tears at the back of her eyes. What a mess. The anger was all on her, because he was right, damn it. She had been so focused on the future that she had missed all the warning signs in the present.

"Hey," he said gently. He reached out to cup her face, tilting her head so that she met his eyes. "I'm sorry. Forget what I said. I should know better than to judge."

She succeeded in blinking back the tears but still needed to sniffle. He offered a wry smile.

"Let's call a truce for the race. If you're still mad at me later, you can punish me in any way you see fit," he said. He raised one eyebrow suggestively and she let out a watery laugh.

"Prepare yourself," she said. "I'm not going to let you get off lightly."

He burst out laughing at her double entendre and gave her a quick, hard kiss before letting her go.

"I wouldn't have it any other way," he said.

They kicked Brock's ass in the race. As Tessa had predicted, he didn't make good decisions when he was angry. He nearly capsized several times, and he made a couple of risky choices that didn't pay off. In the end, Tessa and RJ won handily, with Steve and Mike coming in third behind a husband-wife team they didn't know. The weather had delivered on its promise, providing them with a sunny, breezy day. By the time Tessa and RJ were hauling the boat out of the water, they were back on an even keel, both of them focused on getting the boat buttoned up so that they could get back to his place. Fast.

As they were hitching the boat trailer back onto the truck, Brock and Helen walked by.

"That was some hard racing today," said RJ. It should have been a neutral comment on the race, but the loss had left Brock in a foul mood.

"It won't happen again," snapped Brock. He looked like he was going to keep on walking, but then suddenly stopped and turned on Tessa. "Don't forget that I'm your boss now."

"Oh, I'm not likely to forget," said Tessa. She used her most soothing voice. "But don't worry. I can be patient while you learn the ropes. After all, not everyone is a natural leader."

She tilted her head and watched him sputter, then turned on her heel and walked away, climbing into the cab of the truck and closing—but not slamming!—the door on further conversation. RJ followed suit, thankfully, rather than getting caught up in a cave-man showdown. RJ paused with the key in the ignition as if he were going to say something, then shook his head, started the truck, and they drove away.

She had goaded the king of passive aggression into a direct confrontation, or as close as he was likely to come. She wasn't sure if she should be proud or worried. Maybe both.

By the time they made it back to RJ's place, Tessa's temper had cooled, but she couldn't quite recapture her pre-race playfulness. Instead she found herself thinking about work, and the need to make some decisions. She had updated her resume but she hadn't actually sent it out, and she couldn't put her finger on what exactly was holding her back. She much preferred to let things drift along, both with work and with RJ. The minute she started to think about her future career, she couldn't help thinking about her love life as well. Here they were not even two weeks into their almost-relationship and instead of enjoying it, she was obsessed with its inevitable end.

It helped that he pulled her into his arms for a long, slow kiss as soon as they cleared the kitchen door. That went a long way toward resetting her mood. The trail of kisses along her jawline didn't hurt. She had never thought much about her ears until he paid them close attention, sending a cascade of shivers down her back.

"Want to play backgammon?" he murmured in her ear. Her face was buried in his neck, so she could feel the rumble of his voice. At first she couldn't figure out what he had said. She pulled back and looked up him. He repeated the question, then laughed at the confusion that must have been evident on her face.

"Is that code for something kinky?" she asked.

"It was just an idea," he said. "We can do something else."

"No, actually, that's perfect," she said, surprised to realize that it was true. She didn't want to use him to escape the other crap going on in her life. She just wanted to be with him.

So they set up the game on the coffee table. She hadn't played backgammon in years and needed to look at the directions to remember exactly how to play.

"So Sunny and the boys..."

"...are spending the night at my mom's," said RJ.

Tessa paused in the middle of laying down one of her pieces, then smiled and looked up at him through her lashes.

"So we have the house to ourselves," she said.

"We do," he answered. Her smile widened.

"Excellent," she said. "I'll have to remember to thank Sunny."

She rolled the dice, and the game was on. He won the first game easily, but she was well on her way to winning the second when he distracted her with a question.

"I'm curious about your past relationships," said RJ. "Why would you stay in a relationship that wasn't physically satisfying?"

They had played mostly in silence until now, so the question seemed to come out of nowhere. She opened her mouth to insist that her relationships had been plenty satisfying, thank you very much. However, that would be a total lie. She had already admitted as much.

"I'm not sure," she said. She hoped he would let it go, but of course he didn't. Instead, he looked thoughtful.

"I've always thought that the physical connection between two people was the foundation for everything else. It's hard to imagine being in a relationship without it."

She swallowed hard. That was some seriously sexy, mature relationship talk coming out of his mouth. If only her answer were mature enough to match. Unfortunately, he had zeroed in on the baggage she had been dragging around for, oh, about nineteen years. She gave a half shrug.

"I've never been particularly comfortable letting my physical responses cloud my thinking."

He leaned back on the couch and settled in for what looked like an interrogation.

"Interesting," he said. "Now in the case of you and me, I would say that we have some pretty strong physical reactions going on. Do you feel that they are clouding your thinking?"

"No," she said. "I'm very clear on what we're doing. This is nothing like any of my previous relationships."

Her body started to wake up, as if sensing the underlying intent of his questions. She had never seen him in this mood. She couldn't tell if he was serious or teasing or maybe a little of both.

"What exactly does that mean?" he asked.

"It means this...thing between us is a vacation from reality. When I look for a long-term partner, I look for stability. The physical side of things is a secondary consideration. I look for comfort rather than chemistry. In fact, I avoid strong chemistry. Too much potential for disaster."

"Comfort?"

He actually sputtered as he said the word, the game completely forgotten. Great. Now they were going to drag all her baggage out into the open. Exactly what she wanted to do today. So what if she looked for comfort? She appreciated comfort. And she tried to ignore the fact that she sounded defensive, even inside her own head.

"So if a guy can really turn you on, you run the other way?" he asked.

She flushed. He didn't need to look so appalled.

"In a nutshell, yes." Her mouth tightened. "Don't look at me like that. You of all people should know how awful things can get when you're overwhelmed by lust and make stupid decisions. It can destroy entire families. It can make your children want to kill themselves."

"Whoa," he said. "Talk about overgeneralizing. Yes, passion can be dangerous. People can get hurt. But do you think maybe you're taking it to an extreme?"

She didn't like the way he was looking at her, like maybe she was being illogical. Overreacting.

"You're not the one who walked in on them," she snapped. "Two whole families destroyed, all because two people couldn't control themselves." She didn't try to mask the disgust in her voice. "They didn't even notice we were there."

"And you're not the one who lived through the aftermath," he returned. "It was ugly, but avoidable."

"Yes. Exactly. If your mom and Annabelle's dad had remembered they were married to other people, if they had stayed away from each other, all that destruction could have been avoided."

"No," he said softly. "If they had ended their marriages sooner then they would have been free to live their own lives and love who they wanted to love, and nobody would have gotten hurt."

She sucked in a breath. Now it was her turn to be appalled.

"But we're talking about your family."

"Not every relationship is strong enough to last," he said.

Tessa heard the echo of her mother's words from the barbecue. *Not all relationships last forever—nor should they.* Never had she felt more lost at sea. She needed to find her bearings but couldn't get a fix on true north. She had built a career centered on repairing relationships so that they could stand the test of time. Hell, she had written her thesis on it. Passion was not a reliable foundation for a long-term relationship. Friendship. Common interests. Shared goals. These were things you could count on. Not passion. Passion was fickle. Passion could infect you like a virus and lead you to destroy the people you love. She had seen it with her own eyes.

He seemed to be waiting for her to say something.

"What?" she asked.

"Not all relationships last forever, right?" he repeated.

She could feel the prick of tears but breathed deeply and tried to shake it off.

"Of course not," she said. "But marriage—"

"—is different. Yes. But we're not talking about marriage. Right now I'm worried about you and me."

"Oh."

He moved closer to her on the couch and put his hands on her shoulders.

"Are you sure you're okay with this?" he asked gently. "Good chemistry isn't something you need to fear. We haven't made commitments to other people. Nobody is going to be destroyed."

"I know," she whispered.

He studied her carefully. He didn't look like he believed her.

"You know it in your head," he said, "but do you believe it?"

"I want to," she said. "I need to."

She knew she was all mixed up about sex. She had given herself so many lectures, even given herself explicit permission to enjoy the physical side of relationships, but it didn't seem to matter. The only relationships that felt safe were the ones that were lukewarm. No danger. No chance of losing your head. But RJ was different. He was the only guy in the world who could understand why she was all twisted up about this, and she trusted him. He knew how to handle chemistry, and he would never knowingly hurt her.

She bit her lip. The time had come to take a risk.

"Take your shirt off," she whispered.

He blinked. She had surprised him. Good.

He stood up and peeled off his T-shirt without saying a

word, then stood there looking ridiculously good in board shorts and nothing else. He waited patiently while she let herself appreciate the view.

"Nice," she said at last. Understatement of the year.

"May I help you with your shirt?" he asked.

She shook her head as she stood to face him. Without his shirt, he seemed bigger, somehow, all those layers of muscle surreal. She lifted a hand and placed it on his chest. His skin was hot. She raised her other hand as well, shamelessly exploring the contours and planes of his upper body. Definitely not Photoshopped. He quivered beneath her hands but (smart man!) didn't try to return the favor. His turn would come later.

His skin heated beneath her fingers as she finally got her chance to check out his tattoos. The narrow band around his left bicep revealed a complex pattern that probably had some symbolic meaning. She moved slowly around to his back, inhaling the scent of him and letting her cheek graze his shoulder along the way. The tattoo on his back was more elaborate, an intricately detailed v-shape that connected shoulder to shoulder, right where her hands would go if she gave in to temptation and massaged the muscles that had grown taut beneath his skin.

She smiled. Why not? Reaching up, she placed her hands on his shoulders and whispered, "On your knees, sailor."

He complied so quickly that she laughed out loud. She stood behind him, her hands on his shoulders, which were now at the level of her waist. She began to knead. Did he work out or did sailing alone give him this kind of muscle definition? Because really, who feels this good in real life? He gave a groan of appreciation and she focused her attention on the knotted muscle beneath her thumbs. Poor man. So tense.

· · ·

RJ's brain started to short-circuit when Tessa ordered him to take his shirt off. She seemed suddenly very comfortable with the chemistry between them. Her subsequent slow, thorough exploration of his upper body nearly broke him, but he reined in his reaction and forced himself to stand still. When she placed her hands on his shoulders and ordered him to his knees, he didn't even have to think about it. He simply let himself collapse. The wave of lust that slammed into him would have knocked him over anyway.

But then she started to work his shoulders, massaging away the tension that was the only thing holding him together—the only thing stopping him from scooping her up, throwing her over his shoulder, and carrying her directly to the bedroom. He had promised her that he would follow her lead, but if she kept this up he wasn't sure he could keep that promise.

Her hands disappeared from his shoulders for a brief moment, and when they touched him again, a jolt of electricity shot through his body. She leaned over to bite his earlobe and the combination of bite and breath connected directly with his groin. Her hair tumbled down and around his face, so that he could barely breathe. She was everywhere, her hands sliding down the front of his chest.

"Take me to bed," she whispered.

She didn't need to ask twice. He turned in her embrace, scooped her up, and was halfway up the stairs before she could take her next breath. She undermined him every step of the way, kissing and biting his neck until he nearly killed them both by running into the upstairs wall.

"Hey—"

"Damn it," he said at the same time. She shifted her attention to his ear. He course-corrected and made it through the bedroom door this time, heading directly for the bed and landing on top of her with a growl.

"Enough," he said, grabbing her hands with one of his and pinning them to the pillow above her head. "My turn."

He covered her mouth with his before she could object and with his other hand unbuttoned her shirt. The tiny red bikini was no match for him. He untied the strings and within seconds she was bared to him. When he shifted his mouth down to her exposed breasts, she gasped, then began to writhe beneath him. He released her hands so as to give his full attention to her upper body—returning the favor—and she grabbed onto the headboard, anchoring herself.

When he began working his way down her body, she stopped him.

"Wait," she gasped.

He blinked away the fog of desire and tried to focus on her words.

Tessa had to stop RJ before he could make her shorts disappear. She needed to own this. She needed to make this happen instead of letting it happen to her.

"Stop," she gasped. "My turn."

She pushed him over onto his back and climbed on top of him, feeling gloriously reckless. She was half naked, her shirt hanging open and her bikini top long gone. She leaned over to kiss him and he crushed her against him. Remembering what had happened on the couch, and before that in the tub, she scooted away before he could get her again. She was calling the shots, and she intended to include him in the grand finale this time around.

Tessa took advantage of her freedom to tug his board shorts down. He figured out what she was after and helpfully lifted his hips, allowing her to strip the shorts off in one motion and throw them on the floor. Turning back, she hummed in satisfaction. RJ had never looked so good. He should not be allowed to wear clothing.

She lay down beside him, one hand on his chest to keep him right where he was. He groaned in frustration but stayed put. She smiled up at him, loving the hot hunger in his eyes as she let her hand wander down his stomach. When she clasped him in her hand, his eyes closed and his face relaxed into pure bliss. She studied his face as she caressed him, amazed and aroused by the powerful emotions in play.

"Tessa," he growled, his eyes suddenly open and his hand covering hers. "You need to stop now, please. I want—" He rolled onto his side, tipping her onto her back. "I want to do this together."

She nodded. She wanted that, too. With her free hand, she searched in the pocket of her board shorts. She held up a shiny foil packet between them, triumphant.

"You came prepared," he said. "Impressive."

She grinned at him. "I like to plan ahead."

He reached for the packet but she held it out of his reach and ripped it open.

"I've got this," she said.

Technically, she had never done this part herself, but she had watched and really, how hard could it be?

She fumbled a bit, but managed to roll it on without screwing up. The heat of him, and the throb of his pulse beneath her hand the whole time was very distracting. By the time she finished, her heart was pounding just as urgently. When he would have rolled her onto her back she pushed him down and climbed on top of him instead.

"My turn," she said fiercely.

"Our turn," he corrected. Then he grasped her hips and eased her down onto him.

She gasped, grabbing his shoulders and closing her eyes.

She stayed very still for a moment, absorbing the feeling of holding him inside of her, and then she rocked, slowly, as if they were out on the water. Heat like liquid sunshine warmed her from the top of her head to the tips of her toes. When one of his hands moved around from the side of her hip to the front of her, she moaned and moved against him. She would never stop, never give up the feeling of him both inside and outside, as he matched her movements and her brain started fizzing. She rocked forward and back until she could feel the wave coming. He could feel it, too. He tightened his grip on her hip, and with his other hand, he increased the pressure. She gave herself over to the pleasure that slammed through her, swamping them both. They clung to each other, reckless now as they rode the wave together until there was nothing left but a quivering mass of arms and legs and lungs and heart and satisfaction.

RJ didn't want to move. His memories were hazy, the past hours a blur of nakedness punctuated by the need for food and sleep. They had dozed off sometime after dark, and the early morning glow from the bedroom window told him they had slept through the night. Tessa shifted beside him. He opened his eyes and watched her slide off the bed, clearly trying not to disturb him. She collected her fallen articles of clothing and slipped them on. He thought about letting her sneak away, but he knew from past experience that they should talk now—to acknowledge the massive shift that had just taken place—or their next meeting would be more than awkward.

"Going somewhere?" he asked.

She started, then turned around to look at him.

"You're awake."

He smiled in the way that usually distracted her, but it didn't work this time. She stared at him, serious but not shy. He had expected shy and maybe even a little embarrassed.

"You okay?" he asked. She had seemed so sure of herself earlier. Maybe now she was having second thoughts.

A gentle smile crept across her face as she nodded.

"Better than okay." She took a deep breath. "Is it always like that?"

"Always like what?" he asked. He was pretty sure what the 'it' was, but he had no idea what she was comparing it to.

"Wild. Mind-blowing." She blushed. "Liberating."

Her answer stunned him into silence. He had never, in all his crazy dating history, met anyone as brutally, painfully honest as Tessa. He couldn't believe that he had suspected her of sneaking away. She played no games, and she certainly didn't run from awkward conversation. In response he felt exposed, like he should be equally honest no matter how terrifying that might be.

Her smile faded when he didn't respond right away. He needed to say something.

"I don't know how to answer that question," he hedged. "I don't want to compare this to anything else. I don't want to compare *you* to anybody else."

That brought her smile back, but now it was rueful.

"This is nothing new for you," she acknowledged, "but for me..." She sat down on the side of the bed, seemingly unaware of the fact that she was completely naked. She picked at the sheets as though they might be hiding the right words. "I get it now. I understand why people would put their everyday lives in jeopardy to experience this. Maybe it's the fact that this thing between us is so undefined. Maybe it's because I've never had a fling before. Maybe we just have really good chemistry."

"Does there have to be a why?" he asked, reaching out to cover her hand with his own. She stopped her fidgeting and met his eyes.

"Can't help it," she said. "It's a therapist thing." She shrugged. "Maybe it's a Tessa thing."

"The reason this works," he said, reaching up to thread his fingers through her hair and draw her down toward him, "is because we don't examine it too closely."

She didn't let him pull her closer, and he felt his first twinge of unease. He had avoided admitting it out loud, but the experience had been mind-blowing for him as well. The difference between him and Tessa was that he didn't want to know why. Call it cowardice or self-preservation, but he had no intention of questioning his good fortune. They were going to have a glorious affair, and when the summer ended, the affair would end as well. It would be a summer to remember, not a summer to analyze.

If Tessa was determined to poke around under the covers, he wasn't going to help.

"Stay," he said. Maybe he could take her mind off all those questions.

She shook her head slowly.

"I need to go home and freak out a little," she said. Her words did not sound promising.

"You seem pretty calm to me."

That got him a smile.

"I feel pretty calm," she admitted, "but I need to catch my breath before we dive in again."

He let his fingers slide out of her hair and caressed her cheek as she pulled away from him. He stopped himself before he could ask when he would see her again. He wasn't in high school. He wasn't needy. She would find him when she was ready.

The problem was, he thought to himself as he listened for the squeak of the back door that marked her departure, that he had never been on this side of the need. He didn't want her to leave. He wanted to hold on tight, and that was a really, really bad sign.

CHAPTER TWELVE

Instead of walking directly home, Tessa detoured by way of the troll bridge and sat for a few moments on its steps. This bridge had always been her safe haven, and today she needed its strength. She ignored the rust on the wrought-iron railings and the crumbling concrete foundation. She would have her freak-out here, and then she would go home.

Not that she was freaking out, exactly. It was more like keeping her footing as a storm blew through. Last night everything had changed, and not just between Tessa and RJ. Something inside Tessa had been fundamentally altered by her first chemistry experiment. She couldn't un-know what she now knew: comfort alone was not enough. Not for her. Not anymore. This complicated things, maybe not between her and RJ, but certainly in her search for a life partner. As if she didn't already have enough requirements for her future mate, now they had to be combustible as well.

She sighed and leaned her head against the railing. There was no point in worrying about what came after the affair. The whole point was to enjoy it while it was happening. So instead of dwelling on all the questions she couldn't answer, she focused all her attention instead on the water. The morning mist glowed with the promise of sunrise, softening the glassy surface of the lake and enfolding Tessa in a cool embrace.

It was an odd experience, this attempt to live in the moment, and not altogether comfortable. Tessa had always thought three steps ahead. Sometimes four. She had come out of the womb with a plan, and she felt naked without one. Some people (Mel) had told her (repeatedly) that she was missing out on all the fun in life. She had tried to explain how good it felt to set her own course. She liked being the captain of her own ship, and she didn't have any particular interest in dropping anchor for a quick swim. She wanted to get to her destination already.

But for the first time in her life, she was winging it. She felt unprepared, off-balance, and, frankly, a little scared. On the whole, though, it felt amazing. All the pressure that she put on herself, pressure to do the next thing or achieve the next goal, had disappeared. She had set herself free.

The roar of a motorboat shattered the stillness. She couldn't see it through the mist, but she could guess what they were doing. Only the hard-core water-skiers would be up this early on a Sunday morning. She stood slowly, reluctant to leave, but her in-between moment had ended. Time had restarted with a jolt. Last night would be shelved with her most treasured memories, its meaning only clear with time and distance.

Time to live in the next moment.

She took a more direct route from the bridge to her parents' house. Maybe she could surprise them with breakfast as a thank-you for not asking too many questions about her erratic schedule. However, as she approached the back steps she could see that the kitchen lights were already on, and when she opened the door that led into the mudroom and the kitchen beyond, the voices from the kitchen went abruptly silent. The silence was not followed by happy greetings or even a friendly 'Who's here?' Instead, she stepped into the kitchen and into the middle of a heavy, awkward silence between her parents. She couldn't remember ever feeling this much tension between them, and for the first time in her life, home didn't feel like home.

Her mother recovered first.

"Tessa, honey, what a nice surprise. Well, I guess that answers one question. We weren't sure if you had come home late last night or if you had stayed over at RJ's. Neither of us wanted to bother you if you were still sleeping. Did you two have a nice time?"

Her mother left the question hanging in the air, and Tessa blinked at her, feeling suddenly self-conscious. There was no way she was going to be discussing the details of last night with her mother.

"Yes," said Tessa. "Lovely."

Luke stood abruptly. "I'll be in my office," he said, and disappeared down the hall. The door shut behind him with a soft but firm click.

Her mother forced a smile and thankfully asked no more questions. Instead, she began clearing the table while she talked, and Tessa relaxed. This was much more like the mother she knew. She helped clear a few things and then poured herself a cup of coffee, but she didn't interrupt the comforting flow of words. When the kitchen was put to rights, they took their respective mugs and walked out to the porch to watch the world wake up.

"There was that long stretch while you were so busy with school and work," said Dora. "It felt like we never saw you, though I suppose we saw you more often than we did Callie. It's nice to have our girls back, even for short visits."

Tessa gave her mother a spontaneous hug. Her parents had made it for thirty years. They would get through whatever needed getting through. Even so, Tessa couldn't help asking about the tension from earlier.

"Mom, is everything okay? You and Dad were a little... intense when I got home."

Her mother reached over to squeeze Tessa's shoulder.

"Don't worry about us, sweetie. Your dad has some decisions to make about how he wants to spend his time, now that he's retired. I'm afraid if he hangs around the house all day that I'll kill him. You know what I mean?"

"Do you think he'll start spending time in Nashville?" asked Tessa. "Wouldn't you miss him?"

Dora smiled gently. "Of course I would miss him. We're so accustomed to being together that it's hard to imagine being apart. But even so, I think it would do him good to go. He always missed that life. It's not often we get a second chance to explore the road not taken."

"And you?" asked Tessa. "Have you been thinking about the road not taken?"

Dora kept her eyes on the lake.

"I wondered how long it would take for Callie to tell the two of you."

Tessa didn't say anything. She felt bad enough about throwing Callie under the bus.

"You're right," said Dora. "I have been thinking about how things might have turned out differently. Now mind you, I have no regrets." She emphasized her point with her mug, and Tessa leaned back to stay clear. "Looking back, I wouldn't change a thing."

"You would still have an affair?" asked Tessa. "But I thought..." She didn't know what to say. She had assumed that the affair had ruined her mother's life and resulted in the severing of ties with her entire family, providing yet another example of the dangers of letting your heart rule your head.

"I wouldn't change a thing," repeated Dora. "And that's all I'm going to say about it."

Dora took one last sip from her mug, then walked back in the house, leaving Tessa to gather her scattered wits. If she had been hoping for answers, she was out of luck, because all she had were more questions.

That afternoon, Tessa and Sunny kicked back on the grass at the park while Oscar and Huck played in the sandbox. Tessa still marveled that these two little creatures had come from Sunny and Will, even though she could see the evidence with her own eyes. They both had Sunny's wispy curls. They both had Will's oversized ears. Tiny Huck seemed to be more adventurous, while his older brother approached the world with more caution, but they were both happy kids who loved to play. Their favorite activity (for the moment) was digging and building.

"So, you and RJ, huh?" said Sunny.

Tessa nodded slowly. "Looks that way." She looked over at Sunny. "Does it bother you?"

"God, no," said Sunny. "I'm relieved, actually. He's never had anything real, and you're about as real as it gets. It's about time."

Tessa's heart thumped hard. As much as she herself wanted something real, she didn't want to let her friend walk away with the wrong idea.

"I don't think—"

Sunny burst out laughing.

"Let me guess," she said. "It's nothing serious. Just a summer fling. Don't get my hopes up. He's never even going to consider having a real relationship. Does that about sum it up?"

"Yep."

"He's such an idiot," said Sunny. "And you can tell him I said that."

"I'll leave that to you," said Tessa.

"He fed me that load of crap the other day. I don't buy it. You're different. If he hasn't figured that out yet, he will soon enough."

"I don't know, Sunny. I think he may be right." Tessa hated to say it out loud. She didn't want to jinx a good thing, but she also didn't want to delude herself. "He sees marriage as a trap, a way for two people to lock each other in."

"You could change his mind," said Sunny.

"Maybe," said Tessa doubtfully, "but I'm not sure it's a great idea. You know things would get hard at some point, and when it happened, he would blame me for talking him into it. Besides, things are too intense. We'd flame out for sure."

Sunny threw herself back on the grass. "Is there such a thing as too intense?" she asked. "The beginning is the best part."

Tessa couldn't argue with her. Just thinking about yesterday made her shiver all over again. But she also couldn't ignore the dark clouds headed her way. She had promised to keep things light and easy, and she would find a way to keep that promise, no matter how tempting it might be to talk him into something more.

"It's the best part, but it's also dangerous, don't you think? You get so caught up in the other person that you can't think straight anymore. You forget about all the really good reasons that you shouldn't be doing what you're doing. All the ways you might get hurt."

"You're right, of course," said Sunny. She rolled back up to sit beside Tessa and together they watched the boys dig. "The more intense the passion, the more stupid the mistakes."

Tessa gave her a hard look. Was Sunny thinking of her parents' messy separation, or worse, was she thinking of her own marriage? Tessa thought back over her recent conversations with Sunny. She had mentioned Will only a handful of times. And come to think of it, why were Sunny and the boys spending so much time here? When did they see Will? She had a sudden suspicion about the 'clients' that RJ had asked her to help with. Maybe they weren't clients at all.

"Speaking of passion," began Tessa casually, "where's that gorgeous husband of yours?"

She watched Sunny carefully for any sign of trouble. Sure enough, it was there in the subtle stiffening of her shoulders and the clench of her jaw.

"He's great," she said, keeping her eyes on the boys. "He's got a weird work schedule now, so I figured I could spend a lot of time here with the boys, and we can visit him during the week on his days off." She bit her lip. "He got promoted at work. He's still a detective, but now he's been assigned to a special task force, so he's been putting in a lot of overtime."

Tessa didn't want to worry for no reason. The tension in Sunny's shoulders could be due to a fight, not an impending divorce.

"You guys doing okay?" she asked.

"We're fine," said Sunny firmly. "We'll be fine. We just need to work on forgiveness. People make mistakes."

Tessa thought about digging further, but it was clear Sunny wanted to shut down the conversation. Something in her expression, maybe the mulish set to her mouth, reminded Tessa of Nana Vi, which in turn gave her an idea.

"If your schedule is flexible, I wonder if you'd like to come on a field trip with me," asked Tessa.

"Where?" asked Sunny. She sounded suspicious.

"When was the last time you saw Nana Vi?"

Bringing the kids to see Nana Vi was a sneaky move, to be sure, but one that guaranteed an open door. Nana would do just about anything for extra time with her great-grandchildren. On Tuesday, promptly at ten o'clock, she opened the door to her apartment with a flourish and the two little boys tumbled inside. They knew exactly where to find the secret toy cupboard. Sunny gave Vi a big hug and then released her so that she could follow the boys and prevent them from doing any damage.

Tessa did not get a hug. Not even a smile.

"Smart move, bringing the kids," said Vi, after glancing down the hall to make sure Sunny was out of earshot. "You fight dirty."

"Learned from the best," said Tessa.

Vi pressed her lips together and led the way down the hall.

Tessa followed Vi, intensely curious to see whether or not she had put away the dummy in expectation of the visiting grandchildren. Sunny and the kids were in the living room, but Tessa snuck a peek into the kitchen before taking a seat on the couch. The dummy was still there.

This was going to be interesting.

The boys began building a tower with blocks, and from what Tessa could overhear of their conversation, they would soon be knocking the tower down in spectacular fashion with a dump truck. While they were occupied, the adults made an attempt at conversation.

"Sunny, where's that husband of yours? When are you going to make me another great-grandbaby?" Vi wasn't one to beat around the bush.

"He's working. But he's great. We're great. Everything's going great."

From the way Vi's expression darkened, she now had a pretty good idea that everything was the opposite of great. Before she could quiz Sunny about it, Sunny turned the tables.

"What about you, Nana?" she asked. "What have you been up to lately?"

Vi shot Tessa an accusing look, as if Tessa must have put Sunny up to the question, but Tessa smiled blandly and shrugged.

"I'm fine," she said. "Just fine, thank you very much for asking."

Sunny looked back and forth from Vi to Tessa trying to figure out what was going on.

"What I really want to hear about is these boys," said Vi. "I can't believe how big they are. Oscar, come here for a second. I need to see how much you've grown."

Oscar carefully placed his block at the top of the tower, ordered his brother to leave it alone for a minute, and strode over to Nana Vi. He swelled with pride as she fussed over him, convinced that he had grown at least a foot since the last time she saw him.

As Tessa watched their interaction, Vi's melancholy expression tugged at her heart. Here in the apartment, time stood still. Vi could repeat each day as if her Robert were still here, making do with a stand-in rather than the real thing. But now, in front of her, stood evidence that in the outside world, time was marching on. Oscar was taller, he knew more words, and he was getting very comfortable in the role of big brother. The change in Huck was even more pronounced. Six months ago, at the funeral, Huck would have been more baby than toddler. Now he was steady on his feet and ready to take on the world.

The sound of the tower crashing down startled them all. Huck sat among the scattered blocks, clutching the sides of the dump truck. One of the blocks must have hit him, because he was now sporting a red mark on his cheek and he was doing the long, slow inhale that would precede an ear-piercing wail. Oscar was also doing the slow inhale, ready to burst into tears because his brother had demolished the tower without him.

"Who wants cookies?"

Nana Vi to the rescue.

Two little faces swiveled in her direction, and two sets of tears were interrupted with a hitched breath and, in Huck's case, a hiccup. Huck clambered to his feet and hurried over to Nana Vi, almost tripping several times on the scattered blocks. He clutched her knees and gave her his best angel face.

"Want cookies," he said quite clearly.

"Well, then," she said. "Let's go find some."

Nana led the boys into the kitchen, but Tessa caught Sunny's arm.

"Don't freak out," she whispered.

Sunny gave her a confused look, but Tessa shook her head.

"No time to explain," she said. "Just roll with it."

Tessa stepped back so that Sunny could enter the kitchen first. Sunny stopped short in the doorway, then continued on as if nothing had happened.

"What's that?" asked Oscar. He stood in front of the dummy, studying it, his little arms crossed and his brow furrowed.

Vi turned slowly from the pantry cupboard, a box of cookies in her hand. She avoided Tessa's eyes and kept her attention solely on Oscar.

"That's Papa," she said simply.

"No it's not," replied Oscar. He poked the dummy on the leg.

"Yes, it is," repeated Vi, sounding stubborn this time.

Oscar frowned and crossed his arms.

"It's not real," he said. "Papa is in heaven."

Leave it to a four-year-old to speak plainly. Tessa held her breath, waiting for Vi's response.

Huck marched over to the dummy and patted it on the leg, looking up at its blank face. He hit the leg harder, but still nothing happened. Finally he wiggled hard on the leg and the dummy's torso tilted alarmingly to one side. Huck jumped back, then scurried over to Sunny and wrapped his arms around her legs.

Vi sighed.

"I like to pretend that it's real," she said, speaking only to Oscar. "I get lonely sometimes without Papa, and it's nice to have somebody to talk to—even if it's only a pretend somebody."

Oscar thought about that for a minute, then he nodded.

"When I miss my dad, I cuddle with Mr. Wiggles. He's only a stuffed octopus, but he has a lot of arms and he makes me feel better."

Vi smiled.

"I'm glad you understand," she said. "Cookie?"

Oscar quickly climbed into a kitchen chair and held out a hand for one of Vi's cookies. Huck followed suit, with a boost from his mom, and a moment later they were munching happily away, as if having cookies and milk at the kitchen table with their fake great-grandfather were a completely normal occurrence. Sunny didn't comment, for which Tessa was grateful. Vi needed this time with her great-grandchildren. There would be plenty of lonely hours later for her to think about what it all meant.

Late Thursday afternoon, Tessa finished with her last client and stopped for a cup of coffee on her way back to her office. If she put in another hour today, she would be all caught up and ready for her long weekend. She still had notes to write and some filing to do. She was also taking some time each day to clear out her desk, so that the final departure, whenever it happened, would be quick and painless. Given the rapid deterioration of her working relationship with Brock, she didn't think she would last the summer.

She wasn't gone long, but apparently it was long enough. She stopped short in the doorway of her office, surprised to see Brock sitting behind her desk. He might as well have been rifling through her underwear drawer. The files on her desk were confidential—even from him—as was her email, open on the computer screen. Even her phone lay face up next to the keyboard. What the hell was he doing?

"Can I help you?" she asked, her voice cold and curt. He had no business snooping in here. From now on she would lock her door every time she stepped out.

She stepped into the room and walked around behind her desk, signaling loud and clear that she expected Brock to vacate her chair. He didn't respond immediately. Maybe he was waiting to see if she would take the patient's chair. Fat freaking chance. This was her office. Her territory. He could swagger all he wanted in his new executive suite, but this was her domain, and he would respect it.

He finally rose. He didn't bother to hide the funny little half smile. She hated that look. He knew something that she didn't, and he was enjoying the upper hand. She couldn't believe that she had ever been taken in by him. For Brock, relationships were all about power.

"Just the person I wanted to see," he said. Rather than sit, he chose instead to lean in the doorframe. She reclaimed her seat, took a slow sip of her coffee, and waited for an explanation.

"I'd like to invite you to be a part of the rollout team for the couples counseling program."

She raised an eyebrow, immediately suspicious.

"You seem to have matters well in hand," she said. "I'm not sure what I could add."

"Extra help is always needed," he said smoothly, "I have my hands full managing the construction of the new wing and doing the community outreach."

All the glory work, of course.

"So what will the 'rollout team' be doing?" she asked.

"I need you to create a marketing and PR plan, work with the marketing coordinator to develop the promo materials, and do all the internal training leading up to the grand opening."

Her eyes widened. Did he seriously think that he could offload all that work to her? He had dumped her quickly enough after she had created the initial roadmap and done all the research. Maybe he thought she was desperate enough that she would do anything he asked. Maybe he thought she would start sucking up? She felt more like throwing up.

"I don't know, Brock," she said. *Be diplomatic. Be polite.* "It sounds like quite a bit of work, and I'm pretty maxed out right now in terms of my regular client load."

What would happen if she said no? Was he really prepared to fire her?

"I'm sure we could transfer some of your clients to other colleagues, to free up more of your time."

There was a menacing undertone to his words that put her even more on edge.

"How many people will be on the rollout team?" she asked.

"You, me, and my father," he said. She almost laughed out loud. She would be doing the shit work, he would be getting the glory, and his father would rubber-stamp everything. Great.

"And once the center is launched, what happens then?"

"If it goes well," said Brock smoothly, putting on the hard sell, "I could see this as an ongoing role, almost an assistant director."

She bit her lip to keep from snorting. So he planned to offload his work onto her indefinitely. It just got better and better. If only there were a diplomatic way to tell him to fuck off.

"Brock," she began cautiously, "your offer is very tempting —" He probably viewed it as a command, but she needed to reframe the issue. "—but I love client work, not administration.

This would be a great opportunity for someone else, just not for me. I'm happy doing the work that I'm doing. I'll have to say no."

Was that diplomatic enough? She couldn't tell from Brock's face. She wished she knew what he was holding back.

"Are you sure you don't want to think about it?" he asked.

"I'm sure," she replied. "Thank you for thinking of me."

He nodded and straightened up in the doorway.

"You know," he said, "sometimes I wonder if you're really committed to the success of the Hammond Center."

Now there was a loaded statement. She tiptoed around it as if it were a land mine.

"I'm committed to the success of my clients," she said. "In my mind, the success of the Hammond Center happens one client at a time."

"Of course," he said as he turned to leave. "Who could argue with that?"

She sat staring after him for many long minutes. He was up to something. She didn't know what, but whatever it was, she needed to get her ass in gear. She had finally sent out two resumes, but that wasn't going to cut it. She would need to get serious before he did something mean or stupid. She wanted to quit on her own terms.

She turned to her computer and was about to switch over to her client records program when her phone chirped an alert. Glancing at the screen, she saw the text from one of her grad-school classmates:

Passed your resume along to my boss. Fingers crossed! Will let you know if I hear anything.

Please, please, please let that be the first time the text alert popped up. If Tessa didn't dismiss an alert the first time it appeared, her phone would give her a reminder a few minutes later. And if the first alert had popped up while Brock sat at her desk, well, suddenly his odd behavior made sense.

She forced herself to continue typing up her notes as her stomach sank lower and lower. There was no second alert. Brock had seen the first one, and now he had the ammunition he needed to get her fired. She would need to move up her timetable.

She closed her eyes and thought through her options. If she was smart, she would remove the rest of her personal belongings from her office tonight. She would take the next hour to make sure all her client files were up-to-date and ready for transition to a new counselor. All except one, that is. The thought of leaving Nana Vi in Brock's hands made Tessa's stomach drop the rest of the way to the floor. Tessa needed to make sure Nana Vi's situation was settled before she quit—or got fired, whichever came first.

An hour later, Tessa did one last sweep of her office. She made sure she had no personal files left on the work computer, then shut it down. She took a quick inventory of her bookshelf and determined that most of them could stay, at least for now. Nobody was going to hassle her about taking her books home. Last of all she looked through her file drawers. The only critical item was the hanging file containing her credentials and academic records. Everything else would stay. She shoved that file into her briefcase, along with a few of her favorite books, and headed for the door.

CHAPTER THIRTEEN

Tessa drove straight from work up to the lake. As the miles passed, the pressure on her chest eased. She took big gulping breaths that still were not enough. The pressure must have been the only thing holding her together, because along with her breath came all the emotion she had been keeping in check. Only when her vision began to blur did she realize her deep breaths had given way to full-fledged crying. She pulled off on the shoulder of the road and let the tears fall.

They say people study psychology in order to understand themselves, but she wasn't sure she ever would. This was no time for tears. She wanted to quit. She didn't even like working at the Hammond Center, and not only because of Brock. She wanted to help people make change in their lives. She wanted her clients to graduate from therapy and move on. The Hammond Center took a more old-school approach, offering weekly talk sessions for as long as the client felt they needed support, which was usually forever. The clients loved it. The counselors loved it. Tessa was clearly the odd one out.

She was the one who needed to move on. She just hadn't expected it to be so hard.

Earlier, she had left a message for RJ, giving him a heads up that she planned to come over. Things were moving so fast, for her anyway, that she wasn't sure of the protocol. She assumed they would spend the weekend together, even though there was no race, but he could just as easily have other plans. Which was fine. He had a life and, in theory, she had one, too. Unfortunately, her life for the past few years had centered around work, but she could change that. She needed to change that. If RJ had plans for the weekend, then she would roll with it. She could hang out with her parents, or go back to the city and go out dancing with Mel, or...something. She couldn't really think of any other ideas at the moment, but that wasn't important. She would be fine, with or without RJ.

After her emotional storm had cleared, she got back on the road toward Hidden Springs and drove directly to RJ's house. She knocked, hoping that he had gotten her message, but nobody came to the door. Both his car and Sunny's were here, but maybe he wasn't home from work yet, or maybe they were out somewhere. She knocked again, and when there was still no answer, she opened the back door and stuck her head inside.

"RJ?" she called.

Still no answer, and no sign of Sunny and the boys, either. Then she heard the sound of tiny feet running upstairs and realized that it must be close to their bedtime already.

She closed the door behind her and leaned against it, wondering if it was still okay to invite herself in, now that they were sleeping together. Would he get weird about boundaries? Need his space? She rubbed the tense spots at her temples. Crying always gave her a hangover.

"I thought I heard you come in."

She jumped. RJ stood in the doorway that led down the hall, one towel around his hips and another rubbing his head dry. Her heart had stopped, and when it restarted it pounded double-time against her ribs, partly from the adrenaline and partly from the sight of half-naked RJ. She hesitated for half a second, then launched herself into his arms. He made an 'oof' sound when he caught her.

"Hey, there," he murmured into her hair. He held on tight and didn't try to kiss her or make her talk. "You made good time. I thought I'd have plenty of time to shower and figure out dinner. Rough day?" he asked.

She nodded into the crook of his neck, not letting go even a little bit. Most guys would have lost patience at some point, but RJ just held on. When she finally released him, RJ gave her a sweet kiss.

"Don't move," he said. "I'll be right back, and you can tell me what's going on."

RJ wasn't sure what was up with Tessa, but it wasn't good. He could tell that she had been crying. Most women, in his experience, would have started pouring out the story the moment he put his arms around them, but Tessa did not seem to work that way. She had accepted the comfort of his arms without saying a single word.

He mulled over his next steps while he threw on some clothes, then stopped by the small bathroom to say good night to the boys. When he headed back downstairs, Sunny was reading them bedtime stories. She had them on a strict limit of two stories each, so she would be downstairs in a few minutes.

Tessa had found the bottle of Chardonnay in the fridge, poured three glasses of wine, and carried them into the living room. She was sitting on the couch, feet up, sipping her wine and looking out at the lake. He grabbed his glass and took the seat beside her, settling on the direct approach.

"You want to tell me what happened?" he asked.

She shook her head slowly.

"I'm not really sure," she said. "I guess I'm more emotionally caught up in work than I realized. I thought it would be easy to make the break."

"Did you quit?" he asked, startled.

"What? No," she said, laughing. "Can you imagine? I still don't have a real plan. That would be crazy."

"Crazy," he murmured, wondering what she would say about his impulsive departure from California.

"No," she sighed. "I think I got panicky because my timetable for making a decision got moved up."

He raised an eyebrow.

"I'm almost positive that Brock knows I'm job hunting. That alone may be enough to get me fired. I don't know, and it's freaking me out. I have a...situation that I need to resolve before I leave, and I don't want to be rushed."

"Now this is a problem I can help you with," he said. "You need to relax, and you need some distraction, because there is absolutely nothing you can do about this over the weekend. Am I right?"

She nodded, but she still gave him a skeptical look. At that moment, Sunny walked into the room.

"Is that for me?" she asked, gesturing toward the third wine glass.

"It is," said RJ as he stood up. "Why don't you two ladies take a walk down by the lake while I make you some dinner?"

Now Sunny was looking at him with suspicion as well.

"Are you seriously going to question a guy who wants to make you dinner?" asked RJ.

"You're right," said Sunny, taking her wine glass and heading toward the porch door. "We would be crazy to argue with you. Come on, Tessa, before he changes his mind."

Tessa stood and followed Sunny out the door.

"Don't get every single pan dirty," called Sunny over her shoulder. "I know how you cook."

He smiled as he watched the two of them head down toward the water. He knew a thing or two about comforting women in distress. Wine and food would help. Having someone else do the dishes would help. Talking about it would also help, but neither of them seemed inclined to confide in him. Maybe, though, if he gave them some breathing room, they would talk to each other.

Tessa and Sunny took their time wandering down to the water. The pier was deserted. This wasn't exactly a surprise. Things were usually pretty quiet during the week, and Tessa appreciated the solitude. She wasn't in the mood to make polite chit-chat. They walked all the way to the end of the pier, then kicked off their shoes and sat side by side, dangling their feet in the water. Neither spoke for a few minutes. Tessa wanted to absorb the beauty of the moment so she could take it back with her to the city. Pale blue sky, pale blue water, and the barest hint of a breeze combined to soothe her soul in a way that city lights never could.

"You want to tell me why you've been crying?" asked Sunny.

Tessa shook her head.

"Not really," she said. "You want to tell me what's up with you and Will?"

Sunny pressed her lips together to keep from smiling.

"Not really," she said.

"Maybe we should forget about all that stuff and just enjoy this weekend," suggested Tessa.

A cloud passed across Sunny's face.

"Can't ignore it forever," she said.

"True," agreed Tessa, "but we can ignore it for now, and you can tell me about it when you're ready."

"It would be nice not to obsess about things for a few days."

"It's settled, then," said Tessa, and she emphasized her point by making a big splash with her feet. "For this one weekend, we won't worry about anything. We can start worrying again on Monday."

Instead of wasting a gorgeous evening trapped in the kitchen, RJ threw together a picnic dinner and carried it down to where the girls sat with their toes in the water. He topped up their wine glasses but didn't interrupt their quiet conversation. They seemed perfectly happy to be right where they were. He had even been smart enough to bring the baby monitor so that Sunny wouldn't worry about the boys. She had tested its range upon arrival and determined that it worked all the way at the end of the pier.

The girls gave him shit about not cooking a proper meal for them, but it didn't stop them from devouring their sandwiches or drinking their wine. He smiled to himself. A little food, wine, and girl time and they were both looking better. Sunny had lost the edginess she had brought back with her from the city, and Tessa had unwound. He could see it in the lines of her body and hear it in the tone of her voice.

He kicked back in one of the Adirondack chairs and enjoyed the view. It was his favorite time of day, when the sun's rays hit the calm surface of the water at such a flat angle that the lake glowed more white than blue, the time of day when cinematographers love to film because the light is soft. The two most important women in his life glowed in the soft light as well. He wasn't sure exactly when Tessa had become important, but things were changing fast. He could feel his foundations shifting to accommodate her presence, and he wasn't sure how he felt about it. It had barely been two weeks since the barbecue, and already the lines between them were blurring.

RJ believed in drawing a clear demarcation between his life

and his recreational relationships. The time had come to admit that wasn't going to happen with Tessa. She had been a part of his life for so long that she'd simply bypassed his usual boundaries and waltzed into his inner sanctum. He had never allowed a woman in there before, and it made him deeply uncomfortable in a way that he didn't want to examine too closely.

He realized that he was staring at her so he closed his eyes. He needed to get a grip.

Tessa looked over at RJ, who now appeared to be sleeping in the Adirondack chair. She didn't quite buy it. Maybe he was just trying to give her and Sunny a sense of privacy. She wouldn't put it past him to eavesdrop, but they were talking in low voices. If he wanted to learn any secrets, he was out of luck anyway. They had made their pact to stop worrying for one weekend, and so far it was working.

It was probably for the best that he had stopped staring because she really didn't want him studying her too closely. They had taken a big step last weekend, and the thing that scared her more than anything else was how right it felt. There was none of the usual awkwardness, none of the transition. Either he had way too much experience—a real possibility—or they had known each other so long that even the earthquake of sleeping together couldn't throw them off balance. The idea of a foundation that strong was unsettling, to say the least.

Her past relationships had all been nice. Boring. Tentative when it came to sex, and definitely an awkward transition afterward. Looking back, she blamed herself for the awkwardness. There had been nowhere near the chemistry that she had found with RJ, so the sex had felt perfunctory from the beginning and perhaps a bit forced on her part. Not that the guys involved seemed to mind. On the contrary, they were more than happy to take things to the next level. But now that she had experienced the difference between nice and need, she wasn't sure she could ever go back.

And that was a scary place to be.

RJ kept his promise. He had offered rest and distraction, and he delivered. They spent their mornings sleeping late and their afternoons on the water. They made sure that Sunny got a break from the kids every day. Tessa even put in a few courtesy appearances at her parents' place. As much as her mother loved the idea of RJ and Tessa together, she would be miffed if Tessa blew her off completely.

The memory of the perfect weekend sustained Tessa during the very strange week that followed at work. Each time she passed Brock in the hallway, he gave her that knowing, I-have-power-over-you look. She couldn't help feeling paranoid, wondering if she would be called into Dr. Hammond's office at any moment and fired on the spot. Although that didn't happen, she couldn't shake the sense of impending doom, so she spent her evenings on her job search. She even set up a couple of interviews for the following week. The one thing she did not do was change her weekend plans. She had already requested Friday off, and if she could manage two perfect week-ends in a row, then she would do it, even if it accelerated her departure from the Hammond Center.

Tessa headed up to the lake on Thursday night for the second week in a row. She loved the long summer days, and she could very quickly get used to these short workweeks. Maybe she should make flexible scheduling a priority in her job search. In her line of work, burnout was an ever-present danger. A shorter workweek would allow her to recharge. Filing that thought away for later, she pulled into the parking spot beside RJ's car. She caught sight of Sunny down by the water, so she bypassed the house and walked to the shore to say hello.

She found Sunny watching over the boys—all of them. RJ

lay on his back on the sand while Oscar and Huck built a sand castle on his stomach. He pretended like he was going to get up to greet Tessa, then let the boys wrestle him back down. After extracting his promise to stay perfectly still, they resumed their castle-building. He blew Tessa a kiss, then turned his attention back to the boys.

Sunny and Tessa left them to their silliness and sat down on the grass. Sunny had spent the last few days with her mom down in Chicago, trying to give RJ a break. Unfortunately, spending time with her mother was not much of a break for Sunny. She looked like she hadn't slept the entire time and there was an edge to her that Tessa hadn't felt since things had gotten really bad eight years ago. Tessa wanted to avoid a repeat of that summer if at all possible.

"You ready to tell me anything yet?" she asked. The grimace on Sunny's face said it all.

"Do I have to?" she asked.

"Yes," said Tessa, and Sunny half groaned, half sighed.

"It's bad," she said. "Really bad."

When Sunny didn't elaborate, Tessa took a guess.

"You said something the other day about forgiveness. What happened that needs to be forgiven?"

Sunny wouldn't look at her, which sent Tessa's imagination into overdrive. How bad could it be? Had Will started doing drugs or drinking too much? It wasn't uncommon for people in law enforcement to have trouble coping with the stress of the job. Not everyone handled it well. Or worse, had he taken out some of that stress on Sunny or the kids? Tessa's heart clenched up just thinking about it. Maybe he had cheated on her. In light of the other options, it actually didn't sound so bad.

"What did he do?" asked Tessa. To her surprise, Sunny let out a bitter laugh.

"Why do people always assume that the guy is the one who did something awful?"

Tessa's racing thoughts screeched to a halt and she scrambled to regroup. Instead of making assumptions this time, she asked an open-ended question.

"Can you tell me about it?"

Sunny's eyes filled with tears but she stared at the sky to keep them from falling.

"I hate myself," she whispered.

Alarm bells went off in Tessa's head. Sunny was closer to the edge than anybody had realized. She had gotten very good at putting on a happy face, probably for the kids. Now the mask was slipping, and Tessa could clearly see that she was a mess.

"You know I'll be here for you no matter what happened," said Tessa. "But I can't help unless you tell me."

Sunny was silent for so long that Tessa didn't think she was going to say more.

"Do you remember what I said after everything that happened with my mom?" she asked.

Tessa searched her memories for something meaningful, but came away confused. Sunny had said a lot of things, but none seemed to apply to this particular situation.

"I swore I would never, ever grow up to be like her," whispered Sunny.

Tessa felt her eyes widen in dismay.

"I was just so lonely," Sunny continued. "My world had gotten so small. All I did was take care of babies and then toddlers and then finally, one day, they were both in preschool, and I had two hours, three times a week, all to myself." She laughed that scary bitter laugh again. "I didn't know what to do. I didn't know who I was anymore. I started going to the gym. Nobody knew me there. Nobody even knew that I was a mom. And I never said a word."

She finally looked over at Tessa, probably checking to see if her friend was horrified. Tessa fought to maintain a neutral expression. She didn't even let herself feel sympathy for fear it might show on her face.

"And then what happened?" she asked.

This time it didn't take her as long to answer.

"I left my rings in the locker room," said Sunny. "They cut into my fingers when I use the equipment, you know?"

Tessa nodded. She didn't wear rings, but she could imagine that it would hurt.

"The first time he talked to me, I didn't even think about it. It was so nice to talk to an adult about something other than kids. It was such a relief to remember that there was more to me than being a mom. I loved that feeling."

She sniffled and used the hem of her t-shirt to wipe her eyes. Tessa didn't say anything. She had been down this road before in therapy sessions and knew when to keep quiet. They watched the kids as they industriously worked to bury RJ, and eventually Sunny continued her story.

"The next time we talked, he said something about me having good form. Not in a sleazy way. More flirty. It certainly wasn't the kind of thing you'd say to a married lady. And I almost said something. I almost stopped it right then and there, but I didn't. I saw him double-check my finger for a ring. There's an indentation on my finger, but he must have thought I was divorced or something. I let him make his assumptions because I loved how it felt. I loved it," she said fiercely. "It was like a vacation from my real life, a chance to remember who I used to be."

Now Sunny needed a response, and when she looked at Tessa with all that defiance showing in her face, Tessa knew what to say.

"I understand," she said.

And the tears started to fall.

"I love my kids," said Sunny. "I would never give them back or wish them away, but it's hard sometimes, you know? I get so sick of laundry and cooking and cleaning and runny noses." She dug a tissue out of her pocket and paused to blow her nose, then laughed. "I get sick of always having to be the patient one, the saint who never gets mad. At least Will gets to go to work with grown-ups and feel like he's good at something. Nobody throws food at him, or makes poopy footprints on the carpet during nap time. I just—" She stopped to catch her breath. "I just wanted to feel like me again, and all of a sudden, I did."

She was quiet for a long time. Tessa waited her out.

"At the gym, I felt like a different person. Maybe that's why I let things get out of hand. It didn't feel like I was cheating, because I was somebody else." She looked over at Tessa and shrugged. "Pretty stupid, huh?"

"Not stupid," said Tessa. "Lots of moms feel that way."

"But they don't all sleep around," said Sunny. "They don't all wreck their marriages because they're trying to live a fantasy."

Tessa pursed her lips. What Sunny said was true, but it was also irrelevant. It didn't matter what everyone else did. All that mattered was what Sunny had done, and whether or not she could forgive herself. If she wanted Will to forgive her, she was going to need to make her peace with what had happened.

"True," said Tessa. "Some of them don't even realize they've lost themselves until their kids go off to college, and then they have a major crisis. You're just having yours a little early."

"What am I going to do?" asked Sunny. She sounded so fragile that Tessa almost lost hold of her calm.

"What do you want to do?" asked Tessa simply.

"I want to go back to the way things were," answered Sunny.

"Really?" asked Tessa. "Because you didn't sound very happy in that place. You sounded like you had lost yourself in all the laundry."

"Well, what else am I supposed to want?" Sunny wailed. "The affair is over. I don't want him. I never wanted him."

"You want to feel the way you felt when you were with him," said Tessa.

"Yes," said Sunny. "But I can't have that anymore."

"Why not?" asked Tessa.

That stumped Sunny for a minute.

"All I know is that I want my family back together again. I want to be me *and* have my family. I want both."

Tessa smiled. Now they were getting somewhere.

"We can work on that."

Tessa wandered through the living room picking up toys while Sunny got the boys to bed and RJ took a quick shower to wash off all the sand. RJ made it downstairs first, sneaking up behind Tessa and slipping his arms around her waist. She jumped, startled, then leaned back against him.

"So what were you and Sunny talking about that got her so upset?" he murmured into her ear.

She tilted her head back so that she could give him a peck on the cheek.

"Sorry, honey," she said matter-of-factly. "I pinky-swore years ago never to spill Sunny's secrets. If she didn't tell you, then I can't tell you."

RJ turned her within the circle of his arms so that they were face to face.

"Seriously?" he asked. "This is a big deal. I think I should know what's going on."

"And why is that?" asked a very skeptical-sounding Sunny from the doorway.

RJ's head whipped around and he at least had the sense to look sheepish.

"Look, Sunny, I'm worried about you and I—"

"Save it," she said.

"You're really not going to tell me?" RJ sounded both angry and wounded at the same time. It didn't seem to earn him any sympathy from Sunny.

"Nope," she said.

"How can I help you with the divorce if you won't tell me what's going on?" he pleaded.

Sunny gave him a hard look.

"I'm not so sure that divorce is the right answer," she said. There was a dangerous edge to her voice, like she was daring him to argue with her. He did, of course.

"You'd rather torture the kids?" he asked. Tessa sucked in a breath at the low blow. Sunny flinched as if he had slapped her, but he didn't stop. "I'm really sorry that things didn't work out with Will," he continued, "but now you need to think about the kids and what's best for them. It's not about you anymore, and you know it."

Tessa looked back and forth from Sunny to RJ. Sunny looked like a breath of wind would knock her over, so Tessa didn't vent her anger on RJ right away. She was about to suggest to him that they step outside for a moment when his phone rang. He held up a hand.

"I've got to take this," he said as he accepted the call. "Hi, Mom."

Tessa could hear the murmur of the voice on the other end of the line, but not the actual words. One thing was very clear, however. RJ would not be getting a turn to talk anytime soon.

"Yes, Mom—"

"Sorry, I—"

"Mm-hmmm..."

Sunny stood frozen where RJ had left her. Tessa threw an arm around her shoulders and steered her toward the couch. They sat side by side where they could watch the last of the sunset spread its fire across the water. They could also shame-lessly eavesdrop on RJ. Tessa didn't feel guilty at all. Sunny needed her, and if RJ really wanted privacy he could step outside.

Tessa hadn't seen RJ's mother since the day everything had gone to hell. In Tessa's mind she was frozen in that moment of passion, like Thelma and Louise at the end of the movie. But real life doesn't freeze frame. The world keeps turning. From what she could hear of RJ's conversation, it sounded like this summer might bring them all back together, and she couldn't help but wonder what RJ's mom was like now, and how the events of that summer had changed her.

"Mom, I wasn't kidding," he was saying. "You should come up for the Fourth of July."

Sunny was urgently shaking her head 'no' as RJ listened to the voice on the other end of the line. Tessa could feel her eyebrows rising. Was he serious?

"At some point you need to face these people, Mom. It's been nineteen years."

She must have said something that surprised him, because he stopped moving abruptly.

"Really?" he said. "Are you sure?"

He waited.

"That's great." Tessa thought his enthusiasm sounded forced. "I'm sure we can all manage to get along for one day."

More talking. More surprises.

"Who?"

Tessa couldn't help looking again. RJ's free hand clenched the back of the couch.

"I'll look forward to meeting him," he said evenly.

RJ clicked off his phone and stared at the blank screen for a full minute. For years, his life had worked very well as long as he could keep his family members safely in their own separate corners. He knew how to handle his sister, even when she was at her most fragile. He could manage his mother at her worst. He had even learned how to get along with his father. One-on-one, everything was fine.

All together? All bets were off.

RJ was not looking forward to the coming family reunion. Sometimes he fantasized about running away and letting them sort out their own messes. He would never actually do that, of course. If things ended badly, he'd spend the rest of his life blaming himself. Better to stay and suffer for a weekend than run and suffer for years to come. He could survive a weekend, right?

He just needed to figure out a way to keep Tessa out of it.

CHAPTER FOURTEEN

To Tessa's surprise, it was Sunny who recovered first. Getting up off the couch, she said, "You know, I'm not really hungry tonight. I'm going to bed." Before either Tessa or RJ could object, she set down her still-full glass of wine and disappeared upstairs, leaving Tessa and RJ staring at each other.

"She wants to make things work with Will," said Tessa. "Why do you keep talking about divorce?"

RJ sighed. "I don't expect you to understand. You had the perfect childhood, so you don't know what it feels like when things aren't right between your parents. It's awful, and Sunny knows it. She knows better than to put her kids through that."

"But what if they can work it out?" Tessa asked, truly confused by RJ's logic. "Wouldn't that be better for everyone?"

RJ's cynical laugh sliced neatly through her heart.

"Don't be naive," he said. "Trying to fix things only delays the inevitable. Better to make it quick and painless, like ripping off a Band-Aid."

She stiffened. His words were a slap in the face, although she wasn't sure he even realized it.

"You think I'm naive," she said, fighting to keep her voice

even, "and yet I've seen couples recover from this. It can happen." She set her wine glass next to Sunny's on the coffee table and stood up. "You can be as pessimistic as you like about your own relationships, but don't you dare destroy your sister's marriage. Ease up on the divorce talk until we know for sure it's the only option."

He didn't respond immediately, and she didn't wait. She was out the door before he could say a word.

Tessa stalked down to the beach, grateful that she hadn't bothered to carry her stuff in from the car. The sky and the wind matched her mood perfectly. The sunset glowed a deep, angry red while the wind blew fierce and angry. Most of her anger was directed at herself. She had always known that RJ didn't do relationships. She had simply allowed herself to forget.

She sat down hard on the sand and let the wind whip strands of hair out of her ponytail. She needed to get a grip. It felt like all the strands of her life were coming unwoven, and she didn't know how to weave them back together again.

Her parents were hiding things.

Her career plan was crumbling.

Her summer fling was flaming out after only a few weeks.

Mostly she just wanted to crawl into a hole and dream up a brand new life, one that wasn't so hard.

Tessa closed her eyes and focused on the feel of the wind on her face. She should be out on the water right now, her full attention on keeping the boat upright, rather than trapped on land with too much room to think. She pulled out her hair elastic and let the wind blow through her hair. Sometimes she felt like the wind could blow all the way through her soul, clearing out the horrible, uncomfortable feelings and leaving her empty.

If she were a client, the advice would come easily: Let yourself feel all these horrible feelings and then let them go. Don't deny them. Don't wallow in them. Acknowledge them. Give them the space they need. Then let them go and move on with your life.

The time had come to start over.

RJ sat alone in the fading light. He hadn't moved for a long time after he heard the kitchen door close behind Tessa. When he realized he'd been standing motionless in the middle of the living room, he simply sat down on the couch. He had nowhere else to go. Nothing to do but sit and think about where things had gone wrong.

It was better this way, better that she understood him too soon rather than too late. At least now he was simply making her furious. It was way too early to break her heart.

"Surprise!"

Tessa breezed through the back door, a carefree smile already in place. She caught her parents at the end of their dinner, chatting over their empty plates as if everything were completely normal. As if her father weren't contemplating a move to Nashville and her mother didn't have an ex-lover in New York.

"Sweetie, I didn't know you were coming up tonight," said Dora, hopping up to give her a quick hug. "We would have saved you some dinner."

Tessa set her bag down and shrugged.

"Don't worry about me," she said. "It was a spur-of-the-moment decision. I'm sure I can scrounge something from the fridge."

Before her mother could start fussing and asking questions about RJ, Tessa made a preemptive block.

"I should probably do a grocery run tomorrow," she offered. "It only seems fair."

"Don't be silly," said her mother. "We're happy to have you here. The least we can do is feed you." She headed toward the fridge.

"Mom, seriously, don't worry about me. I had a late lunch, so I'm not even hungry. What I could really use is a bath and an early night. Do you mind if I'm antisocial tonight?"

She tried to look tired and vulnerable. It wasn't that hard.

"Of course, dear," said Dora, giving her another hug. "You know I think you work too hard. Take as much time as you need."

Tessa gave her dad a quick kiss on the cheek and then escaped to her room. She closed the door behind her and sagged against it. She had never been any good at lying, and even pretending like everything was normal for the past five minutes had exhausted her.

There was something incredibly comforting about her childhood bedroom. In this room, she would always be a child, and her parents would make sure everything turned out okay. Although she had cleaned out the clutter a few years back, the room was still packed with memories. Most of them were happy memories, which made the current instability in her parents' marriage all the more difficult to comprehend.

Tessa flopped facedown on the bed. She didn't want to think about her parents right now. She didn't want to think about Sunny and Will, or work, or where things were going with RJ. She wanted to clear her mind and make it all go away. Maybe she could sleep for the entire weekend. It was worth a try.

Tessa knew perfectly well that she was hiding, but she didn't care. The world could wait until tomorrow.

CHAPTER FIFTEEN

KAT ARRIVED EARLY FOR WORK ON FRIDAY MORNING, BUT AS SHE settled into her desk chair, coffee cup in hand, she was startled to hear the noise of someone moving around upstairs. Most likely it was RJ, but he wasn't supposed to come in at all today, and it was wildly out of character for him to make it into the office first. Frowning, she set down the coffee cup and went upstairs to investigate. When she reached the door that led to RJ's workspace, she paused, wondering if it was dumb of her to come up here by herself. What if it wasn't RJ? What if someone had broken in looking for cash or computer equipment? Then she shook herself. This was Hidden Springs. B&E was not a thing around here. Domestic violence, yes. Child abuse, yes. Drugs and alcohol problems, yes. But straight-up breaking and entering was extremely rare.

Still, she braced herself before turning the door handle.

RJ sat as his desk, his back to her and his head in his hands. At the sound of the door opening, he turned and leaned back, trying to look nonchalant and failing miserably.

"Hey, Kat," he said. "You're here early."

244

"I could say the same for you," she said. "You're never here before eight."

He shrugged.

"Couldn't sleep," he said.

"I can see that," she answered. "You look like hell."

He half laughed and rubbed his forehead.

"Well, that makes sense. I feel like hell."

"Everything okay?" she asked.

He hesitated before answering.

"Let me ask your professional opinion on a personal matter," he said.

This could not be good. She leaned against the doorframe and waited for him to explain.

"My sister is having some problems with her husband," he began.

Kat nodded, wondering how much Sunny had shared with RJ. Her guess would be, not much.

"What's the best way to get her to talk to me about it?" he asked. "In the past, she's always confided in me, but not this time. Any suggestions?"

This was not exactly a professional opinion question. This was more of a brother-sister relations question, and Kat was perhaps the least qualified person in the world to answer. She had no siblings, a screwed-up childhood, and very few close friends. But if he was asking, she might as well give it a go.

"Honestly? I'd suggest that you back off. Less talking, more listening. You have a lot of opinions about this stuff, and she probably doesn't want to hear them right now."

He didn't look happy with her answer.

"Sunny should know how hard it is on kids when their parents fight, but when I mention the word divorce, she shuts up. I can't believe she would do this to her kids. She needs to let go."

It must be nice to be so sure of the right answer. Kat now

understood perfectly why Sunny hadn't asked RJ about custody and how it worked. It would have been like opening Pandora's box. She pursed her lips and debated how to answer without breaking Sunny's confidence. In the end, she settled on a generalization.

"Divorce isn't always the right answer, you know."

He gave her a grumpy look.

"Why do women always say that?" he asked. "Relationships either work or they don't. It's pretty simple. If they work, great. If they don't, then end it."

"Every time?" asked Kat. She didn't bother to hide the skepticism in her voice.

"Every time," he answered.

Kat pushed away from the doorframe and shook her head.

"You're hopeless," she said as she turned to leave. "I count myself lucky that we will never date."

"I'm a realist," he said to her retreating back. "I live in the real world."

She snorted. He had no clue.

"Hopeless," she called over her shoulder.

She would do whatever she needed to support Sunny, because the girl clearly wasn't going to get any help from her brother.

Friday morning, Tessa woke up refreshed and ready to tackle not only her own problems but everyone else's as well. Fourteen hours of sleep will do that to a girl. Her parents had disappeared to their respective corners after breakfast. Her dad was in his office. Her mother had run over to the sailing school for the morning. Tessa was left to her own devices, still trying to figure out her next move. She was in the middle of pouring a second cup of coffee when someone knocked on the back door.

She squelched the hope that surged through her. It wasn't RJ. The chances of him coming here to apologize were less than zero. In his mind, he had no reason to apologize. Tessa peeked out the open kitchen window and saw Sunny raising her hand to knock a second time.

"Hey," said Tessa. "Want a cup of coffee?"

Sunny jumped, then looked relieved.

"I'd love one," she said.

They didn't say more until they were sitting at the kitchen table, and then it was Sunny who spoke first.

"I'm really sorry about last night," she said.

That caught Tessa by surprise. "Why are you apologizing? You didn't do anything."

"I left you and RJ in the middle of a fight. I should have stayed. You're both trying to help me, in your own way, but I'm afraid my situation will only screw things up between the two of you. This is my problem, and I can fix it. Really. You don't need to worry about me."

"What if I want to worry about you? You're my friend."

Sunny looked down into her coffee cup. "I know," she said, "but there's a part of me that wonders what you could really do. I can't undo what happened. All I can do is hope he'll cool off and find a way to forgive me."

"If you two are both willing to talk to someone—not me, but someone—then there's hope. Of course he's angry. And you're right, he needs a chance to cool off. For you, the waiting will be the hard part. You probably want to apologize and then pretend like it never happened, but it did, and you both need time and space to work through it."

"Can you help me find someone to talk to?" asked Sunny. "If there's any chance for us, I'll do whatever it takes to make things work."

"Absolutely," said Tessa. "We'll figure this out."

"RJ is going to be pissed," said Sunny. She thunked her elbows onto the table and dropped her head into her hands.

"Hey," said Tessa sharply. "This isn't RJ's marriage. It's yours. If he wants to give up at the first sign of trouble, then he can do that in his own relationships. This is your business, and you decide how to handle it."

Sunny groaned, then looked up at Tessa. "I know, I know. Everything you say makes sense, but RJ's still going to be pissed."

"Don't worry about RJ. I'll keep him occupied. You worry about opening up communication with Will, okay?"

"You'll tell me what to say?" she asked hopefully.

"I can't do that," said Tessa, softening her refusal with a gentle smile, "but I can give you some tips, and I can help with the kids. This is ultimately between you and Will. You don't want anybody else in the middle."

Sunny nodded, then wrinkled her forehead. "I really hope this doesn't mess up you and RJ," she said. "You two are good together."

"We're having a really good time," said Tessa, choosing her words carefully, "but we both know that RJ doesn't do the long term. I promised him that I would keep things light, and I intend to keep that promise." She ignored Sunny's raised eyebrows. "I will," she repeated. "No matter what."

The race on Saturday did not go well. For starters, Tessa and RJ were still at odds. In all his previous relationships, the first fight was the signal to end things, but for some reason with Tessa he was not following his own rules. Instead, he was waiting to see if they could recover.

Tessa wasn't helping. She had texted him that she would be there for the race, and he had texted back to confirm, but apart from the texts, there had been no talking. They rigged the boat, raced, and put the boat away, all without saying more than ten words to each other.

Brock only added to the grim mood. Helen was nowhere to be seen, so he was working with a sub as his crew. This left him in a foul temper, which he vented by making asshole comments to anybody in earshot. RJ was sick of him, sick of his sister shutting him out, and sick of the tension between him and Tessa. They finished the race in the middle of the pack, and his only consolation was that they finished ahead of Brock.

They returned home to find Sunny packing up her car while the boys napped. RJ looked at Tessa sharply, wondering if she was in on this change of plans, but she looked just as surprised as he felt. His first instinct was to interrogate his sister, but he remembered Kat's advice and kept his mouth shut. She was fragile enough right now. She didn't need him going all 'big brother' on her.

"Change of plans?" he asked casually. He stopped next to Sunny and stifled the urge to repack her trunk. She had thrown the suitcases in a jumble, leaving her no room for the bag of toys. She gave up trying to squeeze it in the trunk and instead tossed it in the back seat between the car seats.

"I'm going home," she answered, matching his casual tone. She gave him a look over her shoulder, as if daring him to object to the plan, but he wasn't that stupid. He did jump a bit when she slammed the trunk, then he and Tessa followed her as she strode back inside the house.

Once in the kitchen, she started to assemble what he assumed was a snack for the boys. Cheese, crackers, juice boxes, apple slices. The usual.

Tessa leaned against the counter, also trying really hard to look casual. She wore that infuriatingly neutral expression that he thought of as her 'therapist face.' She had been doing it all day, and it was making him twitchy. He wondered if her patients found it as annoying as he did. He didn't want a thera-pist. He wanted an actual human who would actually respond to him. Screw neutral.

Sunny broke the silence but kept her eyes on the apple she was slicing. "How was the race?" she asked Tessa.

Tessa shrugged. "Fine," she answered.

Sunny gave her a funny look, but Tessa looked at RJ instead of offering any details, so Sunny turned her attention to him. He sighed heavily.

"We lost," he said. "We were a little...out of sync today."

His sister snorted in response. "You think?"

Sunny shoved all of the snack items into an insulated bag, which she put on the counter next to her purse. Then she turned to face RJ and crossed her arms.

"We're going home today," she said. He found the challenge in her voice insulting. As if he had ever been able to tell her what to do.

"So you said," he said. He couldn't help the edge of sarcasm that crept into his voice. "You let me know how that goes."

"Why don't you want me to try to fix things with Will?"

"Do you not remember what it was like?" he countered. He could feel his control slipping. "Do you really want that for your boys? Do you want them to listen in on the fighting, or sit through the silent dinners, or wonder what they did to make Mom and Dad so angry? Do you?"

Damn it, he was making her cry. He hated to see her miser-able, but somebody had to make sure she wasn't living in denial, and as usual it looked like that responsibility fell to him. He looked over at Tessa, hoping for God knows what because he knew she was on the opposite side of this argument, and sure enough all he got was the damn therapist face.

"I remember," said Sunny. "I also remember how quiet it was after Dad left, and how Mom cried in the shower, and how we didn't laugh anymore. So don't pull that shit with me, big brother. I remember everything, and I reject that future. I want better for my kids, and if that means I need to grovel and earn back my husband's trust, then that's what I'm going to do. I'm all in, and I'm not going down without a fight."

Wait, what? How is any of this Sunny's fault? He had assumed that Will was the one... RJ shook his head and pressed on with his objections.

"But things will never be the same," he said.

"Of course not," she said. The 'duh' was implied. "If I wanted everything to stay the same, I never would have screwed up in the first place."

Sunny shook her head in disgust and headed for the hallway. RJ and Tessa were left staring at each other across the suddenly vast expanse of kitchen. He grabbed the back of a chair to steady himself. Nothing about what Sunny had just said made any sense. What had she done? And why would she torture herself or the kids by signing up for a lifetime of penance? It didn't make sense.

"You okay?" she asked. The professional mask melted away and she was regular Tessa again, the concern clearly written on her face. He didn't know who moved first, but they came together in the middle of the kitchen. He wrapped his arms around her and buried his face in her hair.

"It kills me that she won't let me help her," he said. "She won't even tell me what happened."

Tessa nodded against his chest. He was grateful that she didn't analyze, or try to fix, or any of the other things she could have done. She let it be, and they held each other until they heard the sounds of little-boy feet upstairs. He pressed his lips against her forehead, savoring one last moment of peace. RJ couldn't say what he needed to say in words. He had to hope that she would understand anyway. He didn't want their disagreement over Sunny's situation to end things between them. He needed more time.

~

Tessa returned to her parents' house after Sunny left. She used the excuse of needing to spend more time with them, but she and RJ both knew that she needed some space.

Nothing about this summer was going as planned. She was supposed to be reconnecting with her parents, but instead she had never felt more disconnected from them. She was supposed to be coming up with plan B, but instead she found herself daydreaming about plans C, D, and her personal favorite, plan RJ. She was supposed to be finding her feet, but she had never felt more off-balance in her life.

She found her father in his office, working on a song. He nodded a greeting, but he had his 'music face' on, the one that said he was deep in concentration and didn't really want to be disturbed. She found her mother, after some searching, up in her art studio. She also had that grumpy, creative thing going on.

"Only a few hours of good sunlight left. Be down soon, honey."

Tessa thumped back down the stairs, figuring that her mother would show her face about an hour after sunset, when the light was completely gone. That would be eight-thirty or so, and Tessa was hungry now. Shaking her head, she made her way back to the kitchen and dug around in the fridge until she found the makings of a sandwich.

She spent the next half an hour wallowing in self-analysis. Maybe she should go right back to RJ's place and they could make dinner together. If she went back now, she would look needy, though, and she would still have no idea how she wanted to proceed. He was not a 'forever' kind of guy. Which was fine, right? The whole point of the summer was to have fun and enjoy the moment. She knew perfectly well that her time with RJ was limited and that their relationship would end with the sailing season. Maybe she should enjoy every second of their time together and deal with the inevitable hangover when it ended. Maybe she should put the stupid sandwich in the fridge and go see him already.

She needed expert advice, she realized, as she swallowed another bite of the lonely sandwich. She dug her cell phone out of her pocket. Callie was useless right now, so much in love that she thought the entire world should follow suit. Only Mel would know what to do. Mel didn't do relationships. She did passion and flings and love 'em and leave 'em.

Now that she thought about it, Mel was a lot like RJ.

Mel picked up on the first ring.

"What's up, sis? How goes it with the sexy sailor?"

Tessa choked on her sandwich. When she was done coughing, she answered.

"He's great. Mostly."

She squinched up her face, waiting for the smart remark that she knew was coming.

"So, grasshopper," intoned Mel, "you have called the master for advice."

Mel was not going to make this easy, but Tessa didn't care. She was desperate.

"Shut up and help me," said Tessa. "I've never done this before. I'm going to be a basket case when it's over, and I'm starting to psych myself out. What am I supposed to do?"

She heard the panic in her own voice and winced.

"Calm down," ordered Mel. "This is not a life-or-death situation. You need to tell the professional counselor inside of you to take a Vicodin and call me in the morning. Regular Tessa needs to come out to play."

"I am one person," Tessa wailed. "I can't turn off the therapist. It's me. In my own head."

Mel sighed dramatically on the other end of the line.

"Fine. Therapist can stay. She's telling you to calm down. Are you listening?"

"No!"

Mel laughed.

"Okay, then. So let's fix that. How do you get your clients to calm down?"

"Deep breaths. Find an anchor."

"Fine," said Mel. "You breathe and try to think of an anchor. I'm going to put you on speaker while you do that, because I actually have plans tonight, and I need to do my face."

"You're going to multitask while I'm having a panic attack? Seriously?"

"Breathe. Think." Mel's voice sounded more distant on the speakerphone, and she talked in the weird way that meant she was putting on mascara. "What's your anchor?"

Tessa found her irritation with Mel very calming, so she focused on that, using it to ground herself while she tried to think of a better anchor. Something more positive. Something like the feeling she got while she was sailing. There was something about being on the water that brought her peace, and she wanted more of that feeling in her life. She closed her eyes, breathed in and out, and thought about being on the water. In less than a minute, she felt calm.

"I'm better now," she mumbled into the phone.

"Good," said Mel. "Now let's talk about your personal brand of crazy. Your problem is that you don't remember how to have fun."

"I'm having fun," protested Tessa. "That's not the problem. I'm freaking out because I'm in too deep and the end is going to suck."

"So end it," said Mel. "Rip off the bandage. Pull the plug. Do whatever you need to do."

"But—"

"If all you can do is think about how much it's going to hurt, then get it over with. Stop whining."

"But I don't want to get it over with. I like this. I like him."

"Then shut up and enjoy it."

"But—"

"No more buts. Either enjoy it or end it. It's the waffling that's killing you."

"All in," whispered Tessa.

"Exactly," said Mel, her voice suddenly loud in Tessa's ear.

"Ouch. Turn off the speakerphone."

"Go big or go home," said Mel, and this time her voice was normal volume.

"Got it," said Tessa.

"Are you sure?" asked Mel. "I'd like to hear you say it with more conviction."

"Got it."

She said it with so much conviction that she almost fooled herself.

"Good," said Mel, "and good luck."

The call ended abruptly, and Tessa set her phone down on the counter.

All in. Go big or go home.

The advice echoed through her heart like a giant klaxon. *Warning! Danger!* She shook her head. If she wanted to live her life, she was going to have to follow her own advice. She was going to have to open her heart and love, accepting the fact that someday it would hurt. A lot.

Tessa paused at the back door of RJ's house. Things felt different between them now, and she was uncertain how to proceed. Should she knock? Go right in? She had lost the momentum that had carried her from her parents' house to RJ's, and now she didn't know what to do.

She was raising her hand to knock when he walked into the kitchen and saw her through the window in the door. Before she could move, he had opened the door and pulled her into his arms, kissing her as if she had been away for days rather than only an hour. She almost melted onto the kitchen floor. Right before her knees gave way, he took her by the hand and led her upstairs to his room.

She had worried about what they would say, but it turned out she needn't have worried at all. They tumbled onto the bed and worked things out with actions rather than words. Tessa's last coherent thought was that she should recommend this approach to all her clients.

Later, she yawned and stretched, content to stay exactly where she was all night long. She smiled up at RJ.

"Hi," she said.

"Hi, yourself," he returned.

"I came back," she said.

"I noticed."

"I didn't call first," she said, her smile fading. "Hope that was okay."

He grinned and rolled over on top of her.

"I love it when you're spontaneous," he said. "Are you by any chance free to spend the night?"

She nodded slowly and her smile came back.

"Excellent," he said. "I don't want to waste a second."

RJ woke first. He studied Tessa by the glow of early morning that illuminated the room. She slept deeply, her chest rising and falling with her breath and her hand dangling off the edge of the bed. He smoothed her hair and curved his body around hers, content to stay where he was until she woke up. They had recovered from their first fight, but he had few illusions about the next one. Inevitably, there would be another fight, and he was unwilling to jeopardize their friendship by dragging their affair out too long. He couldn't stand to lose her completely.

The confrontation with Sunny yesterday had left RJ with a sick feeling in the pit of his stomach. He loved the confidence of his convictions, and he hated the possibility, no matter how remote, that he might have been wrong all these years. If Sunny succeeded in repairing her marriage, what would that say about his personal mission to rescue people from their misery?

Rather than dwell on his doubts, he began tracing the veins on the inside of Tessa's elbow, coaxing her awake. When she turned her face in to his chest and tried to stay sleeping, he kissed her ear and nipped at her earlobe. He knew he was making headway when she curved her neck to allow him better access.

"Good morning," he murmured in her ear.

She responded with an inarticulate grumble, but her hands moved around his waist and she pressed a kiss against his chest. He rolled onto his back, bringing her with him, so that she could continue dozing on top of him. He moved her long hair to one side and rubbed the nape of her neck, then continued kneading small circles down the length of her spine. By the time he reached the base of her back, she had adjusted her position so that her legs stretched out on top of his. He had only to reach lower to press her hips against him and coax her legs open.

At last she was waking up, and their movements became more purposeful, more urgent. He rolled her onto her back and reached for his stash of condoms in the drawer of the bedside table. It took only a moment to cover himself, and then he eased inside of her, giving them both a moment to breathe before the need to move overwhelmed them both. They remained locked together long after the climax slammed through them, even after she fell back to sleep.

Later, after they had scavenged breakfast from his kitchen, they went out onto the screened front porch. Although RJ's house was only a short walk from her parents' house, the view from here was completely different. Their house was situated at the far end of The Gardens, perched on the top of a hill so that they looked down on the water, their view extending all the way across the lake and beyond. In contrast, RJ's house sat close to the water's edge, only the gentle slope of the commons separating it from the shoreline. Here, the lake filled her field of vision, soothing the deepest, darkest corners of her soul. They sat in silence for a while, drinking their coffee, until Tessa asked if he had heard from Sunny. He hadn't.

"I hope she's okay," he said. "If I were Will, I might be an asshole."

Tessa snorted and splashed coffee on herself.

"Luckily, Will isn't that kind of guy," she said.

"How can you be so confident?" asked RJ.

"Experience," she said. "I've seen this before, and I think their odds are pretty good."

"To Tessa, the marriage whisperer," said RJ, raising his mug.

They clinked and sipped, and then Tessa wrinkled her eyebrows.

"Wait, does that make you the divorce whisperer?" she asked.

He thought about it for a second, then nodded.

"Yes. Yes it does."

She snickered.

He could do this. He could go back to flirting and fun. He would do whatever he needed to do for a few more weeks with Tessa.

"I guess we cancel each other out, then," she said.

"Or maybe we're just highly combustible," he countered, giving her a suggestive wink.

She shook her head in exasperation.

"Some people have a one-track mind."

He cheerfully agreed with her. "We do."

RJ took Tessa's half-finished mug and set it on the table next to his. Then he reached for her, cradling her face in his hands, and kissed her. One kiss and Tessa got muddled. He loved the way that he could make her lose her train of thought.

"Do you think maybe we should go to the bedroom?" she mumbled. "People seem to walk in at the weirdest times…"

A second kiss, and she couldn't quite put her words together correctly.

"I mean…it's daytime…" She sighed, successfully distracted by his mouth on her neck. He eased her back on the couch. He would never get tired of distracting her.

She tried to talk again.

"People could walk by and look right in…"

Her words trailed away on a moan. He had moved quickly, stripping her of the oversized T-shirt she had slept in and leaving her in only a pair of panties.

"Are you really worried about the neighbors?" he whispered as he took one breast in each hand. He rasped her nipple with the stubble on his cheek, earning a ragged breath.

"Weekend," she mumbled as she stretched her hands above her head and arched her back. "Lots of…people." Her words faded away as he dispensed with her panties as well, leaving her completely naked in broad daylight, cloaked only in the long hair spilling loose around her shoulders. She looked up at him and smiled, her eyes dark and her lids heavy.

"More," she demanded. She threaded her fingers into his hair, massaging the nape of his neck and drawing him down toward her. He resisted, drawing out the moment and committing it to memory. He could feel the clock ticking down on their time together, and he wanted to remember moments like this one long after their affair ended.

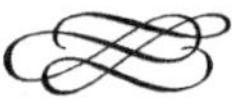

CHAPTER SIXTEEN

Tessa hesitated before knocking on the door. Truth be told, she was nervous. Vi had summoned her to the apartment with little warning, and Tessa wasn't sure what to expect. However, she needed to report back to Dr. Hammond on Vi's state of mind, and she couldn't do that unless she talked with Vi one more time.

Giving herself a shake, Tessa knocked, and the door opened immediately. Vi had probably been watching as Tessa waffled outside her door. Vi stood taller today, and her eyes snapped with challenge.

"About time, missy," she said by way of greeting.

Since she had arrived a few minutes early, Tessa didn't bother to respond. She simply raised an eyebrow and waited for Vi to lead the way to the living room. But instead of heading to the living room, Vi led Tessa to the kitchen, where she had coffee and snacks waiting at the kitchen table. The dummy was nowhere to be seen.

"Sit," she said.

Tessa obeyed and was about to ask about the noticeable absence at the table, but Vi beat her to it.

"Yes, I put the dummy away. You made your point. People think it's weird to talk to yourself, and they think it's weird to talk to a dummy. So I put the dummy in the closet, and I'll keep the conversations in my head from now on."

Tessa tried to hold the laughter in, but it came out as a snort. Vi looked affronted.

"What is your problem, young lady?" she demanded. "It's not enough to be right? Now you're going to laugh at a little old lady?"

"Don't try to play the little old lady card with me," said Tessa. "I only laughed because I thought of something a wise woman once asked me."

"And what was that?" asked Vi.

"'Do you want some cheese with that whine?'" said Tessa.

A smile tugged at the corner of Vi's mouth.

"Did this wise woman have any advice on dealing with sassy little girls?"

Tessa cocked her head to one side and pretended to consider the question.

"Not that I recall," answered Tessa.

"Well, she should have," said Vi.

Tessa picked up a pirouette cookie and munched on it while she gave Vi the once-over. She looked good. There was more color in her cheeks than before, and as grumpy as she might be, she didn't look like she was on her own death watch anymore.

"So you called," said Tessa.

"I did," said Vi. "What do I need to do to get Robert Junior off my back?"

"What's he doing?"

"Fussing," said Vi crisply. "He calls almost every day, and he's threatening to visit."

Tessa snickered at that. "You realize that most mothers would be thrilled with all the attention?"

Vi made a dismissive sound.

"He's worried about you," continued Tessa. "I can reassure him that you're doing much better, but he might need to see it with his own eyes."

In classic middle school style, Vi rolled her eyes and sighed dramatically.

"I'll do my best," said Tessa, "but you might want to prepare yourself for a visit anyway."

"He can visit," said Vi, "but I'm not going to entertain him. In fact, I might have a few chores waiting for him." Her evil grin made Tessa smile, too. Woe to anyone who dared annoy Nana Vi.

Tessa gauged the mood of the moment and decided it was time to broach a more delicate topic.

"Have you thought at all about getting out of the house more?" she asked. "That would go a long way toward reassuring your son."

"Where would I go?" asked Vi. "Nobody wants an old lady hanging around."

"Again with the 'little old lady' sob story?" said Tessa. "You know perfectly well that Sunny and RJ would love to see you, and I assume you've made some friends over the course of your extremely long life. They might want to see you from time to time, too."

Vi looked away. For goodness' sake, she was acting like a little girl, waiting for Tessa to beg her to please come out and play, and as much as Tessa wanted to help, she wasn't going to set that precedent. Vi needed to own this.

Tessa pushed away from the kitchen table. She picked up her purse and moved toward the hallway. Vi crossed her arms, refusing to look at her.

"RJ asked me to invite you up to the lake for the Fourth of July," she said, making up the invitation on the fly. "Sunny and the boys will be there, too. I hope you'll consider joining your family for the holiday."

She didn't wait for an answer. Better to give Vi some time to make her choice. The visit had given Tessa more than enough confidence to write up her report for Dr. Hammond and Robert Junior. Vi was not losing her mind. Boredom would bring her out of her cave eventually, but Tessa hoped that this invitation would provide the catalyst she needed.

The rest of the week flew by. It helped that Tessa knew her time at the Hammond Center was drawing to a close. She spent her evenings making sure that each client file had a written transition plan, and that all her notes were clear. There was something very satisfying about tying up all the loose ends and preparing to move on. She was putting in a full week this week, rather than taking Friday off again. Most of her clients had canceled their sessions next week due to the Fourth of July holiday, so she squeezed in extra appointments and planned to take off much of next week as well.

Sometimes she marveled at how much her life had changed in only a month. She had changed course over Memorial Day weekend and looking back, she had no regrets.

She didn't leave herself time to think, because the only thing she could think about was RJ. It was bad enough that he had taken over her dreams, but he was starting to take over her waking hours as well. She kept catching herself staring off into space, imagining the different ways he might welcome her back on Friday night.

The only other thing she thought about was sailing. How she had gone so long without it? The best explanation she could come up with centered around the brain's ability to deceive itself.

She hadn't had time to sail, so she had conveniently forgotten how much she loved it. Deep down she must have known that even one outing would be enough to break the illusion, because she hadn't made even the smallest effort to get out on the water.

Now that she had tasted the wind again, she knew that she couldn't give it up.

She wouldn't give up RJ either, if she could help it. Her brain was probably tricking her right now, allowing her to enjoy this time with him while conveniently forgetting that it would never be more than a summer fling. She didn't really care. For once in her life, she didn't want to analyze her relationship. In fact, she didn't want to think about it at all. She just wanted to feel her way through.

And no matter what the future held, she would always be grateful to RJ for bringing her back to sailing.

Race day turned out to be gray and choppy. It was exactly the type of weather that made her restless. She had slept over at RJ's house, not even bothering to pretend to stay with her parents this time. They got ready together in the morning, and by the time they got out on the water, they were perfectly in sync and ready to race.

Unfortunately, they didn't time the start well, so they found themselves in third for the first few legs of the race. Tessa wasn't overly concerned, though, because this was a longer course and they were working with a consistently strong wind. There was plenty of time to lose an early lead or catch up from behind. The teenage brothers were in first. Brock trailed behind them. She could tell even from a distance that he was intent on winning. His smug looks back in their direction suggested that he would be happy as long as he beat RJ. Their three teams had pulled ahead of the pack early on, and it looked as if the field had broken into two separate races.

It wasn't until they were ready to round the windward mark for the last time that Tessa realized they had a problem. They had pulled ahead of Brock, but now he was heading back in their direction on starboard, and he wasn't changing course. There was no way he could make it around the mark. He was cutting it too close, but technically he had the right-of-way and they had to yield. He was yelling at them to get the hell out of his way.

Tessa shrugged helplessly at RJ and then eased the sails to slow them down. He adjusted their heading so that they would duck behind Brock before coming about, a move that would cost them time and their shot at catching up to Steve and Mike. Brock was shooting himself in the foot, however, because he would need to re-round the mark after hitting it. She watched, curious, as he headed straight for the mark. They were on the far side of him, so she couldn't see for sure whether or not he hit it, but given his trajectory, she didn't see how he could have missed. He acted as if he had cleared it, however, and made no move to round it again. He bore down on the teens in the lead and left Tessa and RJ to claim third place.

She glanced at RJ, but he kept his mouth shut and clenched his jaw. She knew that look, and she dreaded the coming confrontation. RJ wouldn't simply let Brock walk away after making a dick move like that. They crossed the line in third place and headed directly back to the yacht club.

As soon as they had hauled the boat out of the water, RJ caught up with Brock.

"I assume you're going to disqualify yourself," said RJ.

Brock stiffened. Helen hung back, a pinched expression on her face.

"I have no idea what you're talking about."

"You hit the last mark," said RJ.

"Now, RJ," said Brock. "Don't be a sore loser. There is no way you could have seen whether or not we hit that last mark. You were on the far side of our boat. The angle was all wrong." His expression turned smug. "You're going to have to trust me on this one. We came close, but we cleared the mark. No harm, no foul—and definitely no disqualification."

Brock turned to go, but RJ grabbed his arm, forcing him to turn him back. Helen froze by Brock's side. Tessa tensed as well. The last thing they needed was a brawl.

"You're absolutely certain you cleared the mark?" demanded RJ. He stared into Brock's eyes as if he could read the truth for himself.

"One hundred percent," said Brock, his voice overly hearty and loud enough for all the bystanders to hear.

RJ released him.

"I guess I'll have to take your word for it," said RJ.

"Yes," said Brock, "you will."

He turned to leave, putting his arm around Helen to make sure she came along, too. RJ turned slowly toward Tessa. He looked calm on the outside, but she could tell that he was still furious.

"He hit that mark," said RJ.

"I know," said Tessa.

"He cheated, and then he lied to my face."

Tessa nodded.

"I knew the guy was an asshole," said RJ. "I don't know why I'm surprised."

"I'm not," said Tessa with a shrug.

"Do you mind if we head home?" asked RJ. "I'm not really in the mood for a drink today."

She linked her arm through his and together they headed out to de-rig the boat.

"I'm with you," she said, then cracked a smile. "One hundred percent."

The race had left them both out of sorts, so when they got back to RJ's house, they wandered down to the end of the pier. The lake was still restless, sparkling in spots where the sun had broken through the dark clouds, but for the most part a steely gray speckled by occasional whitecaps. They sat side by side, dangling their bare feet in the water. Tessa knew that she should head back to the city soon—traffic would be a nightmare—but she couldn't bear to leave yet.

"Do you ever miss the California weather?" asked Tessa. "I'm sure it was never this chilly in June in L.A."

He shook his head.

"Nothing ever changes out there," he answered. "The people never age, the grass never grows, and the leaves never fall down. After a while, it gets boring. There were times I felt like I was sleepwalking through my life."

"What made you decide to come back?" she asked. "Mom said you had a really high-powered job. It can't be easy to start from scratch here."

She waited, watching the clouds roll across the sky, until he finally answered with a question of his own.

"Do you remember much about my dad?" he asked.

"Not really," said Tessa. "He was just another grown-up. I don't remember him being here very much."

"He's a divorce lawyer. The kind that does high-profile cases and charges really high fees."

"Did you work for him?" asked Tessa.

"I did," said RJ. "I was in training to be his right-hand man. Suit, tie, briefcase, the whole thing."

She snorted. He was making this up.

"I'm serious," he said. "I'll show you a picture sometime. You wouldn't recognize me."

"So what happened?" she asked.

"I met a girl."

"Oh."

He laughed.

"No," he said. "Not like that. She was a client."

Tessa opened her eyes and looked over at him, appalled. He laughed again.

"Not like that either," he said. "She was a friend of a friend. Called me up because I was the only lawyer she knew. Asked if she and her husband could come meet with me—together. In all the years that I'd worked with my Dad, I had never—not once—run into a couple who were still talking to each other. Our job description included 'translator' and 'messenger boy.' The idea that we could be a partner, a facilitator, was confusing. It didn't fit."

"Sounds a lot healthier than a typical Hollywood divorce."

He barked out a cynical laugh.

"A lot cheaper, too," he said. "My dad was pissed."

"So did you help them?" she asked.

"I did," he said. "And when my dad called me on the carpet and asked me what the hell I was thinking, I just...snapped."

"What did you do?" she asked.

"I quit," he said simply.

"Just like that?"

"Pretty much," he answered. "I had this blinding moment of clarity where I realized that I didn't want to follow in his footsteps. He's not a happy man. He lives for his work, and his work is miserable. Divorce sucks. If it's going to be my specialty, I don't want to make it any harder than it needs to be. I want to make it easier."

She wrinkled her forehead.

"That sounds...admirable," she said, "except for the fact that we're talking about divorce."

"Why is that so bad?" he asked. "For some couples, it's the only solution."

"I know," she sighed, "but for so many it's the first option instead of the last. I find that depressing."

"I guess I'd rather see people divorce too soon than too late," he said. "If you stick it out too long you can do lasting damage."

"The problem is that people don't know what to do when things get hard," said Tessa. "If they would only come see me at the first signs of trouble, they could get some training and work through their problems instead of tripping over them."

"And if they're fundamentally incompatible?" asked RJ.

"Then maybe divorce is the solution," she admitted, "but I wish people would at least try to work things out."

"Your way sounds like a lot of work," said RJ. "Marriage shouldn't feel like work."

Tessa couldn't help laughing.

"Right, and parenting should be all cuddles and rainbows. Please."

"I'm serious," said RJ. "Work is something you do to get along with a roommate, not a spouse."

She raised a skeptical eyebrow.

"Are you speaking from experience?"

"I'm very good at relationships," he said. "Beginning, middle, and end."

"I see," she said coolly.

"You see what?"

"This is the RJ approach to relationships. I keep forgetting you're not a 'for better or worse' kind of guy. You're more 'for better or not.'"

"Why do you frame it that way?" he demanded. "It sounds really shitty when you talk about it like that. I don't think there's anything wrong with enjoying the best parts of a relationship and then letting go when it stops working."

"Do you think parents should let go of their kids when it stops working?" she asked.

"Of course not," he snapped.

"So you would love your kids unconditionally, but your spouse not so much," she said.

That shut him up for a minute.

"It's not the same," he said.

"And that's the problem," she said quietly.

The wind shifted, and the clouds covered the one remaining patch of sunlight on the lake. The sky was gray again, and she was cold.

"I need to go."

As Tessa sat in traffic that night on her way back into the city, she could feel the tension creep up her back and across her shoulders. Her tiny studio felt stifling when she unlocked the door and kicked her duffle inside, but the air outside was no better. She had to choose between hot and dirty city air or cold, clammy air-conditioning. There must be some way to live near the water, so that she could breathe fresh air and sail more often. There must be jobs out there where she didn't have to report to her ex, and where she felt like she and her colleagues had a shared philosophy. There must be a way to have love in her life.

No matter how things turned out with RJ, her life needed to change. She needed to make time for the things that brought her joy. She needed to work in a place where she could be herself. She needed to get a life.

CHAPTER SEVENTEEN

"SHE'S COMING," SAID RJ.

His dad didn't answer right away.

"Dad? You still there?"

"Are you sure?" His father's voice was gruff.

"This is Mom we're talking about," said RJ, "so there's no way to be completely sure."

"Right," said Robert. "I'll book a flight, and we'll see how it goes."

RJ decided not to mention the fact that Mom was bringing a friend.

"Sounds like your grandmother might come up as well," said Robert.

"You're kidding," said RJ. "That's amazing. I've been asking her to visit ever since I moved in, but no luck. How did you convince her?"

"I didn't, actually," said Robert. "You remember that girl Tessa? One of the triplets?"

"Tessa James?" asked RJ. Why would his father have any connection to Tessa?

"That's the one. Your grandmother was starting to act

strange, even by her standards, so I called up my old friend Don Hammond to see if he could help. At first Vi refused to talk to anybody from Hammond's outfit, but then she found out Tessa was working there and agreed to meet with her."

"Tessa met with Nana Vi?"

The more his father talked, the less sense he made. How could Tessa have met with his grandmother and not told him?

"Several times, in fact. She reported back that your grandmother was struggling with grief, but assures me that she's pulling out of it. When I talked to your grandmother a few days ago, she said she was coming up to the lake for the Fourth."

"Who, Tessa?" asked RJ.

His father sighed.

"Your grandmother. Nana Vi is coming for a visit."

"Right," said RJ. "Wow. Great news."

RJ wrapped up the call with his father as fast as he could so that he could bang his head against the wall. Maybe then all of this would make sense. Not the part about Nana Vi coming for a visit. That part was great. No, the part he worried about was the one where Tessa got involved in his family drama and kept secrets from him. The part where she met with his grandmother—multiple times, in fact—and neglected to tell him. The one where she talked with his father behind his back. He was a member of the family, too. Didn't he deserve to be a part of the conversation?

The whole thing left him feeling sick. He and Tessa had been doing so well, but then the fighting had started, and now she was keeping secrets. He knew that the time had come to end things, but something held him back. Whatever it was, he needed to get over it before someone got hurt.

∾

Tessa had always been a good girl. Growing up, she had never once landed in the principal's office. At school and later at work, she wasn't one to make waves, preferring to let her work speak for itself. Today, however, she was getting a taste of life on the naughty list, and she found the adrenaline rush intriguing. Maybe this was why her sister Mel didn't seem to mind getting in trouble.

Frankly, she was surprised she hadn't gotten the call sooner.

Dr. Hammond's secretary gestured for her to go directly into his office. Dr. Hammond sat behind his desk, looking a bit like a king holding court. Brock sat in one of the leather chairs facing the desk. He looked smug, but then, he often looked smug. The general counsel was there as well, which Tessa found oddly flattering.

"Miss James," said Mr. Hammond.

She sighed inwardly. Still no Dr. James.

"Yes, sir," she replied.

He did not invite her to sit down, which made sense because all the available chairs were taken. She was literally being called on the carpet—a very thick oriental carpet with perfectly groomed fringe at either end. She swallowed a giggle.

"Do you know why I've asked you to come here today?" began Dr. Hammond.

"Not a clue, sir," she answered honestly. She knew she was probably getting fired, but she didn't know how Brock planned to justify it.

"It has come to our attention," he began, "that you are not fully committed to your position at the Hammond Center, nor are you supportive of the new couples counseling initiative."

"May I ask what gave you that impression?" she asked.

Dr. Hammond leaned back in his chair and gestured to Brock to explain. Brock's panicked expression delighted her. He wasn't the type to prepare for a meeting, and clearly he had not expected questions. He must have expected her to go on the defensive and babble incoherently.

"You've been taking a lot of time off," he said, as if it were an accusation rather than simply a fact. "And you refused to take on additional responsibility related to launching the new center."

"That's true," she admitted. "I have been making an effort to use my vacation days. In past years, I allowed work to take over my life, and that's not healthy. This year, I'm trying to be more balanced."

"And your refusal to help?" demanded Brock.

"We talked about this, Brock," said Tessa gently. She could see him bristling when she used her professional voice on him. "You offered me an administrative role, but my passion is for client work. I would not be happy in that type of role."

"Your attitude is unacceptable," he snapped.

"As is yours," she replied.

Brock didn't have an answer to that. Instead, he gaped at her like a suit-wearing goldfish. She turned her attention to his father.

"Dr. Hammond, I offer you my resignation."

She pulled a letter from the inside pocket of her blazer and handed it to him.

"As you can see, your son and I do not work well together. Rather than allow this to become a problem, I have decided to pursue my career elsewhere. I wish you all the best on the launch of the new couples counseling program."

She observed Brock in her peripheral vision. He looked stunned, as did both the attorney and Dr. Hammond. Clearly they had expected something else to happen in today's meeting.

"My notes are all up-to-date. It should be very straightforward to transfer my clients to other counselors. I'll remove my personal effects from my office today and turn in my security card."

"There's no way I'm writing you a letter of recommendation," snapped Brock.

She turned to look at him. Was he really that self-involved? Did he think he could force her to stay, somehow blackmail her into working for him? She looked more closely at his face and realized that she had seen his expression before. This wasn't about work at all. It was about winning. It was about sailing, and RJ, and who gets the girl—as if she were the spoils of war.

She smiled, knowing that it would piss him off. He deserved whatever torture she could dish out, the ass. She hoped his new couples therapy center was an expensive failure.

"That won't be necessary," said Tessa.

"You can't go somewhere else," said Brock. "You signed a non-compete."

"Yes, I did, and I will not be violating that agreement. The non-compete laid out some very specific geographic boundaries, and I will be moving outside those boundaries. Trust me," she said, "I'll be taking a job that's as far from here as I can get."

"Not if I have anything to say about it," said Brock. He was practically sputtering with anger. "You can't just walk away from here with all that inside information about the couples counseling program. That's proprietary information. We could sue you."

"Now, Brock," she said, "I don't know what you'd sue me for. The new program is your baby. Don't downplay all your hard work."

She had him on that one. Brock opened and closed his mouth a few times before clamping it shut for good. He could either admit that she had done all the work, or he could keep his mouth shut and continue to take all the credit. In this case, his selfishness came in handy.

She smiled sweetly at him and turned her attention back to his father.

"Thank you for the experience of the last few years, sir," she said. "It's been very...educational."

Dr. Hammond looked from her to Brock and back again. He knew that there was more to the story, and he would clearly extract the truth from Brock later. The thought of Brock's future discomfort made her smile wider.

"Fine," said Dr. Hammond at last. "Today is your last day of work. You and Carl can work out the details of the separation. Keep it simple."

She nodded her agreement and turned to leave, with Carl the attorney following her out. It was an odd feeling, this heady sense of relief, but she liked it.

Today had turned out to be a good day after all.

Tessa drove too fast on her way up to the lake. The single cardboard box containing her last few personal items from work rattled around in the back seat, reminding her with each touch on the brakes that she had permanently changed course. No more Stepford wives. No more posh offices. The future stretched before her, unknown, an adventure waiting to happen. This must be what it feels like to sail on the ocean, when you can't see the far shore, when water and sky stretch out before you to meet at the horizon, and you could sail all day without meeting another soul. Just thinking about it made her blood sing. She put the window down and let the wind dance in her hair.

From now on, her life would be different, both professionally and personally. On the personal front, she knew exactly where she wanted to start. Clearly RJ wasn't ready for a relationship that required work, but they could start small. She had already shown him that a small-scale fight could be overcome. It didn't automatically spell doom. Maybe Sunny and Will could show him that some relationships can recover from a bigger trauma. She was rooting for Sunny on this one.

It was still early in the afternoon, so when Tessa rolled into town, she headed for RJ's office rather than his house. As she parked, she was surprised to see her parents' car parked a few spots down. Lucy's Diner had already closed for the day, and there really wasn't much else here, except...

Her eyes turned to the law office just as the front door opened and her parents stepped out. They chatted briefly with RJ, who leaned against the doorway looking a little too serious and a little too professional, despite the board shorts and the flip-flops. It wasn't the collar on the sporty polo shirt that did the trick. The stubble and the wild hair were actively working against him. It was his body language.

She closed her eyes and tried to be invisible as her parents said their good-byes, shook hands with RJ, and turned toward their car, but it was no use. Her car stood out like a beacon on the otherwise empty street. She sighed and opened her eyes, just in time to see RJ's jaw tighten and her mother's look of dismay. Even her father looked unhappy to see her.

The adrenaline high came crashing down around her ears. The air whooshed out of her lungs as if someone—in this case, RJ—had punched her in the gut. There was only one reason that people talked to RJ in his office, and Tessa couldn't wrap her head around it. It made no sense. Her parents were happy. Her parents were fine. Things had been weird, yes, but not bad. Not toxic. Not nearly bad enough to talk to RJ.

Without thinking, she threw the car in reverse and backed out of the parking space. She didn't squeal the tires, although it was tempting. She held herself tightly under control, worried that if she let go, even for a second, she would hurt someone or something. Very carefully, she drove home, keeping the speedometer under twenty-five miles an hour the whole way. She coasted down the driveway and rolled to a stop by the back door. She put the car in park, shut off the engine, and held on to the steering wheel, breathing in and breathing out, until she felt more calm, more in control. Her parents hadn't followed her down the driveway yet. They were probably still with RJ, frantically talking through their options, asking his advice on how to break the news to the family.

He would be good at that. He was good at endings.

Quietly, carefully, she opened the door of the car and slid out, surprised that the world around her looked completely normal, completely unaffected by the whirlwind inside her. She let the car door swing gently shut and walked in to the back of the house. She could feel the tears and the rage battling it out somewhere inside her ribcage. It made her ache, but she refused to give in. Instead, she put on the kettle and kept her hands busy preparing a tea tray. Perhaps the British were right in thinking that a spot of tea could fix any problem. At least the activity gave her something to do other than smash the dishes and kick holes in the drywall.

Calm. Controlled. Careful.

As the kettle began to whistle, she heard the crunch of tires on the gravel. She carried the tea tray to the kitchen table and sat down, feeling ferociously calm. She folded her hands and waited.

Her parents entered cautiously, as if they weren't sure what kind of reception they would receive. They seemed relieved when she didn't shout at them, but exchanged a worried glance at her silence. That was fine. Better for them to be worried. Her unnatural silence should make them uncomfortable. They should feel compelled to fill the silence with talking.

"Are you okay, sweetheart?" asked Dora, moving slowly toward the kitchen table and taking a seat across from her.

Tessa thought about saying no, but that would be childish.

If she was honest with herself and them, she really did want to know what was going on.

"I just want to know why," she said. "Why now, after all this time? You guys are good together."

Dora moved over to the next chair before answering, making room for Luke to sit down as well. He looked suddenly older.

"We are good together, aren't we?" asked Dora, looking fondly at Luke. He managed a smile for her, but it was a tense smile. He was nervous. Tessa could see that now. "When we first got married, we weren't sure how long we would make it," Dora admitted.

Tessa looked sharply at her mother.

"Why not?" she asked.

"Because we were both in love with other people," Dora answered matter-of-factly.

Tessa didn't know how to respond. The plain and simple answer shocked her. In one sentence, her mother had destroyed Tessa's understanding of their marriage.

Dora laughed.

"You should see your face, sweetheart. Is it that difficult to imagine your father and me? We were so young. I was only twenty-one when you were born. Can you imagine having six-year-old triplets right now?"

Tessa let out a choked laugh. Her parents sat across from her at the same old kitchen table, only they were strangers, cheerfully admitting to a lifetime of lies.

Well, her mother was cheerful. Luke, not so much.

"If you were both in love with other people, why did you marry each other?" asked Tessa, still struggling to put all the pieces together.

Dora hesitated. Tessa could sense that she chose her words very carefully.

"In my case," she began, glancing quickly at Luke, "I was in love with a married man, and his wife was my friend. I couldn't...there was no way. Your father knew about my situation, and he didn't think I was crazy. He was in a bit of the same boat himself."

She smiled wryly at Luke and shrugged. He sagged back in his chair.

"You were in love with a married woman?" asked Tessa, trying to read her father's face. His reaction didn't make sense. He wouldn't meet her eyes.

"He was in love with someone who was on a very self-destructive path," offered Dora when Luke remained silent. "We were both hurting, we both needed a friend, and we were both ready to build a life. We simply decided to do it together."

Tessa ignored her mother and kept her eyes on her father. There was something he wasn't saying, and she wanted to know what it was.

"Dad," she said.

Finally he looked at her.

"We needed each other," he said, deflecting her real question. Tessa followed her father's helpless glance at her mother, and saw something flicker in her mother's eyes.

"Why?" Tessa kept her voice low and calm, using every ounce of her training to stay focused.

Dora and Luke stared at each other for a long minute, then Dora nodded briefly, giving in, it seemed, because she turned to meet Tessa's accusing stare.

"We couldn't let go," she said, "but we couldn't go back, either. We were useless to anybody but each other."

All her life, her parents had told them a giant pack of lies. She tried to hold on to the shreds of her identity, but the fairy tale that had cloaked her all her life fell shredded at her feet.

"So you married out of friendship," said Tessa.

Dora nodded. Tessa could feel the tension creeping across her shoulders as she turned to Luke.

"And you walked away from love."

Her voice broke on the last word, but she didn't cry. She refused to cry. Her parents sat speechless across the table, concerned about her reaction, perhaps, but not bothering to deny the basic truth of her words.

She stood abruptly.

"I need to go," she said, then turned and walked out the back door, leaving her parents and their worries and their questions behind. She couldn't fix this, but she could sure as hell place blame, and she knew exactly where to find the responsible party.

"WHAT HAVE YOU DONE?"

RJ jumped a foot when Tessa burst through the kitchen door.

"What are you talking about?" he asked.

He had been sitting at the kitchen table, rubbing his face and wishing that the hot cup of coffee sitting in front of him could scald away the memories of that summer his parents self-destructed. Working with Dora and Luke James was hard. They were close in age to his parents, and once upon a time they had all been summer friends. Comparing the civility of their separation with the ugliness of his parents' experience, he found himself getting angry with his parents all over again.

Which was good, because it helped him forget that he was also angry with Tessa.

She was breathing hard, as if she had run full-out to get here, or maybe was about to cry, or—judging by the look on her face—both. She was pissed. At him. He understood that much. He just had no idea why. He had heard of this happening to other men, but usually he was so attuned to the women around him that they didn't take him by surprise.

"My parents," she practically spat the words at him. He stayed quiet, waiting to hear what she had to say. Until he knew what Dora and Luke had shared with her, he couldn't talk about their situation, no matter how much he might want to explain.

"What about your parents?" he asked cautiously.

She laughed, a short, harsh sound that made him tense.

"Oh, I think you know full well what I'm here about. How could you? They've been happily married for almost thirty years, and over the course of a couple of quick meetings you're going to help them take that apart? No discussion? No reflection? No, 'Gosh, this is a big step, maybe we should think about it for thirty fucking seconds before we undo the work of a lifetime'?"

She wrapped her arms around her stomach. She looked the way he had felt, all those years ago, when his family had exploded around him. She was hurting, and there was nothing he could do to make it better.

Tessa thought she might be sick. She held on tight to her stomach, pushing back the nausea, and tried to control her breathing. It didn't help. She was so upset that she couldn't calm down, couldn't stop the heaving that was one hysterical laugh away from total meltdown. She had trusted him. She had hoped that maybe, if things worked out for Sunny, that he might start to believe relationships can grow and change and even heal. They weren't all doomed. And now...now he had shoved all that aside and started dismantling her own family.

He might as well have taken an axe and chopped off her legs.

"What exactly did they tell you?" he asked cautiously.

"What exactly...?" she sputtered. "You're going to lawyer-talk your way out of this?"

"What did they say?" he insisted, and she threw her hands in the air.

"Does it matter what words they used?" she cried. "They're separating. Step one toward getting a divorce. Dad's moving to Nashville. Mom's staying here. They're throwing in the towel after all this time because of *you*."

"No," he snapped back, "not because of me."

She took a step back when he shoved back from the table and stood to face her. He had switched from defense to offense in a heartbeat, and she hadn't expected it. This was all his fault. It had to be his fault.

"Then why?" she demanded.

"That's not my story to tell," he said firmly.

She sucked in a breath.

"You know, don't you?" she asked.

"Know what?"

"Everything. They trusted you with their secrets before they trusted their own family."

"Oh, that's rich, coming from you," he said.

"What are you talking about?"

He crossed his arms and the look he gave her was more than just angry. It was cold.

"How's my grandmother doing? Seen her lately?"

She flinched.

"What, no explanation?" he asked.

"I'm not at liberty to discuss it," said Tessa. She crossed her arms, feeling defensive even though she knew she was in the right on this.

"So she shared secrets with you rather than with her family?" His voice had a menacing edge to it.

"I'm not at liberty to discuss it," she repeated.

He spread his arms as if to say, 'How does it feel to be on the other side of this one?' She nearly smacked him.

"The situations are completely different," she said. "I heal families. I heal relationships. You destroy them. I can't believe my parents went to you."

She could feel her breath catching in her chest, like she had scared away the wind and couldn't make the air come back inside her lungs. Tears stung her eyes but she refused to let them fall.

"Why wouldn't they come to me first? What are you to them?"

His mouth tightened, and his eyes got darker. Her questions were making him even more angry, but she couldn't stop.

"A friend, maybe," he bit out. "A trusted advisor. A neutral third party. Take your pick." He spread his arms wide, shrugging dramatically. "I'm a lawyer, Tess. People confide in me all the time. They may not tell me about their difficult childhood, but they ask me to help solve their problems now. Today. And I help."

"But what if it's the wrong kind of help?" Her voice was suspiciously high. She was going to lose it, and soon. His voice, when he replied, had a note of finality to it that chilled her to the bone.

"That's not for me to decide," he said.

"Some relationships are worth fighting for," she whispered fiercely.

"And others you need to let go."

"So that's it?" she demanded. "You let go?" Her voice gained strength. She had wanted to know his secret, how he could get involved with so many women and yet emerge from a breakup with his emotions untouched. Now she knew. There was no secret. You just let go.

"When we start making each other unhappy instead of happy, then it's time to let go," he answered. "*Before* we start hurting each other."

A whirlwind of jumbled thoughts and emotions tore through her. The intimacies they had shared, the laughter—none of it mattered. Now that things had gotten tough, he would let go. For weeks she had been floating, trying to live in the moment like he did, knowing that their time together would end but imagining that it would happen later. Someday.

Someday had arrived. There were no more moments to be shared. They had reached the end of the line.

She cleared her throat, which had grown uncomfortably tight.

"Well, then," she said carefully, "let me give this a try." She swallowed past the lump in her throat and continued. "This... thing between us has grown painful, and I think it's time to let go." The tears were coming, but damned if she would let them fall in front of RJ. "Good-bye, RJ."

She walked out the kitchen door and didn't look back.

RJ didn't know how long he stood there, staring at the kitchen door and willing her to walk back through it. He didn't run after her. There was a part of him—a surprisingly big part of him—that wanted to do just that, but RJ knew better than to let that needy part of himself win. He knew how the story would end. He would run after her, beg forgiveness, tell her whatever she needed to hear to give them a second chance, and then the cycle would begin again. A honeymoon, another fight, another promise. Each time the fights would get bigger, the promises easier to break. And then one day, she would leave for good, and he would be alone, only the hole in his heart would be much, much bigger. Better to suffer today, with only a small wound. The small ones were easier to patch up.

He forced himself to turn away from the door and walk into the living room. He flopped down on the couch, staring unseeing out at the lake until the sun set and he was alone in the darkness. He breathed deep, waiting for the ache in his chest to ease, but there was no relief. There was no peace. He closed his eyes and cursed.

He didn't know how to let Tessa go.

CHAPTER NINETEEN

Dora found Tessa at the troll bridge. It had always been Tessa's thinking place, but tonight the twilight over the lake and the cool evening breeze did little to soothe Tessa's hurts. She was still in shock, really, not quite able to process what had happened with RJ. She expected that she would pass through the stages of grief. Her relationship with him had been brief but so very intense that she would mourn it like any other loss.

Knowing the process did not make it any easier.

When she heard footsteps, she looked up and was surprised to see her mother. Tessa let her forehead drop to her knees and said nothing. She felt her mother sit down beside her on the grass and the gentle touch of a hand on her back. Her mother had always been very good at offering silent comfort.

So wasn't this a karmic kick in the ass? There was nothing she could do to fix her parents, and there was nothing she could do to fix things with RJ. The only thing left to fix was herself. She lifted her head to look out over the water, then closed her eyes to feel the cool air caress her face. She longed to be empty. To feel nothing at all.

"We were friends," Dora said. "Friends first and always, and for a long time that was enough."

Her mother's words picked up the thread of their earlier conversation, but it took a moment for their meaning to filter through Tessa's consciousness.

Friends.

All this time, her model for marriage had been based on a mirage. Not that she didn't believe her parents. Yes, they were friends, and they had clearly sought comfort in each other's arms. She and her sisters were living proof of that. But even after thirty years of friendship, they were ready to part ways in search of something more than friendship. They each wanted to find love, and they were willing to admit to each other that friendship alone was not enough.

So where did this leave Tessa? She had always imagined that one day she would find the right guy and have a marriage as solid and steady as her parents' example. That was her fairy tale—no fairy godmother required. Without realizing it, she had been searching for friendship and calling it love. She had run from passion because of its power to destroy, but what if passion also had the power to create? What if she had learned the wrong lesson?

Maybe she should feel free. She could define relationships on her own terms, without the expectation of doing 'better' than her parents, or even 'as good as.' But she didn't feel free, just lost.

"You okay?" asked Dora.

"I don't know," answered Tessa honestly. "I guess I'm confused. If you guys aren't an example of a strong marriage, then who is?"

"Oh, sweetheart," said Dora. "There are a million ways to build a marriage. Every person is different."

"Like snowflakes," said Tessa. In her work, she tended to

focus on the things that couples had in common, the critical elements of a successful relationship.

"Exactly," said Dora. "You put two unique people together in a relationship, and they're going to build something that suits them, even if it makes no sense to anybody else."

"But what if it doesn't last?" asked Tessa.

Dora shrugged. "Some people build for the long haul, others are only pitching a tent for a little while. There's no universal law that says a relationship is a failure if it doesn't last forever. People grow and change. Sometimes they outgrow each other, and that's okay."

Tessa rubbed her face, wishing she had heard some of these pearls of wisdom from her mother during her formative years. It was turning out to be very difficult to absorb them now. Dora sounded too much like RJ, and that made her chest hurt.

"And now?" asked Tessa. "After all these years, why part ways?" This was the part she really struggled with. Why end a perfectly good marriage?

"Because it's time," said Dora simply.

"Time for what?" asked Tessa.

"A fresh start," answered Dora. "Your father and I promised each other that we would stay together until the three of you were all grown up. We've kept that promise, and then some. You three are so strong and kind and brave. We couldn't be more proud."

Tessa could feel the prick of tears again, and she didn't bother to hold them in. If she couldn't cry in front of her mother, when could she?

"We kept each other company after you three were launched mostly because we weren't sure what we wanted to do next. We had grown very comfortable with each other over the years, and there were times when we talked about staying together. But then…"

"Then what?"

"Circumstances changed," said Dora.

"Does this have something to do with New York?" asked Tessa. "And Nashville?"

Dora nodded. "It's complicated. My friend is dying, and she wants me to be there for her husband after she's gone."

Tessa sucked in a breath.

"And you're thinking about it?"

Dora lifted a shoulder in a half shrug.

"Only one way to find out if there's still something there. It's been a long time."

"Wow," said Tessa. "You're right, that's..."

"Complicated," agreed Dora.

"And Dad is okay with this?"

At this, Dora smiled.

"You should ask him," she said. "He has some plans of his own."

They sat together in silence for a few minutes, then Dora slowly climbed to her feet, stretching the stiffness out of her legs, and brushed bits of grass off her long skirt.

"Come home soon," she said softly, smoothing back Tessa's hair one last time. "Dinner is almost ready."

Tessa nodded absently, keeping her eyes on the water as the sound of her mother's footsteps faded away. Her thoughts had started swirling again. She would need time to sort it all out.

The wind rustled through the treetops and teased loose a few strands of Tessa's hair. She pushed them out of her face, thinking about all the different kinds of relationships she had seen in the course of her work, and wondering if she had ever really known what she was talking about. What business did she have giving people advice when she couldn't even sort out her own feelings, or run her own love life? She had the sinking feeling that RJ might be right about relationships, or at least not completely wrong. Not all relationships last forever.

It was times like these that she wished Lucky were here.

She missed that crazy dog. He had never seemed to mind when she didn't have everything figured out. He had been happy to sit by her side for as long as it took to figure things out. In this case, figuring things out could take all night, so she stood up and rolled her shoulders. She could do the rest of her thinking back at home.

As she turned back toward the house, she smiled to herself. She might not have resolved any of her big issues, but she had figured out one very important thing. She needed a dog.

Luke didn't join Tessa and Dora for dinner, so afterward Tessa knocked on the half-open door of his office and poked her head inside. He looked up from the music notation spread across the desk and waved her in.

"What's up, Tess?" he asked, motioning her toward the recliner in the corner. She curled up in the comfy chair before answering.

"Sorry about freaking out before," she began. "I'm calmer now, but I have questions." She paused, watching his reaction. He had become very still, and she wondered why he would be nervous about talking with her. Maybe he had grown too comfortable with the family narrative. "Will you tell me your story?" she asked softly.

He leaned back in his chair and steepled his fingers in front of his mouth.

"I'm not really sure where to start," he said. "I've only ever talked about this stuff with your mom."

"Well, we're all grown up now," she responded, "and I for one would really like to understand why you two are separating after all these years together. You always seemed so...solid."

He smiled. "We did well together, didn't we?"

Tessa smiled back. "Yeah, you did. So why screw up a good thing?"

"It's complicated." Luke sighed and ran a hand through his thinning hair.

"That's what Mom said."

Luke shook his head and looked to the ceiling for help.

"I just need to figure out where to start," he said.

"How about the part where you fell in love with someone other than Mom?" Tessa suggested. "Who was she?"

Luke rubbed a hand across his mouth, still not meeting her eyes.

"Dad?"

Finally he looked at her, and she didn't like the worry she saw on his face.

"That's the complicated part," he said. "The question isn't 'Who was she?' It's 'Who was he?'"

Tessa stared blankly at her father for a full minute before she managed to say, "Oh."

Luke actually laughed at that.

"Is that how you respond when your clients tell you something shocking?" he asked. "Because if it is, you need to work on that."

She shook herself. *Get a grip!* But her mind was still reeling from the news, and she couldn't put a coherent thought together.

"No, I don't...I mean...arrrgghhhh! Dad, you're not my client, and I'm not in work mode right now, and I'm just...startled, is all," she said. "Is this how you told Mom? Because, I mean, seriously, you need to work on your 'coming out' speech."

He laughed again, almost as if the relief of finally telling her was making him giddy. Meanwhile, she was chasing her thoughts around in circles trying to figure out if her whole life had been littered with clues that she never noticed before.

"This is why you've been spending so much time in Nashville?" she demanded. He nodded.

"Your friend Zeke?" she asked, and her father nodded again, smiling slowly in a way that made her very uncomfortable. Her father was head over heels in love with a guy named Zeke from Nashville. Her head was going to explode.

"Wow," she breathed.

"I know," he said. "It's a lot to take in."

"So start at the beginning," she said, grasping for her professional calm and wrapping it around her like a blanket, even as she pulled up her legs and wrapped her arms around them, resting her chin on her knees. "Tell me the story."

He smiled, as if he could tell that she going into work mode, but he didn't seem to mind. He was ready to talk.

"I knew in high school," he began, "but I never told my family. We lived in farm country down in southern Illinois, not an easy place to be...different. I think Gramps always knew. He and I spent a lot of time together playing music. When my dad figured it out, he wouldn't speak to me anymore. He kicked me out the day after high school graduation. Mom did what she could to find me some getting-started money, and I headed up to Chicago."

"Where you met Zeke?" prompted Tessa.

As he told his story, she couldn't shake the feeling that it was all a dream. Her father was a schoolteacher, for goodness' sake. When he finally caught up to the story of his first meeting with Dora, she was surprised that it was still the same story from her childhood. Her parents had simply embellished the true story with a sprinkling of true love and happily ever after, and she and her sisters had been more than willing to believe.

"I'm sorry that I got so upset earlier," said Tessa softly. "I really want you both to be happy, and for that I thought you needed to be together. I was wrong."

"Are you sure you're okay with this?" asked Luke. "We didn't mean to spring it on you. If you hadn't seen us coming out of RJ's office..."

She closed her eyes, blocking out the image of RJ that immediately sprang to mind.

"I'm fine, Dad," she said, opening her eyes. "Really."

"Don't be angry with RJ," he said. "After all, we went to him."

Her father was too perceptive. She could forgive her parents much more easily than her lover. Ex-lover. She sighed.

"Things aren't going to work out with RJ," she said, "but it has nothing to do with you and Mom. He's a love-'em-and-leave-'em kind of guy, and I find I'm not very good at that sort of thing."

"Good," said Luke gruffly. "If RJ isn't smart enough to stick around, then he doesn't deserve you."

Tess went from calm to mush in two seconds. She sniffled.

"That's very sweet, Dad," she said. "And on that note, I think I need to get some sleep. It's been a hell of a day."

She unfolded her legs and climbed out of the deep cushions, walking around the side of the big desk to give her dad a hug.

"Thanks for explaining," she whispered as he gave her a big squeeze. "It's a lot easier to accept when I understand why."

He squeezed harder, then let go.

"It's a lot easier to do," he said, "knowing that you don't hate us."

She sniffled again.

"Never," she said firmly. "We're family."

RJ must have fallen asleep on the couch, because the clatter of the back door opening woke him up. His eyes snapped open and his heart stopped. She had come back. She was going to give him a chance, and he was not going to screw it up. But then the kitchen light flashed on and an all-too-familiar voice snapped him out of his fantasy.

"RJ, honey, I'm home."

He groaned. He had completely forgotten that his mother was coming today.

"Cute place," said a male voice, and RJ pounded his forehead a few times. He had also forgotten that his mother was bringing a friend.

RJ woke at first light and tiptoed down the stairs. Thankfully, he was the first one up. He wasn't sure he was ready to handle his mother and her boyfriend this early in the day. He started the coffee and then wandered out to the porch to watch the sunrise.

He couldn't decide if he felt relieved or disappointed that Walt had agreed to crew for him today. Walt's foot wasn't quite healed, but he was sick of sitting on his ass, so he had jumped at the chance to get back out on the water. RJ should really count himself lucky. He hadn't wanted Tessa to show up out of some twisted sense of obligation. Maybe she could take that brand of torture, but he was man enough to admit that he couldn't. Maybe she had been relieved to get his text. He would never know. She hadn't even bothered to respond. He had felt oddly voyeuristic watching the message status change from 'Delivered' to 'Read.'

Walt would probably be clumsy and slow, but RJ didn't really care. It wasn't as if he and Tessa were on track to sweep the season. Another loss wouldn't bother him. He had already lost the most important thing, anyway.

The weirdest thing about the unexpected breakup with Tessa was how bad it felt to be on the other side. He had to respect her. She had kept her word and ended it cleanly. Sure, things had gotten tense, but he'd seen worse. This morning's text was the only communication he had allowed himself, and it hadn't been easy. More than once he'd found himself staring at his phone, about to call her. He needed to get a grip and accept the fact that their...whatever it was they had been doing, it was over. She had made the decision to end it, and he would have to live with that.

Still sucked, though.

He would have liked more time with her. Maybe, if her parents had gone to someone else for help, they would have found a way to make it work. He would have gotten over the whole secret-keeping thing eventually. Maybe they could have broken his three-month relationship record. Maybe...

He needed to stop thinking about this or he was going to go crazy. All the maybes in the world were not going to bring Tessa back. They had agreed to these ground rules from the beginning, and he couldn't fault her for sticking to them.

Or could he?

She was the one who believed in working things out. She was the fricking queen of second chances. So what if she had tried to play this round by his rules? What if he wanted to play by hers?

Hell, if his parents were going to give it a second try after nineteen years apart, then anybody could do it.

Even him.

"I can't believe I missed all the drama."

Tessa woke to the sound of Mel's voice, followed by a bounce as her sister landed on the bed beside her. She burrowed her face into the pillow, hoping that this was only a weird dream, but no such luck. Mel poked her a few times in the back and Tessa growled at her.

"Give me a break," said Mel. "I got here last night and you were already sleeping. I ended up going to bed early. Now it's morning, the sun woke me up, and I'm not even a morning person. Stop hiding out and come swimming with me. I'll even let you gloat."

At that, Tessa turned her head and peeked at Mel out of the corner of her eye.

"You heard me," said Mel. "You get to gloat. You had a 'feeling' about Mom and Dad, and yeah, you were right. But no gloating until we're in the water. Be downstairs in five or I'm dragging you out."

With that, Mel wiggled off the bed and left, presumably to get her suit on. Tessa rolled onto her back and stared at the ceiling. She did not want to face a new day. She wanted to go back to sleep so that she didn't have to deal with the first day of the rest of her life. Unfortunately, her sister was relentless. She would have no peace this morning. With a sigh Tessa rolled out of bed and went on a hunt for her swimsuit.

She could hardly believe that tomorrow was the Fourth of July. Not that she should be surprised at how quickly things with RJ had flamed out. Really, she should be surprised at how quickly things had gotten serious. She did her best to put him out of her mind, but quickly realized that was going to be impossible. She couldn't put on a swimsuit without thinking about their time in the bathtub. She couldn't jump in the lake without thinking about her vow not to go in the water again until at least the Fourth. In fact, she couldn't be anywhere near the lake without thinking of him, so she finally gave up and let the memories come out to play.

The first shock of cold lake water was the worst. It seemed even colder than the day they had capsized, but that might be due to the fact that she was wearing a bikini instead of a windbreaker. There was no barrier at all between her skin and the frigid water. She and Mel raced to the Slow No Wake buoy and back. Mel won, of course. She was more alert. She was also more competitive. They swam over to the raft and hauled themselves out of the water to warm up, but the early morning sun didn't do much to help. They stayed anyway, bobbing up and down with the waves. The skiers were out in force this morning. Apparently Mel and Tessa weren't the only ones taking advantage of the calm before the Fourth.

"How much did Mom and Dad tell you last night?" asked Tessa.

"God, I hope it was everything. If there's more I don't know if I can take it."

"I don't think it's really hit me yet," said Tessa. "All my life, when I thought about what marriage should be like—what I wanted it to be like for me—I always assumed it would look like theirs, and now they tell us they've been faking it. What am I supposed to do with that?"

"Lucky for me, I'm not really a white-picket-fence kind of girl," said Mel with a laugh. "This new story is actually much easier for me to understand than the deathly dull Happily Ever After thing."

"What do you mean?" asked Tessa.

"I've always had trouble believing in forever and 'til death do us part.' Maybe that worked when people barely made it to fifty, but now? Let's say I'm skeptical. I'm not holding out for Happily Ever After. I'd be content with Happy For Now."

Tessa didn't answer. She couldn't figure out if the idea was horrifying or freeing. Relationships grew and changed over time. She knew that, and she had helped couples navigate those changes. But after spending time with RJ, she had begun to question whether or not she understood the full range of possibilities. She saw only the people who wanted to stay together and were willing to put in the effort. RJ saw only the people who knew it was over and were ready to say good-bye. These were two complementary pieces of a much larger picture. Neither one made sense by itself.

"I think I screwed up," said Tessa.

"With Mom and Dad?" asked Mel.

"No, with RJ."

"What happened with sexy sailor?"

"Did Mom and Dad happen to mention that he was helping them with the separation?" asked Tessa.

Mel cocked her head to one side as she tried to remember.

"I don't think so," she said. "The wild news just kept coming, and I didn't stop them to ask about logistics."

Tessa told her how she had kicked things off yesterday afternoon, and how the rest of the day had unfolded.

"By the time I got to RJ, I was a mess," admitted Tessa. She thunked her forehead down on her knees.

"How bad was it?" asked Mel. "Did you break anything?"

Tessa laughed.

"Nothing like that," she said. "But before I left I told him it was all his fault and I broke up with him."

"Bummer," said Mel. "You're much nicer when you're getting laid."

"I'm pretty sure there's no going back. He's not exactly the type to work through relationship issues."

"I don't know about that," said Mel. "Did you try groveling? Naked?"

"Um, no."

"Worth a shot," said Mel. She stood and stretched, then bent down to prepare for her dive. "Last one to the pier has to make breakfast." Mel was off the raft like a shot and halfway there before Tessa could even brace herself for the backsplash.

She had screwed up, no doubt about it. It wasn't RJ's fault that her parents wanted to split up after all these years, and it certainly wasn't wrong of him to keep quiet about it until they were ready to break the news on their own. She needed to get over herself and apologize. Possibly naked. She'd have to think about that one.

As she swam at a more leisurely pace than her sister back to the pier, she resolved to make a fresh start. If she wanted RJ to fight for a future together, she needed to show him how it was done.

CHAPTER TWENTY

RJ PLOTTED HIS STRATEGY WHILE HE DRANK HIS COFFEE, THEN took off as soon as the local stores opened up. He was a man with a mission, and he would not be stopped.

When he got back from running his special errand, he found his mother cooking pancakes. He paused for a moment in the back doorway, wondering if the last twenty-four hours had even been real. Maybe it was all a weird dream. Nancy said something and it must have been a joke, because her boyfriend laughed. RJ rubbed his forehead, but it had no effect. His mother really was in his kitchen, making pancakes with her 'friend,' Ken. Not only was Ken named after the anatomically incorrect doll, he also looked like Barbie's boyfriend. It wouldn't be so surreal if Ken were anywhere near his mother's age, but sadly he was not. Ken was maybe twenty-five. Maybe.

He poured himself a cup of coffee and sat down at the table. Might as well roll with the craziness. He would need some crazy if he was going to pull off his plan.

"RJ, honey, do you want a pancake?"

He had to think about it for a minute. Was he hungry? Yes.

"Sure," he said. As a bonus, if his mouth was full, he wouldn't be expected to talk.

His mother dropped a fresh pancake onto a plate and set it in front of him, then turned to see what the commotion at the back door was all about. The door burst open and two small whirlwinds blew in, followed by a more subdued Sunny. RJ couldn't help but laugh as he pushed back from the table. Time to face the tiny invaders.

"My angels," crowed his mother, dropping the spatula on the counter and swooping the boys into a giant hug. "I'm so glad you could come today. We're going to have a very good time."

As his mother stood up to greet Sunny, RJ couldn't help but notice the way she used her grandchildren as tiny human shields. He realized abruptly that this was her master plan. If she had to run the gauntlet of old friends and neighbors, she would do it with grandchildren in tow. And instead of towing them behind her, she would be hustling them along in front of her.

Brilliant. Machiavellian, even.

His mother introduced Sunny to Ken. RJ met Sunny's bewildered gaze and shrugged. Leave it to their mother to knock them sideways even after all these years. Before giving the boys their obligatory upside-down thrills, he gave Sunny a quick squeeze.

"You okay?" he whispered against her ear.

"Not sure yet," she murmured back, "but at least Will and I are talking. Ask me again in six months. Oh, and by the way—"

Over Sunny's shoulder, RJ saw one last person entering the kitchen.

"—I brought a visitor."

"Nana!" he cried. He released his sister and caught Nana Vi in a big hug. A few years ago he would have lifted her off the ground and spun her around, but now he took more care. She had taken a hit when she lost Pops, and it showed.

"Now stop fussing," said Nana as she pulled out of his arms. "I'm not at death's door, and I'm not crazy. You all need to back off and give me some space."

RJ backed off and saluted, earning himself a sharp look.

"Don't sass me, young man, or there will be consequences."

"Yes, ma'am," he said, all innocence.

She swatted his arm and moved past him into the kitchen, stopping short when she saw Ken with his arm around Nancy.

"Hello, Vi," said his mother. She shot RJ a meaningful look, clearly irritated that he hadn't warned her about Vi's visit, but he just smiled.

"Nancy," said Nana Vi. "Who's your little friend?"

Before his mother could explode, clueless Ken stepped forward to offer his hand to Nana Vi.

"I'm Ken, ma'am," he said. "Pleased to meet you. Nancy invited me up for the long weekend."

Vi shook his hand, then gave him a pat on the cheek.

"Why don't you make this old lady a Bloody Mary," she said. She met RJ's eyes across the room. "I have a feeling I'm going to need it."

"Of course," said Ken, looking to Nancy and RJ for help. "Do we have any tomato juice?"

Nancy sighed and began hunting through the cupboards. RJ settled Nana Vi at the kitchen table and sat down beside her.

"You look good, Nana," he said. "Dad had me worried."

She patted his hand.

"Your father is an idiot," she said briskly. "I gave up on him years ago."

"But he said that you—"

"I miss my Robert," she said. "Simple as that. I was dealing with it in my own way and your father did not understand. But not to worry. Tessa got everything straightened out, and Robert

Junior and I had a nice...discussion about the whole thing. There may be hope for him after all."

RJ's skepticism must have showed on his face, because Nana Vi gave him a smack on the cheek.

"People change, sweetheart. Learn to roll with it."

Ken interrupted their conversation to present Nana Vi's Bloody Mary with a flourish.

When the dust had settled, RJ finished his pancake as slowly as possible, keeping his mouth full and just watching everyone. Oscar and Huck were the only reason that it all worked. They required so much attention—and so many teddy-bear pancakes, of course—that it eased the awkwardness among the adults.

A part of him ached as he watched the boys enjoying all the attention. Just the idea that they might have to deal with the same bullshit that still plagued him and Sunny was enough to make him want to put his fist through a wall. He didn't, of course, and he didn't plan to bug Sunny again about divorce. If both she and Will wanted things to work, then maybe—despite all the evidence he had seen to the contrary—they would find a way. He was surprised how much he wanted to believe it.

What he really wanted was to understand how his grand-parents had stayed together for so many years, literally until death had parted them. He couldn't help smiling as he watched Nana Vi suck down her Bloody Mary. She had earned the right to do whatever she wanted, but it was barely ten o'clock in the morning. He hoped the drink was a weak one.

Now that his anger had worn off, he felt guilty about the way he had thrown Vi in Tessa's face yesterday. He should be the last person in the world to resent someone for keeping client information confidential, but the idea that she had kept a secret from him—especially a secret that big—had really rankled. If he was going to be brutally honest in the privacy of his own mind, it had also scared the shit out of him. He had never been involved with someone who had the power to hurt him, but somehow, without even realizing it, he had handed that power to Tessa.

After breakfast, RJ volunteered to do cleanup—yet another tactic to avoid conversation with his mother and Ken. Sunny and Nana Vi took the boys outside to see if there were any other small people looking to play. Although it was still the day before the Fourth of July, many families would arrive today, and soon the neighborhood would be crawling with children.

He also needed to stay alert for his dad's arrival. True to form, his father had neglected to say exactly when he planned to show up. It must be nice to be the center of the known universe.

Unfortunately, his attempt to avoid his mother and Ken backfired when the two of them decided to settle in at the kitchen table for another cup of coffee. He was trapped. Shaking his head in defeat, he began scrubbing industriously and tried to ignore the odd couple behind him.

He had made it through about half the dishes when three sharp raps sounded on the kitchen door, immediately followed by the grand entrance of RJ's father. RJ mentally thanked the powers that be that his hands were wet and soapy. He gave his dad a nod in greeting, but continued washing up. He did glance over his shoulder to see his mother's reaction. She had managed to avoid the man for fifteen years, which was no small feat. He had already resigned himself to the fact that she would be pissed at him for facilitating this meeting. Maybe, if he was very lucky, she would stop speaking to him altogether. He could use a break.

Her lips tightened at the sight of her almost-ex-husband. She shot RJ a look that would have paralyzed him as a child, but he didn't feel even the smallest pang of guilt. She had hidden behind her children for too long. He was done. She couldn't use him as her human shield anymore.

"Robert," said his mother. "How lovely to see you after all these years."

Poor Ken looked back and forth between RJ's parents, clearly confused. Did he have any clue who this was? Had his mother even mentioned his father? She had probably said that he was dead.

"Nancy," he replied. "You haven't changed a bit."

Now that was laying it on a little thick. Even RJ could see that time had eroded her sparkle, but apparently his father remembered his mother all too well. Compliments, no matter how far-fetched, were very effective. RJ could see his mother soften in spite of her anger.

"And who's this?" asked his father, indicating Ken with his gesture and looking to RJ for an explanation. Given Ken's youth, it was probably a logical assumption that he was a friend of RJ's. His mother gave him a pleading look, as if she hoped that he would lie to cover her ass, but that wasn't going to happen. RJ kept his mouth shut. He was not going to let his mom weasel out of this one. She gave him another glare, then straightened her back and lifted her nose.

"Robert, this is Ken," she said crisply. "He's with me."

His father sized up the competition as they shook hands. Ken made the mistake of saying 'sir' to acknowledge the introduction. Nice manners, but he had just made Robert the alpha dog in the room. RJ sighed. Poor Ken had no idea what was going on, and RJ was too softhearted to leave him hanging out to dry.

"Hey Ken," he said. "Could you do me a favor?"

"Sure," said Ken. He looked more than eager to get away from the weird vibes in the room. "What do you need?"

"I just realized that I forgot the hamburger and hot dog buns. Would you mind doing a store run? Maybe grab some extra beer while you're there?"

"Sure, man," said Ken. He looked relieved. "We passed the store on the way into town. I can find it again."

He was out the door in a flash. Now if only RJ could think of a good excuse to make his own escape. Only a few dishes to go, and he could probably fake a check on Sunny.

"What the hell are you doing here, Robert?"

Too late.

"Why Nancy, darling, I'm here to see you."

She made a rude sound.

"After fifteen years, you're suddenly ready to be rid of me?" she scoffed. "What's her name? Am I invited to the wedding?"

"You've got it all wrong, Nancy. I don't want to end things. I want to start over."

RJ risked a peek over his shoulder. If his father hadn't forewarned him about his intentions, he would have probably fallen to the ground in shock. His mother, with no preparation at all, might actually have a heart attack. She stared at him, uncomprehending. From time to time she opened her mouth as if she were going to say something, but then she closed it again. After a minute or two, she shook herself and gave Robert a fierce glare.

"You can't be serious," she said. "Stop being an ass and tell me why you're really here."

"Ah, but I am serious."

His father took his time getting a mug and pouring himself a cup of coffee, probably giving his mother time to believe him. He sat down across the kitchen table from her and took a slow sip, waiting for the right moment to continue. RJ had seen him use this tactic when negotiating a divorce settlement.

"Why?" asked Nancy. Anger had given way to utter confusion.

"I'm going to retire in a few months, and I realized something as I thought about what comes next."

"What did you realize?"

"Life is boring without you."

"Oh, please," she said. "This must be some legal strategy. Have you found a loophole in the community property laws? It won't work. I won't be taken for a fool."

RJ's father laughed. Not a chuckle, but a full-bodied, honest-to-goodness laugh. RJ hadn't heard that laugh in far longer than fifteen years.

"God, you're wonderful. Do you know that? And while I certainly deserve your skepticism, I can assure you that there are no new loopholes to exploit. RJ can vouch for me on that one."

"Like I would believe him," said his mother. "The two of you are probably in cahoots."

Her accusation stung, but he was too fascinated by this new version of his father to get worked up about it. The retirement thing was a total surprise. RJ had expected his dad to work until the day he died. Something had changed. Maybe the loss of Pops had hit him harder than anybody realized.

"Get your own attorney then. There's no risk here. I have a simple proposition for you."

His mother looked at Robert, her skepticism very clear.

"Hear me out," he said. "I'd like you to give me one year. If, after one year of living together, we still can't find a way to make it work, then I let you go. For real this time. No legal shenanigans. No loopholes. A divorce, and we split the money down the middle." He put up a hand to forestall her questions. "It has to be a real try, though. We live together. We sleep in the same bed. We eat together. No easy out, and no comfort on the side."

"How do I know you'll stick to the bargain? As I recall, you were a master at hiding your extracurricular activities."

"Point taken," he said. "I'll agree to whatever form of surveillance you suggest. You may invade my privacy in any way you see fit."

"And if I refuse to have sex with you?" she challenged.

"You still have to sleep in my bed," he replied. "I won't push you to do anything you don't want to do."

His mother crossed her arms.

"You can be very persuasive," she grumbled.

"Yes," said his father. "I can."

RJ really didn't want to know this much about his parents' sex life, so he prepared for a graceful exit as he finished rinsing the last pan.

"We'll need to have a written agreement," she said, "and I'll have my own lawyer draw it up."

"If that makes you more comfortable, then that's what we'll do."

She stared at him for a long minute.

"I accept," she said. She stood and held out her hand to shake on the deal.

He rose as well and clasped her hand, but instead of shaking it, he brought it to his lips and kissed the inside of her wrist. RJ froze, appalled at the realization that he had inherited his charm from his father. From the look on his mother's face, it was working.

"Don't you think we should seal this with a kiss?" asked Robert, still holding Nancy's hand and moving slowly around the table toward her. She snatched her hand away and took two steps back.

"Not so fast, mister," she said. "No kisses from you until we have the paperwork signed and sealed. I'm not falling for that again."

He chuckled, and she gave him a long, slow smile in return. RJ really needed to get out of the room.

"I guess I'll leave you two kids alone, then," he said, setting down the towel and sidling toward the living room. He would have made it, too, if his mother hadn't grabbed his wrist to keep him there.

"Don't leave, RJ honey. I'm not sure I trust your father to keep his hands to himself."

Robert did his best to look affronted.

"Now, darling, I can't be held responsible if you find me irresistible."

"Hold me back, RJ. I'm going to smack him."

RJ tugged his wrist free and headed for the living room.

"I'm definitely not getting in the middle of this one," he said as he fled. "One question, though," he said, pausing in the doorway. "What are you going to tell Ken?"

Tessa saw Callie's number on the caller ID and grabbed the phone before Mel could pick up.

"Hey, stranger," she said. "How's Nashville?"

Her greeting got the attention of Mel and her parents, all of whom were in various stages of eating breakfast. Tessa was tending to the pancakes, but through a series of complicated gestures let Mel know that she was handing off the job. Tessa grabbed her coffee and headed out onto the porch so she could kick back and talk in comfort.

"Oh, Tess, I found the perfect apartment," said Callie. "It's right in the thick of things, walking distance from everything, and they take dogs, thank goodness."

Tessa had almost forgotten about the drool-fest her sister had adopted from the shelter. He was staying next door with Adam and Danny until Callie got her Nashville crash pad settled.

"Sounds awesome," said Tessa. "Do you have to furnish it from scratch, or are you bringing over stuff from the old place?"

Callie made a sound of disgust.

"I don't want anything from that life," she said. "I'm starting fresh."

"Sounds good to me," said Tessa. Callie's ex was bad news. The cleaner the break, the better.

"The other thing that's perfect about it is the extra bedroom. If Adam and Danny come to visit, then Danny has a room of his own, and if Dad comes down for a stretch, he would have an actual bed to sleep on instead of a fold-out couch."

Tessa hesitated before answering. She would leave it up to her Dad to explain that he might be spending most of his time with Zeke.

"It sounds amazing," she said. "Send pictures immediately."

They talked for a few more minutes before Mel demanded the phone, and then Mel passed the phone to Luke. He needed to tell Callie what was going on, and Mel didn't plan to let him wait until he saw Callie in person, even if that was only a few days away. He gave Mel a grumpy look but dutifully took the phone into his office.

Tessa grabbed her plate and coffee mug and sat down at the kitchen table with her mother and Mel. They had each gravitated toward their usual spots, and Tessa found the familiarity comforting. She picked at her pancake, trying to ignore the flutter of nerves in her belly. RJ probably thought she was going to blow off the race today. She needed to let him know that she wasn't going to bail on him, but she didn't really want to talk until afterward.

"Text him," said Mel.

"What?"

"You're overanalyzing. I can see it from here. Text him and let him know you'll be there. You don't need to actually talk until afterward."

Dora looked back and forth between the two girls, then smiled.

"Are you going to work things out with RJ?" she asked, the delight clear in her voice. "I'm so glad. You two are so good for each other. He's been such a gentleman about this whole separation, and so respectful of our privacy. I couldn't be more thrilled that the two of you finally hooked up after all these years. I knew, even all those years ago, that the two of you would eventually get together. And I was right!"

"Mom, don't you think it's a little early to—"

"Of course not," interrupted Dora. "I know a strong match when I see one. You two have some serious chemistry going on, and that's important, but you're also friends, and that will make it last. Trust me on this one. Friendship is a big deal."

Tessa and Mel looked at each other across the table and rolled their eyes, careful to make sure their mother couldn't see. There was no point in arguing when she was on a roll. Tessa eased out of the room, leaving Mel to be the designated listener. She had some phone calls to make.

CHAPTER TWENTY-ONE

THE REGATTA PROVIDED RJ WITH A PERFECT EXCUSE TO ESCAPE his family. Unfortunately, it didn't help him escape his obsession with Tessa. He needed to put her out of his mind just long enough to finish the race, then he could put his plan in action. If he needed any help getting Tessa alone, he would bet money that Dora would help him.

The yacht club buzzed with activity. The annual regatta during Fourth of July week drew sailors from all over the state, turning the parking lot into a traffic jam and raising the level of competition.

RJ checked his watch. Walt was late. He needed to get his ass in gear and rig the boat, and hopefully Walt would show up sooner rather than later.

Tessa leaned against her car and watched RJ from across the parking lot, ignoring the activity around her. The yacht club was always a madhouse on the first morning of a big regatta. She should be grateful for all the chaos because it gave her the opportunity to spy on him unobserved. If only she could freeze this moment forever, while she was still holding on to the fragile possibility that they could make this work. In a moment, he would turn around, and he would see her, and they would have to talk—not that there was much to discuss. He had always been honest and up front about his approach to relationships, and they had clearly passed the point of no return. Of course he would say no to a second try. She should know better than to hope, but found herself hoping anyway.

So she was stubborn, and maybe even a little bit stupid. This must be love, then, this willingness to lay your heart on the floor and ask for it to be stomped on. She smiled ruefully, wondering why she always needed to learn lessons the hard way.

RJ walked around to the far side of the boat, and when he looked up, their eyes met. He froze, then put down whatever he had been holding and walked toward her, which was lucky because she found that her heart was pounding in her ears and her feet couldn't move.

He stopped a foot away and they stared at each other for a long moment. She gave him half a smile, afraid to let the hope show on her face. He looked so serious. Why didn't he say something?

Then he lifted his hands and slid his fingers along her cheeks and into her hair, cradling the back of her head. He moved slowly, watching her reaction. She could barely breathe, but she didn't want him to stop, so she reached for his hips and pulled him closer. His eyes crinkled at the edges and she saw the hint of a smile around the corners of his mouth. Then her eyes closed and his lips touched hers and she felt a rush of relief so strong that she had to hold on to him just to stay upright. He kissed her lips, then moved his mouth along her cheekbone to her ear.

"You came back," he whispered.

She nodded, her head still cupped in his hands.

"I called Walt," she said, her voice husky. "Told him you didn't need a sub anymore. I'm here."

"Stay," he said. It wasn't exactly a question, but she nodded again. If he was ready to give this a real shot, she was completely and totally on board.

He kissed his way back to her mouth, then rested his forehead against hers. His hands moved to gently hold her face, his thumbs caressing her cheeks.

"Marry me," he whispered.

She jerked back in surprise, but his hands, still holding the sides of her face, kept her from retreating too far. She looked into his eyes, his face inches away from hers, and searched his face for an explanation, but saw only determination.

"But—"

"Please," he said. "I can't let you go."

He was hurting. She could see it. He wanted this thing between them so badly that he was willing to build his own prison. She smiled, her heart breaking for him. It didn't need to be this scary.

"I love you," she said. It felt good to say it out loud. It felt right.

The look on his face was priceless. Confused. Panicked. Uncertain. However, he couldn't seem to make his mouth work.

"Do you love me?" she asked, her confidence growing.

He nodded slowly, wary now, as he watched her smile and heard her steady voice.

"Say it out loud," she ordered. He needed to know that it wouldn't kill him.

"I love you," he whispered hoarsely.

Once the words were out of his mouth, his shoulders sagged with relief and he tipped his head forward to rest his forehead against hers again. She chuckled softly and wound her arms around his neck.

"I'm glad that's settled," she murmured, and kissed him

gently. She could feel the tension in his shoulders and kneaded the base of his neck. She bit his lower lip, then left a trail of kisses along his jawline until her lips reached his earlobe. "I'm so sorry for yelling at you, and for leaving. No excuses," she whispered, then bit his earlobe. "I'll try to handle it better when we fight." She pulled back so that she could see his eyes, but left her arms wrapped around his neck. "Because you know we're going to fight, right?"

He swallowed, looking determined.

"Is this a yes?" he demanded, his voice still hoarse.

"Nope," she said, and tried to kiss him again, but he held her away from him, studying her face.

"But I thought..." His voice trailed off. He tried again. "You said—"

"—that I'm a happily-ever-after kind of girl?"

He nodded.

"I don't need a ring, RJ," she said softly.

"But—"

"No handcuffs."

He was still confused. She could tell. But she also felt some of the tension draining from his shoulders. This was a good kind of confused.

"We've both got crazy baggage. You can't shake the idea that marriage is a prison. I've just had my world turned upside down. Everything is a mess, but I don't care because I'm sure of one thing: You. The rest can wait."

He smiled.

"Honey, I don't know shit about relationships, but I do know one thing." He pulled her tight against him. "I don't ever want to watch you walk away again. I'll do whatever it takes to make sure that doesn't happen again."

"Even get married?" she asked.

"If that's what you need," he answered.

She felt the tears fill her eyes and his face blurred.

"I don't," she said fiercely. "I choose you, and you choose me. Every day. We don't need a contract to make it real, and we don't need a lawyer to end it."

He crushed her against him, and she hung on tight.

"I choose you," he growled against her neck, sending shivers through her body.

She nodded her head, which was tucked under his chin.

No more endings. Only beginnings.

"I got you something," said RJ.

She looked up at him, but didn't let go. He gave her a quick kiss on the forehead, then peeled her arms from around his waist.

"Come on," he said. "I want to give it to you before the race."

He grabbed her by the hand and they wove through the crowded parking lot. Sometimes he forgot how crazy things could get during a special event like this regatta. Today, though, it didn't bother him at all. Tessa had come back. She was going to give him a second chance. All was right with the world.

When they got to his truck, he yanked open the door and fished out a shopping bag. She tried to peek, but he didn't let her. He needed to explain first.

"I may never be ready for a white picket fence. It's easier to imagine the two point five children—someday. However," he continued when she tried to interrupt, "I'm more than willing to give the matching track suits a try."

He pulled the waterproof gear out of the bag with a flourish and presented it to her. The color matched the blue of the spinnaker on the M-17, but it was the personalization that made it special. He watched her face as she deciphered what he'd had embroidered on each jacket. On his, it said 'Hers,' and on hers, 'His.' Her delighted laughter unlocked something deep inside him and he relaxed. They would find a way to make this work.

"His and hers?" she asked.

"You belong to me. I belong to you." He shrugged. "Pretty simple, really."

It was truly the perfect day for sailing. Bright blue sky with just a few clouds scuttling across the higher altitudes. Nice brisk wind. They quickly finished rigging the boat and pulled it down to the launch. Tessa glanced over her shoulder at RJ and he gave her a suggestive wink that made her laugh out loud. He couldn't believe his luck. She had come back, and she was going to stay. She didn't need a ring. She was just here, and she loved him.

It made no sense, but he was not so stupid he would blow a second chance.

The race started off well enough. They were surrounded by the usual suspects, all looking as intense—or in Brock's case, as pissed off—as usual. He and Tessa had never been more in tune with one another, and as a result, they found themselves running up front with Brock and Helen trailing just behind Steve and Mike as they prepared to round the orange mark that signaled the final leg of the race.

RJ studied their lay line and realized that something needed to change. Tessa must have realized it at the same time, because she gave him a look over her shoulder that said, 'What do you want to do, Captain?'

They could either cut off Steve and Mike in a jerk move similar to the one Brock had pulled on them in that first race, or they could cut off Brock. If they cut off the teenagers, they would likely win. If they cut off Brock, they would clear the way for the Steve and Mike to win and would end up racing Brock for second. RJ grinned at Tessa. For him, it was really no decision at all, but this was her call. He raised an eyebrow in question and she gave him a sharp nod.

Instead of gybing when they reached the port lay line, they continued just far enough to cross paths with Brock. They had the right of way, and Brock knew it. When he shouted at them to gybe already, RJ shrugged, grinned, and saluted. Brock spewed curses in their direction as he changed course to avoid them. Mission accomplished, RJ signaled Tessa and they made their move. Late, yes, but their tactic had succeeded. The teenagers had executed their moves perfectly and now held a strong lead. RJ and Tessa trailed them in second. Brock, who had been surprised by the unexpected maneuver, had not recovered well and lagged behind, ending up in fifth place.

Tessa didn't bother looking back at Brock during the final leg. She knew what his expression would be, and she didn't feel like seeing it right now. She had wasted more than enough of her life dealing with him already. She would much rather enjoy their second place finish and then get RJ alone—the sooner the better.

After the race, as they got the boat out of the water and hauled it toward the parking lot, the two teenagers stopped them.

"Dude, I don't know why you pulled that move at the last mark, but we certainly appreciate it," said Steve.

"Thanks, guys," echoed Mike. "You rock."

RJ didn't offer an explanation. He was pretty sure these kids had it all figured out.

"Nice racing out there, gentlemen," said Tessa, offering a hand, which they shook in turn.

"Until next time," said RJ.

They might have made their escape, but Brock had hopped

off the boat at the pier, leaving Helen behind to hold it in place. He stalked over to confront them.

"What the hell was that stunt you pulled?" he demanded.

RJ cocked his head and considered.

"Well," he said, "I suppose I could have cut off those kids for the win, but that wouldn't have been sporting, now would it?"

"Sporting?" Brock spat out the word like it was something vile. "Who says that?"

"Haven't you heard it before?" asked Tessa, all innocence. She took satisfaction in knowing exactly how to push his buttons. "You know: sporting, sportsmanship, good sport. I'm surprised you're not familiar with the concept."

Brock looked like he might explode.

"I would buy you a drink," said RJ, "but we have plans. See you around."

Before Brock could get worked up again, Tessa and RJ turned and walked away. He reached over and linked his fingers with hers.

"Plans?" she asked, giving him a sideways look from under her lashes.

"Yes," he answered. "Let's get this boat put to bed. We have plans to make."

EPILOGUE

TESSA CROUCHED BY THE BONFIRE, ONE ARM AROUND HUCK'S belly to keep him from tipping over into the flames, and the other holding the marshmallow stick. Huck liked to help with the stick, but he couldn't yet be trusted with it on his own. At the slightest distraction, he would turn his head, the stick would point down, and the marshmallow would dip into the ashes or start on fire. Tessa kept a firm grip on both her responsibilities. Sunny knelt beside her, doing a similar thing with Oscar, but he required less assistance. He was now big enough to hold the stick himself, and smart enough not to fall into the fire.

"I'm so glad you guys came back for the Fourth," said Tessa, giving Huck's potbelly a squeeze.

"Me, too," said Sunny.

When Sunny smiled, she looked less strained than she had only a week ago. The pinched look had been replaced by a calm optimism that had Tessa feeling optimistic as well.

She looked around at the people scattered across the commons. All twenty homes were filled this weekend. All twenty families accounted for. She had known these people all her life, and though her heart ached for Nana Vi and her generation as they slowed down, she found new hope in small potbellies and sticky fingers. None of them would be here forever, but they were part of something that would continue long after they were gone.

Tessa didn't have any expectations about her future with RJ. They were going to take things one day at a time, and for now, that was enough. The extent of their planning had been to talk about the possibility of her moving up here, depending on where she found a job.

She didn't want to him to panic, so she hadn't mentioned the fact that she was researching how to open her own practice, and she intended to talk with her mother about maybe, possibly taking over the sailing school. After all, if her mother was going to be spending time in New York, and her father was going to be spending time in Nashville, somebody would need to hold down the fort. Tessa didn't dare hope that she could have it all—part-time counselor, part-time sailor, and full-time lover of a certain sexy sailor. She didn't want to talk about it out loud yet. She didn't want to jinx it.

She laughed, earning herself an inquiring look from Sunny.

"I just realized that I started wishing again," she said.

Sunny looked startled, then said, "Good. It's about time."

Tessa smiled and shook her head. She might be planning to take things one day at a time, but her pent-up wishes, held tightly for too long, came tumbling out of her heart and floated toward the sky along with the smoke from the bonfire.

A life with RJ.

A career that combined all her favorite things.

A potbellied toddler of her own. Maybe two. Hell, maybe six. RJ would make an amazing father someday.

Was that too much to wish for?

When the marshmallows turned the perfect shade of toasty brown, Sunny and Tessa helped them make their s'mores and then plunked them down on a split-log bench on either side of Nana Vi.

Sunny caught sight of Nana Vi's rings in the firelight. She knew, deep down, that her grandmother would never take them off. When she died, the rings would go with her to her grave. She glanced at her own rings, but even by firelight they didn't sparkle. She had tarnished them. She probably shouldn't even be wearing them. She needed to earn back the right to wear them, after her massive screw-up. In that moment, she made a promise to herself, to Will, to the kids, that she would find a way to earn those rings back, even if it took the rest of her life.

"You girls go make your own s'mores," said Vi. "I'll keep these rascals out of the fire."

The boys would be occupied for a while with the sticky treats, so Sunny and Tessa wandered over to the picnic table and claimed their own roasting sticks and marshmallows. As Tessa turned back toward the fire, she caught sight of Sunny's parents standing together in the shadows just outside the light of the bonfire. Sunny followed her gaze and then smiled.

"Weird, huh?" she asked.

"I never would have predicted it. Not in a million years," agreed Tessa.

"That makes three of us," said Sunny. "Four, counting Nana Vi."

"Any idea what made your Dad change his tune?" asked Tessa.

"Not a clue," said Sunny, "but I have to admit, it gives me hope."

Tessa studied them for a moment longer, but their body language revealed only what she already knew. Robert had turned on the charm and was slowly but surely working his way back into Nancy's good graces. The older woman still held herself at a distance, but she was beginning to soften. Tessa could see it, even in the fading light. Very intriguing, but she would need to be patient if she hoped to learn more. In the meantime...

"You seem like you're feeling better about things with Will," said Tessa. "Did any of the referrals work out?"

Sunny sighed.

"There's one guy that I thought would be good, but Will isn't on board with the idea of talking to a stranger. He wants to work things out, but he's not ready to ask for help."

Tessa didn't respond. She didn't want to squash Sunny's optimism.

"What?" whispered Sunny. "You don't think it will work? Damn it, I knew I should have pushed harder."

"No, don't," said Tessa. "If he's not ready, you can't force it. I do think that your chances over the long term are better if you talk to someone, but some couples get through on their own."

"Are you just saying that to make me feel better?" asked Sunny.

Tessa laughed.

"Of course not. I want you to be happy, and it's hard that I can't help. I shouldn't help. I'm too close."

"But you'll give me some tips every now and then?"

Tessa put her arm around Sunny and squeezed.

"You bet."

At that moment, RJ poked his head between theirs and slung his arms over their shoulders. In each of his hands was a perfectly prepared s'more.

"Treats for my two favorite ladies." He gave them a double-squeeze, then traded the finished s'mores for their not-yet-toasted marshmallows, handing off their sticks to some nearby kids. "Mind if I borrow Tessa for a minute?" he asked Sunny. She waved them away, her mouth too full to respond, but her gestures indicating that she was going to talk to Kat, who stood alone on the opposite side of the fire roasting her own marshmallow. RJ slung an arm around Tessa and steered her toward the privacy of the shadows at the edge of the commons.

"My hero," she said, her mouth full of marshmallow.

"S'mores are my superpower," he answered with a grin.

"You're good, I'll admit," she said, "but there are a few other things that you do even better."

She laughed at his raised eyebrows.

"Yes, that's exactly what I was thinking," she said.

When he stopped, she turned around to look at the people illuminated by the firelight. The people she loved most in the world were all here. Her parents walked down toward the little beach, hand in hand. If she didn't have inside information, she would have no idea that they were, for all intents and purposes, just friends. Her sister Callie, along with Adam and Danny, had already claimed spots on the strip of sand where they would watch the fireworks. Roscoe had been left behind in the house because he was not a fan of loud noises. Mel stood at the fire, toasting one last marshmallow. Tessa eyed her sister thoughtfully, realizing that Mel's wish lanterns had set the wheels in motion with RJ only a month ago. She would need to find a way to return the favor.

The lake twinkled with the lights of a hundred motorboats, all moving slowly toward the packed municipal beach as darkness fell. The police boats would stop them before they got too close, of course, but they jockeyed in slow motion for front-row seats. Tessa jumped at the boom of the warning shot that signaled the start of the fireworks display, and RJ put his arm around her.

"Scared?" he asked.

She leaned her head on his shoulder.

"Nope," she answered. "You?"

He knew she was asking about more than just the fireworks.

"Nope," he echoed.

Tessa turned her head to look up at him. He laughed.

"Yep," he said. "That look has got to be considered a super-power. I can't lie to you."

She stopped and turned to face him, wrapping her arms around his neck.

"Good," she said.

"I just thought of the perfect place to watch the fireworks," he said.

"Where?"

"The troll bridge," he said, as if the answer should have been obvious. She laughed.

"Lead the way," she said. "I'm all yours."

Thank you so much for reading *Love Story (Confidential)*!

If you loved Tessa and RJ's story, return to Hidden Springs for Kat and Rob's story in *Love Me Not*.

SIGN UP for Lisa McLuckie's eNewsletter at www. LisaMcLuckie.com to receive new release alerts, insider information, and bonus content.

THANK YOU for helping to spread the word about *Love Story (Confidential)*. Reviews help readers discover new authors, so please pay it forward by leaving a review on your favorite book site, and be sure to tell your book-loving friends if you enjoyed the story.

And now, an **EXCERPT** from *Love Me Not*.

EXCERPT

Love Me Not

Kat licked the last of the marshmallow from her fingers and debated making one more s'more. Already starting to buzz from the sugar high, she decided against it. Truth be told, she really should have stopped at two.

The bonfire had mellowed to a warm glow. Firelight flickered on the split log benches surrounding the fire pit, while the rest of the commons had faded into semidarkness. Teenagers clustered together, caught up in the end of summer and the imminent return to school. Younger children raced around in the dark, flashlights bobbing wildly. Adults stood around in groups of two or three or five. Looking out across the grass toward the lake, the pinpricks of light on the far side of the water felt awfully far away. It was easy to imagine herself at a camp in the remote north woods.

In reality, though, they were all too close to civilization. The twenty or so houses that comprised The Gardens circled the edge of the commons. This swath of lakefront property served as a haven for summer people up from Chicago. A handful of families lived here full time, but most were weekenders, and most of these families had been coming up to the lake for generations. The tight-knit community reflected those bonds.

Kat had never felt more like an outsider.

Her lawyer brain did not let her get away with a sweeping statement like that, even in the privacy of her own mind. Technically, she had felt like more of an outsider on multiple occasions, including the first time she had come to a barbecue at The Gardens, not even three months ago. Or her first day of kindergarten, when she had understood that she belonged to no group—not the milk-pale farm girls, or the already-friends town girls, or even the Spanish-speaking Mexican girls, daughters of immigrant farm workers, who puzzled over the girl who looked like them but couldn't understand them.

Mentally scrolling through the years between kindergarten and today, Kat concluded that she had spent more of her life as an outsider than an insider. No wonder she was so comfortable in the role. She had trained for it her whole life.

So why had she accepted another invitation to a gathering here in The Gardens, knowing that she would always be on the outside looking in? She didn't even socialize in her own neighborhood, not that the tidy row of townhomes where she lived could really be considered a neighborhood. She wrinkled her forehead, considering the possibility. Maybe, if you used the term loosely. They certainly didn't have barbecues. They exchanged friendly waves as they passed each other going in and out. She knew the names of the people in the next townhome. Did that add up to a neighborhood?

One stark contrast between her tidy group of townhomes and this sprawling neighborhood was the trees. A spindly sapling accented the front "lawn" of each townhome, each the same size and species, although Kat couldn't put a name to them. Perhaps one day they would be as majestic as the trees here on the commons, but Kat suspected they had been chosen for their modest size and good behavior. The trees here in The Gardens were neither modest nor well-behaved. Scattered randomly across the otherwise open expanse of grass, these trees anchored the neighborhood, bearing witness to generation after generation of tradition.

Kat drained the last of her beer and contemplated heading home. Better to think deep thoughts in the privacy of her own living room. But before she could come to a decision, a girl approached the picnic tables on the edges of the firelight. She was so intent on her goal that she didn't seem to notice Kat sitting quietly in the shadows. Kat watched with interest as the girl filched something from the buffet and began to back away slowly, moving toward Kat and the bonfire. As she inched closer, Kat realized three things. First, she couldn't be older than fifteen. Second, that was a bottle of vodka clutched behind her back. And third, she was about to trip on one of the split log benches surrounding the bonfire.

"Look out," called Kat. The girl jumped, dropping the vodka as she whipped around to see who had caught her. Luckily it landed in the dirt and not on the log. Kat gave her a brisk nod. "Have a seat."

The girl promptly sat down on the bench that had nearly tripped her. Kat didn't recognize her, but then, she really knew only two families here.

"Why don't you pick up the vodka before someone trips over it?"

The girl picked the bottle up gingerly, as if it were a Molotov cocktail about to blow, and set it beside her on the very end of the bench. Both the girl and the bottle were poised for a quick getaway.

Kat waited while a pack of smaller kids ran past, playing some kind of tag in the dark, then she continued. "So, was this your idea, or did your friends put you up to it?"

The girl looked startled before she put her bland talk-to-the-adults face back on. "It's on me," she answered.

The lie was convincing nobody.

"If it was your idea, you wouldn't be so nervous."

"I'm not.... Nobody. It was my idea."

Kat studied the girl for a long minute, but it looked like she wasn't going to give up her friends, and Kat didn't really have jurisdiction here. She was just a guest. She also admired the girl's willingness to stick up for her friends, even if they were being idiots.

"Leave the vodka. You're free to go."

The girl was gone before Kat could say another word, leaving behind the bottle of vodka teetering on the bench. Kat sighed. She hated playing bad cop.

Thank God it was the last night of the summer. Even without kids of her own, the summer wreaked havoc on her schedule. She was looking forward to fall, and to a return to "normal." She made a disgusted sound in the back of her throat. Normal wasn't that great these days. She'd been working crazy hours these past few years building her practice. It was work she loved, but she didn't have anything outside of work that could be called a life.

She had done much better in those first couple of years after law school. There had been an entire cohort of newly minted lawyers all working for the big firms in Milwaukee. Sure, they had worked crazy hours then, too, but they had done it together. She had great memories of late-night after-work drinks, concerts, and comedy clubs—even the occasional weekend away. Not anymore. Ever since she had ditched the big money and the big firm to come home, her world had grown smaller and smaller. Sure, she kept up with friends on Facebook, but on a day-to-day basis, she had no social life. No dates. Nothing but work.

"Hey."

Kat had been so absorbed in her own thoughts, staring into

the fire, that she hadn't heard Mel approach. It was weird how she could tell the triplets apart so easily now. Maybe it was because they were all older, or maybe it was just repeated exposure. She didn't expect they would be close friends anytime soon, but over the summer, she and Mel had reached a tentative truce, leaving their high school animosity behind.

"Hey, yourself," she answered.

Mel took a seat beside Kat on the bench and stuck a marshmallow into the fire. They sat in an oddly easy silence while the marshmallow toasted. Only when it was done—a little overdone, in Kat's opinion—did Mel break the silence again.

"This is definitely my last one," she said as she clamped the skewer between two graham crackers (and the chocolate, of course) and slid the pointy end out from the s'more. She leaned her skewer against the bench and took a giant bite.

"That's what I said after my third, but I can feel the fourth one calling my name."

Mel choked on a laugh, then swallowed. "I hear you." She gestured toward the bottle of vodka still sitting on the opposite side of the fire. "Vodka keeping you company tonight?"

"Confiscated," said Kat. "Pretty sure we don't want a bunch of teenagers puking their guts out later."

Mel snorted, her mouth full of the next bite of s'more.

"Are there fewer people than usual tonight?" Kat had been to only two other events here at The Gardens. The group tonight fell far short of the Memorial Day weekend or Fourth of July crowds.

"Illinois kids are already back to school. Not all the families make it back up for Labor Day weekend."

That made sense. "It must be exhausting, living your life in two different places, running back and forth all the time."

"I don't mind. The city revs you up, and then the lake calms you down. It's actually a nice balance."

They sat in silence for a few minutes until Mel asked, "Do

you ever think about taking off and exploring the world?"

An unexpected question—one that must be on Mel's mind because it certainly had nothing to do with their conversation so far. It also felt strangely intimate, at least for their fledgling friendship. Maybe Mel had drunk enough wine to be feeling philosophical?

Kat considered her answer, and realized to her surprise that the idea didn't interest her at all.

"I've never had itchy feet," she said. "I guess my mother did, or she never would have left Colombia to come here to school." One of the logs shifted, sending a flurry of tiny sparks into the air. Kat watched them float and fade away as she continued speaking. "I've been on a few vacations—Florida, up north, Canada, even—but I haven't found anywhere else that feels like home." The expression on Mel's face made Kat curious to know what had prompted the question. "I was away for long enough. This is where I want to be right now. It's where I need to be." Her personal life would sort itself out eventually. "What about you?"

A brief silence before Mel answered. "Sometimes I wonder what's wrong with me. Chicago is amazing, and Hidden Springs is one of the most beautiful spots on the planet. The fact that I get to split my time between the two makes me very lucky. I shouldn't be daydreaming about someplace else."

"Why not? Dreams make the world go 'round."

Mel grimaced. "Dreams make me fight with my mother."

"She doesn't want you to travel?" That was a surprise. Mel's mother, Dora, seemed like the kind of person who would be up for any kind of adventure.

"She's been pretty clear about wanting me to settle down here and make some babies."

"You do know that you're an adult, right? You don't have to do what your mother says." Kat delivered the observation with an arched eyebrow and got a dirty look in return.

"You try saying no to my mother and see what happens."

Mel shoved the last of the s'more in her mouth. Kat turned back to the fire to hide her smile. Everyone in town knew Dora, and to her knowledge, nobody had ever successfully told her "no."

This was nice, Kat decided. She and Mel were having an actual conversation, one that wasn't tense or heavy with unspoken baggage. It made her feel less like an outsider and more like a human with a social life. It also made her miss her friends from law school a little less.

It occurred to her that Mel might be lonely, too. With her two sisters neatly paired off and in the throes of "true love," she seemed a bit lost.

Mel stood abruptly. "I need to head home before I eat another ten s'mores."

Kat stood, too, realizing this could be her chance for a graceful exit. "Me, too."

"What should we do with the vodka?"

Kat had completely forgotten about it, but Mel was right. If they left it unattended, the teens would reclaim it in about two seconds.

"Do you want to take it home?" asked Kat.

With a shrug, Mel said, "I could stick it in the liquor cabinet, but I doubt anyone will drink it. You?"

"Same. Why don't you take it?"

Mel grabbed the bottle, and they started walking up the hill, Mel heading home and Kat toward RJ's house, where she had parked her car. They had almost made it to the edge of the firelight when a voice rang out behind them.

"There you are!"

There was too much satisfaction in that declaration for Kat's peace of mind. She turned to face Dora with a tiny sigh. So much for a quiet fade from the party. Beside her, Mel did the same, although she might have hesitated a second longer and turned more slowly.

"Here I am," said Kat.

Mel crossed her arms, the vodka bottle dangling against one hip. "Mother."

Dora was about the same age as Kat's mother would have been, if she were still alive. Maybe a few years older. Kat remembered her own mother as quiet, at least around other people. Dora, in contrast, was never quiet. She was a force of nature. You always knew where you stood with her. No hidden agenda. No games. She was like a giant beating heart that never stopped talking.

"Come with me." Dora claimed Kat with one hand and Mel with the other and led (some might call it dragged) the girls back downhill, veering off toward one of the clusters of adults. "Mary Evelyn and I were just talking about the library project. You remember Mary Evelyn, don't you? The librarian?" Dora paused only long enough to take a breath and hear Mel's and Kat's murmured affirmations that they did indeed remember Mary Evelyn. "Of course you do. Everyone knows Mary Evelyn. Anyway, this mural project at the library is very exciting. They've won a grant to fund an artist from Chicago. He's going to do a mural on the side of the library building, and there's going to be a new garden put in. It will be beautiful." They arrived at a small knot of people, and Dora announced, "I found them."

The group included Mary Evelyn Bennett, the librarian, as well as several other retired ladies who were quite active in the community. Kat began to wonder if she should be nervous.

"Just the women we needed," said Mary Evelyn. "Kat, we're hoping that you know the right person to talk to up at the county. We're wondering if there are any teenagers in need of community service hours who could help on the library project. We thought you would know the right person to call."

Kat breathed a sigh of relief. Dora and her friends weren't trying to rope her into some huge volunteer project. They just needed help making connections. This she could handle.

"I'm not sure exactly who's running the juvenile programs right now, but I'd be happy to make a few calls. Connect you to the right person."

"That would be wonderful!" said Mary Evelyn.

"See, I knew she would know what to do," crowed Dora. "Thank you so much, honey. There's no way we can do this without some volunteer labor, and kids these days are just so busy. I think the community service angle will be much better than an open call for helping hands."

"Happy to help," said Kat.

"And now you, sweetheart," began Dora, but Mel quickly interrupted.

"Mom, you know I'm swamped—"

Dora interrupted her right back. "I know you're between apartments right now—" She packed a lot of disapproval into that short phrase. Kat was exceedingly happy not to be on the receiving end. "And that you're planning to spend the next few weekends up here."

Mel had the look of a trapped rabbit, and she was making some kind of growling noise in the back of her throat.

"It will be so nice to have your helping hands on Saturday mornings."

They had a brief staring contest. Mel lost, and Kat bit back a smile.

"I'm afraid I have to head out," said Kat, "but I'll make some calls first thing in the morning and let you know what I learn."

She escaped as quickly as she could, their calls of "thank you" following her as she tromped back up the hill toward her car.

～

Rob was finishing up his breakfast at Lucy's Diner the following morning when Dora breezed in. Everyone knew Lucy, in much the same way that everyone knew Dora. They were always in the thick of things, always up to something. Rob was sitting at the middle of the counter, so he could overhear very clearly as Dora ordered doughnuts to go and the two women started chatting.

His ears perked up when he heard them mention Kat. As far as he knew, there was only one Kat in town, and that was Katherine Rodriguez, attorney-at-law, whose offices happened to be right next door to this very diner. Kitty Rodriguez, back in town as if she'd never dropped off the face of the earth in the middle of their senior year of high school, leaving behind dead parents and a lot of unanswered questions. She had opened that office a few years ago, just after he had launched his business, and only the intense pressure and long hours of that startup year had kept him from stopping by to welcome her back to town. Well, that and possibly nerves.

The pressure had eventually eased off, but not the hours, leaving him little opportunity to casually drop by and reconnect. You'd think, living in a small town, that they would have crossed paths at some point, but the universe appeared to be working against him on this one. His least favorite people he saw all the time, but not once had he seen Kat around town. Not at the grocery store. Not at the post office. Not even at the gas station. He didn't really go anywhere else.

Clearly, he needed to get out more.

Last week, as his company marked its three-year anniversary, he had realized that if he wanted to see Kitty sometime this century, he was going to need to get creative and make it happen. Today's breakfast was a first attempt at reconnaissance. His workday started at seven, and he was unlikely to catch Kat in her office this early, but he was hoping that Lucy might drop a hint as to her habits. He didn't dare ask, though, without drawing attention. He would need to play this just right.

"That girl works too hard." This comment was from Dora.

"All the young people do these days. They've lost the ability to have fun. Did you have any luck?" asked Lucy.

"Yes!" crowed Dora. "She's going to make a few phone calls, put us in touch with the right person up at county."

"But is she going to help?"

"Small steps," said Dora. "Small steps."

Dora headed out with her doughnuts, and Rob pondered their conversation. Clearly, they were trying to rope Kat into one of their schemes, and so far she was managing to stay clear. If Dora and Lucy had joined forces, however, chances were that she would end up doing whatever they needed her to do. It was just the way things worked.

Lucy came over to freshen up his coffee and give him his check. When she came back with his change, she paused. He did not like the gleam in her eye.

"You're Rob Murray, aren't you? Peggy's son?"

At his nod, she continued. "And you have a landscaping business, isn't that right?"

"Yes...?" He shifted on the rotating stool, realizing that he was about to be roped into something as well.

"You know my mother, don't you? Mary Evelyn Bennett, the librarian?"

He nodded slowly. It seemed safe enough to confirm this fact.

"Of course you do. I remember seeing you there when you were small. My girls are older than you, but I always chatted with the other mothers while my girls looked for books to check out."

Rob set down some of the change to leave a tip, putting the rest in his wallet and standing to slide the wallet into his back pocket. As he has hoped, this prompted Lucy to get to the point.

"Mom just won a grant to put in a mural on the side of the library building, the side that faces the empty lot that's all full of scrub brush, between the library and the church. You know where I'm talking about?"

He considered saying he had no idea, but he just couldn't bring himself to lie to her. He nodded again despite the sense of impending doom.

"There's some money available in the budget for new plantings, but she doesn't even know where to begin, that lot is such a mess. Do you think you might be able to swing by and give her some advice? She really needs to talk to an expert."

Rob breathed an internal sigh of relief. Advice he could do. He didn't have time to take on a big project—particularly a free one—but he could offer a little advice, especially for Ms. Bennett.

"Why don't I swing by there after work today and see what she's dealing with?"

"That's wonderful of you, sweetheart. I really appreciate it. I'll give her a call and let her know you're coming."

Another customer called for Lucy's attention, and Rob took the opportunity to escape. As he walked out to his truck, he wondered if Kat would be helping with this same project. He had no intention of getting sucked into something big, but if she were involved, maybe he could volunteer a few hours here and there after work. If they happened to cross paths, well, then that was just good luck. He slid into the truck with a smile, started the motor, and turned up the volume on the radio. Today was going to be a good day.

Want to read more of Kat and Rob's story? Look for *Love Me Not* at your favorite bookseller.

ACKNOWLEDGMENTS

Writing may be a solitary pursuit, but without the support of friends and family, I would never have finished a book, much less two of them.

I'd like to thank my subject-matter advisors for their help with Tessa's story. Jon Carlson and Jennifer Keefe provided insight into the mind and life of a professional counselor. Jon has written some amazing books about his experiences, including *The Mummy at the Dining Room Table: Eminent Therapists Reveal Their Most Unusual Cases and What They Teach Us About Human Behavior*, which he co-wrote with Jeffrey A. Kottler. It's fascinating reading even if nonfiction isn't usually your thing. Julie Navin acted as my sailing consultant. She's a lifelong sailor who knows her stuff. Without her help, my limited experience would have been all too obvious. If, despite their best efforts, I've still managed to get things wrong, I take complete responsibility. They tried their best.

This story grew and changed with the help of my writing crew: Kelly, Sarah, Barbara, Bill, Andy, Marilyn, Amey, Sara, Erika, Karen, and Simone. Some of you are family. Some are friends who feel like family. All of you contributed by reading drafts, bouncing around ideas, or simply offering moral support. Special thanks to my amazing editor, Diana Plattner, whose collaboration makes me a better writer.

And finally, thank you to my husband, who has always supported this crazy endeavor, and to my three boys, who understand that staring into space counts as "working."

With love and gratitude,

Lisa

ABOUT HIDDEN SPRINGS

Growing up, I spent a lot of time in the lake country of south-eastern Wisconsin. This area may not be quite as famous as the Finger Lakes region in upstate New York, or Lake Tahoe out west, but for me that makes it better. A little more down-to-earth. A little less crowded. The fictional town of Hidden Springs is a wonderful mash-up of all the different lake towns I love, past and present, large (relatively speaking) and small, fancy or not.

If you want to know more about the real-world lakes of southeastern Wisconsin, these websites provide a great starting point.

http://www.travelwisconsin.com/southeast/walworth-county
http://www.visitwalworthcounty.com/
https://www.visitlakegeneva.com/
http://www.discoverwhitewater.org/
http://www.cruiselakegeneva.com/
http://www.atthelakemagazine.com/

See you at the lake!

Lisa McLuckie was born a wanderer. She has lived in four states and two foreign countries, had twenty-four different addresses, and explored five of the seven continents. Her debut novel, *Love Song (Instrumental),* earned two honors from the Independent Book Publishers Association in 2015: the Benjamin Franklin Gold Award for Romance Fiction, and the Bill Fisher Silver Award for Best First Book (Fiction).

She currently lives on the fringes of Chicagoland with her husband, three sons (sizes small, medium, and extra-large), and a ridiculously adorable dog named Daisy. Learn more and sign up for new book announcements at LisaMcLuckie.com.

Books by Lisa McLuckie
Love Song (Instrumental)
Love Story (Confidential)
Love Met Not
Love Letters